# Brighter Skies in the Dales

Betty Firth grew up in rural West Yorkshire in the UK, right in the heart of Brontë country... and she's still there. After graduating from Durham University with a degree in English Literature, she dallied with living in cities including London, Nottingham and Cambridge, but eventually came back with her own romantic hero in tow to her beloved Dales.

# Also by Betty Firth

## Made in Yorkshire

*A New Home in the Dales*
*War Comes to the Dales*
*A Wartime Christmas in the Dales*
*A Wartime Wedding in the Dales*
*A Little Miracle in the Dales*
*Brighter Skies in the Dales*

# Betty Firth
# Brighter Skies *in the* Dales

**hera**

First published in the United Kingdom in 2026 by

Hera Books, an imprint of
Canelo Digital Publishing Limited,
20 Vauxhall Bridge Road,
London SW1V 2SA
United Kingdom

A Penguin Random House Company
The authorised representative in the EEA is Dorling Kindersley Verlag GmbH. Arnulfstr. 124, 80636 Munich, Germany

Copyright © Betty Firth 2026

The moral right of Betty Firth to be identified as the creator of this work has been asserted in accordance with the Copyright, Designs and Patents Act, 1988.
All rights reserved. No part of this publication may be reproduced or transmitted in any form or by any means, electronic or mechanical, including photocopy, recording, or any information storage and retrieval system, without permission in writing from the publisher.
No part of this book may be used or reproduced in any manner for the purpose of training artificial intelligence technologies or systems. In accordance with Article 4(3) of the DSM Directive 2019/790, Canelo expressly reserves this work from the text and data mining exception.

A CIP catalogue record for this book is available from the British Library.

ISBN 978 1 83598 414 7

This book is a work of fiction. Names, characters, businesses, organizations, places and events are either the product of the author's imagination or are used fictitiously. Any resemblance to actual persons, living or dead, events or locales is entirely coincidental.

Printed and bound in Great Britain by Clays Ltd, Elcograf S.p.A.

Look for more great books at
www.herabooks.com | www.dk.com

*Dedicated to the memory of Rachael Lee: a wonderful, warm, caring, talented person who it was a pleasure to know and a privilege to share a stage with. Always missed but never forgotten xxx*

## Chapter 1

### December 1942

The darkness was thick when Bobby Atherton was awoken by the shifting of the little life inside her. It wasn't a kick yet – more like the butterflies that went with the anticipation of something pleasant. It reminded Bobby of how she'd felt when she had seen her sweetheart Charlie, now her husband, striding towards her during their courtship.

The baby had proven as good as an alarm since he'd started moving, always waking his mother shortly before the clock rang to rouse her for work. As she snuggled close to Charlie, Bobby wondered if their child would always be so punctual in his timekeeping.

Charlie was murmuring fitfully while he slept. Bobby had grown accustomed to the sound, and no longer tried to wake him from the nightmare. Dr Minchin, who had been treating Charlie for neurasthenia since he'd been invalided out of the RAF a month ago, had warned Bobby not to wake her husband unless he showed signs of extreme distress. This, the doctor said, was how Charlie's brain was dealing with the things that had happened to him as a bomber pilot. As upsetting as it might be to witness, Bobby must let sleep, the great healer, take its natural course.

The doctor was right: it was upsetting to witness. Bobby had grown up with a father whose mind had been disordered by war and thought she knew all that it had to show her, but every mind was different. Her father she could soothe with prayer or drink, but with Charlie she felt so powerless. If he suffered a nervous attack whilst awake, she could comfort him. But when the horrors came in his sleep… every night Bobby had to watch him relive terrible experiences in his dreams, unable to offer relief.

Charlie rarely woke himself with crying out as Bobby's father did, but he tossed and flailed, and mumbled the names of friends he had lost, and sobbed softly in a way piteous to see. For all that the doctor said he needed this fitful sleep, Charlie often awoke more exhausted than when he had gone to bed. But when Bobby asked if he could remember his dreams, he always told her he couldn't.

The right sleeve of his pyjama shirt had rolled up, and Bobby ran her fingers along his exposed arm. The skin from wrist to shoulder was mottled with cordite burns – a stark reminder of Charlie's dramatic final mission, which had so nearly cost him his life.

She tried to make out what he was muttering. It sounded strangely melodic.

More than melodic, in fact. Was he… singing?

She laughed softly. He was! Bless the boy, he was singing a jolly little song in his sleep.

The sound of her laughter woke Charlie, who tensed, then relaxed when he realised he was in her arms.

'Sorry,' Bobby whispered. 'I didn't mean to wake you.'

Charlie rolled over to plant a kiss on her lips. 'Did I wake *you*?'

'No, your wicked offspring did. He's dancing a foxtrot in my belly this morning.'

'Too fond of a good time, that boy.'

'Then he obviously takes after his father,' Bobby said, returning the kiss.

'What were you giggling about?' He rested one hand on her burgeoning stomach. 'Was naughty Marmaduke tickling you?'

Marmaduke was the temporary name they had bestowed on the baby, until his true sex – and hopefully, true name – became apparent.

Bobby smiled. 'I was laughing at you, daft lad. Did you know you were singing?'

'Was I? What was I singing?'

'It sounded like' – she let out a snort – 'I swear, it sounded like "Do You Know the Muffin Man?"'

'Gosh, that's right,' Charlie said, laughing too. 'I was dreaming I was in our mess at Binbrook. The lads used to sing it as a dare, balancing a pint of wallop on their heads while they walked from one end of the hut to the other.'

Bobby smiled, pleased to hear that happier memories of the RAF sometimes inspired his dreams.

'I remember O'Rourke tripping over his big feet and landing head first in Forrester's lap, beer and all.' Charlie laughed, but it faded away in a sigh. 'Both gone now. Them and so many others.'

Bobby held him for a moment before she reached for the lamp.

'You might as well go back to sleep,' she said. 'I can light the fire, then it'll have the house warm for when you get up.'

'No, I'll do it.' Charlie eased himself into a sitting position. 'Bad enough you have to go out to work. At least let me manage the house until I'm back in a job. You shouldn't be exerting yourself.'

'Honestly, darling, it's all right. It's Saturday, don't forget. It's only a half day so I'm hardly going to wear myself out doing a few chores before work. I juggled my job and keeping house for my dad long enough, didn't I?'

'Not with Marmaduke to weigh you down.'

'Marmaduke's barely the size of a nectarine yet, the doctor says.' Bobby fixed him with a stern look. 'He also says I'm to make sure you're getting enough rest. You're still healing, Charlie.'

'Oh, he's an old mother hen. Sitting on my backside isn't healing anything.'

Bobby got up to put on her dressing gown, the chill in the air making her shiver. 'At least let me bring you a cup of tea.'

'Bobby, there's no need to fuss. I can make my own tea.'

'Please, let me. I want to make you one.'

There was an embarrassed pause.

'Go on.' Bobby forced a smile. 'Let me feel like a wife before I go out to work, eh?'

Charlie caught her arm and pulled her down so she was sitting on his legs.

'Oh, you want to feel like a wife, do you?' he said huskily, nuzzling her neck. 'You should have said.'

Bobby giggled. 'Charlie, get off. We don't have time for that.'

'I won't have you complaining to Mary that your conjugal rights aren't being respected. Why don't you come back to bed for quarter of an hour?'

'You can lure me into bed this afternoon if you like. Not now.'

'Why not both?' he murmured against her skin. 'I'm a hot-blooded young husband.'

He pulled aside her nightdress to kiss her shoulder. Bobby let him continue for a moment, relishing the softness of his lips, before wriggling away.

'We can't, love,' she said. 'I've been late twice since I went back to work because of morning sickness, and you know how your brother gets. We can't risk Reg realising I'm in the family way until we're ready. He's bound to let me go once he knows, and with you out of work we need the money.'

Charlie slumped against his pillow. 'You had to remind me.'

'Oh, you know I didn't mean it like that.' Bobby sat down by him. 'It's a fact, that's all. Our savings won't last long with neither of us bringing in a salary. We need to be putting aside as much as we can while I'm still able to work.'

'What if I can't find anything, Bob?' Charlie said, rubbing his temple. 'No veterinary practice wants a large-animal vet with a bad limp and one arm practically useless, and if I'm too broken for that, what else is there? I was only good at three things my entire life: charming girls, fettling beasts and flying. The RAF's ruined me for the last two, and I imagine you'd have something to say about the first.'

'I certainly would. I expect all your charms to be reserved for me,' Bobby said with a smile. 'There's plenty of things you could do. You've a good brain, a good education, and you're hardly long in the tooth at twenty-eight. Something's bound to turn up.'

'Huh. I wish it'd hurry.'

'You only left hospital a month ago. Be patient.' Bobby reached up to stroke his hair. 'We're all right, aren't we?' she said softly. 'I've got my job, for now at least. We're adding to our nest egg, little by little. We're home, we're together, and best of all we've got Marmaduke. It wasn't long ago that my every waking minute was filled with worry about whether you'd survive the night, so I'm not going to complain that things aren't quite perfect yet.'

Charlie wrapped her in his arms.

'You're right. I've been given the moon and I'm complaining they forgot to put sugar on it for me,' he said. 'It's a good thing I've got you to remind me what an enormous fathead I am.'

'Yes, but you're my enormous fathead.' Bobby kissed his nose. 'Come on. You can build the fire and I'll make breakfast. How does that sound?'

'Perfect.' He released her so he could put on his dressing gown. 'Just make sure you don't spend too long jawing with Mary and Lilian after work. I haven't forgotten that promise to let me lure you into bed on your afternoon off.'

Dawn was breaking when Bobby left for work. She paused to look at the cottage before setting out. She had only moved in two months ago following compassionate discharge from the Women's Auxiliary Air Force, with Charlie joining her a month later, so married life was a novelty yet.

Number 4 Church View was the middle home in a row of seven that had once been almshouses. It was small, the best she and Charlie could afford to rent: bedroom, parlour and kitchen, all on one floor, and an outhouse with a flush privy. There was no garden, only a yard, but they did have the luxury of indoor plumbing.

It was modest, yes, but neat and snug, and Bobby couldn't help feeling houseproud. The place wasn't only her first marital home. It was also where she and Charlie would truly become a family when Marmaduke joined them there in spring.

Before leaving for work, Bobby had prepared breakfast, swept the flagged kitchen floor and made the bed, to lighten Charlie's load when he tackled the daily chores. When she left, he had been sitting with *The Veterinary Record*, frowning over the vacant positions while he smoked a cigarette.

Bobby had cast a worried glance at his hands while she said goodbye. They shook so, these days.

She couldn't help feeling a little guilty too, knowing she wasn't being entirely frank with her husband. Whenever Charlie bemoaned their lot, Bobby delivered a stern reminder that they ought to count their blessings. She never confided to him her own occasional feelings of dissatisfaction in the life they now shared.

Or, not dissatisfaction exactly, Bobby hastily corrected herself. She had never felt happier or more loved than she had since she and Charlie had moved into their little home. This was more a sort of… yearning.

She knew it was foolish. She was grateful, so grateful, to be back home in Silverdale with her husband. She relished being close to the people she loved – her sister, her father, her sister-in-law Mary, and Florence and Jessica Parry, the little Londoners she had grown close to when they had been evacuated here. Every day Bobby looked up to the fells and said a quiet prayer of thanks that Charlie had made it back from a war which had taken so many. With the baby that had seemed an impossible dream on the way, they had everything they could have hoped for.

Even Bobby's much-loved job on *The Tyke* magazine had been restored to her. Yes, Charlie's injuries would make a difference to their lives, but nothing was insurmountable. Nor was there anything Bobby regretted about the course her life had taken.

Yet still there was that hungry feeling, as of something promised yet never fulfilled. She had been about to do important work in the WAAF – had dreamed of a codes and ciphers commission, an overseas posting, really making a difference. She didn't regret the path she had taken, but there was still curiosity, even longing, about the one she had failed to take.

Bobby wondered if she was destined never to be completely happy with her lot. To long always for fresh challenges, and stimulation for her busy brain. What would her little world look like when Marmaduke came along? It was so strange to think that before summer came again, she would – God willing – be a mother.

Silverdale had an eerie appearance when Bobby stepped off her doorstep. St Peter's churchyard was opposite, and the silhouettes of the stubby gravestones made her shiver. One memorial topped by a stone angel had nearly frightened her witless the day she had gone back to work, rising out of the darkness like an avenging spirit.

Her heart almost stopped again when she saw one of the squatting silhouettes rise and take on human shape, but Bobby was soon laughing at herself when she recognised what a familiar shape that was. It belonged to her sister, Lilian Scott.

'Honestly, Lil, you frightened me to death,' Bobby said when she had joined her twin. 'I thought you were the Ghost of Christmas Yet to Come.'

Lilian laughed. 'I doubt you need an old sinner like me to show you the error of your ways.'

'How long have you been here?'

'Half an hour.'

'You should've knocked. You could have warmed up inside while I got ready.'

'I didn't like to wake your Charlie.'

'He's scouring the paper for jobs already. I don't think either of us will be able to break the habit of early rising now we've been in the services.' Bobby glanced at her sister, who looked washed out, as she so often did these days. 'What brings you out so early?'

'I couldn't sleep.' Lilian gestured to the gravestone she had been kneeling beside. 'Annie was sleeping soundly so I thought I'd come and have a little talk with her sister.'

Bobby looked down at Georgia Scott's gravestone. As always, it was scrubbed clean and adorned with fresh greenery – even in winter, there was always something living to give colour to the stone. Lilian took exceptionally good care of the plot where her baby slept.

'What have you been talking to her about?' Bobby asked, slipping an arm through her sister's as they set off walking.

'Oh, just foolishness.'

'You can always tell me your foolishnesses.'

'Honestly, it's nothing.' Lilian laughed. 'It was mostly moaning about not being able to get any tinned pilchards on points and the quality of the National Loaf. Dad and Tony's eyes glaze over whenever I vent about housewife business, and I'm not sure Annie's don't as well. But Georgia's always happy to listen.'

'You come down here too much, Lil,' Bobby said softly. 'You're still recovering from the birth. You shouldn't be squatting in cold, damp churchyards.'

'You sound like George Parry.'

Bobby frowned. 'The captain?'

'Yes, he gave me some advice too in his quiet, serious way.' Lilian smiled. '"Grief is a necessary thing but don't neglect the people alive who love you, Lilian." That's what he said to me.'

'That was bold of him. Still, he's right.'

'I have to come.' Lilian swallowed. 'I… think about her, when I'm in bed. Think about how lonely she must be, alone in the dark.'

'And about how lonely you are, alone in the dark,' Bobby said quietly. 'Can't you talk to Tony? He's grieving for her too.'

'I know, but it isn't the same for him, is it? I'm her mother, Bobby.'

'Have you tried talking to him?'

'I used to.' She laughed bleakly. 'He tries to make me feel better, bless him. It's absurd really.'

'What is?'

'The way he acts like he can fix it with words. He reminds me that we ought to be grateful to have Annie, that I'm lucky to be alive, that there'll be other babies.' Lil turned wet eyes to her twin. 'But I don't want to feel better, Bob,' she whispered. 'That's what I can't make Tony understand. I don't want him to fix it. I want him to share it.'

'It's harder for men. Dealing with feelings and things.'

'I know. Tony does his best. And I know he loves me, although I often wonder why. We're so little alike.'

Bobby had wondered this herself. Tony had long admired her twin, and that was natural. Many men back in Bradford had sighed over pretty, vivacious Lilian Bancroft. But Bobby hadn't realised the depth of Tony's feelings for his wife until the night Lilian had nearly died in childbirth, when Bobby had overheard Tony's desperate prayer that God would take him instead.

Yet it was true the pair had little in common and struggled to relate to one another. Perhaps it was Lilian's need for Tony, her vulnerable state when she had found herself carrying his baby, that had inspired his fondness. He had always had a weakness for a damsel in distress. All Bobby knew was that she had seen Tony in love a handful of times since they had known one another, but she had never seen him display the tenderness he showed to Lilian.

'I wish you'd come to me when you can't sleep, Lil,' Bobby said. 'I'll always be there to listen, about tinned pilchards or anything else.'

'I wouldn't wake you for my trivial mitherings. You've got Marmaduke to think about.' Lilian forced a smile. 'Anyhow, never mind me. Did the doctor give my niece or nephew a good report at your last appointment?'

Bobby glanced warily around. They were still some distance from Moorside Farm and the converted barn known as Cow House Cottage, where Lilian lived with Tony and her father. However, they weren't far from the place George Parry shared with his daughters, Florrie and Jess. The two Londoners had been evacuated to Silverdale after losing their home in the Blitz. They had formed a strong bond with Mary and Reg Atherton, their hosts, which had persuaded Captain Parry to make a home here when he had been medically discharged from the army. Now, Athertons, Parries and Scotts felt almost like one big family.

'Not so loud,' Bobby murmured to Lilian. 'I don't want any rumours to get back to Reg. With Charlie out of a job, I need to stay in work as long as I can.'

Lilian lowered her voice. 'Would Reg really lay you off right away? It is his brother's baby.'

'I have a horrible idea he'd try to give us money,' Bobby said, pulling a face. 'I'd rather earn my keep while I can.'

'How long do you think you can get away with it? Reg is one thing, but there isn't much gets by Mary.'

Bobby felt a twinge of guilt that she hadn't yet shared her news with her good friend – Lilian was the only person she had confided the secret to. There were twenty years between half-brothers Reg and Charlie, and Mary had raised her brother-in-law as a son after the death of his mother. She would be thrilled to learn she was to be a grandmother, in spirit if not in blood. But while Bobby trusted Mary with a secret, it didn't feel right asking her to conceal one so significant from her husband.

'Mary wouldn't tell tales on me,' Bobby said. 'I'm hoping it'll be at least another month until I need to confess to Reg. Maybe two, if I adjust my clothes cleverly. I'm barely showing yet.'

'Oh, but you'll feel rotten traipsing about getting stories when you're six months gone.' Lilian looked appalled at the idea. 'I don't understand why Charlie can't just reopen his practice.'

'It isn't that simple.'

'Why not?' They had reached the packhorse bridge now, and Lilian glanced at the cow house in the distance. 'His surgery's been kept as it was before he went to war. Tony, Dad and I can work around him if he needs it again.'

In civilian life, Cow House Cottage had been Charlie's bachelor residence, and he had run his veterinary surgery from a more modern extension. However, he had arranged for his practice to be absorbed by the one in the nearby village of Smeltham when he had left for the RAF, and since then the surgery had sat unused.

'Charlie couldn't start practising again just like that,' Bobby said. 'He made an arrangement with the Smeltham vet, Bill Lawrence, when he moved away eighteen months ago. Bill extended his premises and took on a couple of lads to cover the work. It wouldn't be very fair to expect him to just hand back all Charlie's former customers after laying out all that expense. And… well, things are different for Charlie now.'

'Because of his injuries?'

Bobby nodded soberly. 'With just his bad leg he could still practice, but his arm… I hadn't realised until I moved to the countryside how *strong* vets need to be. Battling huge brawny bulls to get them vaccinated, and the way Charlie describes birthing a calf, it sounds more like a wrestling match than a delivery.'

'Won't his arm ever heal?'

'Not entirely. There's been a lot of nerve damage. It's always going to be weaker than it was.'

'Well, then couldn't he tend the smaller animals and leave the big ones for the stronger men? A terrier can't put up much of a fight.'

'His specialism is large animals. Maybe he could retrain, but…' Bobby paused. She didn't like talking about this, knowing it humiliated Charlie. But she and Lilian had shared care of their father from childhood, and she knew her sister would understand. 'It isn't just the weakness in his arm,' she said in a low voice. 'He shakes, now. His hands tremble constantly, even when he's calm.'

'Yes, I've noticed,' Lil said quietly. 'His nerves, I suppose, like Dad. Will he always?'

'Dad does, doesn't he? You can't be a fumble-fingered vet, Lil.'

'I guess not.'

'Poor Charlie,' Bobby said with a sigh. 'He had interviews with two practices last month, but as soon as they saw his stick, his hands shaking and his arm burnt, they didn't want to know.'

'That makes me so cross,' Lilian said, scowling. 'Why should men injured for their country lose because of it? We owe them a huge debt.'

'I expect the vets who run these practices are just thinking about their businesses,' Bobby said. 'They don't owe Charlie a living, war or not. If he can't do the work, why should they give him a job?'

'Doesn't that make you angry?'

'I've been angry about so many things in this war, I've none left to spare for ordinary people just trying to make the best of things.' Bobby sighed. 'I do hate how being out of work makes Charlie feel though. Cooking and cleaning like a housewife while I'm out trying to earn enough to support us. It humiliates him.'

'My Tony acts aggrieved if he has to make his own cup of tea,' Lil said with a dry smile. 'Men, honestly. It'd do the lot of them good to learn one end of a kettle from the other.'

'It's more than that. Charlie's never been stuffy about me working, and he lived alone as a bachelor so he's no stranger to chores. It's more… I suppose that he feels it's his job to take care of me and Marmaduke, and if he can't, he feels useless.'

'That's understandable.'

'It's funny, isn't it?' Bobby said dreamily.

'What?'

'How different they all are. Men. Charlie's experience is the mirror of Dad's in some ways, and there's Reg and Captain Parry – all scarred by war, physically and in their minds. Charlie and Dad both struggle with feelings of uselessness when they can't do what they feel is their duty as men. Yet they each deal with it in their own way.'

'What's Charlie's way?' Lilian flashed her twin a worried look. 'He doesn't try to cope… like Dad did?'

'He doesn't knock back spirits, no,' Bobby told her. 'But he hates to lean on anyone, even me. Especially now when he thinks I'm fragile.'

'But you two are all right, aren't you? I thought you and Charlie were signed, sealed and delivered when it came to living happily ever after.'

Bobby smiled. 'Yes, we're all right in that sense. I never expected the things that happened to Charlie – to both of us – when we were in the RAF would just fade into the past once we were back on Civvy Street. We need to take each day as it comes, I suppose, and count our blessings whenever we feel inclined to grouse.'

'Do you miss the WAAF?'

They had reached Moorside now. Bobby discovered on glancing at her watch that she was a few minutes late for work.

Mary Atherton was on the doorstep beating out a rug, and she called to Bobby that Reg was waiting to speak to her and Tony in the parlour. Bobby was grateful to be spared answering her sister's question as she hurried into the farmhouse.

## Chapter 2

'Good afternoon,' Reg observed dryly when Bobby walked into the parlour. The editor was seated behind his desk with Tony on the other side, looking like a naughty schoolboy summoned to the headmaster.

Bobby wondered what Reg wanted to speak to them about. Nothing bad, she hoped. Running a rural magazine in these days of paper shortages and wartime uncertainty was a fraught business. The little mag seemed to be doing well – enough for Reg to increase their salaries to two pounds a week – but still, Bobby thought he must struggle to afford two staff reporters.

Two pounds wasn't a large salary – quite the reverse. Bobby and Tony had earned a pound more a week when they had worked together on the *Bradford Courier*, and even that was a modest wage. Nevertheless, eighty shillings a week was still a lot for Reg to be paying out.

When Bobby had left for the WAAF in spring, her brother-in-law had been taken on as *The Tyke*'s only staff reporter in her place. She hadn't expected her old job back when she left the Air Force six months later – indeed, she had assured Reg she wouldn't want it if it would mean laying off Tony. It had knocked her for six when Reg had said he wanted her back on *The Tyke*, working alongside her old *Courier* colleague. Bobby believed Reg might actually have missed her, although it was the last thing the gruff Yorkshireman would ever admit.

She was glad to be back, but her old job came with new challenges, not least of which was the lack of space. With three workers and their desks crammed into the parlour, there was precious little space for anything else – in fact, the room had now abandoned any pretence of being a parlour at all. It looked like what it was – an office – and the Atherton family were forced to retreat to the kitchen for their living space.

Mary bore it stoically, but Bobby knew it was devastating for the houseproud Daleswoman to have no room in which to rest and entertain. The space was foggy with tobacco now as Tony chain-smoked his way through the day, and every weekend Mary diligently scrubbed the ceiling above his desk to remove a persistent yellow ring.

Tony himself was the other challenge. His work had improved since he and Bobby last worked together, but as at the *Courier*, he was prone to belligerence if he felt his female colleague was being favoured over him. As a man, he saw himself as naturally Bobby's superior at work. It rankled whenever he was reminded that they were, in fact, equals.

'Sorry I'm late,' Bobby said in answer to Reg's sarcastic 'good afternoon'. 'I'll make it up before I leave.'

'Aye, see you do. No, don't start work,' Reg said, seeing she was heading for her desk. 'I want to talk to the pair of you.'

Bobby pulled her chair over to sit beside Tony. She flashed her fellow reporter a questioning look, but Tony just shrugged.

She felt her stomach lurch with anxiety, and winced at a movement from the baby in response. Was she going to be sacked? Could Reg have discovered her secret? He was a kind man underneath his sternness, and Bobby knew he both respected and liked her. Nevertheless, he had traditional ideas about women in the workplace. It had been difficult enough to persuade him to keep her on once she became a wife. As a mother, he'd never accept she ought to be anywhere but at home.

Tony looked worried as well. Bobby wondered if he, too, was fearful his head was on the block. Feckless and workshy for most of his career, Tony had earned a reputation back in Bradford that had rendered him virtually unemployable there.

This job, low paid as it was, had been a lifeline to him when he had been an out-of-work new husband. It had allowed him to move his pregnant wife nearer to her family, and provided them with a grace-and-favour home in the form of Cow House Cottage. He would be in an even worse position if he lost his place than Bobby.

'Um, did we do anything wrong?' Bobby asked Reg. She was determined, if paying their salaries was the issue, to offer her resignation in place of Tony's. God knew she needed to be earning, but if Tony lost his job he might never get another. Worse, he might follow through on a plan to move his family to Liverpool, and take Lilian away from her.

'Since you mention it,' Reg said, frowning. 'Third time you've been late since I took you back on. Not like you, lass.'

Bobby flushed. It had been Lilian who had distracted her today, but early-morning vomiting had caused her lateness on previous occasions. She couldn't tell Reg that, of course, but she was fast running out of excuses.

'I know, and it's not good enough,' she said. 'I'm still getting into a routine at home and... but you don't care about that. It won't happen again.'

'See it doesn't.'

'What about me? What did I do?' Tony demanded. 'I'm always at my desk before nine.'

'Aye, smoking with your feet up.' Reg looked faintly amused. 'Have the pair of you got guilty consciences or what?'

Bobby felt another stab of worry. Did he know?

'Um, how do you mean?' she asked.

'I summon you both here and straight off you're trying to work out what you've done wrong. I've summat to tell you, that's all.'

Bobby and Tony exchanged puzzled looks.

'Well, boss, what is it?' Tony asked, lighting one of his smelly Egyptian cigarettes.

'Just this.' Reg handed Bobby a lumpy envelope. 'My missus has given *The Tyke* its marching orders at long last. I think those fags of yours were the last straw, Tony. You're moving out.'

Bobby looked at the envelope. 'What do you mean, moving out?'

'Into new premises. There's a key in there. I'm trusting you to open up, Bobby, so mind you knock this lateness on the head.'

'Where are we moving to?' Tony asked. He didn't look particularly perturbed by the news. Bobby supposed it was all one to Tony where he smoked. But to her, for whom Moorside Farm and *The Tyke* had always been inextricably linked, it felt earth-shattering to think of their little team working anywhere else.

Reg coughed as a stream of smoke from Tony's cigarette hit him in the face. 'For God's sake, lad, turn to one side if you must smoke them things. As to where you're moving to, there's a shed behind Ginger Parry's place. You seen it?'

Tony snorted. 'A *shed*?'

'Aye, well, best I can do at the minute.'

'We can't run a magazine from a shed.'

Reg shrugged. 'Why not? It's in good nick, and I've had the place fettled smart.'

'Did you say it's on Captain Parry's land?' Bobby asked.

'Aye, the field behind his cottage. Ginger's not using it so he said we could have it in exchange for a couple of eggs a week from our hens. Pete Dixon's coming round to shift the desks this afternoon so you'll be ready to start there Monday.'

Bobby felt like she was in a dream. A new office! That meant no more cosy chats with Mary during her dinner hour. No more friendly hand snuffles from Reg's old wolfhounds, Barney and Winnie, as they lay across her feet while she worked. No more would she look up to the welcome sight of Mary's tea tray appearing round the door...

She frowned as something else Reg had said registered.

'What do you mean, *you'll* be ready to start on Monday?' she asked. 'You're coming too, aren't you?'

Reg gave a hoarse laugh. 'Me, sit in an old shed all day with mustard gas on the lungs and shrapnel in one leg? Nay, that's for young folk. Dick Minchin would have my guts for garters.'

'You're going to keep working here? How will we know what you want us to do?'

Reg sighed. He looked suddenly older as he slumped back in his chair.

'You don't need me to tell you what to do,' he said quietly, and the way he met Bobby's eyes told her these words weren't intended for Tony. 'You know the mag as well as I ever did. Happen even better.'

'But it's yours, Reg. Your baby.'

'Half the letters we had while you were off to war were about you,' he told her, somewhat wistfully. '"What happened to the nice young lady who wrote the bits to make us laugh?". Well, now I've got two of you trained up, seems daft not to let my old bones have a rest. Mary's been nagging me about it ever since I gave you your job back, Bobby.'

Reg was seized by another coughing fit. Bobby wondered if there was more to these than Tony's smoke. She hadn't realised Reg's lungs had been affected by gas in the last war. And he did look tired – she'd noticed the change when she'd returned from the WAAF. Still, Reg must really be feeling his age if he was willing to take a step back from *The Tyke*. As Mary often complained, he lived and breathed for that magazine.

'I don't get it,' Tony said, stubbing out his cigarette in one of the ashtrays Mary had placed discreetly around the room. 'Who's in charge then? Someone has to be.'

Reg mopped his mouth with a handkerchief and nodded to Bobby. 'She is. I'm promoting her to deputy editor. I'll still be editor-in-chief, but that don't mean I'll be hovering over your shoulders, don't worry. I'll just stop in from time to time and cast my eye over things.'

Bobby sat up straighter. 'Deputy editor! Really?'

'Aye.' Reg smiled. 'Told you there'd be an editor job in your future, didn't I? There'll be a bit extra in your pay packet to reflect the promotion. Not a lot, mind, but another three bob a week. That's as much as I can afford for now.'

Tony looked appalled. 'You're promoting her over me?'

'Oh, don't sound so shocked,' Reg said, rolling his eyes. 'She's got more experience, that's all.'

'She might have more experience on this rag but I'm the more experienced journalist. I was a seasoned newspaperman when she was just the girl who made the tea.'

Bobby glared at him. 'You know, I can hear you, Tony.'

'Save it, son,' Reg told him shortly. 'Don't matter if you've got fifty years' experience in papers. It's this magazine you need to know – this magazine and this place.'

'And what about when she buggers off to have a baby?' Tony demanded. 'Waste of time employing women.'

Bobby felt her colour rise, and hid her cheeks by pretending to blow her nose.

'We'll talk about that when the time comes,' Reg said firmly. 'Now get to work, the pair of you.'

Bobby floated to her desk in a daze.

Deputy editor! It was everything she'd dreamed of when she came to work here. Perhaps Reg was even thinking she'd take over from him as editor one day. When the war ended and paper became once again plentiful, who knew to what heights the little magazine might rise?

Bobby felt elated for a moment, until her fluttering belly brought her back to earth. Her excitement had awoken Marmaduke. It reminded her that this was only temporary – just for a month or two, until she left to take up her duties as a mother.

What would happen then? Reg would promote Tony to deputy editor, she supposed, and hire a junior reporter to work under him. It would be unlikely there would be any way back for her once the baby was born. Bobby knew well enough from Lilian how all-consuming the responsibilities of a new mother were. There would be no time to think of writing between changing napkins, washing, cooking and cleaning.

The irony of it – of being offered everything she had dreamt of, only to then have it snatched away – brought a lump to her throat.

She forced it down, feeding a sheet of paper rather violently into her typewriter. Ridiculous to be crying over good news. Marmaduke's fault, she supposed. Her emotions seemed to lurch between extremes far too easily these days.

–

Too curious to wait until Monday, Bobby hurried to the Parrys' cottage as soon as she finished work at midday, stopping only to promise Mary that she would return shortly to help her and Lil with the Christmas baking.

The captain might well be working a shift at the department store in Bradford where he was employed as a tailor, but if he was at home, Bobby was sure he would let her peep inside her new office. If he wasn't, she could at least peer over the wall.

'Shed' didn't sound too promising. It made her think of the rotting wooden construction on her dad's old allotment in Bradford. Then again, in the Dales, 'shed' could refer to buildings of many sizes. It might just as easily be a large cowshed as one of the garden variety.

More importantly, though, what condition was it in? Bobby didn't relish the idea of an office reeking of animal dung, with rainwater leaking through the roof and wind whistling through cracks in the wall.

She spotted Tony a little way ahead, also heading for the Parrys' place. Bobby should have guessed he would have had the same idea.

Well, she supposed it was no bad thing to have an opportunity to clear the air. Her brother-in-law had been casting her resentful glances all morning, her promotion over him clearly rankling, and she knew from long experience that there was nothing harder to extract work from than Tony Scott in a sulk. She hailed him, and he slowed to let her catch him up.

'You should have waited and we could have walked over together,' she said when she fell into step beside him. 'Don't forget it's me who's got the key.'

'Not likely to forget, am I?' he said grumpily, choosing to interpret this as an attempt to rub her seniority in his face.

Bobby nodded to the cottage up ahead.

'What do you think of all this?' she asked. 'I suppose it's a good sign. The magazine must be in a strong position if Reg is willing to put it in our hands.'

'I just hope he's not dying. Never thought he'd retire while he was still able to hold his blue pencil.' Tony turned a resentful gaze on her. 'Followed me to gloat, did you?'

'Don't be daft, Tony.'

He thrust his hands into his pockets. 'It was bad enough when Don Sykes made you his pet at the *Courier*, but Atherton really seems to think you're God's gift to journalism.'

Bobby shrugged. 'Well, I've worked for him longer. You shouldn't take it so personally.'

'Helps your career prospects if you're married to his brother, I reckon.'

'Perhaps it does.' She smiled warmly. 'And since you're married to my sister, that makes *The Tyke* a thoroughly family affair. Let's not fall out over it, eh?'

'Bloody humiliating when I'm made junior to a bird on a tinpot rag like this, after ten years in the newspaper business,' Tony muttered.

'It's that attitude that's going to keep you junior as well,' Bobby said sharply, her patience thinning. 'Reg promoted me because I understand what's special about *The Tyke*. All you ever do is sneer at it.'

Tony ignored this.

'Not going to put on airs and start ordering me about, are you?' he demanded. 'Don't forget who gave you your start in this business.'

Tony often threw this in her face, which Bobby felt was rich considering what 'giving her her start' actually meant – getting her to write his copy back when she was still a humble typist, while he took his girlfriends out on the newspaper's time. She felt that now wasn't the time to bring this up, however, and adopted a conciliatory tone.

'Things won't be any different, I promise – except that with Reg stepping back, we can both have more creative control,' she told him. 'It'll be a partnership.'

'Apart from the extra few bob you'll be pocketing.'

'I'll gladly split the difference. One and six a week is a small price to pay if it's going to stop you sulking.'

'No thanks,' Tony said, adopting a superior expression. 'I won't take charity.'

She squeezed his arm. 'But you'll take a pint at the Hart later, won't you? You, me, Lil and Charlie can make up a foursome, and my dad can mind Annie. Show there's no bad blood, eh?'

Tony looked slightly mollified. 'Aye, all right. Just don't be getting ideas above your station because you've got "editor" after your name. It don't mean owt.'

They'd reached the cottage now, and Tony rapped on the door.

It wasn't Captain Parry who answered but Florrie, with Ace the border collie at her feet. The dog immediately hurtled out and flung himself at his old friend Bobby. He was a sizeable hound now, quite capable of winding her, but no one could persuade him he wasn't the same ball of fluff as when he'd first joined the family. Bobby laughed as she made a fuss of him.

Ace was full of beans but Florrie seemed rather tired, Bobby thought. She wondered if growing pains had been costing the child sleep. Florence was really getting quite grown-up now – she would be celebrating her thirteenth birthday in the summer.

Already she was nearly as tall as Bobby, seeming to gain inches whenever the adults turned their backs on her. But tired as she looked, Florrie grinned to find a friend on the doorstep.

'Hullo, Bobby.' She turned dutifully to Tony. 'Good afternoon, Mr Scott.'

Tony gave an awkward 'good afternoon' in return. Unused to the company of children, he often seemed ill at ease around the Parrys. The girls sensed his wariness and rarely prattled to him as they did to other members of the family, reserving their best formal manners for him.

Having observed the social niceties, Florrie turned her attention back to Bobby.

'I'm glad you've come,' she said. 'Me and Jessie want to go to Moorside and help Mary with the mince pies, only Dad said we'd to wait till he came home. But if you go with us, I bet he won't mind.'

'I'm sure Mary will be grateful for extra help, as long as you're not just after her carefully hoarded raisins,' Bobby said, laughing. 'Mr Scott and I were hoping to talk to your dad. Is he at work?'

'No, he went into Skipton for summat. Jessie says she bets it's Christmas presents.' Florrie looked at Bobby hopefully. 'Do you think it is?'

'I'm sure I couldn't say,' Bobby said with a smile.

'You can come in if you want. Dad says we're not to let people in when he's out, but I think he meant strangers, not you. Jess is in the garden, feeding her hens.'

'We came hoping to look at something. Reg told us your dad's got a shed we're to use for the magazine. Do you know about it?'

The girl's eyes kindled. She had always taken a lively interest in the magazine, earnestly working on stories of her own in the hope that one day, she too could join the staff of *The Tyke*.

'Yes, it's the shepherd's hut in the field behind our garden,' she said eagerly. 'I didn't even know it was ours. We've never been allowed to play in it, because there used to be rats and stuff.'

Bobby shuddered. Rats! She hoped Reg had been thorough in evicting these former residents.

'Can we have a look inside then?' Tony asked Florrie, more gruffly that he probably intended.

'I guess that's all right,' Florrie said. 'I'll take you to it.'

She led the way through the house, swaggering a little in her role as guide. Bobby tried not to smile.

In the garden, they found Jessie sitting by her little chicken coop, singing to the two young hens that Mary had given her from her brood of chicks.

Jessie, too – now all of nine years old – was growing up. This was reflected in her new fascination with what her big sister scoffingly called 'the lovey pictures'. Jess was an avid reader of the film magazines Lilian saved for her, sighing besottedly over every big-screen romance and cutting out pictures of her favourite stars. Her hens, therefore, had been christened Joan and Olivia, after the leading ladies she most admired.

Jessie had been convinced of the power of song to produce more and better eggs ever since she had tended Mary's elderly biddies at Moorside, and every day spent half an hour singing earnestly to her own girls. Bobby smiled when she heard what the child was chanting.

'Old Hitler's a funny 'un, he's a face like a pickled onion,' Jess warbled in a dirge-like tone. 'A nose like a squashed tomato, and eyes like green peas.'

'I dread to think what flavour eggs you'll get with that song, Jess,' Bobby said with a laugh.

The child squealed and jumped up to hug Bobby around the waist. Bobby lifted her up to swing her around, pleased to see the girl but fearful lest Jess noticed her thickening waist. She would have to be cautious about hugs from the children if she wanted to keep her pregnancy secret.

'It's all right,' Jess said when Bobby had put her back down. 'Dad says Joanie and Livvy lay their best eggs when I sing songs about Hitler being bad. I bet they hate him as much as us human beings do.'

'Well that's mightily patriotic of them.'

'Have you come for a game?' the girl asked hopefully. She glanced at Tony. 'You can both play.'

'I'm afraid not,' Bobby said. 'I promised to help Mary with the Christmas preparation after work, and then I have to make tea for your Uncle Charlie. Mr Scott and I came to take a look at your dad's shed.'

Jessie jutted her lip. 'Aww. You promised you'd play Spy School next you saw us.'

'This isn't an official seeing you. Spy School is for tomorrow at Moorside, after Sunday dinner.' Sundays were family days, when Athertons, Scotts and Parrys would gather for a convivial meal and an afternoon in each other's company.

'But a quick game though?' Jess asked. 'Half an hour isn't long.'

'I really don't have time, sweetheart.' Bobby bent to kiss the child's head. 'But I know Mary's desperate for help with her baking, and I'm certain Lilian would let you help put Annie to bed afterwards.'

'Ooh, yes please!' Florrie said. 'And may I read her a story from my book? I've written a new one.'

'You'd better ask her father.'

'May we, Mr Scott?' Florrie asked, turning to him with pleading eyes.

Even Tony had to smile at the children's fondness for the baby, who they cooed over as if she was the most precious thing in the world.

'She'd like that,' he said, in a softer, less awkward voice. 'She loves stories and lullabies.'

'I'll do the lullaby,' Jessie said eagerly. 'I'm best at singing and Florrie's best at stories.'

Bobby laughed. 'All right, but nothing about Hitler. We don't want to give baby Annie nightmares, do we? Flor, can you show us the shed?'

Florrie pointed to a building at the end of the field behind their garden. 'That's it. I haven't got the key but you can look through the window.'

'That's all right, I've brought the key Reg gave me. I hope your father won't mind if we peek in.'

'We'll show it to you,' Florrie said, and Bobby and Tony followed her and her sister to the shed.

## Chapter 3

Bobby was relieved to find that the wooden hut wasn't too dilapidated. It had been given a fresh coat of distemper, and the walls and roof were in good repair. It was a fair size for a shepherd's hut too: not large, but big enough for a couple of desks.

Still, it was hardly what one would picture as the headquarters of a magazine. It was going to be cold in these winter months, and there'd be damp from condensation – Bobby wouldn't dare leave her typewriter or books overnight. That would mean a lot of lugging things about.

She could see Tony curling his lip and had to sympathise. Reg had gone to some effort to get the place shipshape, but it still felt like a step down. They could call it an office all they liked but at the end of the day, a shed was a shed.

'Nice place if you're a sheep,' he observed, under his breath so the children wouldn't hear.

'All right, I know,' Bobby whispered back. 'We'll just have to make the best of it.'

But while the adults might be unimpressed, Jessie was fairly skipping at the thought of the magazine office at the bottom of her garden. This, it seemed, was a far more exciting prospect than the usual fairies.

'That means you'll be here nearly every day, Bobby,' she said breathlessly. 'And at dinner time we can have games, and me and Florrie can help with the magazine, and—'

Bobby laughed. 'I think you're forgetting a little thing called school, aren't you?'

'No, but in the holidays though,' Jessie said, not to be discouraged. 'Can we look inside? I want to see if there's still rats. I'd like to make a pet from a rat. Jimmy in my class says you can train them to do tricks.'

Bobby suppressed a wave of nausea. She wasn't a fan of rats, and judging by the way her body was reacting, nor was Marmaduke.

She didn't need to worry, however. When she climbed the wooden steps and unlocked the door, she found the hut had been spruced up smartly by whoever Reg had paid to do it – Pete Dixon, she imagined. Pete was Silverdale's resident poacher, spiv, scrap metal merchant, lifter, mover, painter, decorator and general maid of all work.

It almost did look like a real office. The walls had been painted, the floor carpeted, and a couple of pictures hung on the walls. Bobby recognised the style as Mary Atherton's, who was a talented painter. There was even a stove, and a gas burner and kettle next to a tea caddy. There were certainly no rats, much to Jessie's disappointment.

Tony strode to the gas burner and picked up a note.

'"Take it easy with the gas. I'm not made of money. Reg",' he read. 'Huh. Might've guessed.'

'He's gone to a lot of effort.' Bobby glanced at the paintings. 'Mary too. I suppose she feels bad for throwing us out.'

Florrie blinked. 'Is Mary throwing you out?'

'Oh, I was only making a silly joke,' Bobby said, annoyed with herself. She'd forgotten the children were listening. 'Mary wants her parlour to sit in, that's all, so Reg said he'd find a new place for us to work.'

'So you don't want to come and work here?'

Florrie's lip was wobbling all of a sudden. Bobby blinked. The girl had been all smiles a moment earlier, yet now she was emotional over something quite trivial. Even Bobby's Marmaduke-related moods couldn't compete.

'Of course we do,' she said, resting a hand on Florrie's shoulder. 'It was a surprise, but not a bad one. It'll be lovely to see you every day.'

Florrie stared at her for a moment, then without warning she ran out of the hut and started sprinting back to the house. Ace ran after her, clearly thinking this was a great old game.

'Well!' Bobby turned to Jessie. 'What on earth was behind that?'

Jessie scuffed her shoe. 'Not s'posed to tell.'

Bobby cast Tony a helpless look, but he was no use. He had retreated back into awkwardness.

'I'd better get home to our Lil,' he muttered. 'You coming, Bob?'

'No.' Bobby glanced at Jessie, who was frowning at the carpet. 'Not just yet.'

'Right.' Tony wasted no time in hurrying off.

When he'd gone, Bobby turned to Jessie.

'What is it you're not supposed to tell, my love?' she asked gently.

'Can't say,' the child murmured. 'Florrie made me double cross my heart.'

'But it's something you're worried about, isn't it?'

Jessie nodded.

In the absence of chairs, Bobby sat on the floor. Jess hesitated a moment, then sat beside her.

'Perhaps you can give me a clue without breaking your promise,' Bobby said, putting an arm around the girl. 'Is it something that's making Florrie upset?'

Jessie nodded emphatically. 'She's been crying about it all the time. But she said no one's got to know.'

'And it stops her sleeping?'

Jess tugged thoughtfully on her earlobe. 'I guess so. Sometimes when I wake up, she's awake already. And two nights this week, she woke me up to—' She stopped. 'But I ain't supposed to say about that.'

'Can't you give me any clue?'

Jessie shook her head sadly. Bobby's heart ached for the girl. Now she looked at her closely, she could see that Jess looked tired too.

'And you're concerned for your sister?'

Jess nodded. 'She won't tell anyone what's up, not even Dad or Mary, and she says I can't tell anyone either now I've promised. But... but...' She buried her face in the crook of Bobby's arm and let out a sob. 'But I wish Mary'd get the doctor.'

'The doctor!'

'She said she was going to before, when Florrie kept having nightmares about Uncle Charlie getting killed.'

'Is that what's wrong? Is she having nightmares about the war?'

Jessie shook her head.

'But it is something you think a doctor could help with?'

Jessie hesitated, then gave a little nod.

'What on earth can be so wrong that Florrie would need to see a doctor?'

'I *promised*, Bobby,' Jess said unhappily. 'I'm not to say or I'll die. I double crossed my heart, and Florrie made me have one hand on the Bible.'

'If your sister's poorly then you ought to tell someone, Jess, promise or not. God won't be angry if it's to help someone.'

The little girl looked so miserable while she wrestled with the moral dilemma of seeking help and keeping her promise that Bobby's heart filled with pity.

'You ought to ask Florrie,' Jess said at last. 'She might tell, if you promise not to tell Dad.'

'I'll go to her now.' Bobby gave the child a kiss. 'You go and sing to Livvy and Joanie while I see if I can fix this, all right?'

Having deposited Jess by the coop to find solace in her hens, Bobby sought out Florrie in the bedroom she shared with her sister. She thought she might find her weeping. In fact, Florrie was aggressively stuffing a basket with things to be washed.

'Florrie?' Bobby said gently. 'Are you all right?'

The girl shrugged.

'You seemed upset before. I didn't say anything to hurt your feelings, did I?'

Again the shrug, Florrie avoiding eye contact as she pummelled linen into her basket.

'Can we have a little talk?'

'Can't,' Florrie said shortly. 'Got to wash some things before Dad gets back.'

'I thought Mrs Wilcox took in your washing.'

'Not all of it.'

'I only wanted five minutes,' Bobby said, smiling as warmly as she could. 'I just wondered if there was anything you might like to speak to a grown-up about.'

Florrie shook her head, her eyes fixed on the floor.

'Nothing that's upsetting you?' Bobby persisted. 'Anything bad at school, or worries about the war? You look ever so tired, Flor.'

Once more, Florrie shook her head. Bobby tried again.

'Because if you did want to talk to someone, I'd always listen,' she said. 'And I wouldn't tell your dad or anyone without your permission.'

That was at least a half-fib. If the child was really concealing some sort of illness, then Bobby would tell whoever she had to to get Florrie what help she needed. But it was obvious the girl was struggling to open up, and Bobby had to earn her trust.

The promise not to tell Captain Parry seemed to produce a glimmer of hope in Florrie's eyes, but this quickly died.

'Don't matter,' Florrie said gloomily. 'You couldn't help.'

'Help with what, sweetheart?'

'It don't matter,' the girl said again.

Bobby sighed as she admitted defeat. She wasn't going to give up until she'd got to the bottom of the mystery, but she couldn't force Florrie to confide in her. Mary was the person the girls were closest to, other than their father. Perhaps she would know what to do.

'Bobby?' Florrie said in a small voice as she turned to go.

'Yes, my love?'

Florrie hesitated, then blurted out, 'Do you know about the law?'

Bobby blinked. 'The law?'

'Yes. I read how journalists have to know about the law.'

'Well, yes, I know a little,' Bobby said, feeling puzzled at the abrupt change of topic. 'When I worked as a newspaper reporter, part of my job was to cover court cases. Did you want me to teach you about it?'

'No. This is for... summat else.'

'What is it?'

Florrie started rummaging in a chest of drawers. Bobby watched her, wondering what this was all about. Could the child believe she had committed some sort of crime?

After a moment Florrie thrust out a piece of paper, covered in her handwriting.

'Will you make this proper on your typewriter?' she asked Bobby. 'I mean, will you make it proper like with the law? And don't tell Dad, please. You promised you wouldn't.'

Bobby frowned as she took the thing. It looked like a list of Christmas presents. Her own name jumped out as she scanned it.

> *Bobby – story book with the monkeys' tea party story she loved.*

'I can type it, yes,' she said.

'And you won't tell Dad about it?'

'Not if you don't want me to.' The list looked innocuous enough, so Bobby felt no responsibility to take it to the captain. 'What's it for, Florrie?'

But Florrie had grabbed her basket of washing and was hurrying to the bedroom door, head bowed and cheeks on fire. Bobby watched her go, utterly bewildered.

—

Bobby puzzled over the strange little list as she walked back to Moorside.

She couldn't make it out. It read like a list of presents that Florrie was intending to give. But they weren't new things; they were Florrie's things – all her favourite toys, books and keepsakes. She couldn't be planning to give away her most precious possessions as Christmas gifts, surely? And why would she want the thing typed, and what had she meant about the law?

> *Jess – my half of our doll house and tobboggann and Ace. All my clothes when she grows into them, and my ivery hairbrush that she loves*
>
> *Lilian – pickture of Tyron Powere in the seashell frame I made, and my coral knecklace*
>
> *Dad – all my most preshush things, and the juwelery what was ma's, except the pearls that are for Mary*
>
> *Annie – my best doll Susie, and any of my toys that Jess is too big for*
>
> *Louis Butcher – my whistle Reg made me, and my bow and arrow*

And so on. Every person Florrie was close to in Silverdale was listed, and some from her old life in London.

Bobby looked again at the item next to her own name. *Story book with the monkeys' tea party story she loved* – that was the book Florrie had written herself, beavering away to fill it with stories. She prized it above all things. Why would she give something so precious away for a Christmas present? The other things too – her mother's valuable pearls, and the coral necklace her Uncle Jack had given her before he had been killed in the war?

Suddenly, it hit Bobby what the list really was. Why Florrie had been so concerned the list should be made legal and 'proper'. Why she had written out this inventory of her possessions alongside the names of the people she loved most.

'Oh, the poor, poor love,' Bobby murmured.

This wasn't a list of Christmas presents. It was Florrie's will.

## Chapter 4

Bobby wasted no time in bearing the sombre document to Mary in the kitchen at Moorside. It was she who had always been the girls' confidante, and was the closest thing they had to a mother.

'Her will!' Mary said as she looked over the document. 'What on earth can have prompted her to do that?'

'I was hoping you might know.'

'Nay, she's noan said a word to me.'

Bobby was silent while she wrestled with nausea. The kitchen was filled with what under other circumstances would be the delicious fragrance of cinnamon and candied fruits, but right now it wasn't agreeing with her at all.

'She must believe she's ill,' Bobby said when she had the sick feeling under control. She pulled up a chair next to Mary at the kitchen table.

'Nonsense,' Mary said stoutly. 'I've never seen such a healthy specimen of a bairn.'

'She looked ever so tired today, Mary.'

'Oh, that's nobbut her age.'

'Well she's obviously worried about something. And Jess seemed so frightened for her.'

Mary smoothed Florrie's will down in front of her. 'She'd have left me her mother's pearls,' she murmured. 'The most precious thing she has. My poor lamb.'

'She can't really be sickening for something, can she?'

'It'll be nowt. The child's always had too much imagination for her own good. You remember how she was about our Charlie flying, half convinced she could see into the future.'

'What should we do?'

'I'll speak to the girl. Happen she'll open up to me. And if not… we'll have to talk to her father about calling the doctor, I suppose.'

They were interrupted by the arrival of Lilian.

'Sorry I'm late,' she said. 'I took Annie out for a walk. Tony's got her now so I'm ready to do my share of the work.' She glanced at the neglected mince pie ingredients. 'Not that there's a lot of it going on. Is everything all right?'

Mary beckoned her over. 'Look at this.'

'What is it?' Lilian asked, approaching the table.

'Young Florrie made it out. Her will.'

'Her will! Whatever for?'

'That's what we can't work out,' Bobby said. 'She won't talk to anyone about it. Jess is in on the secret, but Florrie made her swear on the Bible not to say anything. The poor love seems to believe she might be dreadfully ill.'

Lilian's gaze skimmed the list. 'What would make her believe that, do you think?'

'I'm not sure. She seemed tired when I saw her, and a little moody, but vigorous enough otherwise. Jess told me she'd woken to find her sister crying a few times recently though.'

Mary was looking seriously concerned now, and Bobby went to put an arm around her.

'I'm sure it's nothing,' she said gently. 'Like you said, anything can seem like the end of the world when you're a bairn.'

'I was just thinking of the poor child's mother,' Mary murmured. 'I don't believe George has ever said what illness took her off. Do you girls know?'

Lilian looked up from perusing the list.

'It was a cancer of some kind,' she said quietly. 'Poor Rose. It sounds as though she just wasted away after Jess was born.'

'Could Florrie be thinking of that?' Mary suggested. 'She's old enough to remember her mother getting ill, even if only vaguely.'

'Lil, what do you think?' Bobby asked. 'You see more of them than I do.'

Since Mary had joined the ranks of the Women's Voluntary Services, which claimed much of her time during the week, Lilian had taken over collecting the girls from school and minding them until their father came home from work.

'Hmm.' Lilian was still staring at the list. 'I suppose… I suppose someone's had a talk with her, haven't they?'

'I tried to, yes, but she wouldn't tell me what was wrong,' Bobby said.

'I mean *the* talk. You remember how Mam sent Dad out with the boys and sat us down to explain everything, when we were ten or so?'

Bobby turned to Mary as realisation dawned.

'Jess told me Florrie had woken her in the night for help with something,' Bobby said quietly. 'And when I saw her in her bedroom, she was filling a basket with washing.'

'Oh my word.' Mary pressed her forehead. 'Oh, the poor motherless thing. Of course she thinks she's dying, if no one's had a talk with her about her monthlies.'

'Poor Jess too,' Lilian said with feeling. 'She must have been scared out of her wits to find her sister bleeding.'

'I don't suppose it occurred to their father to talk to them,' Bobby said. 'What an idiot I've been! It's natural, growing up without a mother, that some facts of life might have passed them by.'

Mary groaned. 'It's my fault. It's me they look to to fill their mam's place, but the only experience I've had of raising bairns that age was with Charlie. It never occurred to me that some woman they trust ought to speak with them about it.'

'One of us ought to put the poor child's mind at rest right away, before she worries herself into a real illness.'

Mary shook her head. 'No. I mean you're right, Bobby, but George ought to be spoken with first. I'm sure he'll be relieved to have one of us offer, but it isn't right to be discussing the facts of life with his daughters without his knowledge.'

Lilian nodded. 'That is true.'

'He ought to be made aware of what his daughter's going to need as well,' Bobby observed. 'Sanitary napkins and so forth. We can offer to buy them.'

'He's at home now,' Lilian said. 'I saw him when I was walking from the village.'

'We should tackle him right away, before the girls lose any more sleep,' Mary said decisively.

Bobby grimaced. 'To talk about it with a man though. I feel like I'd want the earth to swallow me.'

The way Mary's cheeks coloured suggested that even the redoubtable old Daleswoman would find this difficult. However, she squared her shoulders. 'For Florrie's sake, I'll force myself.'

Lilian rested a hand on Mary's shoulder.

'Let me go to him,' she said quietly.

'Could you do it?'

'Perhaps it's because George was the one to find me the night I nearly died in labour, but… yes, I believe I could. I mean I'm sure I'll blush myself silly, but I won't dry up. A father raising girls alone ought to know about these things.'

'I could come with you, if Mary doesn't mind deferring the baking for another hour,' Bobby suggested.

'He'll be less embarrassed with only one of us,' Lilian said. 'I'll call at the cow house and tuck some bunnies into my bag, then when I've spoken to George I can see Florrie. It's no bad thing for her to get the talk from a new mother. I can help her understand that her monthlies are a natural part of growing into a woman.'

'I suppose you are the best suited of the three of us,' Bobby said. 'Come back afterwards and tell us how it went.'

Lilian nodded. She took Florrie's will and left.

'Well!' Mary said when she and Bobby were alone. 'Nowt like a bit of drama on a Saturday afternoon.'

'I'm just glad it's nothing truly dangerous.'

'It's good of your sister to speak to Florrie. I'm sure the child would only be embarrassed to have an old lady like me explaining the facts of life to her.'

'Do you think the captain will be shocked? I wonder he never asked us to have a talk with the girls before.'

'Well, he's a man, isn't he?' Mary said, rolling her eyes. 'A good father, but a man all the same. They rarely think about women's problems unless they're forced to.'

'Still, he was married.'

'Married too long ago when he's daughters to bring up, if you ask me.' Mary started weighing out ingredients. 'I'm surprised he hasn't looked elsewhere before now. He's not forty yet, and eight years a widower.'

'I don't know if the captain would marry again,' Bobby said. 'He seems to have been devoted to his wife.'

'He ought to find himself someone who can be a mother to those girls.' Mary passed Bobby a bowl of flour to sift. 'Happen she might put a smile on his face while she's about it. It's no sin to love again.'

'They've got you for their mothering,' Bobby said, giving her a squeeze. 'They've grown close to Lilian too since she started minding them – and to me, I suppose.'

'Aye, but the three of us don't live with them, do we? Look at Florrie. Fretting herself sickly over the most natural thing in the world, and all of us so busy with husbands and homes that we never noticed until she'd fairly made herself ill.' Mary started rubbing fat and flour together with a vigorous, housewifely arm. 'They need someone in the home. Someone young, who can help them do their growing up. It's high time George realised that.'

It was nearly 2 p.m. when Bobby left Moorside. She only made one brief stop on the way home, to pop an envelope into the pillar box outside the post office.

The contents of this envelope had been kept a secret from nearly everybody. The only people in on it were Bobby's WAAF friend Scarlet, who was the entertainments officer at RAF Wykeness, and her pal Archie Sumner, currently touring with an ENSA party. Bobby was trying not to pin too much on this letter, but she couldn't help hoping it might give her the lifeline she was craving when forced to stop work. The address was Broadcasting House, London.

This task completed, Bobby fairly rushed to get home. She hadn't forgotten her promise to let Charlie lure her back to bed after work. The novelty of being able to hold each other whenever they wanted would, she was sure, take a long time to wear off.

Bobby could have left for home quarter of an hour earlier, the mince pies having been consigned to the oven, but she had been waiting for Lilian to return with news.

Lil had looked pale when she had come back, as if the experience had tired her, but she had been smiling. The captain had taken the news with little embarrassment, she said, although he had been angry with himself for failing to address this aspect of his daughters' growing up. Naivety and not neglect had been the reason – not that he wasn't aware this was a natural part of every woman's life, but that he had never been told at what age he might expect it to begin. He had seemed to believe it would be four or five years until Florrie would experience this particular phenomenon. In his eyes, Bobby supposed, his daughter was very much a baby still.

Anyhow, it was a comfort to know the little girl's mind had been set at rest. Florrie had been relieved, of course, but this had been paired with horror when Lil had told her that the bleeding would be a monthly occurrence until Florrie was – in her own young mind, at least – a quite elderly lady.

Once Lil had explained that the bleeding was only the sign of a normal, healthy growing-up body, however, Florrie began to seem a little pleased at this mark of encroaching womanhood. There was little that appealed more to twelve-year-old girls than the prospect of joining the ranks of the grown-ups. The icing on the cake had been the promise of a girls' shopping trip for Florrie, Jess and Lilian, to buy not only the things Florrie would need for her monthlies but some other little luxuries as well – perhaps even her first lipstick, if her father agreed and she only wore it for play. Lilian said she had left the girl tear-stained but smiling, secure in the knowledge that the afterlife wasn't beckoning just yet.

Honestly, it was a foolish world, Bobby reflected. Women were supposedly the naive ones, many of them kept so in the dark about sex that they were little better than children. This made them easy prey for a certain type of man. Bobby was aware of too many girls who had suffered at men's hands not because of what they knew but what they had been kept ignorant of. Some who, even on their wedding night, had no idea how one would go about creating a baby.

The poorer a girl was, the more likely she was to learn the facts of life at a young age – especially if she came from a big family. It was hard to avoid if you were growing up in a two-up-two-down terrace, sharing a bedroom with older siblings and even, sometimes, with parents. This could lead to a very wobbly understanding of what reproduction involved if it came without any explanation from elders, however. Bobby was thankful that her own mother, a progressive woman for her age and class, had never been shy about such things. Nelly Bancroft had made sure her daughters knew all they needed to prepare them for adult life.

Female naivety was taken for granted, yet men, too, were kept ignorant of things they ought to know about. Why?

Why had Bobby and Lil been warned never to mention their monthlies in the presence of their father and brothers, or any man? To spare those poor fragile males embarrassment, or disgust? Men might not experience monthly bleeding but they would be husbands and perhaps fathers to those who did, yet girls were taught to cover up their natural functions like something shameful. It seemed to Bobby that if men were to fulfil their role in the creation of new life – and all of them seemed eager enough to be involved in that part of it – then they should be aware of all it entailed.

She wondered how Charlie would be about these things. It wasn't something that had cropped up in their married life so far. For the first few months, they had been separated by their respective roles in the RAF. By the time they began sharing a home, Marmaduke had put in an appearance and Bobby's monthly bleeding was temporarily no longer an issue. She liked to think her husband wasn't the sort of man to react with revulsion to matters of nature, although he might be a little embarrassed, perhaps. If Marmaduke turned out to be a girl, she would want Charlie to be better prepared than George Parry had been for what his daughter's future held.

## Chapter 5

Bobby found Charlie and her father sitting by the fire, smoking companionably. Her dad often called on them when he had finished work in the patch of woodland where Bobby's friend Topsy employed him as gamekeeper.

Bobby greeted Charlie with a kiss, then went to plant another on her dad's bald crown.

'It's nice to see you here,' she said. 'Have you had a cup of tea?'

Rob smiled complacently at her. 'Aye, your young man were good enough to brew up. Quite domesticated now, isn't he?'

Charlie smiled at the good-natured teasing, but it looked rather forced. Rob noticed this too.

'Oh, no offence meant, son,' he said, standing up and clapping Charlie on the shoulder. 'No one knows better than me what a beggar it is to get work when a war spits you out.'

'None taken, Rob.' Charlie stood too. 'Come again, eh? Next time, I won't neglect my duties as househusband by failing to have some beer in the pantry.'

'Aye, a half pint wouldn't go amiss after work. You're a good lad.' Rob shouldered his shotgun, which was resting on the fireplace. 'Tell you what, Charlie. If you want to earn yourself a few bob, come out with me Monday afternoon and help me lay some stoat traps. I could use a big, strong lad.'

Charlie hesitated, glancing at his leg.

'Don't worry about that,' Rob said. 'I'm none so quick on my feet nowadays either. We'll walk nice and slow.'

'You don't need to do me any favours.'

'I'm talking about you doing me a favour. Not as young as I used to be. I ought to speak to Her Ladyship about hiring a lad to help, I suppose, but I don't want her to think the work's getting beyond me.'

'Well… all right. If you really think I can be useful.'

'Good man.' Rob turned to Bobby. 'How was work then, daughter o' mine?'

'Rather good actually,' Bobby said. 'Reg told me he's promoting me to deputy editor. Mary's persuaded him to take a step back from the mag, so I'll have a lot more creative control in future. He's moving me and Tony into new premises near the Parrys' place.'

Rob put his arm around her shoulders. 'Well done, lass. Your mam always said you'd do great things wi' that writing brain of thine.'

'Thanks, Dad.'

Charlie raised an eyebrow. 'Reggie's promoting you to deputy editor?'

Bobby laughed. 'You sound surprised.'

'I am, but not because I don't know what a clever, talented wife I've got. I'm just amazed my brother's letting someone else take control of his precious magazine.'

'I know, I didn't see it coming either. It'll mean a few shillings more in my pay packet too.' She pulled a face. 'I just hope Tony isn't going to make life difficult. He was sulking all morning about having to play second fiddle to a woman.'

'Hurt pride, that's all,' Rob said. 'Thinks too much of his pride, that lad. Your sister'll sort him out.'

Charlie nodded to a letter on the coffee table. 'That came for you, Bob. It's addressed to Athy Atherton.'

'That'll be from Scarlet then,' she said, smiling. 'Was that all?'

'Yes. Why, were you expecting something?'

'Thought I might hear from our Jake. His letter writing's been shocking lately.' She turned to her father. 'Have you or Lil had anything?'

'Nay, not recently.'

'I hope there's nothing wrong at his barracks.' Bobby's youngest brother was a sapper with the Royal Engineers, defusing bombs down in London.

'Oh, you know what the lad's like,' her dad said. 'Walking out wi' a new lass, I shouldn't wonder, and no time for writing home.'

'You're probably right.' Bobby grimaced. 'I almost forgot, I've got bad news for you, Charlie. As a peace offering, I said we'd take Tony and Lil to the pub tonight. I know we can't really afford nights out, but it'll be worth parting with a few bob to make my life easier at work.'

Charlie, who found Tony Scott difficult company when the man was awash with beer, pulled a face. 'Oh, all right. If it's for the sake of your career.'

'Dad, I'm afraid I volunteered you to mind Annie,' Bobby told him. 'Do you mind? We wouldn't be late.'

'Always happy with a bit o' grandad time,' Rob said jovially. 'Might as well get some in while I can.'

Bobby frowned. 'How do you mean? Are they increasing the Home Guard parades?'

'Nay, nowt like that.' Her dad started putting his macintosh on. 'I was thinking it were time to be flitting, that's all. Your sister and young Scott don't need me taking up space in that little barn, especially if they're minded to add more bodies to it.'

'You're moving out of Cow House Cottage?' Bobby said, blinking.

'Well, you and Lil have got your own lives to lead. Husbands to mind, and more bairns to come for both of thee, I hope. Your sister's a good girl to want to look after me and Tony's not nearly the rum lad I once believed, but it don't stop me feeling rather surplus to requirements.'

Bobby cast Charlie a worried look.

'Where would you go?' she asked her dad. 'Not back to Bradford?'

'Nay, not when I've a good job here. I was thinking I might as well put the house in Bradford up for sale. I've been too thoroughly countryfied to want to be back in a city now.'

'You'd sell our house?'

'Well, it's not needed by t' family, is it? Must be worth a few bob. Enough to get me set up somewhere, and happen wi' a bit left over to share out among you bairns.'

Bobby framed her next question carefully.

'Um, are you sure you ought to live alone, Dad?' she asked. 'Lil and me could take your washing, but we can only do so much with our own homes to run. You'd have to get a woman in to cook and clean for you.'

'Who said I'd be alone?' Rob jammed his cloth cap on. 'I've a friend in a similar boat. A daughter grown up, with not enough room in t' house for elderly relatives. We thought, why not throw our lot in together? Two can live as cheaply as one, they say, and we'd be company for one another.'

'A friend? Who?'

'Someone from the pub – but I'll not say more till it's settled. Just know you don't need to worry about me, eh, our Bobby? Sithee both at dinner tomorrow.'

With a kiss for his stunned daughter and a handshake for his equally stunned son-in-law, Rob left.

'Well!' Bobby said to Charlie. 'What do you make of that?'

'It's... good, isn't it?' Charlie said. 'Your dad's right – the cow house is small for a young family and him too, and we're no better placed to offer him a home. I know you've always worried about him living alone, but if he's got a pal willing to share then that solves everybody's problems. He can have independence without being left by himself.'

'I suppose so,' Bobby said cautiously. 'Certainly I don't feel nearly so worried as I would have done a year ago. Oh, but selling our house! I was born in that house. I... I lost my mam in that house.'

'I know it'll be emotional for you, darling. But realistically, were you ever going to live there?'

'Well, no. It's like my dad said – I've been too countryfied to want to live anywhere but here. Lil and our Ray have their own homes, and I don't suppose Jake will want to settle there.' She sighed. 'It's just... as long as we had a family home, even with no Bancrofts living in it, it felt like our memories had a place that went with them. It's strange to think of another family making it theirs. Still, you're right, Charlie. Better for it to be sold, and the money used to help the family.'

'I wonder if he's said anything to your sister about moving out.'

'I don't think so, otherwise she'd have mentioned it.'

Bobby thought about how Lilian had looked that morning – so tired and drained. She looked that way far too often nowadays.

Bobby knew her sister was struggling with the life she was leading. Struggling with her responsibilities as a mother to Annie, and her grief over Georgia. Struggling to sleep. Struggling to be the wife of a man who, try as she might, she found it hard to love.

Yes, perhaps this would be for the best. It would be better for Tony and Lilian's marriage to have their home to themselves. Lil would be less tired without her father to wash and cook for in addition to a husband and child. No longer weary and harassed constantly, she and Tony might grow closer.

'I wish I knew who this friend is Dad's considering moving in with,' Bobby said to Charlie. 'It needs to be someone who understands... how he is. His nightmares and everything. And someone who won't encourage bad habits either. He's been doing so well, I'd hate for him to fall into that state where he starts relying on spirits.'

'He said it was someone from the Hart,' Charlie said thoughtfully. 'Maybe it's Stan Henderson. He's been at a loose end since his old woman died, and I did hear he was keen to move out of his place now his daughter's expecting a second baby. He was in the trenches too. They could be good company for each other.'

'Yes. Perhaps.'

'It'll be all right.' Charlie smiled. 'And now, Mrs Atherton, I insist you stop looking so worried and sit yourself down on my lap.'

Bobby allowed him to pull her on to his knee, where she treated him to a long kiss.

'You should get promoted more often,' he said breathlessly when she released his lips again. 'I never realised these deputy editors were so amorous.'

'That was to say thanks for spending time with my dad,' she said, smiling. 'He likes your company, and I know it does him good.'

'I think he feels sorry for me,' Charlie said with a sigh. 'Poor washed-up Charlie Atherton, stuck at home playing housewife with his bad arm and his bad leg and his...' He held up one trembling hand. 'You know.'

'You remind him of himself, I suppose. Don't be offended by it.'

'I'm not offended – not when it's him.' He scowled. 'If it was anyone else, I'd make them eat their damn pity. But your dad understands.'

'I'm glad the two of you have got each other to talk to.' She looked into his face. 'Do you talk? I mean, do you talk about the wars and your injuries and... you know, things like that?'

'Not really. He just likes to share a smoke and read the paper.'

'He certainly seems jolly these days,' Bobby observed. 'I've never seen him happier than he's been since I came back from the WAAF. And he adores the baby.'

'Being a grandfather does seem to agree with him.'

'He's always loved little ones.' Bobby wrapped her arms around her husband's neck. 'I can't wait until we can tell him about Marmaduke, darling,' she said softly. 'You know I don't care what the baby turns out to be so long as it's healthy, but with Ray's girls and little Annie already in the family, my dad would be thrilled to have a grandson.'

'Well, if it's a girl then we'll just have to start trying right away for another, won't we?' Charlie kissed her nose. 'We can start practising now if you like.'

Bobby smiled. 'I wondered how long it would be until the conversation took a turn in that direction.'

'I do seem to remember a certain promise you made this morning. You can't go back on your word now you're a deputy editor, you know. It would undermine your journalistic integrity.'

'Would it now?'

'Oh, absolutely.'

'Don't you want to hear about my eventful day?'

'I want to hear all about it, in…' Charlie looked at his wristwatch. '…no less than an hour. Come on.'

Laughing, Bobby let him lead her to the bedroom.

## Chapter 6

An hour later, Bobby was resting her head on Charlie's bare chest in a state of complete contentment. His heart thudded against her, making her body shake slightly with each rhythmic beat. It was comforting to feel his heartbeat rippling through her, like… well, like life, she supposed. It seemed to soothe Marmaduke too.

Charlie's attempts to make love to his wife weren't always successful. Sometimes the excitement brought on one of his nervous attacks, curtailing bedroom activities. As long as she could be close to him, though, Bobby was content – and if his struggle with impotence in the wake of the crash that had killed two of his crew had taught Charlie anything, it was a slow and thorough enjoyment of his wife's body that she felt privileged to experience. There hadn't been any problems today, however, and they lay naked, satiated and happy in each other's embrace.

'We ought to get up,' Bobby murmured, pressing kisses into the dusting of hair on Charlie's chest.

'Why? There's nowhere I'd rather be than here.'

'I've got to make the tea before we meet my sister and Tony in the pub. Besides, I'm sure the neighbours must be whispering about us, drawing the curtains every Saturday afternoon and never emerging until it's time for church next day.'

'Let them talk.' Charlie rolled on top of her and started kissing her neck. 'They're just jealous.'

'You think old Mrs Barraclough next door wants you for herself?'

'Of course she does. The woman's only human, even if she is seventy-four.'

Bobby smiled as he started nibbling her earlobe. 'Leave off that a minute.'

'I thought you liked that.'

'I do, but give up. I want to look at you.'

Charlie detached himself from her ear to look into her face. 'What's up, love?' he asked gently.

'Nothing.' She drew her fingers over the deep white flak scar on his cheek, a permanent reminder of his last fateful mission. 'I just want to remember how you look right now. I do love you, Charlie.'

He smiled. 'I know you do. What's got you talking soft?'

'I suppose I was thinking… will it always be like this?'

'I might not be quite so sprightly in the bedroom in another sixty years, but other than that, I don't see why not.'

'I just worry about how things will change when Marmaduke arrives. I mean I can't wait to be a mam and dad together, but…' She looked into Charlie's dark brown eyes, which always looked a little sad these days even when he was smiling. 'It won't change anything between us, will it?' she whispered.

He stroked back her hair. The puckered, leathery skin of his burnt arm felt rough against her cheek.

'Of course it won't, except for the better. Why should it?'

'Only I see Lil so washed out all the time, forever worrying about money, and I wonder how I'm going to cope. I rely on my job to give my brain something to do, and to have to replace that with—' She bit her lip.

'With what? Motherhood?'

The word that had actually risen to Bobby's tongue had been 'drudgery', but she didn't say this to Charlie.

'Things are so nice now, just the two of us, loving each other,' she said. 'I want it to always be that way, even with a baby to share it. I don't want to become a cross, tired, frumpy wife who you'll find it hard to stay in love with.'

He smiled. 'Do you ever stop worrying about what might happen and try to enjoy what you've got?'

'I try, but I'm a worrier by nature. As soon as one problem's solved, my brain throws up another.'

'Well now it's throwing up problems that won't exist, if you're talking about me finding it hard to love you.' He tapped her temple. 'I'd have a stern word with that overworked old brain of yours if I were you. You're not doing yourself or Marmaduke any favours worrying about what-ifs.'

'You're right. I'm being daft.' She tilted her head. 'You can take my mind off it by kissing my ear again if you like.'

'I do,' Charlie said, burrowing into her hair. 'Tell me about your day while I do it. I want to see how long it'll take me to distract you.'

Bobby shivered as his lips tickled her skin. 'Well, it began with your brother saying he wanted to talk to me and Tony, which put the fear of God into me for a start. I was worried one of us was for the chop. But he just wanted to tell me I was being promoted, and we were to have a new office in George Parry's shed.'

'A shed?' Charlie murmured, trailing his fingertips delicately over her lightly rounded stomach. 'That doesn't sound comfortable.'

'It's a very nice shed,' Bobby said, somewhat defensively. If she was to be a deputy editor, she didn't want anyone casting aspersions on the workplace she'd be in charge of. 'It's an old shepherd's hut, quite big. Reg has had it done up for us.'

'You went to see it, then?'

'Yes, Tony and I went over after work.' She experienced a pleasant shiver as his lips moved to her shoulder. 'How was your day?'

'Oh, thrilling. I black-leaded the fireplace, did the ironing, polished the brasses and then — and this was the really exciting bit — I got the Vim out and scrubbed the lav.'

'You don't need to do all that,' Bobby said, with a twinge of guilt. 'I could have done the lav tomorrow. I know it must hurt your arm.'

'It's fine, Bobby. No worse than being on fatigues.'

'Still, remember what Dr Minchin told you. You need rest to heal.'

'It's you who needs rest, not me.' He was kissing her collarbone now. 'You know, I'm rather offended that my kisses aren't distracting you from this endless stream of small talk. I mean, as brimming with sex appeal as the image of me scrubbing the outhouse in my pinny undoubtedly is.'

Bobby laughed. 'You're doing splendidly, I swear. I'm just a little too parched to enjoy it properly. Do you think you can bear the separation if I fetch a glass of water?'

He glanced up. 'Only if you give me your solemn promise that you'll come back immediately, and there'll be none of this "making the tea" nonsense until I've kissed all the bits of you I'm minded to.'

She tilted his chin up to kiss him. 'I promise.'

'Then you have my permission to depart, Aircraftwoman.'

Smiling, Bobby put on her dressing gown before going to the kitchen to get a glass of water.

Her throat was very dry, and she gulped the water rather too quickly. She was pouring herself a second tumbler when she spotted a torn-up envelope in the salvage bin. The letters 'OHMS' caught her eye.

What could that be doing in the bin? It must be military with those initials.

The envelope was addressed to Charlie, and the postmark showed it had probably come that morning. Yet he had told her there'd been no post except her letter from Scarlet. Why would he tear up an official letter?

Too curious to mind her own business, Bobby fished the thing out of the bin, extracted the two halves of the letter and pieced them together.

It was from the Air Ministry.

> *Sir,*
>
> *I am directed to inform you that His Majesty the King has graciously approved the award of the Distinguished Flying Cross in recognition of your gallant conduct during aerial action on the night of 30th August, 1942. The announcement of this award will appear in an early issue of the* London Gazette. *Details of the investiture ceremony at Buckingham Palace will follow in a future correspondence...*

Bobby stared at it. The DFC!

She remembered that Wing Commander Butler, Charlie's commanding officer at Wykeness, had talked of recommending him for the honour. Since nothing more had been said, however, she had assumed the CO hadn't gone ahead – perhaps because of the circumstances under which Charlie had been invalided out, with what his doctors called 'shattered nerves'. That could so easily have led to the ignominious classification of LMF – lack of moral fibre – if it hadn't been for the intervention of a sympathetic RAF medical officer. But it looked as though Butler had recommended Charlie for the gong after all.

One of the most prestigious awards in the military, and more than deserved given Charlie had saved the lives of four men at great personal risk. And he had torn up the letter! Why on earth would he do that?

Bobby jumped at a knock on the door. She stuffed the fragments of Charlie's letter into her pocket.

Who was calling? She could hardly answer the door wearing nothing but her dressing gown. Bobby was sure the neighbours were already gossiping about 'those newlyweds at Number 4, who always put their blackouts up early every Saturday, *if you take my meaning*'. She and Charlie would just have to pretend to be out.

She was curious about who it was, though, and tiptoed to the parlour window to peep behind the blackout curtains.

This she quickly regretted when she found a face on the other side, trying to peep in just as Bobby was trying to peep out. It was her friend Topsy Nowak, who waved enthusiastically.

Oh well, so much for pretending to be out. Bobby raised her voice to speak to Charlie.

'You'd better put some clothes on, darling. We have visitors.'

'Damn all visitors to hell,' he called back cheerfully. 'Tell them we're busy and come back to bed.'

'I can't, it's Topsy – with Jolka, I think.' Bobby had caught a glimpse of someone with silky black hair behind Topsy, and assumed it must be her Polish friend. 'It would be rude when they've walked all the way here.'

'Is a man never to have a moment's peace to enjoy an afternoon in bed with his wife?' He sighed. 'Oh, all right.'

Bobby heard him swearing to himself as he got up.

She went to answer the door, trying to hide behind it as she ushered in the visitors. Of course, Topsy started smirking as soon as she saw what her friend was wearing – or rather what she wasn't wearing.

'Oh Lor,' she said. 'What on earth did we interrupt, Birdy?'

'I was… having a lie-down,' Bobby said, feeling her cheeks heat. 'I had a headache.'

'Tops, I hope you won't take it personally if I tell you to make this a quick visit and beggar off home,' Charlie called from the bedroom.

Jolka shook her head solemnly. 'And your poor husband suffers with a headache too, Bobby. I see he also has been in need of a lie-down.'

The three women looked at each other, then broke into laughter.

'Oh, Birdy, I am sorry,' Topsy said. 'I should have known better than to drop in on newlyweds unannounced.'

Bobby smiled, her embarrassment dissolving in their laughter.

'I'm not sure we count as newlyweds any more,' she said. 'We've been eight months married now. But we were forced to spend so much of our early married life apart that, um...' She blushed. 'Well, it does rather feel as if we're still on our honeymoon.'

'This is most natural,' Jolka said in her rolling Polish lilt. 'Piotr and I are the same whenever he has leave.'

'Are you really?' Topsy said, regarding her with interest. 'I can't imagine you as a giddy, giggling bride, Jolka. You're always so sensible and grown-up.'

'Well, perhaps I do not giggle,' Jolka said, smiling. 'But Piotrek says it is good for me sometimes to be giddy.'

'I'll make tea, if you can allow me five minutes to make myself respectable,' Bobby said. 'Please, sit down.'

'There is no need to hurry,' Jolka said. 'I am sure between us, Topsy and I can locate the tea caddy.'

'We'll send Charlie to the Golden Hart so we can have a jolly girls' gossip,' Topsy said. 'We've got such a lot of news, and one piece is going to make Charlie just green with jealousy, Birdy.'

Charlie emerged fully dressed from the bedroom. With none of the shyness that Bobby struggled with, he pulled his wife to him for a deep kiss. This gave every indication of going on for some time, but Bobby pushed him away.

'We've got guests, Charlie,' she said, laughing. 'Behave yourself.'

'I'm just staking my claim, before these wicked women take you away from me. I did hear that threat to evict me.' He greeted both ladies with a peck on the cheek before turning to Topsy. 'What's going to make me green with jealousy, Tops?'

'Only that there's an old friend of ours come back to the village,' Topsy said, managing to look both cryptic and smug. 'But I shan't tell you who. It's for Birdy's ears only, then she can tease you about it later.'

'Well, I suppose I can make myself scarce for a little while so you girls can chat about knitting patterns and Robert Taylor's swoon-inducing eyes.' Charlie put on his macintosh and extracted his walking stick from the umbrella stand. 'I've been meaning to call on Gil Capstick and congratulate him on his engagement.'

Bobby gave him a kiss. 'Thanks, love. Give Gil my congratulations as well.'

The news of the cheery sub-postmaster's engagement to Mabs Jessop, long the object of his unrequited affection, had been announced a week ago. It was bittersweet news, coming as it did on the back of a tragedy for the Jessop family: the death of Bobby's old friend Andy, Mabs's grandfather, at the age of eighty-three.

Bobby had discovered Andy confined to his bed after her discharge from the WAAF, in the throes of his final illness. She had been heartbroken to say goodbye to one of the first friends she had made in Silverdale, but Andy himself had been sanguine. He had lost so many people he loved at a young age that he considered it a privilege to have seen so many years, and to have enjoyed so much happiness.

But one good thing had come of Andy's death. Mabs, a flighty young lady of nineteen with an eye for a man in uniform, had grieved heartily for the grandfather she adored. The support and comfort Gil had offered her at this difficult time had finally given Mabs perspective. She had at last learned to value the caring, steady young man who loved her over and above a handsome face. Andy would be glad to think his death had helped his young granddaughter find happiness.

When Charlie had left to visit Gil, Bobby went into the bedroom to dress, put on some lipstick and arrange her dishevelled hair.

It was when she was hanging up her dressing gown that she remembered the torn letter in the pocket. She took it out and frowned at it.

There must be some reason Charlie had torn it up. But why conceal it like something shameful when it was such an honour?

There was no time to worry about it now, however. Bobby thrust the pieces into a drawer and went out to her guests.

## *Chapter 7*

Bobby attempted to put the letter out of her head as she joined her friends. Perhaps it had been a mistake. It was an easy thing to muddle one piece of waste paper with another. Perhaps Charlie had even concealed it on purpose so he could surprise her. There were a hundred innocent explanations.

What a fine thing it would be for him, though – the DFC! He would be invited to Buckingham Palace, and be decorated by the king himself. They would be able to show the medal to Marmaduke one day, and he would be proud to know what a brave man his father was. It might even help Charlie find work. The award was widely respected in the civilian as well as the military world.

'Birdy, you look a million miles away.' Topsy patted the settee in Bobby's small, neat parlour. 'Sit by me.'

Jolka had claimed the armchair, and was engaged in pouring them each a cup of tea. Bobby sat down by Topsy, smiling.

She could understand why Charlie resented this intrusion. After spending much of their early married life apart, he jealously guarded their precious Saturday afternoons. Bobby, too, looked forward to those contented, peaceful hours in his arms, when the world and its wars could be shut out for a while. Still, it was a treat to spend time with her female friends during what Charlie called their 'mothers' meetings'.

'It is a shame we do not have Lilian,' Jolka observed. Lil usually made up the fourth in their group of young wives. 'It was on the edge of the moment that we decided to pay a visit. Topsy is bursting with news for you, Bobby.'

'What is this news?' Bobby asked. Topsy did seem to be bouncing in her seat, filled with girlish glee at having a secret.

'Well, darling, it's actually a whole lot of news, and all of it jolly exciting,' Topsy said. 'But I shall save the part that concerns you for last, because I know how you like to tease Charlie out of his glum moods with a little healthy jealousy.'

Jolka handed Bobby a cup of tea. 'How does he do?'

Jolka and Topsy had airmen husbands of their own, both of whom had suffered dramatic experiences in the sky, so Bobby felt no bashfulness confiding in them. They knew what it was to live with a man damaged by war.

'Better, I think,' she said. 'He still sleeps restlessly, but the neurasthenia attacks aren't so frequent. Still, I suppose it will be a long time before his brain understands he isn't in danger any more.'

'If it ever does,' Topsy said soberly. As a nurse at the airmen's hospital at Sumner House, and with a burnt and disabled husband at home, she had encountered more horrors than most.

'His moods are improved, I'm sure,' Bobby said. 'The hardest thing for him is not having any paid work. I know he feels like he's failing as a husband, keeping house while I'm supporting us.'

Jolka nodded. 'Men can be sensitive about playing what they see as the woman's part. Yet it is not Charlie's fault that the war has made it impossible to do the work he is trained for.'

'It's still humiliating for him, feeling he isn't doing his duty as head of the house.' She sighed. 'I know it's wrong to look back, but I do miss my days in the WAAF sometimes. Not only the important work I was doing, but the way it allowed me to live.'

'I suppose it is not unusual for ex-servicewomen to feel this way,' Jolka said, sipping her tea. 'Many will not have experienced independent living before.'

'It isn't only that. It's the way we all sort of... mucked in, you know?' A smile flickered on Bobby's lips as she thought back to her brief but happy career in the WAAF. 'Some of the women could be toffee-nosed, but mostly everyone was happy to do their share. We all took our turn on fatigues, and we divided up chores in our billets equally. I've been keeping a home since I was fourteen but I'd never experienced that sort of communal living. It does make it harder to accept the housewife's lot when the military drops you back on Civvy Street.'

'For too many wives, a home can be a prison,' Jolka said soberly. 'Always for women, the world would try to make us be *what* we are at the expense of *who* we are. Still, I do not fear for you, Bobby. You are strong, and your husband loves and respects you.' She leaned forward to press Bobby's hand. 'But for as long as you are able, earn your own money. Always find a way to do this, no matter how little. It is an absence of financial independence that traps women in the home. Even to happy wives, I would say this.'

'That's good advice,' Bobby said, thinking of the letter she had posted earlier. 'But tell me all your news. Is Piotr still at Ryland Moor?'

Jolka's husband Piotr, formerly an air gunner with a Polish bomber squadron, was one of the lucky few who had managed to survive a full tour of operations. Having completed the required thirty missions, he had been transferred to an instructor position ten miles away.

Jolka smiled. 'He is. Tommy is delighted to see his father so often.'

'Will he apply for a second tour?'

'He talked of it, but I believe something I told him recently may have changed his mind.'

'What was that?'

Jolka didn't answer. She only smiled, and rested one hand on her stomach.

'Oh. Oh!' Bobby jumped up to give her friend a hug. 'That's wonderful news! I'm thrilled for you, Jolka.'

'I told you we were brimming with exciting news, didn't I?' Topsy said triumphantly. 'Jolka let it slip when she brought over some tablecloths she borrowed. Of course we simply had to rush into the village and tell you. We'll call on Lilian on the way home, then everyone in our little gang knows.'

'You were very sly not to have told me right away, letting me chatter on about myself.' Bobby held Jolka back to look at her beaming face. 'When is the baby due?'

'In five months. I did not wish to make it public until the most dangerous time had passed.'

Five months! That meant Jolka's baby and Marmaduke would arrive at nearly the same time. Bobby longed to tell her friends that she, too, had news to share, but she would have to hold on to her secret just a little longer.

'Well, I think this calls for something sweet to celebrate,' she said. 'I've got a little fruit cake I've been saving for a special occasion. I can't think of any more special than this.'

'Oh no, please,' Jolka said. 'We would not take your precious cake.'

'Nonsense, I insist.'

Bobby went to fetch the cake tin and served them each a small slice.

There was silence as each woman sank her teeth into the treat. You learned to savour sweet things in wartime.

'However will you manage your painting with two young children, Jolka?' Topsy asked when she had swallowed her morsel of cake.

Jolka shrugged. It was clear that the idea of combining work with motherhood didn't worry her the way it did Bobby.

'There may be a little expense, if I find I cannot manage the house alone and need to pay for some outside help, but we are able to afford it,' she said. 'Still, it is difficult when Piotr must be away from us. I may have to be more selective about the commissions I take.'

'You wouldn't give up work for a while?'

'Oh, no. I would go mad if I did not have my painting.'

'I know how you feel,' Bobby said. 'I couldn't bear not to have something to do with my brain. I hope I'll never be in a position where I have to give up writing entirely.'

'Things go well at your work?'

'I'm to be promoted actually,' Bobby told them with some pride. 'Reg is taking a step back and making me deputy editress.'

Jolka raised an eyebrow. 'Indeed? And your brother-in-law, he will work under you?'

'Yes. That's the part that's worrying me,' Bobby said, pulling a face. 'Tony's never been good at taking orders, and when it's a woman giving them... I just hope he can learn to accept the situation.'

'You must make him accept it,' Jolka said firmly. 'No doubt he will attempt to undermine you, but ultimately he must accept that you are in charge or seek another position.'

'He's my brother-in-law, Jolka. I wouldn't want him to lose his job, for my sister and niece's sake.'

'Yes, this is a consideration. Just make sure that when he challenges you, he is challenged right back. Be alert for little things that undermine your authority.'

It was sensible advice. But how far should she push back against Tony, given that she would have to leave her position soon? She didn't want to push him so hard that he resigned.

Bobby nodded to the last morsel of Jolka's fruit cake. 'Don't forget your celebration cake. I'm sure it's supposed to bring luck to the baby or something.'

Jolka smiled as she popped it into her mouth. 'These days, I like to make the sweet things last.'

Topsy arched an eyebrow at Bobby. 'I must say, Birdy, I think it's high time you and Charlie started making beautiful, clever babies as well. You can't leave it all to Piotr and Jolka.'

Jolka laughed. 'Perhaps they might, Topsy, if their friends were not so rude as to turn up when they are... ahem. Recovering from headaches.'

Bobby could feel her cheeks pinkening and hastily shifted the focus of the conversation.

'What about you, Topsy?' she said. 'Have you and Teddy gone any further with plans to adopt a child?'

Topsy tossed back her tea gloomily. 'What point is there, when we can barely fit ourselves into that tiny cottage? Already I feel horrendously guilty that poor Maimie is sleeping in such a small room.' Maimie Hobbes was Topsy's former nanny, who in retirement lived with her one-time charge as a companion. 'I'm glad the big house is helping those boys get better but it is frustrating, to be lady of the manor and all that rot while I'm having to live like a… a shepherdess or something.'

Bobby laughed. 'More like the little goose girl, with Norman and his family filling the place up.'

'What of the other house you own – Woodside Nook?' Jolka asked. 'That is bigger, is it not?'

'Yes, but it's ever so draughty, and hardly in the healthiest environment in the middle of a damp wood,' Topsy said. 'It wouldn't do Teddy any good, and it would be dreadful for Maimie's arthritis.' She sighed. 'Poor old Maimie. I really ought to take better care of her now she's getting older.'

'She isn't so very old, is she?' Bobby asked.

'She's not fifty yet. Still, she gets a lot of aches and pains, and I feel guilty about every one of them. I wish this bally war would just end, then I can have my house back, Maimie can be comfortable and we can start filling the place with children as Teddy and I long to.'

'How strange it will be when the war is over,' Jolka said, rather dreamily. 'I have only known this house of yours as a hospital, Topsy. It feels odd to imagine it without men and nurses.'

'It will be strange,' Bobby agreed. 'And happy too, of course. Still, I've got used to seeing uniforms in the village, and hearing London accents whenever I pass the playground. There'll be an empty feeling when our wartime guests go away.'

'This is true, yet I would not wish another day of war. I would so desire my children to grow up in peace, and be taken to see our country free once more.'

'I hope it's soon,' Topsy said fervently. 'It's what Teddy wants more than anything: to go back to Warsaw, and find his parents and siblings.'

There was a moment's silence as a thought too grim to be spoken hovered between them – that when Teddy Nowak was able to return to his native country, there may be no loved ones there for him to find. His family were Slavs, and of some Jewish descent. If they had been taken to one of Hitler's monstrous camps... but it was too bleak even to think such a thing, let alone voice it.

'I miss our pantomime this year,' Jolka said after a moment, obviously deciding a jollier subject was needed. 'How do rehearsals for *Dick Whittington* go, Topsy?'

At this time last year, all three women had been involved in the pantomime Topsy had organised for the village children. Bobby had played Cinderella and Jolka had been her Prince Charming, while Topsy had been producer, director, financier and generally in charge. It seemed a lifetime ago.

Neither Bobby nor Jolka were involved in this year's production. Bobby would have loved to be in the cast, but rehearsals had already been well advanced when she returned from the WAAF. Besides, she had always been prone to stage fright, and she wasn't certain that was going to mix well with pregnancy nausea. Jolka had told Topsy she was too busy with work, but now they knew her secret, Bobby wondered if the same thought had been troubling her.

'Well I don't think it's a patch on last year, when we had the pair of you contributing your talents,' Topsy said, somewhat accusingly. 'We're desperately short of men this time too. Still, it's looking good in spite of having to make do.'

'I hope I can be part of it if we put on another next year,' Bobby said wistfully. 'No doubt you're going to be very smug reminding me how you had to twist my arm to do it, Topsy, but I loved being Cinderella.'

'I shall have to bow out again, I suppose,' Jolka said. 'It is a shame, but with a new baby I will struggle to find time.'

Bobby stifled a sigh as she thought that she, too, would be in that position. How different her world would look by then!

'You don't know how close you both came to being drafted in this year,' Topsy said, putting down her teacup. 'I was badly let down by the airman playing Idle Jack, who rudely allowed himself to be discharged from the hospital two weeks ago. I know it's usually a male role, but I'd gladly have taken anyone who could learn the part.'

'You managed to find someone then?' Bobby asked.

'I did.'

'Is it another airman?'

'Yes, but not one of those in the hospital.' Topsy grinned. 'That was the news I brought especially for you, Bobby. You'll never guess who's back in his old billet.'

Bobby felt a stab of worry. She asked the question she knew Topsy was longing her to ask, even though she suspected she already knew the answer.

'Who?'

'Who do you think? It's Ernie King, of course.'

## Chapter 8

After her friends had left, Bobby spent some time making herself pretty. She carefully styled her hair, put on her best dress and applied her make-up. The news that Flying Officer Ernie King of the Royal Canadian Air Force was back in the village produced a sensation of guilt, and she felt the need to make herself attractive for her husband.

She didn't know why she should feel guilty. She didn't even know who the guilt was focused on: Charlie, who had always had a healthy jealousy of her former suitor, or Ernie, for rejecting the proposal he had made seven months ago and leaving him broken-hearted. Perhaps it was both.

It was a foolish guilt. Bobby hadn't done anything wrong in her dealings with Ernie, other than naively failing to notice that he had developed romantic feelings towards her. Nor had she done anything to betray Charlie. Yes, she had briefly considered Ernie's proposal when she had falsely believed Charlie's love for her had cooled, but she had never felt anything for the young Canadian beyond warm friendship and respect. Their entire relationship had consisted of a handful of dances and a kiss, of which Ernie had been the giver and Bobby the startled recipient. But the affair had caused pain to both men, and she couldn't help feeling a certain responsibility for that.

Topsy, who had an inkling of Ernie's partiality for Bobby even if she didn't know all the details, seemed to think the whole thing was rather a joke. Something Bobby could use to tease her husband out of a dark mood, arousing his jealousy before reassuring him with kisses that it was unnecessary. But Bobby wasn't in a humour for teasing Charlie today.

How would Ernie react when they inevitably bumped into one another? With a jovial 'Hey, Slacks' as before? With sad eyes and sighs? Perhaps he would ignore her entirely. That would be painful, when he had been a good friend. Did his feelings for her still linger, or had he moved on to fresher love affairs?

It didn't give Bobby any pangs of envy to consider the latter. She hoped Ernie had found someone else – someone better suited to him than she had ever been. If he did still carry a torch for her, it could only hurt him to see her regularly now she was a married woman.

About an hour after Bobby's friends had left, Charlie arrived home from his visit to Gil Capstick. He smiled when he saw his wife's rouged cheeks and trim floral dress.

'I didn't expect to find you so pretty and fragrant,' he said, putting his stick away so he could take her in his arms. 'Is this for my benefit?'

She smiled. 'Who else's would it be for?'

'One of your many gentleman admirers, perhaps. I bumped into Ernie King on my walk back.'

Bobby blinked. 'You saw Ernie?'

'I did. He offered to buy me a drink at the Hart, but I said I had an important liaison arranged with my wife. Did you know he was back?'

Bobby felt relieved that Charlie knew about Ernie already, and she didn't need to confess the man's presence like some guilty secret.

'Yes, Topsy told me,' she said. 'That was the news supposed to turn you into a raging Othello, I think.'

He smiled. 'And you were looking forward to teasing me about it. Sorry for ruining the fun.'

Bobby hesitated. 'Did Ernie seem… all right?'

'As hail-fellow-well-met as he ever was. I suppose the offer of a drink was a peace-making gesture after trying to steal my girl back in the spring. I'd have accepted, but I knew you were waiting for me so we could meet Tony and your sister. I told him I'd be happy to join him another day, though.'

Bobby smiled. 'That was big of you.'

He shrugged. 'I won, didn't I? You're wearing my ring and carrying my baby. No need to rub the poor chap's face in it.'

Bobby rewarded him for his magnanimous behaviour with a kiss.

'I must admit, it's tempting to tease you if only as revenge for all the flirtations you had going on when I first came to the village,' she said. 'But I prefer knowing you trust me.'

'Completely, Mrs Atherton.' He released her so he could take off his coat and hat. 'What's for tea, love?'

'Potato pie with at least one chunk of stewed steak per serving. It's in the oven. How was the bridegroom-to-be?'

'Still stunned he got a yes, I think,' Charlie said with a laugh. 'He thought he'd never get Mabs to look at him twice with all these handsome airmen around.'

'You're including yourself in that, of course.'

'Of course.' Charlie swapped his boots for slippers and went to sit by the fire. 'He wants me to be groomsman for him. I said yes, naturally.'

'I wish Andy had been here to see them marry,' Bobby said with a sigh. 'He'd have been so proud.'

Charlie watched her appreciatively as she bent to poke the fire, making the flames dance.

'You're very dressed up for the Hart,' he said.

'Not for the Hart. I told you, this is for you.'

'Why for me?'

'I was worried you'd be jealous when you heard Ernie was back. I wanted to make myself pretty for you.'

'Then you can come here and sit on my knee. You're too good to waste, looking like that.'

He pulled her on to his lap and kissed her heartily.

'We don't have to go to the pub,' he whispered when they broke apart. 'It's chilly out. Best to stay in and keep warm.'

Bobby smiled. 'In bed, by any chance?'

'Best place to warm up.'

'We can't, Charlie. Believe me, I'd rather be in bed with you than trying to get Tony out of a sulk, but if I don't he'll make work hell for me on Monday.'

He sighed. 'Oh, all right. I'm really starting to wish we didn't know quite so many people around here. Did you girls have a nice time gossiping about the menfolk?'

'I'm sure your egos would love to believe we talk about nothing else,' Bobby said with a laugh. 'Actually we had something more interesting to discuss.'

'Can you tell me?'

'I think I'm allowed. It's Jolka and Piotr. They're expecting another baby.'

'That's good news. When?'

'Five months, the same as Marmaduke. I felt awful that I couldn't share my news in exchange. I had to assuage the guilt with fruit cake.' She gave him a kiss. 'Don't worry, though, I saved you a slice for after tea.'

'I hope it won't be long until we can start telling people. As soon as I've found a job, you can give Reggie your notice and start spreading the news.'

Bobby thought about the letter she had found in the bin. The DFC could make a big difference to his employment prospects, she was sure.

'Charlie?' she said hesitantly. 'Can I ask you about something?'

Charlie was engaged in kissing her neck. 'If you like.'

'It's just... I'm sure I'm worrying over nothing as usual, but earlier, in the salvage bin, I found, um, a letter.' She took a deep breath. 'From the Air Ministry.'

Charlie stopped kissing her and looked up, his expression wary. 'What of it?'

'I wondered why it was torn up, that's all. You can't have meant to do it.'

'Can't I? Why not?'

'Well, because it's the DFC.'

He turned his face away from her. Feeling awkward, Bobby removed herself from his knee.

'You threw it away on purpose?' she asked.

'I told you when I came back from that last op. I'm not interested in some meaningless bloody gong.'

'But whyever not, Charlie? I can't think of anyone who deserves it more. Climbing out of the plane to put out the fire... that was real heroism. Everyone at Wykeness said so.'

Charlie gave a harsh laugh. 'Everyone said so, did they? And yet I came so close to being classed LMF when I told them I wouldn't fly again. Having my commission stripped from me, reduced to the ranks, disgraced. Wasn't it you who told me there's a fine line between cowardice and heroism?'

'That doesn't make you any less a hero.' Bobby knelt in front of him and took his hands. 'It makes you more of one, if anything, because you had to battle your nerves every step of the way to do what you knew was right. I bet there are a tiny fraction of men who would have done what you did that night.'

'What I knew was right,' Charlie repeated tonelessly. He extracted his hands from hers and took up his newspaper, then turned to a page he'd folded over and pointed out a story. 'Look at this.'

Bobby skimmed it. It was only a couple of paragraphs: a report on the success of recent bombing raids over Germany.

There was no mention of specific ops or squadrons: just a lot of statistics about damage to enemy manpower and things. She was struggling to see what might have upset Charlie. It seemed very dry and unemotional to her. There was a single mention of Mannheim, but no other details.

'I'm not sure what you want me to see,' she said. 'Were friends of yours involved in the Mannheim campaign?'

'It's just so bloody *clinical*,' Charlie said, his face working feverishly. 'How many "manpower hours" the Germans have lost. How many German civilians have been "dehoused". You know what that means, right? It means we wiped the poor buggers out. Loss of manpower means loss of men. Dehoused means some residential area's been reduced to rubble, and its people killed or made into refugees. I did that, Bobby. Me.'

'Well yes, but it's war,' Bobby said helplessly. 'I know it seems heartless, but if it'll end this thing faster then it saves more lives in the long run, doesn't it?'

'I hope that helps the other boys sleep at night, because it doesn't me.' Charlie took the newspaper and held it in hands that trembled so violently, he could barely keep a grip. 'Look here. It says that due to the amount of damage the new heavy bombers can inflict, a Lancaster has paid for itself even if it only makes one trip. No mention of the seven men who would have been killed on that one trip, not to mention those on the ground. At the beginning of this war, people in this country wouldn't have stomached the idea of bombing civilians. Then the Blitz came, our men started dying in the skies and our people on the ground, and it hardened us. Made us vengeful. And if you show any sign of giving a damn what happens to those people, you're scorned as weak or womanish. The RAF can stick their bloody gongs.'

Bobby took the newspaper away and seized the trembling hands. She kissed them softly, looking up into Charlie's face until the black cloud dissipated. It was replaced by weariness as he sagged in his chair.

'I do understand,' Bobby said softly. 'You're right to care, and I love you for it. There's nothing weak about compassion, Charlie.'

He summoned a shaky smile. 'I'm sorry. I ought to have talked to you about it. I was angry, and I tore the thing up and tried to forget it so we could enjoy our afternoon. But I'll have to let them know I'm refusing it, I suppose.' He sighed. 'Why am I like this, Bobby?'

Bobby went to perch on his knee again, wrapping her arms around his neck. 'Like what?'

'Why does it bother me so much?' He rubbed his eyes. 'I didn't meet many airmen who truly hated the enemy when I was in the RAF. Yes, you'd get the odd one who muttered darkly that the only good German was a dead German – those who'd made it personal. But for most, it was just the job. They were doing a job when they flew out to drop their bombs, and they recognised that the Luftwaffe men were doing a job when they tried to shoot them down. They told themselves that there was nothing more important than stopping Hitler, so they put feelings aside and got on with it. Yet it seemed that no matter how often I told myself the same thing, I couldn't detach myself the way they could.' He hid his face in her shoulder and choked on a sob. 'I never should have passed the aircrew selection process.'

'You're that way because you're you,' Bobby said softly. 'You can't help feeling because it's the person you are.'

'I don't have a monopoly on feeling, do I? I met a lot of good men in the RAF, but being good men didn't stop them doing their duty.'

'Compassion combined with imagination is your curse. You visualise too much, Charlie. You're right, they never should have passed you as suitable for aircrew.'

'No.' He closed his eyes. 'Still, I loved flying. I was good at it, and I did want to use that to help win this thing. I wish I'd been stronger.'

'You are strong. It's just a different kind of strength.' She stroked his hair. 'You know that whatever decision you make, I'll support you. But just remember that they're not offering you the DFC for killing Germans. They're offering it to you for saving lives.'

'Why should I deserve it? Every man who's still flying deserves it more, because they kept going when I failed. They're risking their lives while I'm keeping house like a woman with a discharge certificate that says "wounded in the course of duty" where it should say "cowardice in the face of the enemy". I might have saved the men who flew with me on that op, but two others are dead because I made the wrong call on another one.'

'I know you feel guilty, Charlie. I know it's complicated, but you do deserve it.' She kissed him. 'But like I said, it's up to you.'

## Chapter 9

Later, Bobby and Charlie walked to the Golden Hart to meet Lilian and Tony. They found the Scotts already there, although not together. Tony was at the bar talking to Pete Dixon, while Lilian sat by herself with her knitting and a glass of sherry.

The Hart had an almost cosmopolitan flavour these days compared to the staid, old-fashioned place it had been when Bobby had first entered it. It had been a man's domain then, its only female patron being eccentric Maimie Hobbes, Topsy's former nanny. The regulars had evinced a certain wariness when this girl from the city had first appeared in their midst.

It was true that in appearance, the Hart had changed little. The floor was still bare stone flags, the air thick with smoke. High-backed wooden settles still lined the walls. The clientele was decidedly more varied than the cloth-capped farmers who had been the sole patrons two years earlier, however. There were several women in here now. A couple of Land Girls laughed as they leaned against the bar. Mabs Jessop was in one of the settles with her fiancé Gil Capstick, who whispered sweet nothings to his blushing bride-to-be.

And here and there was a flash of blue or khaki: soldiers home on leave, off-duty Home Guard troops, airmen billeted locally. There was even the odd hospital uniform as some of the wounded men recuperating at Sumner House found their way into the village for a drink. It was the slate blue of the regular Air Force uniforms that drew Bobby's eye, however, making her wistful for her days in the WAAF.

She had been granted compassionate discharge by the Air Force with the idea that she would be needed to make a home for her injured husband. Bobby couldn't help feeling guilty that in their reversed roles, it was actually Charlie who was making a home for her.

It made her wonder if she'd have been better off remaining in the WAAF, where there were higher wages to be had, and sending money home until Charlie was able to find work. Except that Marmaduke would have made staying in the services impossible before long, of course.

Bobby hoped something would turn up for Charlie soon, but it worried her what this was likely to be. The jobs in their farming community were all active, and his injuries meant he was no longer fit for prolonged outdoor work. Nevertheless, he had a private education and a good brain. That had to count for something, even if he needed to travel for work.

He could be a clerk in an office, perhaps, where his injuries wouldn't be such an issue. True, the pay was likely to be lower than he was used to, but work was work. It would still be more than Bobby earned on *The Tyke*. She'd miss the little mag, but working for it was never going to make her rich.

Bobby watched Charlie's hands tremble as he lit a cigarette and suppressed a sigh. He had been so good with his hands, before. She remembered the wonderful dolls' house he had carved and painted for the Parry girls last Christmas. Now, he would struggle even to grip the paintbrush.

It reminded her that there was one injury which might always pose a problem, and that was the one in Charlie's brain. His handwriting was often barely legible thanks to the tremor in his hands. That could mean even work as a clerk would be impossible.

This bloody war, that chewed men up and spat them out with never a care for how they would survive in civilian life! Lilian was right: Bobby should be angry. It made her sick that people who had given everything for their country should be forced to suffer for it. But what was there to be done, when men were no longer fit to work?

'You go and join Lil if you want,' Charlie said. 'I'll buy drinks and play at happy families with Tony. I just hope he's not too well-oiled. It always brings out the worst in him.'

'All right, I'll have the same as our Lil. You'd better offer Tony a pint, since I told him I'd be buying.'

Charlie flushed. 'Have you, um, got any money? I don't want to spend the housekeeping.'

'Oh. Yes, of course.' Bobby surreptitiously pressed a note into his hand, knowing how humiliated he would feel if the other men saw her giving him what looked like pocket money. 'See you in a minute, love.'

When she joined Lilian, Bobby found her sister's knitting needles frozen in mid-stitch as she watched Tony talking to Pete. Lil's eyes had an odd, feverish sparkle to them.

'Are you all right?' Bobby asked, sitting down opposite. 'You look a world away.'

Lilian roused herself. 'Sorry. Just hoping that old rogue isn't trying to get my other half into trouble.'

Bobby frowned. Lil's words were clear enough, but her pronunciation seemed slow and deliberate, as if she was having to focus to enunciate.

'How long have you been here?' Bobby asked, glancing at Lil's sherry.

'Ten minutes or so.'

Bobby lowered her voice. 'Lil, have you been drinking?'

Lil laughed. 'Well, yes. We're in the pub.'

'I mean before. You seem a little… off.'

'I had some tonic wine after I'd put Annie to bed.' She shook her head. 'Oh, don't give me that look. This is doctor's orders, Bob. He says I need it to get my strength up.'

'All right,' Bobby said, with a curious glance at her sister's unnaturally sparkling eyes. 'Just don't overdo it, eh?'

'I'm fine. Stop worrying, please.' Lilian glanced around as if she had a secret to share before pressing something into Bobby's hand. 'I brought you a present.'

'Oh my goodness! Knicker elastic?' Bobby fixed an awed gaze on the coil in her palm before stowing it away in her handbag. 'Where on earth did you find it? I haven't been able to get any since I left the WAAF.'

'It's a gift from George Parry. His department store had a fresh delivery yesterday and he bought us all some.' She smiled. 'He asked me to be the distributor though. I can just imagine how the poor man would blush if he had to hand it out himself. I've some for you and some for Mary.'

'Thank the Lord,' Bobby said fervently. 'This rubber shortage has been the devil. My WAAF friend Dilys wrote that she had an incident in the NAAFI last week. How the lads wolf-whistled! Dilys just laughs it off, but I'd blush fit for anything if it happened to me.'

There was plenty in the press about the impact of war shortages, but the difficulty of getting new knicker elastic was one issue on which the papers remained primly silent. Every woman had at least one friend who'd suffered an 'incident' when their worn elastic had given out, if they were lucky enough to have avoided it themselves. There was nothing to be done in such situations except step demurely out of your fallen undergarments, stuff them into your bag and hurry to a public convenience to fix it with a safety pin.

'Do give the captain my thanks, and tell him I'll pay whatever it cost,' Bobby said. 'It was thoughtful of him to make sure we got our share.'

Lilian shook her head. 'I already tried to press payment on him, but he insisted it was a gift. He's going to get us some nylons when they next get any in. Tailors can be useful men to know when there's a war on.'

'I do hope he can. I've darned my last good pair so many times that they're nothing but lumps and bumps. Oxo cubes are all right for summer but it's too cold for bare legs now, and Reg doesn't approve of me wearing slacks to work.'

Lilian nodded to the slate-blue uniforms that had caught Bobby's attention earlier. 'Speaking of slacks, there's an old friend of yours over there.'

Bobby winced. She couldn't fail to have noticed Ernie King drinking with his billet mate Sandy, and had quickly looked away before she met his gaze. Luckily the pub was busy, and he hadn't spotted her in the throng.

'I know, he's just come back,' Bobby said. 'Charlie said Ernie was very pally when they bumped into each other earlier, so I'm hoping things won't be too awkward.' Of course she had told her sister all about her Canadian suitor's proposal in the spring.

Bobby had her back to the Canadians, but Lil had a good view of them.

'He's looking at you,' she told Bobby.

Bobby grimaced. 'Oh Lord, is he? I hope he doesn't come over.'

'Why? You'll have to talk to him sometime.'

'I know. I'd just prefer not to do it tonight.'

'Just because you're married, it doesn't mean you can't appreciate a handsome admirer.' Lilian took a sip of her sherry. 'Enjoy it while you can, love, before you turn into a sack of potatoes.'

'All right, keep your voice down,' Bobby murmured. 'I don't want any admirers, especially not Ernie. I hurt him, Lil, and I feel dreadful about it.'

'A supremely Bobby-like answer.' Lil finished off her drink. 'I wish a handsome officer or two would fall in love with me. I could do with a few compliments from the opposite sex.'

'Tony doesn't pay you compliments?'

Lilian laughed. 'Only of the "cracking cup of tea, love" variety. But that's Tony. I've learnt not to expect love talk from him.'

'Was Dad all right being left with Annie?'

'He'll be fine. Mary said that if he needs a woman's help, he can take the baby to sit with them. They've got the girls over too, so it'll be a jolly party.'

'Is the captain there?'

'No, he's going out,' Lilian said. 'Mary offered to have the children.'

Bobby hesitated, wondering if she should mention what her dad had told her earlier. He hadn't made any secret of it, so she supposed it was all right.

'Has Dad said anything to you about housing arrangements?' she asked.

'How do you mean?'

'Only, he was talking about finding somewhere else to live earlier.'

Lilian blinked. 'Why, has something happened to put him out?'

'I don't think it's that. He just feels guilty about taking up space in that little house.'

'I know it must be difficult for him feeling as if he's living under another man's roof. But he can't move out, can he?'

'Why?' Bobby asked. 'Has he been any worse lately?'

'Well, no. Actually he's been full of buck these past few months. He still has the occasional nightmare, but he never drinks anything other than beer now. Still, he couldn't live alone.' Lilian looked at Bobby with burgeoning hope. 'Could he?'

'You'd like him to,' Bobby said softly. 'Wouldn't you?'

Lilian sighed. 'Yes and no. I want to know he's being looked after by someone who understands his needs, and realistically that has to be one of us. But the cottage is so small, Bob.' She picked up her knitting, a matinee coat for Annie, and idly worked a couple of stitches. 'It does feel awkward when we're practically living in each other's laps. It makes it difficult for me and Tony to be… intimate as often as he'd like.'

'It would make a big difference for you two to have a home to yourselves.'

'It would. But it can't happen, so what's the point dreaming?'

'Perhaps it can,' Bobby said. 'I admit that when Dad mentioned it, I thought the same as you. But he says he wouldn't be alone. He's got a friend who wants to take a house with him.'

Lilian frowned. 'What friend?'

'He didn't say, but Charlie heard Stan Henderson was looking for someone to share with. Stan was in the trenches too, so I guess he'd understand the way Dad is.'

Hope started to blossom in Lilian's eyes.

'Yes,' she said slowly. 'Yes he would.'

'It isn't confirmed yet, Dad said, but that could solve all our problems, couldn't it? I'm still cautious, but it could work out best for everyone.'

'I'll try not to get my hopes up, but oh, to have a nursery room would make such a difference!' Lilian glanced towards the bar, where Charlie and Tony were collecting their drinks. 'Don't say anything to Tony, though, will you? Not until it's certain.'

## Chapter 10

A sherry soon materialised in front of Bobby, with a second for Lilian. Charlie sat down by Bobby, and Tony stretched an arm around his wife.

'What were you talking to Pete about?' Lilian asked him, nodding to Silverdale's resident rogue-of-all-trades at the bar.

'Just collecting on a bet and seeing if he's got any game to sell,' Tony said. 'He's going to bring a hare down when I stop in after parade on Tuesday.'

Lilian shook her head. 'You shouldn't. It's the black market, Tony.'

'Them nobs who own the land can't eat all of the beasts running wild on it. Surely us poor peasants are entitled to a bite of meat too.'

'I wouldn't mind if it wasn't for Dad. It could get him into trouble if Topsy finds out her gamekeeper's family have been filling their bellies with animals poached from her land.'

'She'll never notice one or two missing.' Tony gave her a squeeze, and the gentleness that sometimes appeared when he looked at his wife kindled in his eyes. 'This is for you, love,' he said softly. 'The doctor says you're to keep your strength up. You need good, hearty food for that, not gravy and carrots. Have to look after you, don't I?'

'I'm all right.' Still, Lilian rewarded him for his concern with a peck on the cheek.

Tony turned to Bobby and Charlie with the bawdy joviality that a second pint usually produced in him. 'How're we doing then, you two? You going to be producing bairns of your own soon, or are you still working out how to do it? I don't mind drawing you a picture if you need help, Charlie.'

Charlie looked irritated, but Bobby, anxious though she was to avoid talk of babies, flashed Tony an amused smile. She was used to his crude humour, and that joke was mild by Tony Scott standards. Besides, seeing his concern for Lilian had put her in a humour to appreciate his better qualities.

'Shut up and have a cigarette, Tony,' she said, taking the liberty of offering him one from Charlie's pack. 'I hope now we've bought you a pint, you're going to stop sulking about work.'

Tony shrugged, lighting the cigarette. 'Wasn't sulking. I just think the natural order ought to be preserved, that's all. A married woman's place is at home – no offence, Charlie.'

Charlie didn't say anything. He just lit a cigarette of his own and smoked it from between his trembling fingers. Bobby squeezed his knee to thank him for making an effort to keep his temper. Tony's teasing, even when friendly, always seemed to hit on some sensitive issue guaranteed to rub his brother-in-law the wrong way.

'That might have been the way it was before the war, Tony, but things are different now,' Lilian observed, sipping her second sherry. 'It's changed things for women.'

'Aye, for the worse.'

'In some ways, but in other respects it's opened a lot of doors – and a lot of eyes. Now we've shown what we can do, why shouldn't we girls expect more?'

'Jobs are all right for the single girls, get them a bit of pocket money, but those who've got husbands to keep them ought to be at home. Call me old-fashioned if you want but that's the way I feel.'

'Not every household has that luxury,' Bobby said. 'Working-class women have always had to work, married or not. Our mam was back in the mill a few days after Ray came, and even when she had four of us at home she took in washing. She couldn't afford not to work.'

'Aye, well, that's different, isn't it?' Tony said, exhaling a column of smoke. 'When you need the money, I mean. But it's not the natural order. Men must work and women must weep, as the old song says.'

'Who was it created this "natural order", Tony?' Charlie asked. 'You never struck me as the religious type.'

Bobby flashed him a surprised look. Before going to war and even in his RAF days – at least, prior to the crash that had killed two of his crew – Charlie had been a social being. He still could be, when the mood took him, but at other times he was often quiet in company. Tony in particular was someone he found it hard to be companionable with. Bobby wondered if he had felt the need to come to her support when he spoke up.

There was no need, though. She was used to Tony, and felt comfortable challenging him. He took it better from her, as a friend and non-threatening female presence. Already she could see him fixing Charlie with a resentful look, although he didn't rise to the bait – perhaps mindful that he was currently drinking a beer his brother-in-law had bought him while smoking one of his cigarettes.

'Perhaps "natural order" is the wrong phrase,' he said. 'It's about doing what we're fitted to. Men earn a crust; women keep home and raise the bairns. Men toil; women nurture. We'd be in a hell of a mess if we turned it around, wouldn't we? We can't rebuild the world with a lot of hard women and weak men.'

'Perhaps it's not so black and white as that,' Charlie said quietly. 'Perhaps that's the lesson we ought to take from this war.'

'Besides, women aren't only good at nurturing. We've got individual talents,' Lilian said, her second sherry making her bold. 'It seems hard to me that those of our sex who've found something they're good at, like our Bobby has, should have to give it up to dust and polish. It's a waste of clever girls to give them nothing to do besides make a home. Well, thanks to the war those girls are finally starting to realise there can be more for them.'

'Gawd's sake,' Tony muttered, stubbing out his cigarette. 'I thought I was coming out for a drink, not a ruddy meeting of the league of militant suffragettes.' He glanced at the robust, hardy girls of the Women's Land Army drinking at the bar. 'I don't see what's so wonderful about the war working you girls until you've got calluses all over your hands and muscles like blokes.'

'What's so wonderful is that we're needed now,' Bobby said. 'Not just by our husbands and children but by the world.'

Lilian nodded. 'It's going to be hard to put the cork back in the bottle now the war's shaken things up. A lot of men are going to find things are rather different when they come marching home.'

Bobby gave her sister a smile of solidarity. Lilian had always been the traditional one. While Bobby had been ambitious, dreaming of making it as a journalist, all her twin had ever wanted was to fall in love and make a home. Yet it seemed the war had made a difference to Lilian's view of the world too. Bobby wondered if her sister thought wistfully of her career in the Wrens, cut short by her pregnancy after an ill-fated night with Tony, just as Bobby did about the WAAF.

Lilian's words made Bobby think of their mam. Nelly Bancroft had been a clever woman who had encouraged her daughters to study hard and aim for a better life, yet despite her innate intelligence, Nelly had had little education, leaving school at fourteen to work in the mills like generations of her family before her. Her short life had been one of toil and penny-pinching, until she had been taken by cancer aged just thirty-five. Bobby often wondered what her mam could have been if her sex and class hadn't condemned her to a lot far below her natural capabilities.

How many people in the history of human existence had been forced into lives of drudgery and illiteracy when they could have been great men and women? All because the Tony Scotts of the world decreed that they had no right to more than what had arbitrarily been designated 'the natural order'. Jolka was right when she said that too often, the world only allowed women to be *what* they were rather than *who* they were.

'You're very full of your opinions tonight, Lilian,' Tony said, turning a look of disapproval on his wife. 'You sound like your sister.'

'Do I? Good.'

'It wasn't a compliment.'

'You know, Tony, I'm right here,' Bobby said, glaring at him.

'Am I not entitled to opinions then?' Lilian demanded. 'Women don't give up their brains when they marry, Tony Scott, however much you might wish they did.' She threw back the last of her sherry.

Now Lilian had finished her second drink, her speech had become noticeably slurred.

'Better make that your last one, eh?' Tony said. 'Can't afford to have you drinking away my wages in the pub.'

'Funny you don't say that when you're out with your Home Guard mates.'

'It's not good for you, Lil. You girls can't take it like a man can.'

'Leave me alone, Tony, for God's sake. You nag worse than a fishwife.'

Bobby felt awkward, not knowing where to look while Tony and Lil bickered, and Charlie was shifting uncomfortably as well. Luckily, the argument was halted when Tony's attention was caught by a new arrival.

'Heyup,' he said with a grin. 'Here comes a dark horse, eh?'

Bobby turned to see who he was looking at. George Parry had come in, looking bashful as he escorted a willowy blonde woman to the bar. She was somewhat showily dressed for wartime, looking proud and a little smug at being on the arm of the handsome former officer.

Bobby blinked. 'Well that's a turn-up. I didn't know the captain had a lady friend.'

'He's a sly dog, keeping a corker like her to himself,' Tony said as he helped himself to another of Charlie's cigarettes. 'Not bad, eh, Charlie? Could've sworn for a minute it was Betty Grable on his arm.'

'Yes, very personable,' Charlie agreed. 'Not from the village, I think. You'd notice hair that colour.'

'Who is she? Either of you girls know?'

'Her name's Veronica Simpson,' Lilian said quietly. 'She works with him at the department store.'

'And they're walking out, are they?'

'I don't think they're what you'd call walking out. When I spoke to him earlier, George told me he was going to telephone her to make a date. That's why Mary and Reg are minding the children.'

'Could it be the children he's thinking of?' Bobby asked. 'Mary was saying she was surprised he'd given up on courting, with two motherless girls. I assumed he'd never got over the death of his wife.'

'No, I don't think he has. Still, I'm glad he's looking to find happiness again. He's too good a man to be lonely.' Lilian hadn't removed her gaze from the pair. 'She's very glamorous, isn't she? I wonder where she gets such nice clothes.'

'Perk of working in a department store, perhaps.'

Lilian smiled dryly. 'I bet her knickers never fall down in public.'

'Oh, I don't know,' Tony said with a grin. 'Maybe if Parry strikes lucky tonight.'

Bobby shook her head. 'Show a little class, could you, Tony?'

Tony was too busy running appreciative eyes over Veronica Simpson's curves, however.

'Never would've thought Parry could hook a woman like that,' he said. 'I thought his type would be a librarianish sort, all oversized cardigans and specs.'

'You might want to stop ogling the poor girl before George looks this way,' Lilian observed.

Tony turned to give her a kiss. 'Looking's just looking. I keep my heart for you, darling.'

Lilian, partially appeased, treated him to a half-smile.

'I'm sorry, Lil,' he said in an undertone. 'I never meant to nag. It's only because I worry about keeping you well. Love you, don't I?'

'I know.'

'I'll fetch you another drink, eh? My horse came in yesterday so I've got an extra few bob in my pocket to treat you with.'

'No, you're right. Two's enough for me. You have another though.'

Bobby beamed, pleased to see the row of earlier made up. As Lilian had observed, Tony wasn't someone to whom 'love talk' came naturally, but he knew his wife appreciated it and tried for her sake. In his unpolished way, he was a bit of a romantic.

Bobby had barely drunk any of her sherry. She was worried the sweet, strong drink might upset her stomach, where Marmaduke was stirring. Her baby-related sickness wasn't as severe as earlier in her pregnancy, but strong tastes and smells could still set it off. The smoky environment of the pub was unpleasant enough, especially with Tony chain-smoking his way through Charlie's cigarettes right in her face.

And always she could feel the eyes of Ernie King on her. She knew she was being ungracious by ignoring him, but Bobby was feeling far too sickly to make polite conversation with jilted suitors.

'I need to go outside for a moment,' she said to the others.

Charlie frowned. 'Are you all right?'

'I'm all right. It's just all this smoke.'

'I'll come with you then.'

'No, you stay here. Have another drink. I'll only be five minutes while I fill my lungs with some clean air.'

Bobby put on her coat and made her way outside. She sat down on a horse trough and gulped in mouthfuls of crisp winter air until the feeling she might be sick abated. There was a full moon that night, glinting off the water in the trough.

A clear night would mean another raid over Germany. It made Bobby think of what Charlie had said earlier. All those people on the ground who would be suffering. Women. Children. Women like her, their babies unborn inside them...

She shivered, and tried to push the thought away.

Bobby smelt Ernie before she saw him. Even with the heavy scent of pub smoke on him, she recognised the distinctive smell of the Canadian shaving soap he used.

'Hey, Slacks.'

As anxious as she'd been to avoid him, Bobby couldn't help smiling. She'd missed Ernie's teasing. He sounded gentler than usual but not exactly sad, and certainly not cross or bitter. That was something.

'Ernie,' she said. 'I, um, didn't notice you in there.'

He grinned. 'Yeah, like hell.' He leaned against the trough. 'Avoiding me, kid?'

'OK, yes,' she said, deciding to meet frankness with frankness. 'I've had a bugger of a day, pardon my language. I could have done without one more awkward conversation.'

'All right, Bobby, no need to get all mushy on me. I missed you too, OK?'

She smiled. It was better if he was joking.

'I did miss you actually. Life wasn't the same without you to mock me for my clothing choices. Where's Chip tonight?' She had noted the absence of Ernie's other billet mate when she had spotted him drinking with Sandy.

Ernie was looking up at the stars, his eyes moving over the constellations as if he was counting each pinprick of light.

'Gone.'

Before she had served in the Air Force, Bobby might have assumed his friend had been posted back to Canada. Not now, though.

'Oh Ernie, I am sorry,' she whispered. 'I know you two were close.'

He shrugged. 'Just one in a long line of pals I've lost in this thing. Still, I miss him. Good man.'

There was a moment's sombre silence.

'So, um, did you know I'd left the WAAF?' Bobby asked.

'Not when I came back. Her Ladyship was good enough to fill me in on the changes round here when she roped me in to the latest Topsy Nowak production.' Ernie lit a cigarette. 'Shame. The uniform looked good on you.'

'I thought you didn't approve of women in uniform.'

'No, but I've always approved of Bobby Bancroft in a skirt.'

Bobby closed her eyes. One of them was going to have to tackle the subject that was hovering unspoken between them, and if he wasn't going to do it, she supposed it would have to be her.

'Ernie, I'm sorry,' she said quietly.

He didn't meet her eye, continuing to smoke as he gazed carelessly at the stars. 'About what?'

'You know what.'

'Oh, that?' He glanced at her with a hint of his old grin. 'I'd forgotten all about that.'

'You know that's not true. I never meant to hurt you. But I did, and I feel awful about it.'

'Ancient history, Slacks. If you must know, I've been engaged this past month.' He took his cigarette out of his mouth, noticing her wince of nausea. 'Sorry, is this bothering you? Should've asked before lighting up.'

'No, it's all right.' Bobby swallowed as she battled the sick feeling. 'The smoke in the pub was making me feel ill, that's all.'

Ernie looked at her curiously as he stamped out the cigarette. 'Oh?'

'That's why I came outside.' She flashed him a weak smile. 'I hope you didn't think it was a ruse to lure you out here.'

'If anything, I thought it might be an attempt to run away. You seemed very keen to pretend you hadn't seen me in there.' He smiled. 'Thought I ought to corner you before we ended up dancing round each other in every public place in the village.'

'So... are we still friends then?'

He took her hand and shook it in a frank, manly fashion that made Bobby smile. 'You got it. Friends.'

'And you're engaged.' She summoned her warmest smile. 'Congratulations, Ernie. I knew a handsome boy like you would meet the perfect girl before long. Is she Canadian?'

'No, one of your lot. A WAAF from Cambridge – Barbara. Pretty. Vivacious. The boys think she looks like Dorothy Lamour.'

Bobby laughed. 'So not at all like me then. That's for the best. You and I could never have suited.'

'In some ways you're alike,' Ernie said. 'She's a smart cookie, and she likes to tell me off if she thinks I'm being "stuffy", as you used to put it.' He dabbled his fingers idly in the horse trough. 'She's going to come to Canada with me if I make it through. Help me run the family farm.'

Bobby felt comfortable enough now to squeeze his arm.

'I'm thrilled for you, Ernie,' she said softly. 'I'd love to meet her. Charlie and I can make up a foursome with you and show her the sights, such as they are.'

Ernie smiled. 'That sounds mighty civilised. By which I mean, mighty British.'

'And listen, thanks for being chummy with Charlie. He told me you offered to buy him a drink. I'd like you two to be friends.'

Ernie was silent, watching the water break the full moon into pieces as his fingers moved through it.

'Doozy of a scar he's got since I saw him last, your Mr Atherton,' he observed after a while.

Bobby nodded soberly. 'Flak during his last op.'

'Anything else get broken?'

'His arm was badly burnt. The nerve damage is quite extensive – that's why they invalided him out. He was trying to put out a fire on the wing with his parachute.'

Ernie raised an eyebrow. 'You mean he climbed out the hatch?'

'That's right. He saved the lives of his entire crew.'

'Whoa. Brave guy.'

She laughed grimly. 'Don't say that to him, for God's sake.'

'Why do you say that?'

'He has strong views about being called a hero when so many of his pals are dead, that's all.'

'Can't say I'd feel any different.' Ernie turned to her, all traces of teasing gone. 'A man goes through all that, it's bound to leave him with a few problems.'

Bobby flushed. 'It's not my place to talk about it.'

'But he's good to you? Treats you right?'

'Very much so.'

'Then I'll make sure he lets me buy him that drink next time I run into him. Sounds like the least he's owed.'

'He'd like that. Thank you.'

'He knows, I guess. About what I asked you in spring.'

'You mean the thing you've forgotten all about?'

'Yeah, that.'

'He knows, but he isn't one to hold a grudge,' Bobby reassured him. 'Besides, you didn't do anything wrong. I wasn't his girl then – or at least, it had become rather complicated. I'm sure that now he and I are happily married and you've moved on, we can put it behind us, can't we?'

'Happily married?' His eyes sought hers in the pale glow of the moon. 'You swear to that?'

'I'd be lying if I said marriage was hourly bliss, but… yes. It isn't always easy but it's always… right, I suppose.'

'Well, if you're genuinely happy then that makes it all bearable.' He smiled. 'I do feel cheated of my opportunity to kiss the bride though. I was a mite too heartsick to offer my congratulations when you came back to Ryland Moor after your wedding. Am I too late to claim it now?'

Bobby smiled too. 'You aren't too late,' she said, presenting her cheek.

Ernie planted a gentle kiss there.

'All the happiness in the world, Bobby Bancroft,' he said softly. 'I guess the right guy struck lucky in the end, but every time I hear "The Lambeth Walk" I'll think of the first girl I ever fell for. See you around, kid.'

He strode back to the pub, passing Charlie, who had emerged in search of his wife. Charlie gave him a curious look, but Ernie only nodded in friendly fashion before heading back inside.

'What did he want?' Charlie asked when he joined Bobby at the trough.

'To clear the air.'

'If I'd spotted him following you, I'd have come out right away. I hope he wasn't pestering you.'

'He was the perfect gentleman. We talked, that's all.'

'About what?'

'Just... things. I'll tell you at home.' Bobby took his stick and rested it against the trough. 'Now stop being jealous and hold me, will you?'

'I can't refuse that, I suppose.'

When she was in his arms, Bobby rested her forehead on his chest and breathed his scent deeply.

'I think I've had enough of other people,' she whispered. 'How about we say goodbye to the Scotts and you take me home to bed?'

He smiled. 'Now there's a plan I approve of.'

## Chapter 11

Four weeks passed. Christmas came and went, and Bobby settled into a fresh routine at *The Tyke* as she and Tony got used to the new arrangements.

Her morning sickness had ceased, but her clothes had become very tight now she had passed the five-month point in her pregnancy. Bobby had always insisted on cooking the evening meal, unwilling to entirely relinquish the homemaking role to Charlie. However, in the end she was forced to hand over cooking duties just to keep on top of her sewing. Most of her free time was now spent adjusting the waistline on her knickers and skirts, praying none of her circle would notice her thickening frame until she was ready. Trousers she had been forced to abandon altogether. Bobby knew she wouldn't be able to conceal her pregnancy for much longer, but she was still determined to keep it secret as long as she could.

Charlie had been pestering her about giving her notice again that morning. He was still out of a job, although he had an interview that day for a clerk's position at the Yorkshire Penny Bank in Skipton. However, he was increasingly opposed to his wife going out to work, saying he'd never forgive himself if Bobby made herself or the baby ill through working in a cold shed.

In vain did Bobby remind him of what she'd said to Tony in the pub: that the women of her family had always worked when they'd needed to. It was no use telling him that she felt well and strong, and was sure work did her good. It made no difference to remind him that their pot of savings would only last a few months with no other money coming in. Charlie was adamant she ought to be at home, taking care of herself, and Bobby wasn't sure how much longer she could stop him taking matters into his own hands by sneaking on her to his brother.

The thing was, it wasn't really about the money. Bobby loved her job. She loved *The Tyke*, and she adored being the deputy editress. Deciding what went in the magazine, commissioning articles, going out to interview interesting people... it was all so stimulating, so enriching. Now she'd experienced what it felt like to run a magazine, Bobby didn't know how she could give it up – but she knew the day wasn't far away when she would have to. And once she left work to raise a child, it was unlikely there would be any way back.

Not that Bobby regretted the choices she had made. Two years ago, when she had first come to work for Reg, she had all but sworn off love and marriage. She had known that career ambitions had to be put aside when family life beckoned – at least, for women they did – and she'd had no intention of giving up her dreams so she could bake and wash smalls for some man. Then along had come Charlie, making her love him in spite of her best efforts, and the Parry girls, who had shown her how much she wanted to be a mother.

Those feelings had only been deepened by Bobby's experiences in this war, reminding her how fragile life could be. A successful career was cold comfort without the loving family relationships that gave life its sweetness and richness. She understood that, but it didn't mean she wasn't hankering for mental as well as emotional fulfilment in life.

Bobby thought of the letter she had posted to Broadcasting House four weeks ago. She had been wise not to pin her hopes on it. There had been no word of reply, not even a pre-typed rejection slip.

She still hadn't got used to working in a new place. A couple of times she had been late for work because she had walked all the way to Moorside, then cursed her forgetfulness when she'd had to retrace her steps back to the Parrys' place. Bobby didn't allow her concentration to lapse this Saturday morning, however, and arrived at work in good time. She entered the Parrys' back garden through a gate in the wall.

The outhouse key hung on the gate, which meant the captain must not be at home. Bobby guessed he had a Saturday shift, and she knew the girls had gone out shopping with Lilian.

She knocked on the back door to ask Ida Wilcox, who cleaned for the family, if she could collect her typewriter. Captain Parry was kind enough to allow Bobby and Tony to leave their machines in the house to protect them from damp. Then she squeezed through the gap stile at the back of the garden, her Remington in her arms, and went to unlock the hut-cum-office that was now the home of *The Tyke*.

There was no sign of Tony yet, although it was now five to nine. He had rarely been late for work at Moorside, but Bobby had noted a tendency to be tardy over the past week. It was seldom more than a minute or two, but still, it was irritating.

She didn't like to ask her brother-in-law to make the time up lest it created tension in the office, but she did wonder if this was what Jolka had been talking about – an attempt to undermine her authority. Of course, it could also be Tony's typical desire to do only as much work as he needed to in order to collect a pay packet. Without Reg keeping an eye on them, Tony might have decided he could get away with shaving a few minutes off the working day. Bobby really hoped he was going to be on time today, otherwise it would make the fourth time this week he had been late. That would leave her with no choice but to speak to him about it.

Bobby plonked her typewriter on her desk and lit the stove. It was an icy morning, and while she tried to use fuel sparingly, she and Tony would both have fingers too numb to work if she didn't take the chill out of the air. Then she set the kettle to boil.

She whistled while she prepared for the working day. It reminded her of basic training in the WAAF, and their Nissen hut dormitory with its temperamental stove. She hadn't enjoyed it much at the time, when gnawing homesickness, worry that Charlie had forgotten her and a feeling of alienation had marred her days, but Bobby felt strangely nostalgic now it was behind her.

This made her think of something Andy Jessop had once said to her. Nostalgia was all well and good as long as it was in the past, but people would rarely care to relive it – that had been the gist, delivered in his thick Dales dialect. Well, he hadn't been wrong. Bobby wouldn't care to go back to that unhappy time, although she could look back now through rose-tinted spectacles.

She smiled sadly on remembering the homespun wisdom of her old friend. She missed their talks now Andy was gone.

Bobby sat down at her desk while the water boiled, wincing at the ache in her lower back. Next to her typewriter was last month's issue of *The Tyke*: the Christmas number. She flicked through absently.

It included the piece she had written over a year ago, about how the pantomime they had organised had brought Silverdale's wartime guests together. Bobby didn't know if it was Marmaduke's influence or her own foolish brain, but she couldn't help feeling emotional while she read it.

How much had changed since then! She was a whole other Bobby from the naive Miss Bancroft who had played Cinderella. She even had a new name – Mrs Atherton. By the time Christmas came around once more, she would have another. To one person, at least, her name would be 'Mam' forever afterwards.

Quickly she tapped her fingers against her desk. It was a daft superstition, but every time Bobby found herself thinking about her future as a mother, she instinctively reached for some wood to touch. After Lilian's difficult labour and the loss of little Georgia, it felt like tempting fate to be too complacent.

A thought occurred to Bobby, and she pressed a hand to the bump under her loose-fitting skirt.

Oh Lord, it couldn't be twins, could it? Dr Minchin would surely know if it was. Then again, Lilian's doctor had had no idea she had been expecting two babies. The heartbeat of the stronger child had masked that of poor weak Georgia. And twins ran in families, didn't they? Bobby's sister had had twins, and so had their mother...

Two babies at once! Not that she wouldn't be grateful for two healthy children, but however would she and Charlie *pay* for them? Even if her husband was lucky enough to get the bank clerk job, it was such a small salary. Charlie had no experience of banking so he'd had to apply for a junior role, with wages of less than five pounds a week. He had earned a similar amount in the RAF, but then he hadn't had rent, food or clothing costs to consider, let alone a wife and two children to support. As a vet, he had earned more than double what he'd get as a junior clerk. They would be better off than they were on Bobby's paltry salary, certainly, but with two babies to support, any difference would quickly be swallowed up.

And yet Bobby knew Charlie would be lucky to get it. With his damaged arm, his trembling hands and his nervous attacks, he would be lucky to get anything.

Bobby was roused from her thoughts by the arrival of Tony. She blinked back a foolish tear and glanced at her watch. This revealed that her colleague was once again late – nearly five minutes this time. He made no apology for this as he nodded good morning.

'What's upset you?' he asked as he put his typewriter down, noting her full eyes.

'Oh, nothing. Being daft, that's all.'

'Told you, didn't I?' he said with a grin. 'Too emotional for the workplace, women. Don't matter how well you do the job if you're weeping all over the stock.'

Since this comment seemed intended as a joke, Bobby ignored it. Still, it irked her. Tony sat at his desk and immediately lit a cigarette.

'How can you afford to smoke like that?' she demanded irritably. 'Charlie's had to cut back to five a day now. You puff on the things like you're bloody Diamond Jim Brady, Tony. It must play hell with your asthma.'

Tony exhaled a leisurely stream of smoke. 'Language, love. There's ladies present.'

'All right, go and fetch your smelling salts then,' Bobby said, feeding a sheet of paper into her typewriter. 'And while you're up, you can make us both a brew. Kettle's just boiled.'

Tony snorted. 'You what? It's your turn.'

'You know full well it isn't. It's been my turn for the last five tea rounds.' She looked up from her notebook, which contained a page of shorthand she needed to turn into an article on 'the village blacksmith' before she finished at midday. 'Make sure you brew it properly this time. Don't think I'll let you off tea rounds because you make a bad cup. And if you must be late, you can make the time up before you leave.'

He shook his head. 'What's got into you today? Women's problems? It was only a couple of minutes.'

'It was five minutes. Yesterday it was three minutes. On Tuesday it was two minutes. You're shaving a bit more off every time. Don't forget I've worked with you before. I know every Tony Scott shirking trick there is.'

'Going to blab to Reg, are you?'

'Not if you don't do it again. But if you think I'm going to cover for you like I used to do at the *Courier*, you're wrong. That Bobby's long gone.'

Bobby wasn't sure what had done away with the last of her tolerance for Tony's inability to accept her superiority at work, but whether it was Marmaduke-related or just her own frayed temper, she had no patience left with him.

'This is exactly what I was talking about in the pub,' Tony muttered. 'Work makes women hard.'

'What it makes this woman is gagging for a cup of tea,' Bobby told him shortly. 'If you think you're being hard done by, take it up with Reg. Be sure to mention what time you turned up to work when you do, won't you?'

Tony glared at her before getting up to do as he was told. Bobby watched him from the corner of her eye as he filled their tin mugs.

She softened a little, however, when she saw how tired her brother-in-law looked. He did have a six-month-old baby at home, and Bobby also knew how difficult it could be to share a home with her father when his nightmares came frequently. Perhaps she had been too hard on the man.

'How are Lilian and Annie?' she asked in a softer tone.

'Annie's fine.' Tony smiled at the mention of the daughter he doted on. 'Always a smile for me when I give her a cuddle before work. Lucky she didn't take after her miserable old man, eh?'

Bobby smiled too, ready to let bygones be bygones if he was.

'And Lil?' she asked. 'I haven't seen her for nearly a week. She always seems to be out.'

'I've not seen much of her myself,' Tony said, carrying a thinly brewed cup of tea to her. 'Always she's at that ruddy graveyard.'

'Still?'

'Aye.' He sighed. 'Seems harsh to tell her it's time to move on but it's doing her no good, Bobby, spending more time with the dead than the living. It's been nigh on seven month now. Happen you might have a word.'

'It'd be better coming from you. You're the father.'

'Don't you think I've tried?' Tony sat down with his tea. 'Not got the words, I reckon. Seems like it's a woman's thing. Babies and that.'

'Well, I'll try.' Bobby paused. 'Does she... what does Dr Minchin say about Lil's health now? Is she getting stronger?'

What Bobby really wanted to know was if the doctor was still recommending the tonic wine Lil had become increasingly dependent on. It worried her, given everything they had been through with their dad, that her sister was using alcohol to get through the day.

'Your guess is as good as mine,' Tony said. 'All she tells me is that she's fine. Still, she seems happier since Christmas. I reckon she'd be right as rain if she stopped hanging round that damp cemetery.'

'I'm sure it's her spirits that are weighing her down. Don't you think you could take her out more often? Not to the Hart but to a movie or a dance. I'm always happy to mind the baby.'

'Take her out on what? Fresh air?' Tony glanced listlessly at his typewriter. 'Wish Old Man Atherton could see his way clear to a bit more in my wage packet of a week. I could afford to get a woman in to help Lil at home then.'

'You always seem to be able to afford beer at the pub,' Bobby observed dryly.

'Aye, well, that's business. Puts me in the way of odd jobs.'

'Like what?'

'Jack Foster from our platoon's offered me a oncer to whitewash his place this weekend. That's worth the price of the pint I bought him.' He lit another cigarette. 'Ridiculous for a professional man to have to make money on the side painting bloody houses, but I can't afford to turn down work.'

'I know,' Bobby said quietly. 'Maybe when the war's over, Reg will be able to pay better salaries. It's the paper ration that holds us back.'

'Huh. Churchill's in no hurry to open a second front, is he? We could be in for a long haul yet.' Tony fed some paper into his typewriter. 'Well then, what do you want me to do this morning? Letters page?'

Bobby smiled at him. She knew Tony hated doing the letters, which he saw as typists' work and therefore beneath him. Nor was it usual for him to ask what she wanted him to work on rather than selecting some piece he liked the sound of. He was offering a gesture of peace, and she felt she ought to do likewise.

'I'll do the letters page,' Bobby said. 'Why don't you get the bus out to Redmire and interview the organiser of this new Dales Drama Festival? They're expecting someone at ten.'

'Thought you wanted to do that. You're the one with theatre experience.'

'One village pantomime and a concert party revue doesn't exactly make me Dame Sybil Thorndike. I'll get the women's page ship-shape and type up the letters.'

'Aye, all right. If that's what you want.'

This was what Bobby had found worked best with Tony. A little give, a little take. If she showed herself willing to take on the less popular jobs sometimes, he proved more tractable in other matters.

One wrong word, however, and she knew she would have to wring every ounce of work from the man until she could appease him. Honestly, it was like managing a spoiled puppy. Bobby had never regarded her friend Don Sykes, erstwhile editor of the *Courier*, with so much fellow-feeling.

## Chapter 12

Without Tony to do battle with, Bobby made good progress that day. By the time noon arrived, she had managed to type up the letters, sub the knitting pattern and recipe for the women's page and finish her piece on blacksmiths. She was regarding it with satisfaction when the door opened and George Parry appeared.

'Oh, I am sorry,' he said when he saw her. 'Frightfully rude of me not to knock. I thought you would have gone home. I just came to check the typewriters hadn't been left here. It looks as though we might have some snow tonight.'

'That's thoughtful of you,' Bobby said. 'Sorry to be lingering on your property after working hours. I was just finishing off an article.'

'Stay as long as you like,' the captain said in his usual gallant, soft-spoken way. 'I'm glad this old shed of ours is some use.'

'It's good of you to let us use it, and store the typewriters in the house. I'd have done myself an injury carrying my Remington from home every day.'

'It's the least I can do, when all of you have been so kind to my girls. I'm only glad there's some little thing I can offer in return.' He blushed slightly. 'Speaking of which… is your brother-in-law not here?'

'No, I sent him out to get an interview. Why?'

'Ah. Good. Then I don't need to feel embarrassed about giving you these.' He took a packet from his coat, a little stiffly due to the shoulder wound he had received at Dunkirk. 'Lilian informed me that they'd be appreciated by the womenfolk. I'll be highly insulted if you offer to pay for them so please don't.'

'Oh! Stockings!' Bobby had to restrain herself from diving over her desk to snatch the precious packet from his hand. 'That's really too kind of you, George.'

'Like I said, I owe your family a lot.' He smiled. 'If I can't pay you back with a few perks of the job, then what can I do?'

Bobby smiled too. 'Well, they'll be appreciated. It's ever so long since I had a new pair. Thank you.'

She was grateful for the stockings, but there was also a feeling Bobby couldn't quite put her finger on. Relief, she supposed. Relief that George had given them to her directly and not to Lilian, as he had with the knicker elastic.

She didn't know why it should worry her. It was Lilian who minded the girls after school, so naturally it was Lilian he had most contact with of the women in the family. Bobby knew a friendship had sprung up between her sister and George Parry, but it wasn't one she had felt she need be concerned about. Lilian was younger than Mary, and in the absence of his wife, George felt less embarrassed consulting her about the girls' problems than he would the older matron.

That was perfectly natural, and besides, George Parry was hardly someone who would form designs on a married woman. Everyone who knew the man spoke of him as a paragon of honour and decency. Nevertheless, the idea of George giving intimate gifts like stockings and knicker elastic to Lilian and Lilian alone – even with the intention that she passed them on – unsettled Bobby. She still recalled the fur coat he had given her sister the previous summer, and how it had worried her that he would make her a present of such an expensive item. At the very least, it could give rise to gossip that might cause tension for Lilian at home. Rumours soon spread in a place like Silverdale.

'I did wonder if I might find the girls here,' George said, pulling Bobby from her thoughts. 'Veronica's in the house waiting to meet them.'

That was another thing. The captain was spoken for now, and there was no reason to worry that his friendship with Lilian might be anything other than strictly platonic. He and Veronica Simpson had been walking out for nearly a month, with every sign that things were becoming serious. The fact he had brought her home to meet his daughters seemed to confirm this.

'Lilian was taking them shopping today,' she told him. 'I don't suppose they'll be much longer. Lil was planning to have them home before dinnertime.'

'Oh yes, their shopping trip. It slipped my mind. In that case I'll do my best to entertain the guest until they arrive. You'll join us when they do, I hope?'

'I'll certainly stop in and say hello, if I won't be intruding.'

'Of course not. You and your sister are both welcome. We're all family now.'

Bobby smiled. 'I suppose we are. I never had a large family growing up, but I seem to have acquired one since I moved to the Dales.'

'No, nor I,' the captain said, smiling back. 'Yet here we are.'

He said goodbye and left. Bobby started tidying away, pondering what the captain's lady friend would be like. She had seen Miss Simpson on a few occasions but never been formally introduced. She wondered if the girls knew that their father's glamorous new friend was waiting to meet them.

Before she could leave the hut, however, a deluge arrived: not only Lilian and the girls, but Reg and Mary too. The children piled in with Lil. It was a tight squeeze, and Reg and Mary were forced to wait outside at the bottom of the steps.

'Well! What are you all doing here?' Bobby asked. 'I was about to lock up.'

'Young Scott turned up with a report for me on that drama festival,' Reg called. 'Thought I'd see how things were getting along, seeing as Mary's banned work talk over Sunday dinner.'

Bobby frowned. 'Tony came to you with the report?'

'Aye. Told him to leave it on your desk Monday morning for subbing.'

'He might have left it on my desk this afternoon,' Bobby muttered. She had hoped they'd taken a step forward that morning when Tony had asked her for instructions, but it seemed he still hadn't accepted that it was her and not Reg who was responsible for approving his copy.

'Not much room for us in there,' Reg observed. He turned to Mary. 'Come on, our lass. We'll take a turn around the garden while the bairns tell Bobby their news, eh?'

'Aye, I wouldn't mind seeing how those chicks I gave Jess are getting along.' Mary took her husband's arm and they sauntered off.

'Your father's expecting you at the house, girls,' Bobby said to Jess and Florrie. 'He was just here looking for you.'

'Florrie wanted to show you something before they went in,' Lilian said. 'I told her she'd have to wipe it off before her dad saw her.'

'What is it, Florrie?' Bobby asked.

'Can't you see?' Florrie pouted like a star of the silver screen, and Bobby noticed that the child's lips were significantly pinker than usual.

'Oh! You got some lipstick?'

Florrie nodded eagerly. 'Aunty Lil bought it me. Dad told her she could, only I'm not supposed to wear it outside.'

Bobby raised an eyebrow at her sister. '*Aunty* Lil, is it?'

Lilian shook her head to suggest they ought to discuss the newly conferred title when they were alone.

'Do I look grown-up?' Florrie asked Bobby.

'Yes, very glamorous indeed,' Bobby said with a smile. 'Be sure to save it for special occasions though. Lipstick's hard to get hold of these days.'

'When will I be old enough to wear lipstick, Aunty Lil?' Jessie asked.

'Not for a few years yet, I'm afraid, Jess,' Lil said. 'But if we do a play, perhaps a little stage make-up.'

Jessie clapped her hands. 'Ooh, yes, let's do a play! We can practise when you look after us. A pantomime like the one Bobby was in. I'll be Cinderella, Florrie can be Prince Charming, you'll be Wicked Stepmother and Annie can be...' Jessie paused, thinking back to the plays she had seen over Christmas. 'Um, Baby Jesus.'

'That sounds an interesting pantomime,' Bobby said with a laugh. 'Now, Florrie, you had better wipe off your lipstick and run up to the house. Your dad's got someone there who's come especially to see you both.'

Florrie scowled. 'It's not *her*, is it?'

'That depends on who *her* is.'

'That lady he goes out with. *Veronica*.' Florrie said the name in an affected, singsong voice, as if this was the way she imagined Veronica would talk. 'We don't want to meet her. She's always taking Dad away from us. And she's trying to get him to forget our ma, I know it.'

'Now, Flor, that isn't fair,' Lilian said gently, resting a hand on the girl's shoulder. 'Miss Simpson isn't trying to take your mother's place. She's just someone whose company makes your dad happy. You want him to be happy, don't you?'

'Me and Jess make Dad happy,' Florrie muttered. 'He don't need no one else.'

'But you won't always be at home with him. One day you'll be grown-up, and leave to have families of your own,' Lilian pointed out. 'Wouldn't you like to meet Miss Simpson? I bet she knows lots about make-up and things. She's ever so pretty, like a film star.'

'If Dad wants to get married again, he should marry you or Bobby,' Jessie said, a black look on her face too. 'We'd like it much better if you lived with us than *her*.'

Bobby laughed. 'I think our husbands might have some objections.'

'Well, all right,' Jess conceded grudgingly. 'But it don't have to be her though.'

'Why not meet her before you make up your mind?' Lilian suggested. 'I'm sure if your dad likes her, she must be a rather special person. It would grieve him if you went into a pet after he's brought his new friend especially to meet you. And since you're both so grown-up now, it would be the mature thing to do.'

'Wellllll, I suppose,' Florrie said, her dislike of this perceived usurper of her father's affections doing battle with her desire to prove she deserved her new grown-up status. 'We'll be nice to her if she's nice to us. But I wish she hadn't come.'

'You'll like her once you get to know her.' Lilian handed the child a handkerchief. 'Here. Wipe off your lipstick and go on in. It isn't polite to keep her waiting.'

Reluctantly, Florrie wiped her lips clean and the two girls ran off to the house.

'For George's sake, I hope they make an effort,' Lilian said to Bobby when they were alone. 'He's been ever so anxious about introducing them.'

'It sounds like he and his Miss Simpson are getting serious.'

'Yes. I wouldn't be surprised if he was considering popping the question, between us.'

Bobby raised an eyebrow. 'Already?'

'It took him long enough to start courting again. I suppose now he has, he feels why waste time?'

Lilian sounded dreamy, gazing through the window towards the house. Bobby was pleased to see that her sister was looking healthier. Even in the week they hadn't seen each other, some plumpness had returned to Lil's cheeks. There was none of the feverish sparkle that Bobby had come to dread seeing in her eyes, which meant Lilian had been bolstering her flagging spirits with tonic wine.

'Have you met this Miss Simpson?' Bobby asked.

'Not properly, no. I must admit, I was surprised when I saw her that night at the pub. She didn't seem the type to attract someone like George. Still, if he likes her, there must be something to her.'

'Where's our Annie?'

'With her dad, sleeping. She was tired out after going shopping. The girls have been spoiling her rotten.'

Bobby raised an eyebrow. 'So, what's this "Aunty Lil" all about?'

'Sorry,' Lilian said, flushing. 'I hope your feelings aren't hurt, when you've known them longer. I was sure Mary looked a little upset over it.'

'What brought it on?'

'They asked if they could while we were shopping.' Lil smiled. 'It was touching really. We were in Woolworth's, Florrie picking out her lipstick with me trying to nudge her towards the less garish shades. She started talking about their Aunt Sadie – the one they were living with in London when their house was bombed.'

'Their late uncle's wife,' Bobby said. 'Yes, I remember them telling us about her. She didn't sound like much of a foster mother. Florrie said she was always leaving them alone to go out with boyfriends.'

'That's what she told me today. I could tell it hurt that this Sadie hadn't loved them the way an aunt should. For a year of their lives, she was all they had.' Lilian smiled slightly. 'Poor souls, they did so crave a mother. I can see why George doesn't want to waste any time with Miss Simpson. Florrie starting her monthlies really opened his eyes to how much they miss out on without a female presence in the home.'

'What happened then?'

'They asked if I'd ever been an aunty. I didn't mention Marmaduke, of course, but I told them I had two little nieces in Bradford. They asked what my nieces called me, and when I told them, Jess announced, "Well then we should get to call you that too, because you're really as much our aunty as theirs, and anyhow, our real aunty doesn't want us." You know, all defiant about it.'

'I suppose they're jealous any other little girls should have a claim on you.'

'Yes, that was it,' Lilian said. 'It could as easily have been you, or Mary. I'm surprised it wasn't Mary to be honest, when she's been like a mam to them. But mentioning Rosie and Sue got their jealousy fired up, so it was me. I didn't have the heart to tell them they couldn't.' Lilian glanced outside, where the Athertons were walking back towards them. 'We ought to be discreet in front of Mary though. I'd hate her to be hurt.'

'Yes, you're right.'

They fell silent as Reg pushed open the door.

'Happen you might have room for a couple of old folk now them tornadoes have disappeared,' he said, holding the door for his wife.

Her boss sounded almost jovial, Bobby noticed as he limped in after Mary. He looked healthier than a month ago too, and younger somehow. She wondered if this was the effect of Tony's cigarette smoke disappearing, or if – something she never would have suspected of Reg Atherton – semi-retirement actually suited him. Mary had told her that now he had time on his hands, Reg had got back into his old hobby of birdwatching. This was testified to by the binoculars hanging around his neck.

'Well then, lass, how are things?' he asked, glancing at the various papers on Bobby's desk. 'All set for deadline?'

Mary shook her head. 'Now, Reg, must you always be talking shop? The poor girl's not on the clock. She'd be on her way home if it weren't for us.'

'I'm in no hurry,' Bobby said. 'Charlie's gone to Skipton for that bank interview so he won't be back until later.'

'Still, you don't want to be hanging around cold sheds when you could be beside a warm hearth.'

'Not at all. It's nice to see you both. I do miss our little household at Moorside.'

'Aye, it's good to see you too.' Mary came forward to embrace her, but Bobby held up a hand, conscious of the bump her broad skirt was barely concealing.

'You'd better not hug me. I think I'm coming down with a cold.'

As if to prove this, Bobby took out her handkerchief and theatrically blew her nose.

'I do feel guilty about evicting you,' Mary said with a sigh. 'It's no wonder you're catching cold in this old hut. It's Reg's lungs that had me worried. Those cigarettes young Tony smokes are the devil for bringing on his cough.'

'Thought it was your precious parlour ceiling you were bothered about,' Reg said.

Mary smiled. 'Aye, that too. But I'm almost as fond of you as I am of the parlour ceiling, love. Happen even a mite more.'

'Soft lass,' Reg said, giving her a kiss. He turned to Bobby. 'Well, is the February number done?'

'Yes, we're on schedule, assuming Tony's report on the drama festival can be signed off on Monday,' Bobby said. 'We still need your editor's report and some other bits, then I'll take everything into Settle and have the printers make up a set of proofs. Do you want to take any copy home to check?'

'Nay, you know your business.' Reg paused, with a guilty glance at Mary. 'Well, happen I might take a couple of pieces. Does no harm to get another pair of eyes on them.'

Mary shook her head. 'I was a fool to myself thinking I could get this old man to retire. He'll be subbing copy on his deathbed.'

'Shall we go up to the house and meet this young lady of the captain's?' Bobby said. 'He told me we wouldn't be intruding if we stopped in to say hello.'

'Rude not to pass the time of day, I suppose,' Mary said. But Bobby noticed how her friend's lips pursed, as they generally did when talk turned to the captain's lady friend.

'I'll take Tony's typewriter,' Reg said. 'Should be able to manage it and the stick, since it's a portable. Bobby, can you carry yours?'

'I'll carry it,' Lilian said. 'You shouldn't be lifting heavy things, Bob.' She caught the look her sister gave her and hastily added, 'Not if you're getting a cold.'

Bobby allowed her sister to take the Remington. She locked the door while Lilian and Reg went ahead with the typewriters. Soft snow had started to fall.

Mary hung back, however. The look on her face suggested she was keen to have some confidential talk, which worried Bobby. Had her refusal of a hug given away her secret?

'I thought you'd be running up to the house to get an introduction to this Miss Simpson,' Bobby said brightly. 'Aren't you desperate to know what she's like?'

'Huh. I know what she's like,' Mary said, sniffing. 'All fur coat and no drawers.'

Bobby was starting to feel quite sorry for poor Veronica Simpson. She didn't have many friends in her suitor's family circle, with both the Parry children and now Mary taking against her.

'You don't like her?' Bobby said, taking her friend's arm. In her overcoat with bump well concealed, she felt a lot more secure.

'I'm only surprised George would be interested in such a flashy type.'

'I thought you approved of him courting.'

'Aye, with the right sort. Someone who'll be a mam to them little girls. That one's no good. Too young, too pretty and thinks far too well of herself. She'll be out gadding every night, same way Violet was.'

'Violet... Charlie's mam?'

'Yes, she was another such. Some women aren't made to be mothers, Bobby.'

'It was lucky he had you,' Bobby said softly.

'Lucky for both of us. I often wonder whether I'd have been able to pull myself out of the darkness after we lost Nancy, if there hadn't been another little one who needed me.' She glanced at Bobby. 'Jess and Florrie have christened your sister with a new title, I see.'

Bobby flinched. 'Yes. I'm sorry, Mary.'

'What for? It's good there's a younger woman they feel is family to them.' She pursed her lips again. 'They'll need it if their father decides to make an honest woman of that Miss Simpson.'

'You don't mind? I thought you might be hurt.'

'Why would I be?'

'Well, that they asked Lil and...' Bobby hesitated, feeling awkward. '...and not you.'

It did seem strange that Mary had never earned any title from the pair. They had bestowed an 'Uncle' on Charlie almost as soon as they had arrived, warming instantly to the fun-loving, carefree young man he had been then, who made up games for them and went out of his way to help them settle into their new home. Everyone else, however, had remained as they were when they had first been introduced. Bobby had never felt hurt by it — she was sure the children saw her as more of a big sister than anything, since she had never been responsible for their care — but she had been certain Mary would be upset at such a favour being conferred on Lil when it was Mary who had been mother to them for nearly two years now.

'Are you really not hurt they didn't ask you?' Bobby asked.

Mary smiled a little sadly. 'Well, and who says they didn't?'

'You mean they did?'

'Aye, they asked. It were just after last Christmas that Jessie came to tell me she and her sister wanted to call me summat else, if I'd let them.'

'Then why, um...'

'Because I told them no is why.'

'I don't understand.'

'It wasn't "Aunty" they wanted to call me.' Mary sighed. 'It was "Ma".'

'Oh. Oh!' Bobby stared at her. 'Goodness.'

'Well, I had to say no. Not saying it didn't cost me a tear to do it, mind.'

'I never knew they'd asked you that.'

'Aye, well, you had your own worries. I didn't like to trouble you.' Mary fell into a thoughtful silence before speaking again. 'I told them I thought their dad wouldn't like it, because they'd a mam in heaven and he wouldn't want a stranger acting like they were taking her place. They saw the sense in that. I suppose I had in my head as well that they'd be taken away from me one day, so I oughtn't to let them get too attached. But it wasn't only that.'

'It was Nancy,' Bobby said softly. 'Wasn't it?'

Mary nodded. 'And not the first time I'd had that conversation. Your Charlie asked me the same thing at Jess's age, and I'd to give him the same answer.' She swallowed. 'I often wonder if that was wrong of me. Lord knows he needed a mother, poor lamb. But when you've lost a little one who was the only one ever to use that name, it can feel like... a betrayal, I suppose. Like I was trying to fill her place with other women's childer.'

'Oh, Mary.' Bobby felt tears welling and pressed her friend's hand tightly.

'You understand?'

'Of course. Grief is never simple, is it? And Charlie feels you're just as much his mother no matter what he calls you. A name's just a name, but family is in how we feel.'

'You're wise beyond your years, Bobby,' Mary said, smiling.

Bobby smiled too. 'Well, I'm certainly starting to feel every one of my years. Let's go in, shall we?' They had reached the house and were lingering by the back door.

'We should. If you've a cold coming, hanging about in the snow won't help.' Mary gave Bobby's arm a squeeze. 'But I want you and Charlie to know that there's one name I'd love to be known by, and that's Nana. If it was what you pair wanted.'

'Of course it is. You and Reg would always be Nana and Grandad to any bairns of ours. I mean, when the time comes.'

'Aye,' Mary said, smiling. 'When the time comes.'

## Chapter 13

In spite of Mary's misgivings, Bobby rather warmed to Veronica Simpson. She was forced to confess that she too had felt Miss Simpson, with her flashy clothes and platinum-blonde hair, was unlikely to make a good mother figure to the girls. Bobby had had a stern word with herself, however, reminding herself that George Parry was hardly the sort to make a fool of himself over a pretty face. So she had withheld judgement until she could form a closer acquaintance.

Bobby had quickly reached the conclusion that what might appear as pridefulness was really simple shyness, somewhat disguised by Miss Simpson's film-star looks. The young lady shook hands politely with her suitor's extended family, made softly spoken enquiries about their work, homes and health, and generally came across as a quiet, ladylike person rather than the gadabout Mary had feared from the passing resemblance to Charlie's mother Violet.

What did worry Bobby, though, was Miss Simpson's interactions with the children. She spoke stiffly to them, interviewing them about their schoolwork and other dry topics. She didn't ask what games they liked, what books and comics were their favourites or what they enjoyed at the pictures. When Jess had attempted to introduce their sheepdog Ace, Miss Simpson had drawn her skirts about her and explained that she'd had a horror of dogs since childhood.

Miss Simpson was very young – little more than twenty-two, Bobby would guess. This made her closer in age to Florrie than Captain Parry, who must be a good fifteen years her senior.

And yet, a lack of experience with children couldn't completely explain the stiffness of her manners with them. She didn't seem to dislike the girls, but nor did she relish their company. It was their father who interested her, and his children were merely something to be borne so she could continue to keep company with him. Bobby couldn't tell if the captain was disappointed in the meeting, but he would be justified in feeling so.

Florrie and Jessie had been polite, but Bobby could see the looks that passed between them. The opinion they had formed, their looks said, was that while this wasn't the wicked stepmother of fairy tale, it was a decidedly dull stepmother and that was just as bad. If Miss Simpson was just going to grill them about school and give dirty looks to their dog, why had she wanted to meet them at all?

Perhaps Miss Simpson's stiffness would wear off when she got to know the children better. Bobby hoped so, since the captain seemed besotted with the woman. His expression rarely betrayed his feelings, but he spent a lot of his time gazing at his girlfriend as if amazed this beautiful young person could really belong to him. If Veronica's relationship with the girls remained frosty, would it be too late for their father to extricate himself? Was he already so deeply in love that Miss Simpson was as good as Mrs Parry?

Still, it wasn't Bobby's business. All she could do was be there for the girls, and hope everything worked out for the best.

She was keen to get home and prepare dinner before Charlie arrived back from Skipton. Bobby was dying to know how his interview at the bank had gone. He might be nearly home by now. Despite her eagerness to get back, however, something drew her into the churchyard.

Bobby had to agree with Tony that visiting Georgia's grave so often was doing her sister more harm than good. She knew cleaning and decorating the stone brought Lil relief of a kind, but it was a patchwork sort of help – something that covered over the problem rather than fixing it at the root.

Physically it wasn't good for Lilian, who was still building her strength, to be lingering outdoors. Bobby felt sure it was even less healthy from a mental point of view though. Lilian's grief surely shouldn't still carry such a sharp edge, nearly seven months after Georgia's death. It detached her from her family instead of binding her to them, taking her away from her living child and the husband who, for all his faults, loved her deeply. It worried Bobby that something which ought to bring the couple closer – their shared grief over the baby they had lost – seemed to be pushing them further apart.

Georgia's headstone was scrubbed clean as always, fresh greenery arranged with tender solicitude around it. It made Bobby sad to see how well-kept it was. That meant Lilian was still spending a significant amount of time here.

Her gaze drifted to the writing on the headstone.

Georgia Scott, born sleeping.

A tear slid down her cheek.

'Your mam says you're a wonderful counsellor, Georgie,' she murmured. 'So tell your Aunty Bobby what she ought to do. What does your mother need? How can I help her?'

But all was silence within Bobby's brain. It seemed Georgia's counsel was for Lil and Lil alone.

Bobby glanced at the name on the grave again. Georgia. She had never given much thought to it before, but why that name?

Annie had been named Antonia for her father, of course. Bobby had always assumed Georgia had been named for her and Lil's maternal grandfather, George Goggin. They had never been particularly close to Grandad Goggin, who had died when they were small, but he was the only George in the family.

But now Bobby thought of Captain Parry. It had been he who found Lilian the night she had gone into labour and fetched the doctor to her. Lil often said he had saved her life, and their friendship seemed to have sprung from the bond they formed that night. Could it be *that* George who was the namesake of Lilian's lost child?

The thought unsettled Bobby. It wasn't unnatural that her sister would want to name her child in honour of the man she credited with saving her life, but she knew Tony wouldn't like it. And… Bobby didn't know why, but something about it didn't sit right with her either. While it was clear Captain Parry's heart was now in the possession of the fragrant Miss Simpson, Bobby did worry about her sister becoming too fond of the man. She was a married woman, after all. If Lil's feelings developed beyond those of a disinterested friend, it could only lead to heartbreak.

The captain was a handsome man, with polished, gentlemanly manners. A man to admire. A war hero. Whereas Tony was just… well, Tony. It would be difficult to place the two men side by side and not have Tony Scott lose in the comparison. In her loneliness and alienation from her husband, could Lil's head have been turned by her good-looking friend?

Bobby sighed as she turned from the grave. Suddenly she wanted to be with Charlie, and feel his arms around her. She wanted to spend the afternoon in bed with him, his warm body against hers. She needed that.

Poor Lil though. If she could only have with Tony what Bobby had with Charlie, perhaps she could move on from her grief. Yet Lilian remained emotionally detached from the man she had been forced by circumstances to tie herself to.

–

At home, Bobby picked up a couple of letters from the mat. One was addressed to Charlie, but it didn't look to be anything official, although it carried the RAF censor's stamp. She turned it over, and found the name and service number of a pal from his old squadron on the back – Pilot Officer Willis. The man was an occasional correspondent, and his letters usually cheered

Charlie up. Bobby put it on the coffee table, glad he had something to make him smile after today's interview.

The second letter was addressed to her. She wondered if it might be from Jake, her youngest brother, who hadn't written since his Christmas card a month ago. However, the address was typewritten and there was no military stamp. Full of curiosity, Bobby tore it open. She blinked when a postal order fluttered to the floor.

There was a letter as well. She took it out and started to read.

*Dear Mr Bancroft…*

*Mr* Bancroft! Bobby looked again at the envelope. She hadn't noticed that it bore her maiden name. Jake had been uppermost in her thoughts, and the lad often forgot to use his sisters' married names when he wrote. Now she looked closely, however, Bobby could see that the envelope was addressed to Mr and not Miss R. Bancroft. That was the name she had used in writing to Broadcasting House…

Bobby turned her attention to the letter, which was on BBC-letterheaded paper. It was succinct, no more than a few lines, but the emotions they produced were enough to wake Marmaduke up and set her stomach fluttering.

> *Dear Mr Bancroft,*
>
> *Mr Handley has asked me to convey his sincerest thanks for the sketch you were kind enough to send in. While he will not be able to use it in its entirety, there are a couple of gags he can make use of in a future episode of* It's That Man Again *and he has asked that I enclose a ten-shilling postal order in exchange for the copyright. Five shillings a joke is our standard fee. If you have more material of the same quality, Mr Handley would be glad to consider it.*
>
> *Yours sincerely,*
> *M. Shepherd (Mrs)*
> *Secretary, Mr Thomas Handley*

Under this, a postscript gave the two lines Tommy Handley wished to purchase. It felt very strange, seeing her words typed there on official BBC paper.

Bobby stared at the letter for a long time. Eventually she retrieved the postal order from the floor, and stared at that for a long time too.

Ten shillings wasn't much in the grand scheme of things, but to Bobby it felt like she'd won the pools. It was nearly a quarter of what she earned on the magazine each week. And all for two little lines that she had scribbled down in about ten minutes!

What should she do? She would have to write to Scarlet. Her friend would be thrilled for her. Or perhaps she ought to write to Archie first, who had given her the idea and advised her to use a male pseudonym. She had paired the male version of her Christian name with her maiden surname, knowing that anything addressed to Mr Atherton would be opened by Charlie. Oh, she felt so flustered that she didn't know who to tell first!

What was Charlie going to say? Bobby hadn't breathed a word to him about her secret plan. She had been certain she would get a rejection, and to be honest had felt rather foolish about the business. It had only been the encouragement of Scarlet and Archie that had persuaded her she could write anything good enough for the BBC. Wouldn't her husband be proud?

It would be a lifeline for her too, when she was forced to leave *The Tyke*. Not only because of the money but because it would give her something to stimulate her brain – something she could surely fit into her new life as a housewife and mother. Marmaduke could sense her exhilaration and was practically dancing a hornpipe inside her.

After a moment's calmer thought, Bobby decided against sharing the news with Charlie right away. She knew he struggled with feelings of failure while he wasn't providing for his family. No doubt he would be proud of her achievement, but it might gall him, too, to know Bobby had felt the need to find other ways to support them. If his interview today had gone badly, she might be rubbing salt in a wound already tender.

Would it not be better to squirrel away any little earnings she could get from this, to surprise her husband with when the time was right? Bobby couldn't guarantee it would be a significant amount, or that she would ever write a joke worthy of the five-bob fee again, but if she did, she could keep it hidden away in her own secret pot. When Charlie had a job again, they could celebrate the achievement with everything resting in its proper place.

Bobby couldn't deny, too, that she rather relished the idea of the smug little smile she would conceal behind her handkerchief if one of her jokes came over the air when she and Charlie listened to the Forces Programme. That would be a thrill, hearing her words spoken by Funf or Mrs Mopp or one of the other famous *ITMA* characters.

She heard Charlie's key in the lock, and hastily stuffed both letter and postal order into her pocket.

## Chapter 14

Bobby could see at once that things hadn't gone well at the bank. Charlie's face was grey and strained as he hung up his hat and coat.

He didn't have his walking stick, Bobby noticed. It was still in the umbrella stand. Surely he hadn't gone all the way to Skipton without it? Charlie could walk unsupported over increasingly longer distances as his injured leg grew stronger, but it still hurt him to put weight on it for extended periods.

She went to put her arms around him. He hid his face on her shoulder, and Bobby felt his body convulse.

'Darling, what happened?' she asked softly. 'Why didn't you take your stick?'

'I didn't want them to see,' he whispered. 'Thought if I could hide how broken I was, I might have a sliver of a damned chance.' He laughed. 'What an ass.'

'Come and sit down.'

Bobby led him to his chair by the hearth, cursing herself for lingering at Georgia's gravestone instead of hurrying home to get the fire lit. After Charlie's difficult day, all she could offer him as comfort was a cold, dismal house. Some wife she was.

'Let me make you a cup of tea, then I'll light the fire and get some soup on,' she said. 'I'm sorry there's nothing ready for your dinner. I got held up at the Parrys' place.'

'No. Don't go.' Charlie caught her hand. 'I'm not hungry. I just want to feel you, that's all.'

Since this was what Bobby wanted as well, she didn't object when he guided her to his knee. She held him, burying her lips in his hair.

'Do you want to tell me about it?' she asked gently.

He flinched. 'I'll try.'

'Surely it couldn't have been very awful? You were more than qualified.'

'Oh God.' Charlie hid his face on her shoulder, as if it would be less humiliating to tell his tale if he didn't have to look at her. 'I thought it might be all right. I'd been gossiping with the manager's secretary while I was waiting to be called in. She told me not to worry about disguising my limp, because Miller – the bank manager – had one of his own from the last war. He'd been decorated after Verdun. The staff were very proud of having a war hero for a boss, she said. I thought, well, if he's a veteran too then…' He laughed hoarsely. 'Then at least he'll be on my side.'

'Wasn't he?'

'I don't think he was on anyone's side, except his bank's. One of those snooty-looking fellows with pince-nez on the end of their nose, who regard you as if you're some form of insect life. Within a few minutes, I was shaking so much I could barely keep in my chair.'

'What did he ask you?'

'About my schooling. How my arithmetic was, and if I could provide a reference from my commanding officer. And then he asked…' Charlie closed his eyes. 'Why I'd left the RAF.'

'Did you tell him?'

'I gave him the official reason. That the nerves in my arm had been damaged, which prevented me flying. He seemed sceptical. Wanted to know why they hadn't moved me into an instructor post or some desk job. I told him I could provide my discharge certificate if he wanted – probably sounded pretty defensive. Anyhow, he said that wouldn't be necessary. He was only interested in whether there was anything that would stop me doing the job.'

'What did you say?'

'I said my penmanship wasn't as neat as it once was, but it was legible as long as I took care.' Charlie swallowed another sob. 'But I couldn't stop shaking, Bob. Couldn't stop. This man Miller stared at me for what felt like an hour, and the shakes were getting worse all the while. Then he reached into his desk and took out this bag of coins.'

Bobby frowned. 'Coins? Whatever for?'

'He wanted me to count them.'

'That's a funny sort of test, isn't it?' Bobby lifted his chin to look into his eyes. 'I'd have thought he'd give you credit for at least being able to add up.'

'He didn't want to know if I could add up,' Charlie said quietly. 'The coins went everywhere, Bobby. I couldn't grip them. I fumbled so much that I could barely get them out of the bag. Mr Miller just watched calmly as it rained pennies, told me not to bother picking them up and said they'd be in touch. Didn't even shake my hand.'

'Oh, Charlie.' Bobby held him tight. 'I'm so sorry, sweetheart. But perhaps something will come of it.'

'I can delude myself about a lot of things, but I know a complete disaster when I see one.' He gave a depressed little laugh. 'All for a four-pounds-ten-a-week job that any kid with his School Certificate could do. It's hopeless. I'm unemployable, Bob.'

'You can't be. You're clever and presentable and... and likeable. There must be dozens of jobs you could do well.'

Charlie snorted. 'No one's going to pay me enough to support a wife and child for being professionally likeable, are they?' He rested his forehead against her chest. 'I've let you down, darling,' he whispered. 'I'm sorry. I did try, honestly.'

'You haven't done any such thing.' She planted a firm kiss on his forehead. 'You did your best and I'm proud of you. The shaking is outside your control.'

'I don't know how we're going to make ends meet, Bob,' he muttered in a hollow voice. 'You can't work much longer. You shouldn't be working now. Even if we're careful, our savings will have dried up by the time the baby arrives. If I have to beg Reggie for a loan, I will, but he and Mary are hardly swimming in cash either.'

Bobby shivered as she thought about what had popped into her head at work: that there was a possibility she was carrying not one but two babies. She was glad no such idea had occurred to her husband. In this sort of mood, a worry like that might push him over the edge.

Her thoughts turned to the postal order in her pocket. She hated to see Charlie this way: looking so utterly defeated. For a moment, Bobby considered telling him of her windfall in the hope it might cheer him up, but then she thought better of it. Telling him now, when he was tortured by his own inability to provide for his family, wouldn't do his spirits any good.

Another thought occurred to her, however. It was a subject she hadn't liked to bring up before, but it felt like the right time now.

'Charlie?'

'What?'

'I just wondered... did you write back to the Air Ministry? About the DFC, I mean.'

Charlie's brow lowered. 'Do we have to talk about that now?'

'I'm sorry. I only thought that... well, it might help, mightn't it? You said the staff at the bank were proud their manager had been decorated. I know it's complicated, but people do care about that sort of thing. If potential employers knew you'd been awarded the DFC...'

She trailed off in the face of his black expression.

'I won't masquerade as a hero to get some damn bank job,' he said, his tone grim.

'You wouldn't be masquerading. You deserve that award. I only thought, since you're struggling so much—'

'No, Bobby. Absolutely not. It would be an insult to every airman killed in this war to exploit something like that for personal gain. I'm surprised you'd even ask.'

Bobby flushed. 'I'm sorry. I... hadn't thought of it like that.'

'Never mind. Forget it.'

'I didn't mean to upset you. It was just an idea.'

'All right. Let's put it behind us.'

'Yes. Sorry.'

Bobby pressed a kiss to his forehead. Charlie's expression had turned blank, however, and he merely gazed into the distance.

She stood up, mumbling something about needing to get the dinner on, and went to hide in the kitchen. There, Bobby rested her overheated forehead against the wall and stifled a sob.

Oh Lord, what a stupid thing to say! She ought to have guessed Charlie would react that way. Now he was hurt, and worse, he was disappointed in her.

It was his pride she had been thinking of – the feeling he was failing in his duty as head of the family. But in thinking of his pride, Bobby had neglected to consider his grief. What a fool she had been! How callous, how calculating she must have sounded, to suggest using a decoration to improve his employment prospects. Charlie would never stomach that, after all the friends he had lost. Would he ever be able to forgive her?

Charlie had turned on the wireless. Bobby was glad of it. It meant he couldn't hear her cry. She put a pan of soup on the hob, seasoning it with salty tears.

It couldn't have been more than five minutes later that she felt a pair of gentle arms slip around her waist, and soft lips on her neck.

'I'm sorry,' Charlie whispered.

Bobby wiped her wet cheeks with the heels of her hands. 'You don't need to apologise. I'm the one who—'

'No you're not.' He turned her around and kissed away the tears. 'I was being selfish. Thinking only about my own feelings, as if I was a single man with no one but myself to consider. It was perfectly good advice.'

'I ought to have thought before I spoke. Of course you'd never do anything so cynical. It was insensitive.'

'And I ought to have remembered that it's about you as much as me. Ethical quandaries are bachelor luxuries.' He kissed her again. 'You were absolutely right, sweetheart, and I'm sorry I made you cry.'

Bobby flashed him a shaky smile. 'You aren't going to divorce me yet then? Because Jess was keen to matchmake for me with the captain earlier.'

'What with him and Ernie King, there seems to be quite a queue forming.' Charlie hugged her fiercely. 'For all the good it'll do them, because I'm not planning on letting you go.'

'So what have you decided to do about the DFC?'

Charlie didn't answer right away. His face was against her neck, and Bobby wasn't sure whether it was his tears or the remnants of her own that caused the dampness there.

'I read that letter from Willis you left on the table,' he said after a while.

'What did he have to say?'

'Nothing good. A friend from the Twelves, Hynes, is in a bad way in a London hospital. Burnt head to toe. They're not expecting him to linger.'

'Oh Charlie, I'm sorry.'

'Willis and some of the lads are making a trip down to see him. He wants to know if I'll join them. I know we can't afford to make frivolous journeys but I would like to go.'

'When is it to be?'

'The boys have arranged leave for next Friday, if Hynesy's still with us. I'd have to stay overnight. Would you be all right by yourself?'

'Don't worry about that. Of course you should say goodbye to your friend.'

Charlie massaged his cheek. 'Poor kid. Not even twenty-one. They can pin gongs on those boys all they like but it doesn't keep them alive, does it? Doesn't bring them back when they're gone, or take away their pain when they've been half burnt alive.' He sighed, and rested his forehead against hers. 'But you're right. I can't allow myself the indulgence of righteous anger, with a baby coming. If you think the DFC could help... well, I'll think it over.'

'You do deserve it, Charlie.'

'Please let's not have that conversation again. It's not really about what I deserve. I don't know how to explain it to you.'

'Can you try?'

'If I had to stand in front of the king while he pinned the thing on, I'd feel like such a... a phoney,' he said quietly. 'Like it ought to be Hynesy or Bram or one of the others standing there, instead of lying in graves they were too young to fill. Not me. Not the man who was invalided out with "shot nerves" as if he was some highly strung Victorian dowager. The man who refused to fly and left others to die in his place. Can't you understand that?'

'I understand you feel guilty about having to give up flying, but that doesn't mean you did anything wrong,' Bobby said. 'It's grief that makes you feel that way. The guilt goes with knowing you survived when others didn't, but it isn't a sin to survive, Charlie.'

'But I feel it all the same.'

'They want to give you the DFC for climbing out of that plane to save your crew. That was an act of bravery and self-sacrifice by any measure. You wouldn't be insulting your friends by accepting it, and I'm sure if Bram and the others were alive, they'd say the same. They'd be proud of you.'

'It's what I didn't do that haunts me,' Charlie murmured. 'When I joined up I made a promise to see this thing through, but I soon folded when the going got tough, didn't I?'

'You were right to refuse to fly with your nerves in the state they were. You said yourself that you could have got your crew killed if you'd had one of your attacks in the air.'

'Other men don't have attacks.' He turned away from her. 'Other men don't think and think and think and think until their brains ache. They don't cry in the night like bairns – or if they do, they don't let it stop them doing their jobs. They keep on until we've won this thing, like I vowed to do.'

'Not everyone is the same, Charlie. You're you. You can only *be* you. I wish you wouldn't keep comparing yourself to others.'

Charlie only sighed, and Bobby realised her words were useless. He would never accept that this award was something he deserved, no matter how she tried to persuade him.

## Chapter 15

The following Friday, Bobby was woken as usual by Marmaduke squirming in her womb. He could deliver some hefty kicks now she was approaching the six-month point in her pregnancy.

She lay with one hand on her belly, feeling the baby's movements. She slid her palm over the swell, trying to work out how many little feet were kicking up a storm against her insides. But they were just tiny thumps, hard to pin down. The baby might have one leg or eight for all Bobby could tell.

A thought popped up: of the famous Dionne quintuplets who had been born in Canada ten years ago.

Lord, five babies in one labour! Poor Mrs Dionne. Surely Dr Minchin would know if there were that many babies in residence in her womb, wouldn't he?

Bobby reached for her husband, but Charlie's side of the bed was unoccupied. She turned on the lamp.

'Charlie?' she called out. She wasn't used to him not being there when she woke up.

'I'm here, love.'

He came into the bedroom, wearing his best suit. For a moment, Bobby's sleep-addled mind wondered if he had another job interview. Then she remembered the rather grimmer reason he had to be up early and dressed in his best.

'Oh. Sorry.' She rubbed her hair. 'I forgot about your trip. I ought to have been up to make breakfast for you.'

'You need your sleep, and so does Marmaduke.' He sat by her on the bed and kissed her hair. 'I'm quite capable of making my own breakfast.'

'I know, but I like to do it.' She pressed a hand to her belly again, wincing. 'Anyhow, Marmaduke seems to have had enough sleep. Right now he's practising his football skills with my internal organs.'

'Then I ought to administer some paternal discipline.' Charlie rested his head against her belly. 'You behave for your mother while I'm away, young man, or it'll be no pudding for you for a week.'

Bobby smiled. 'But that means it'll be no pudding for me either.'

'True. It's difficult doing your fatherly duty with your child hiding from you.'

Charlie started to sit up, but Bobby rested a hand on his head.

'Stay like that a minute,' she said softly. 'Marmaduke's still when you rest your head there. He knows when his dad's nearby.'

Charlie smiled, and planted a kiss on the stomach filling out her nightdress.

'You're beautiful, you know, Bob,' he said quietly. 'Never more than now.'

Bobby laughed. 'You must be joking. I feel like a half-inflated barrage balloon.'

'Well, there's a lot to be said for half-inflated barrage balloons.' He glanced up. 'I don't want to harp on about it, but I wish you'd give up work. I hate to think you might make yourself or the baby ill.'

'We need the money, Charlie.'

'I'll find a way to keep us from starving. It's more important that you stay healthy.'

'But I like working, and I'm sure it doesn't do me any harm. I feel fine. A bit tired, but none the worse for that.'

'Still, it's a lot of stress on your body. How long do you think you can keep it up? It can only be a few more weeks.'

'I know. But a few more weeks is five pounds, and five pounds buys a lot of terry towelling.'

'I'd rather have a healthy wife and baby than five pounds. Stop worrying and let me take care of you.'

'Did you hear back from the bank yet?'

Charlie lifted his head from her stomach.

'I wish you wouldn't pin any hopes on that,' he said. 'They probably won't even bother writing to tell me it's a no when it was as plain as the nose on my face. But I'll find some way to make money.'

'Selling your gigolo services to Mrs Barraclough next door?'

'Now there's an idea. I could make our fortune in no time.' He paused. 'I've decided though… you're right, I ought to take that damned gong. I don't feel good about it, but you and the baby matter more than my foolish principles.'

Bobby wasn't sure what to say.

'Oh,' was all she could manage.

'Aren't you pleased? It's what you wanted, isn't it?'

'Well, yes. I mean I thought you ought to take it, but… I wish you wanted to, Charlie. Not for my sake or the baby's but your own. I wish I could make you understand how much you deserve it.'

He looked away. 'Isn't it enough that I'm accepting it?'

'Not for me. I feel like I'll want to swell half out of my frock when the king pins it on, but I won't be able to if I know you're only accepting it because you feel you have to.'

'It's the only way I can feel. I'm sorry, Bob.'

Bobby sighed. 'All right. It's your grief. It isn't for me to tell you how you ought to feel it. I just wish you could be as proud of yourself as I am.' She swung her legs out of bed. 'Have you got everything you need?'

'Yes, I'm all packed.'

'Did you get your sandwiches from the pantry, and put pyjamas and clean underwear in your case?'

Charlie smiled. 'Yes, Mother.'

'And have you packed your wash things?'

'I was an airman, you know. Packing's one thing I ought to be good at.'

'Well, but have you got the scarf and jumper I knitted you?' Bobby persisted. 'There might be an air raid. You'll need to wrap up warm if you have to spend hours in a shelter.'

'I've got plenty of layers, don't worry. I'm only away for one night, Bobby.'

'Clean handkerchiefs?'

Charlie laughed. 'All right, you've caught me out. I forgot the clean handkerchiefs. Do you feel better now?'

Bobby did feel a little better at finding he hadn't remembered quite everything. It made her feel useful. She pushed on her slippers and went to fetch some freshly starched handkerchiefs.

'And don't forget your stick,' she begged him as she tucked the hankies into his case. 'I know it makes you feel self-conscious, but I'd worry half to death if I thought you'd gone all the way to London without it.'

Charlie took her in his arms.

'I'll miss having you fuss over me,' he said softly. 'Think of me while I'm away, won't you?'

'I will.' Bobby stroked his scarred cheek. 'How are you feeling about it?'

'I don't know if this makes me the most callous man alive, but… in a way, I'm looking forward to it. To seeing the boys, and feeling like I'm part of a gang again. I miss that bit of RAF life. Is that terrible?'

'No, love.'

'I'm even looking forward to seeing Hynesy. I know what state he's going to be in, and yet…' He paused. 'It feels like a privilege to be granted a chance to say goodbye. We've lost so many pals who just went out one day and never came back. I know it's going to be emotional, I know he'll be in terrible pain, but I'm glad to have the opportunity to shake his hand and wish him luck in the next life.'

'You think about death differently, when you've had to live with so much of it,' Bobby said quietly. 'I know it isn't the same for me, but I lost friends in the RAF too. Here.' She gave him a kiss. 'You can have that one on account, and I'll be waiting with more and better when you get back. Hurry home, won't you?'

'I will. You take care of yourself, all right? And no running off with Ernie King while I'm away.' He rested a hand on her stomach. 'Look after this little one. I love you both very much.'

'We love you too.'

With a last kiss, he left. Bobby heard him slide his stick from the umbrella stand, then the front door closed behind him.

—

Bobby didn't go straight to work. She'd brought the corrected magazine proofs home the day before so she could take them into Settle first thing. There she would drop them off with the printer so they could be turned into the February number of *The Tyke*.

Her thoughts were filled with Charlie as she walked to the bus stop, some two miles from their cottage. It was going to be draining for him, saying goodbye to that poor boy. Bobby could only imagine how emotionally wrung out she would feel if she had a similar deathbed visit to make.

She took out her purse to see how much of her wage was left.

Hmm. Barely three shillings. It wasn't much to last until Sunday, yet she would have liked to get a few nice things in for Charlie. They had enough points for a can of salmon and some tinned fruit, if she could only spare the money. Bobby knew she oughtn't to fritter money away on luxuries, but the blackout hours felt so long and dreary in winter that it would be bleak to dine on nothing but vegetable soup and gritty slices of National Loaf every day.

Her gaze fell on the ten-shilling BBC postal order in her purse, and her mouth twitched.

Yes, that's what she'd do. It was really bonus money, after all. She had earned it herself, entirely unexpectedly, and Charlie deserved a little treat after his emotional journey. She would get the salmon and a tin of pears or peaches, which would go well with some custard powder she had been hoarding, and a jug of beer from the Hart. When her husband came home, they could have a proper beano tea: just the two of them, snuggled in front of the fire.

It was the first time Bobby had thought about the letter from Broadcasting House since the day it had arrived. Other things had pushed it from her mind. She thought about it now, however.

Charlie was right: her employment at *The Tyke* would have to end soon. But she still had this, didn't she?

Perhaps she had been lucky with the two jokes she had sold. Perhaps there would be no further postal orders. Then again, it was Bobby's brain that had furnished those jokes and who was to say she didn't have more of the same in there? And tonight she had a whole evening to herself. If Bobby could pen... say, a dozen jokes good enough for Tommy Handley or one of the other radio comics, then that would be three pounds, wouldn't it? Maybe she was aiming too high, but still, more than a week's wages for an evening's work – now that would be something!

The thought of being able to add to the family pot, and even more of having a goal to aim for, cheered Bobby immensely. Giving up work didn't feel so daunting now she had this. She hummed as she strolled along the narrow road, beaming with maternal fellow-feeling at some of the pregnant ewes in the fields.

The expectant sheep were just one of the signs of spring starting to appear as January advanced. Showers of white snowdrops stood out against the grass, and although it was cold, with patches of snow on the fells, the winter sun shone as brightly as an afternoon in June. Bobby smiled on it all, pleased to have made a plan and pleased to think she had the resources to do something nice for Charlie.

She spotted Jolka walking towards her from the direction of Sumner House. Bobby pulled her coat around her, conscious of the bump she was still keen to hide. Jolka's own bump was now clearly visible. She carried her pregnant frame proudly, and a little defiantly. Bobby, however, was only grateful she had spent the previous weekend adjusting her old coat so it billowed out from under her bust rather than her thickening waist.

She might have known Jolka, always stylishly dressed, would notice this.

'Bobby.' She beamed when she met her. 'How glowing you are today! That is a flattering new cut for your coat.'

Bobby was glad it was cold, which would explain any pinkness in her cheeks.

'Thank you,' she said. 'I've become quite the seamstress since this war started. I could barely sew a stitch before without breaking my needle. Have you been to see Topsy?'

'I have, to collect some clothes I loaned for her pantomime.' Jolka indicated a bag she was carrying. 'Piotrek has taken Tommy to feed the ducks, so I am at liberty. Where are you heading?'

'Into Settle.' Bobby raised her shopping basket filled with magazine proofs. 'I have to take these to the printer.'

'I will walk with you to your stop.' Jolka fell into step beside her.

'How was Topsy?' Bobby asked.

'She is all at sixes and sevens, as I think is the English expression. Teddy laughs at her, but you would think the world was ending from the way she behaves. I was very sorry I did not wait a few hours to pick up my costumes.'

'Oh my goodness! Why, what can have happened?'

'Do not upset yourself. It is no great disaster, except to Topsy, and she will soon recover. It is the old lady, Mrs Hobbes.'

'She's all right, isn't she?'

'Yes, but she has given Topsy the unwelcome news that she is to leave her. Grown-up married ladies do not need nannies, she says, and she does not want to take up room when she knows Topsy and Teddy desire a child. I believe she is right, but Topsy is distraught to lose her company.'

'Oh, poor Topsy. Will Mrs Hobbes go back to Scotland?'

'My understanding was that she would remain in the village, with that menace of a pet goose and his family.'

'I wonder where she'll live.' Bobby smiled. 'It'll have to be close to the beck or Norman will kick up a stink.'

'Well, we shall see. It is no great loss to Topsy, who will see her friend often, but I suppose she has grown accustomed to having her Maimie at hand.' Jolka smiled dryly. 'It is rare that Topsy is thwarted in getting what she wants, I suspect. I should say it is no bad thing for her now and again.'

'I hate to think of her upset, though. Mrs Hobbes is like a mother to her.'

'I doubt it will be long until she sees it is for the best. With an additional room, she and Tadeusz can pursue their desire to adopt a child.' Jolka raised an eyebrow. 'Your Charlie's nickname for our "mothers' meetings" may prove prophetic, do you not think? It could be that before the year is over, all those in our little group of wives will be mothers also.'

Bobby flushed. 'Um, well, it's rather soon to be thinking of that.'

'I think it is not so soon,' Jolka said, glancing at her billowing coat. 'But I will not say more if it discomforts you. I am sure you have reasons to wish concealment.'

Oh Lord, so Jolka had guessed the secret? Perhaps Bobby wasn't so adept in hiding her bump as she had believed. She was sure she had noticed Mary glancing at her waist recently too, and her comment about wanting to be known as Nana 'when the time comes' had seemed loaded with meaning. Had her cover been blown? If so, that meant her days at *The Tyke* were truly numbered.

Bobby wouldn't want the news to get out through whispers. It would hurt her father if he were to find out he was expecting another grandchild from village gossip instead of from her. As much as Bobby wanted to keep working as long as she could, she did want to break the news to her nearest and dearest herself.

Anyhow, it was no use trying to fib her way out of it now. Bobby was a terrible liar, for one thing, and Jolka far too clever to be fobbed off.

'Is it so obvious?' Bobby asked quietly.

'Not to everyone, perhaps. You conceal it cleverly. But why do you do so? I am sure the news would be received joyously.'

'I wanted to keep it hidden while I was still able to work. Reg would dismiss me if he knew I was expecting. You won't say anything, will you?'

'Your secret will be safe with me.' Jolka glanced at her. 'Still, it is a shame you must give up the work you love.'

'Yes,' Bobby said with a sigh. 'Charlie's desperate for me to leave my job. He's convinced it isn't good for me or the baby, yet I'm certain it would be worse to let my brain and skills stagnate at home. It's only the fact we need money that's persuaded him not to tell tales on me to his brother.'

'You are sure Reg would want you to give up work? Surely you can do some of your writing at home. There could be no harm to your health in that.'

'I could, but I feel sure he wouldn't approve. He has set ideas about mothers working. It was only the difficulty of finding anyone else with my skills that persuaded him to keep me on after marriage.'

'The roles of women and men are so carefully controlled within this world,' Jolka said with a sigh. 'Even our language is loaded with ideas of the functions we must perform. When we talk of a woman mothering a child, we mean that she will nurture and care for him. When we talk of a man fathering a child, it speaks only of his role in the creation of life. People like your editor are unable to think beyond ideas that have been driven into them over generations. It is most frustrating.'

'It is, but what can we do about it? What can *I* do about it?'

'You ought to be like me, Bobby. Do not pin your fortunes on the Regs of the world. Who is it that runs his little magazine now?'

'Well, I do,' Bobby said, shifting the basket of proofs to her other arm. 'I decide what goes in the magazine and take overall responsibility for each number.'

'Quite. You have the skills you need to do this work. You are used to managing it. Why not manage it for yourself?'

Bobby frowned. 'I don't understand.'

Jolka stopped to stretch her back before she carried on walking.

'When I was a young woman, before I met Piotr, I worked for an agency that produced illustrations for advertisements,' she told Bobby. 'There were several of us, all struggling artists who aspired to better things. Nearly all were men, and as men they were paid a third again what I and the one other woman artist earned. One day I said, "To hell with pictures of soap flakes and matchboxes for a handful of *złoty* a week", and I resigned. After that I said I would paint only what I wanted to paint for the people I wanted to paint for, and I would accept no less for my work than a male of the same skill. Times were lean at first, but eventually it brought me my independence, and even some wealth. By the time I met Piotr, I had no need to marry for the financial support of a husband. I was free to choose for love.'

Bobby thought about this.

'You mean I could start my own magazine?' she asked.

'Why not? To create your own employment could bring you independence, as it did for me.'

'You were young and single though,' Bobby said. 'It was brave of you, Jolka, but it wasn't a risk everyone could afford to take. Not if they had people to support. And you had a skill rare enough that it could earn you a living.'

'But you too have skills – skills that mean you do not need a man to tell you what to do or put money in your pocket.

Tell yourself what to do. Put money in your own pocket. It is something women rarely consider.'

'I couldn't do what Reg did when he started his business. He didn't have dependants to feed and care for as I will, or a home to keep. Besides, I wouldn't want to start something in competition with *The Tyke*.' She sighed. 'I wish I could do some of my work at home, though, just a few hours a week. But Reg is so stuffy about mothers working, I don't know if he'd ever consider it.'

'If you wish for it then find a way,' Jolka said firmly. 'You can write for other publications as well as *The Tyke*, I suppose. Do not allow your own ambitions and desires to become lost because you have others to care for. It is not a sin to also care for yourself.'

–

Bobby pondered Jolka's advice as she travelled into town.

Making her own employment was something to consider, certainly. *The Tyke* had a number of freelance writers it commissioned work from. Those writers produced pieces for other publications as well, Bobby imagined. Could she do the same?

The difficulty was in knowing where to begin. She had no idea how someone went about selling their writing services. It wasn't like the BBC, presumably, sending in gags in the hope someone might want them. Periodicals commissioned their pieces well in advance. Was it a case of sending your portfolio to an editor and hoping they took a fancy to your work?

What Bobby did know was that the clock was now ticking for her job at *The Tyke*. Jolka had guessed her secret, and while Bobby knew she could trust her friend's discretion, if Jolka had noticed then it couldn't be long before others began to do so. Reluctant though she was, she would have to speak to Reg about it soon.

Soon… but not just yet. She could put it off another week, perhaps, if she was careful. Maybe even two.

In Settle, Bobby dropped off her proofs then took the liberty of taking an early dinner hour so she could cash her postal order and buy the things she wanted for Charlie.

She was lucky enough to find a tin of salmon at the grocer's – the last tin, much to her joy, which felt like fate's seal of approval for her plan to treat her husband. She also found a tin of peaches and some evaporated milk to make up her custard, and a packet of Charlie's favourite cigarettes. By the time she returned to Silverdale, she had a basket of goodies on her arm. All she needed now was a jug of beer from the Hart, then Charlie would have a veritable feast to return to.

One incident from her trip into town stood out. It had been when she emerged from the grocer's to see George Parry, talking earnestly with an elegant woman in a fur coat and feathered hat. Bobby had thought the woman must be Veronica Simpson – the glamorous fur and jaunty hat looked like her style – but on drawing closer, she realised that this woman had a pram. When the woman turned her head, Bobby saw that it wasn't Miss Simpson but her sister.

Lilian had immediately waved her over to have a cuddle with Annie, who was full of giggles and sunshine that spring-like morning. The captain shook Bobby's hand warmly, explaining that he had bumped into Lilian while doing some shopping.

Neither seemed furtive. They hadn't been standing close, or touching in any way that hinted at intimacy. Nevertheless, Bobby felt unsettled at running into them alone together, with Lilian all dressed up and the captain talking in what had seemed such a significant manner. She felt even more unsettled at the sight of Lilian wearing that fur coat, which Bobby recognised as the one George had given her. Her sister had told her months ago that she was going to give the thing away, before Tony discovered it. Clearly the wrench had been too much, however.

But it was probably nothing. Why wouldn't two friends who ran into one another stop to pass the time of day? They had looked earnest, yes, but the captain generally did look earnest. Bobby had worked herself up into a state of worry after her idea about Georgia's name, she supposed, and now she was imagining things that weren't there.

Anyhow, it had been good to see Lilian looking so bright and vibrant. Today she'd looked truly young and healthy, as she had before her babies had been born. Male heads had turned as they passed her. All the same, Bobby determined to call on her sister after work and ask what she had been discussing with the captain.

## Chapter 16

When Bobby got back to her office-shed, she found Tony leaning back in his chair, smoking.

'You took your time, didn't you?' he observed.

'I took my dinner hour early to run some errands in town.' Bobby's eyes stung in the fug of smoke. 'I hope you've done more this morning than make yourself cough, Tony.'

She sat down at her desk, unfastening her pixie hood but not removing her coat. After the encounter with Jolka, Bobby felt self-conscious about her bump. Tony was less astute than a woman was likely to be, but still, she ought to be cautious.

'I've been working, don't worry.' Tony took out his cigarette. 'Been hard at it, in fact.'

'What have you done then?'

'Take a look. It's on your desk.'

Bobby glanced at his copy: an article on the fairy legends of the Dales.

'Oh,' she said. 'Well, thanks. I'll sub it now.'

'Not sure what you were trying to say, getting me to write that one,' he said, grinning. He nodded to her coat. 'Not going to take that off? You won't feel the benefit when you go outside.'

'In a bit. I'm freezing.'

'Not that cold, is it? Stove's on.'

'Yes, but it was a chilly walk from the Bull. If you're that concerned about me, you can get a brew on.'

'It's your turn.'

'No it isn't.'

'Yes it is. I've been making my own brews all morning. About time someone else made me one.'

Bobby sighed. Every day the same argument. Just by virtue of her sex, it seemed, the rota of tea rounds was expected to tip five to one against her. But she had no energy to do battle with Tony over the tea.

'All right, I'll get one on in a minute.' She glanced up from his fairy article. 'I suppose the captain's out, is he?'

'Aye, he went shopping. Left the back door key in case he's not here when we leave, so we can put the machines inside. He says to pop it through the letterbox.'

'Right. Good.' Bobby paused. 'I bumped into our Lil in Settle, taking the baby out.'

'She was going in to change her library book, I think,' Tony said vaguely. 'All right, was she?'

'Yes, she looked better than I've seen her for ages.'

'You think so too?' Tony seemed pleased to have her confirm this. 'I thought the same. Happen she's getting back to normal at last.'

Bobby felt relieved that Tony's version of events tallied with Lil's and Captain Parry's. It meant she was being foolish, and there had been no clandestine liaison arranged.

'Hope she don't have such a rough time of it with the next one,' Tony observed as he finished off his cigarette. 'Our mam says it's never as bad with the second.'

Bobby frowned. 'The next one? You don't mean—'

'Nay, she's not in the family way yet,' Tony said complacently. 'Want to get her strong and healthy again first. We've not got space at the moment anyhow.'

Bobby thought about what her dad had told her before Christmas. She hadn't heard any more about his plans to move in with a friend. Was he still considering it? The unsettled feeling about her sister's friendship with George Parry had only made Bobby feel more keenly that it was imperative the Scotts had a space to call their own if their marriage was to thrive.

When work was over, Bobby walked to Cow House Cottage with Tony. He and her father had a Home Guard parade that evening, so she could have Lil and Annie to herself.

She found her sister and the baby out, however. Tony disappeared to get changed into his uniform, leaving Bobby with her dad. Rob was fastening his denim tunic by the fire, his trembling hands fumbling with the buttons.

The tremor in her dad's hands made Bobby think of Charlie. He would have said goodbye to his dying friend by now, she supposed. She wondered how he was feeling, now it was over.

'Lil's not still in town, is she?' Bobby asked her father.

'Nay, she stepped out to take them little lasses back to their dad.'

'Oh yes, of course. I wonder Tony and I didn't run into her on the way.'

'Happen she's dropped in at Moorside for summat,' Rob said. 'So, that lad of thine found hissen a job yet?'

'Not yet. He had an interview for a clerk's position at the bank in Skipton but he isn't optimistic about it.'

'Why, what were wrong with it?'

'Oh, I'm sure he's worrying over nothing,' Bobby said vaguely. 'Still, he's right not to pin too much hope on it. He's got no experience in that kind of role, and he'll be a fair bit older than the other applicants.'

Bobby felt it best not to mention what had happened in the interview. She knew Charlie wouldn't like her discussing it, and bringing it up would no doubt force her dad to dwell on his own similar problems.

'Well, tell him I'm always ready to slip him a bob or two to come trapping wi' me,' Rob said cheerily.

'I will. Thanks, Dad.' Bobby paused. 'Does Lil tend to hang around when she takes the girls home? I was planning to wait, but if she's going to be ages…'

'Sometimes she stays for a brew while Ginger has a hold of the baby, but on parade nights she always comes straight back to make sure us fellers have got us sandwiches and whatnot. Doubt she'll be long.'

Her dad didn't seem to think there was anything amiss in Lil's relationship with the captain, at any rate. Bobby felt a certain relief at this. Rob had always been fierce about protecting his daughters from male attention, both wanted and unwanted. He had passed that baton on to their husbands now, of course, but she was sure he would be alert to anything not quite right.

She smiled at her dad's tunic. He had done the buttons up unevenly, so the bottom buttonhole hung empty.

'Come here,' she said, stepping closer to rebutton it. 'Honestly, Dad, however do you think you'll get on living with Stan? The pair of you will be going about in odd socks and with holes in your vests with no woman to look after you.'

He frowned. 'Stan? Stan who?'

'Well, Stan Henderson,' Bobby said, blinking. 'Or has the plan changed? I was meaning to ask.'

'What plan's that?' Rob asked, looking rather puzzled.

She lowered her voice in case Tony was listening. 'Your own place. Did you change your mind?'

'I've not changed owt. I don't see what Stan Henderson's got to do with it though.'

Now she thought about it, Bobby wasn't sure what Stan Henderson had to do with it either. She thought her dad had said Stan was the friend he would be setting up a bachelor establishment with, but now she considered it, hadn't it been Charlie who had made that suggestion?

'Sorry, I think I'm muddling two conversations,' she said. 'Who is it then, if not Stan?'

Rob rubbed the back of his neck.

'Well, I can't say just yet,' he said. 'There's a question I need an answer to first. But if it goes the way I'm hoping, I'll let you know on Sunday.'

'It's the wedding on Sunday. Gil Capstick and Mabs Jessop. We'll be having our family dinner later than usual.'

'Oh aye. Well, there'll be time after for news.'

'All right.' Bobby adjusted his forage cap so it stood at the smartest angle. 'I don't know why there needs to be all this mystery though, Dad.'

'I just want everyone together for it. Saves me repeating missen.'

Bobby might have pressed further, but Lilian arrived at that moment with Annie in her pram. The baby gurgled happily.

'Oh. Bobby,' Lil said, looking flustered. 'I wasn't expecting you. Let me sort the men out, then I'll pump some water for the kettle.'

'I can do that,' Bobby said. 'Least I can do when I'm dropping in on you unannounced.'

'Well, I'm not saying it isn't nice to see you,' Lil said with a smile. 'Leave the water to me though.' She flashed her sister a significant glance, which Bobby could interpret as meaning she oughtn't to be pumping water in her delicate condition. 'You mind the baby while I send these two off to their parade. I'd better go and check Tony's found his way to some clean socks.'

Lilian disappeared into the bedroom to minister to her husband's sock needs and Bobby picked Annie up. The baby grinned, showing off her single milk tooth as if very proud of her achievement in growing it. Bobby held her close as she inhaled her soft, powdery baby scent.

'Corker, i'n't she?' her dad said, smiling proudly at the wriggling infant. 'She's another little tooth coming through, looks like. Won't be long till she's got a full set of gnashers.'

'She's certainly growing up fast. She'll be walking before we know it.'

'She don't half look like our Jake at that age, for all that she's a lass. Funny really, when he's grown up to be more like the Bancroft side than you and Lil. Don't reckon you two got owt off your old man but your noses and a store of bloody-mindedness.'

'And we're very grateful for both,' Bobby said with a laugh.

Rob dusted down his uniform. 'What do you think then, will I pass muster tonight?'

'Yes, you look very smart. We ought to get a photo of you at the studio in Skipton, Dad. I'm sure your grandchildren will want a keepsake of their grandad in uniform. I mean, in uniform for this war.'

'Oh, us old lads are only laiking at soldiers. No cause for photographs.' Still, he looked rather pleased at the suggestion.

Once Tony and Rob had been furnished with sandwiches and a tea-filled Thermos, they left to catch the bus into Settle and Lilian went outside to pump some water. Bobby pressed a kiss to the dozing baby's soft, dark hair and put her back in her pram. Then she looked around the barn-cottage that had once been her home.

Not much had changed since she had lived here with her father. Lil had purchased new curtains, but everything else remained just as it had been.

The main difference was in the presence of Annie – not only her little self but the many baby items that now littered the house. Two clothes horses filled with terry towelling were standing by the fire, beside the bucket Lilian used for soaking them. Pieces of matinee coat were bundled on the settee waiting to be sewn up. Annie's tiny tin bath hung on a hook above the fireplace, next to the larger one that served the full-grown members of the family. On wandering into the kitchen, Bobby found it filled with glass bottles, rubber teats, tins of Household Milk and other signs of the infant resident around which life in Cow House Cottage now revolved. It must be trying for Lilian, living in such a small space with all this clutter.

It would be difficult for the other residents too – her father particularly. Bobby knew he must feel more keenly than he let on that he was occupying a home he could no longer be the head of.

She wondered how her own home would be transformed when Marmaduke arrived. Her parlour wasn't so confined as

Cow House Cottage's, but there was only one small bedroom. There wouldn't be much space for her little family once they had to squeeze in a cot, bath and other baby items.

Still, at least she and Charlie had running water, unlike poor Lilian. Bobby well remembered how she had ached after drawing water from the cow house's stiff outdoor pump. With two men and a baby to provide for, bottles to sterilise and napkins needing constant soaking, Lilian must have to visit the evil thing several times a day.

Bobby found her eyes drawn to the door that led from the parlour to the extension that had housed Charlie's veterinary practice. She went to peep inside.

Everything was as it had been when Charlie had left for the RAF: the steel examining table, the metal instruments hanging in their customary places. Lilian had clearly been keeping everything dust-free in there.

Bobby winced to think that her sister, whose days were already long and hard, should have been spending time polishing Charlie's old instruments. She vowed to have a word with him about it. There was really no need for this room to be kept as it was, when his veterinary days were over. He might as well sell his equipment, and let Lilian and Tony have the room for a nursery.

How would Charlie feel about gutting his old surgery? Bobby had a suspicion it would be a wrench for him, for all that he accepted it would be impossible now to return to veterinary work.

It reminded her of how she had felt when her dad had talked about selling the house in Bradford. Bobby had no wish to live in the place again, now her home was here. It wasn't even as if she'd been particularly happy there – or at least, the happy memories were tainted by the recollection of her mother's illness and death. But it was a part of her past, synonymous with growing up and with family. The idea of another family making it their own…

She could imagine Charlie feeling the same about the surgery, symbolising the job that had been such a big part of his pre-war life. But what else was there to do? It would be foolish to make a shrine of the place.

As she scanned the room, Bobby's eyes flickered to one of the lockable cupboards. When she had lived here, she had used it to keep the spirits she gave her dad after a nightmare safely locked away. Bobby had handed custody of the key to Lilian when she had moved out.

The spirit was one Bobby's friend Don Sykes got for her, distilled by a pal of his from potato peelings. Bobby had made sure to stock up the last time Don had been on leave from the army, in case it was a while until he could get more for her.

She wasn't sure why, but something drew her to the cupboard. She found herself trying the handle.

Strange. It was open. Surely Lil hadn't been so remiss as to forget to lock it? She said their father hadn't been drinking, but if a low mood struck, the temptation of an unlocked cupboard full of spirits might prove too much.

Bobby stared when she opened the door. It was empty.

Empty! But she had bought a dozen bottles from Don a few weeks before Christmas. Even in his worst drinking days, her dad hadn't knocked it back at that rate.

She felt a cold dread settle on her.

'It isn't what you think,' a quiet voice said from the doorway. Bobby looked up to see Lil, baby Annie in her arms.

'There were twelve bottles in here less than a month ago,' Bobby whispered. 'Dad didn't... he couldn't have...'

'No. Not him.'

Bobby stared at her. 'You didn't.'

Lilian laughed. 'Mercy, Bob, is that really what you think of me? I'm not quite on the road to becoming a dope fiend just yet.'

'Then where is it?'

'I... all right, if you really want to know – I sold it,' Lilian said, flushing.

'Sold it? To who?'

'Pete Dixon.'

'Pete! But why on earth…?'

'Dad asked me to get rid of it. Told me to pour the lot down the drain. He said he didn't need it any more and he'd rather be rid of the temptation.'

'Dad said that?'

'Yes, a couple of weeks ago. But it seemed such a waste, and I struggle so on the housekeeping Tony gives me…' She sighed. 'I'm sorry. It was wrong to do it without telling you. You've every right to be cross.'

'I'm not cross. Just relieved, if that's all there is to it.'

'I've been meaning to tell you, but I wanted to make sure there was no chance of being overheard.' Lilian rocked Annie, whimpering in her sleep as her second little tooth made its presence felt. 'It seemed better than letting it go to waste after you'd laid out money for it. Still, I guess it's against the law to sell illegally distilled alcohol to a black-market trader. I wouldn't want to get us into trouble.'

'No,' Bobby said, rather dazed. 'That was… good thinking.'

'I'll pay you back with interest, I promise. Pete gave me a good price for it – fourteen shillings a bottle, six bob more than you buy it off Don for. I've been using it to eke out our rations. Tony's on so little that even a couple of bob extra a week makes a difference.'

'You don't need to pay me back,' Bobby said, getting to her feet. 'I wish you'd told me, though, Lil. My heart nearly jumped out of my mouth when I saw it was all gone. I thought Dad must be slipping back into bad habits.'

'Or that I was,' Lil said with a smile. 'I'll put Annie in her cot and we'll have that cup of tea, eh?'

## Chapter 17

Lilian put the baby to bed while Bobby made the tea. They moved the racks of towelling into the bedroom and sat on the settee in front of the fire. It had dwindled to embers now, but Lil didn't bank it up.

'We're on the last of our coke,' she explained. 'I don't want to waste it on myself when the men are out. On parade nights, I usually go to bed with a hot water bottle and my book.'

'You ought to take care of yourself, Lil. Never mind spending extra money on Tony. It's you who needs to be getting stronger. Come to me and Charlie if you're worried about saving fuel, then we can share heat.'

Not that there was anything wrong in Lil's looks today. Bobby had wondered if the healthful glow she had observed when they bumped into each other in town had been an illusion brought on by the cold, but she was pleased to see that the sparkle in Lil's eye and pink glow in her cheeks persisted.

'Don't worry about me,' Lilian said. 'Honestly, I feel much better. I know you think I always say that, but it's true.'

'You do look better.' Bobby hesitated. 'Is the doctor still recommending that tonic wine?'

'Oh, I'm off that stuff,' Lilian said breezily. 'I don't believe it was doing me any good. I felt better after a few glasses, but once that wore off I felt worse than before.'

Bobby smiled. 'I am glad. I hated the thought you might come to depend on it. What made you decide to stop? Did Dr Minchin tell you to?'

'No.' Lilian flushed as she bent over the teapot to top up their cups. 'Actually it was something that happened a week ago. You mustn't tell Tony though.'

'What happened?'

Lilian leaned back in her chair and closed her eyes. 'It was a bad day. A very bad day.'

'Bad in what way?'

'I just felt so... I don't know. Life seemed so empty, suddenly. Annie was colicky and spent the whole day wailing, I'd done nothing but pump water and boil napkins, and I felt guilty that I hadn't paid a visit to Georgia for days. My head was aching, my back was sore from pumping, and I couldn't help thinking how different my life was from the one I used to dream of. Whenever I thought about Tony coming home, of being in bed with him, I burst into tears. By three o'clock, I couldn't cope any more. I just... broke down.'

'Oh, Lil. Come here.' Bobby put an arm around her sister and guided her head to her shoulder. 'So you had a drink?'

'More than one. Annie was sobbing and I was sobbing, unable to get it under control, half hysterical. I felt like such a fool, but I couldn't stop. And I...' Her cheeks coloured. 'I'm not proud, but I drank half a bottle in no time at all. Just to blunt the misery. Just to make it feel like life was something I could deal with.'

'Half a bottle! That's a lot, isn't it? It's as strong as sherry.'

'It was enough to knock me out anyway,' Lilian murmured. 'I fell into such a deep sleep that I never fetched Jess and Florrie from school. The poor things must've waited for ages before they made their own way home in the dark. The next thing I knew there was their father, banging on the door worried I was dead in here or something. Annie was screaming and screaming, but even that hadn't woken me. It's lucky I woke up to his knocks or I'm sure he would've broken the door down.' She smiled. 'George quieted the baby right away. She always behaves for him.'

'Wasn't he angry you'd put the girls in danger?'

'You'd have thought so, wouldn't you? I felt so ashamed when I answered the door. I was sure he'd be able to tell the condition I was in, and he'd…' Lilian swallowed a small sob. '…he'd ban me from having anything to do with him or his daughters ever again.'

'Oh, Lil.' Bobby stroked her hair. 'What did he say?'

'Well, I was right. He knew I'd been drinking.'

'He was shocked, I suppose.'

'That's just it. He wasn't at all. I was certain he'd think I was in that state all the time, around his girls as well, and despise me as a lush. But he didn't.' Lilian gave a damp laugh. 'He was just… kind. I don't know what I've ever done to deserve that man's kindness. He sat me down and made me tea as if I was a poorly child, looked around at those foul napkins I'd boiled and boiled until I wanted to hurl every damn square of towelling into the fire, and told me he understood.'

'Did he really?'

'He did,' Lilian said quietly. 'And it wasn't just words, Bob. He really did understand. He told me he'd almost fallen into the same trap after his wife died, but having two little girls who needed him had pulled him back from the brink.'

'Gosh,' Bobby said, blinking. 'I'd never have imagined that. He's always so calm and stoical.'

'Of course then it all came pouring out. How empty and pointless my days felt. How different my life looked to the one I'd dreamt of, and how it was my own stupid fault for letting Tony persuade me to go to bed with him. And I told him…' She hid her face in her hands. 'Oh God, I wish I hadn't. I never would have if I hadn't drunk that dreadful tonic wine. I told him how hard I found it to feel the way a wife ought to about her husband. How lonely I was. And how guilty I felt knowing Tony had feelings for me I was unable to return.' She rubbed her tear-stained face and looked up. 'That was wrong, wasn't it?'

'I... don't know,' Bobby said, rather stunned. 'I understand why you needed someone to talk to, but I wish you'd come to me, or to Mary. These aren't the sort of confidences it's wise to share with a man. It could sound like... well, like an invitation.'

'I don't suppose I'd have talked to anyone, if George hadn't turned up at that moment. I needed someone so badly, and he just happened to be here. And thank God he was, or I can't honestly say there might not have been another binge the next time I was at the end of my tether.' She gave a bleak laugh. 'I must be more like Dad than I thought.'

'You mustn't let it, Lil,' Bobby said earnestly. 'Come to me if you feel that way. Let me help you.'

'Oh, it won't happen again. By the time George left I felt thoroughly ashamed of myself, although he'd never said a word that wasn't kind and understanding. But he showed me the error of my ways in his gentle fashion.'

'Was he shocked when you told him why you married Tony?'

'No.' Lilian sighed. 'No, I don't think so, although he had every reason by then to want to run away from this fast dipsomaniac he'd made the mistake of trusting with his daughters. He never said a word about it after I'd sobbed the whole miserable tale out on his shoulder. But he did talk earnestly about the dangers of drowning my sorrows. He asked how I'd feel if Annie needed me, and I'd incapacitated myself to such an extent that I couldn't care for her. That was what brought home how foolish and selfish I'd been. As soon as he'd gone, I locked the remainder of the wine away, gave Annie a big cuddle and vowed I wouldn't touch the stuff except in sickness.'

'That doesn't change the feeling that caused it though,' Bobby said gently.

'No.' Lilian was quiet for a moment. 'No. But I need to find another way to cope. If I put Annie in danger, I'd never forgive myself.' She smiled. 'She's one of the few things in my life that brings me moments of true joy. I married Tony for her, and when I look into her face, I feel that in spite of everything, it was worth it.'

'Did the captain say anything else?'

'Only that he'd always be there to listen if I needed someone, even after his marriage. He really is a very kind man.'

'His marriage!' Bobby said, blinking. 'Is it definitely happening then?'

'I don't think he's asked the question yet, but he doesn't seem in any doubt that the answer will be yes when he does.' Lilian sighed. 'The girls will be upset, I suppose. They haven't taken to her much.'

Bobby looked into her sister's eyes. 'And how will you feel about it?'

Lilian shrugged. 'I'll miss picking them up from school. We have some fun times here in the afternoons. But I suppose Veronica will give up work once they're married, and their care will fall to her.'

'I didn't mean on the girls' account.'

'Then what did you mean?'

Bobby hesitated, sipping her tea. Lilian looked genuinely puzzled.

'Lil, who is Georgia named after?' Bobby asked eventually.

'After him, of course. George Parry. I told you that, didn't I?'

'No. I thought you named her after Grandad Goggin. What made you think of naming her after him?'

'He saved my life, didn't he? I thought that was something worth commemorating.'

'Tony doesn't know, I suppose?'

'I've never mentioned it, but I thought everyone must realise that was where it came from.'

'And when I saw you and George in Settle, had you really just bumped into each other?'

'Well, yes,' Lilian said, blinking.

'What were you talking about? You looked very earnest.'

'He was asking my advice on the sort of engagement ring Miss Simpson would like. He was going to look at some this weekend.' Lilian frowned. 'What are you hinting at, Bob? This is as bad as the interrogations I used to get from Dad when a boyfriend brought me back late from the dance hall.'

Bobby sighed. 'Well, come on. I mean, Georgia's name, the fur coat, those intimate little gifts like knicker elastic and stockings, and then there's all the time you've been spending with him and his children. You must realise that to the casual observer, that looks a certain way. And when I know you're not in love with your husband... I mean, what was I supposed to think?'

Lilian laughed. 'You don't really think I'd have an affair? Was this before or after I'd swigged the twelve bottles of whisky from the cupboard? Your faith in me is stupendous, little sister.'

'I didn't say I thought you'd have an affair,' Bobby said. 'But feelings aren't so straightforward, are they? I never thought you'd be foolish enough to go to bed with him, but I was worried you might be... starting to think too well of him.'

'I do think well of him,' Lilian said, with a little smile. 'I like his company and conversation. The thought of seeing him when I take the girls home is a bright spot in my day. But there's nothing more to it than friendship, I promise.'

'What about Tony?'

'He's jealous, naturally, but that's just Tony. He knows George would never think of me that way. Actually, Tony's seemed a lot happier about me minding the girls since George started walking out with Veronica Simpson. I think he was mostly worried people would gossip, and that hurt his pride. If he really thought George was after me, he'd have thumped him long ago.'

'I meant, what about you and Tony?' Bobby took her hand and gave it a gentle press. 'I worry about you, Lil. I know you two aren't happy. When I see you getting close to the captain, it isn't that I think you'd do anything wrong. I'm more concerned that you're setting yourself up to get hurt.'

'I made my bed the day I let Tony talk me into his,' Lil said in a toneless voice. 'I married him for the baby's sake, but that doesn't mean I've got anything to complain of. He provides us with a home and food, even if money's not so plentiful as we might like. He takes care of me, he's faithful, he never raises a hand to me in anger and in his own way, he loves me. You say we aren't happy, but we're not unhappy either. We just... muddle along, like thousands of husbands and wives who find once the honeymoon's over that they don't really suit.'

'But you don't love him.'

'No.' Lilian gazed into what was left of the fire. 'I wish we had more in common. I wish he understood all the thousands of things I want to be able to talk to him about. I wish... I wish I could admire him more. And it's silly, but I can't help harbouring a little resentment – I mean about the way we were forced into marriage. I've really got no right, when it's my fault as much as his. If anything, I ought to be grateful that he stepped up when he could easily have walked away.'

'Huh,' Bobby muttered. 'Well, let's not take things too far.' Although she and Tony had since made their peace, Bobby was holding on to her own resentment over the way her sister had been pushed into marriage. She hadn't forgotten how the relationship began, with Tony practically blackmailing Lilian into a date in exchange for suppressing a *Courier* article about their father's black-market activities with Pete Dixon.

'You and Charlie seem to suit each other so well that I can't help being a little jealous,' Lilian confessed. 'But Tony's a doting father, and a good husband in his fashion. I do try to love him. I don't know why I can't. It almost feels like I don't have the energy. I've felt so utterly wrung out since I became a wife that there's nothing of me left for Tony.'

'That's understandable, when you've been ill.'

'Have I? There's nothing physically wrong with me. There never was, Dr Minchin says, other than the usual toll giving birth to two babies takes on the body.' She swallowed a sob.

'I just feel so very, very tired. Tired of the effort it takes to get through every day. Tired of trying to understand Tony, and trying to make him understand me. Tired of life.'

Bobby reached out to embrace her. 'Oh, love. Please don't say that.'

'Tired of my life, I mean,' Lilian said softly, returning the hug. 'Don't worry, I'm not getting into that state Dad was in. But there seems so little joy in each day, just hard work and aching limbs, and at the end of it a husband I struggle to relate to on any level. Even when he makes love to me I feel numb, just desperate for it to be over so I can sleep.' She glanced up. 'It isn't like that for you and Charlie, I suppose.'

Bobby thought of her husband, and how it felt when he held her in bed. She couldn't imagine ever feeling numb in Charlie's arms. It sounded so unutterably bleak and cold.

'No,' she said quietly. 'No, it isn't like that at all.'

'And I have to admit that George Parry has been a little spot of colour in each grey day,' Lilian went on. 'But I know he can never be more than that. I threw my lot in with Tony Scott, for better and for worse, and that's that. I'm not going to do anything silly, Bob, I promise.'

'I'm sure things could be better for you and Tony if you worked harder at it. He loves you, which is halfway to a strong marriage.'

'I try to be a good wife. I think he's been happier the past fortnight, since I stopped taking tonic wine. It did tend to make me irritable with him.'

'I mean be a lover as well as a wife. You two never really had a courting period, but that doesn't mean you couldn't have one now.'

'How do you mean?'

'You looked so pretty today, Lil, in your fur coat and that hat, but at home I never see you in anything except a housecoat and curlers. Perhaps you could dress up for Tony once in a while — I mean, not in the fur coat, obviously, but you've got other nice things.'

Lil gave a weak smile. 'I was only wearing my best hat to hide the fact that it's over a month since I was able to afford a shampoo and set.'

'Here.' Bobby took out her purse and held out half a crown. 'Take this into Settle and get your hair done. My treat.'

'I can't take that. You're even more hard up than we are. At least we've got Dad contributing to the housekeeping.'

'But we haven't got a baby to provide for – not yet, at least.' Bobby pressed the coin into her sister's hand. 'Take it, please. I had a little windfall earlier in the week – never mind what from, I'll tell you another time. I've bought Charlie some nice things for when he comes home, but I'd like to treat my sister too. I know you'll never be able to justify using your own money.'

Still Lilian hesitated. 'Are you sure? You'll have plenty of baby things to buy soon enough.'

'I know,' Bobby said with a sigh. 'But this is bonus money, and I've made up my mind to spend it making the people I love happy. Make yourself pretty and go dancing with Tony. I'll look after Annie.' She rested a hand on her swollen stomach. 'I need the practice.'

'It feels like such an effort to be pretty when I'm practically hunchbacked after hours of pumping water, with my hands chapped all over from boiling napkins.' Lil put the half-crown away. 'But you're right, I ought to do more to please him. After all, what's the alternative? I'm married to Tony and I have to make the best of that.'

Yet Lilian sounded more resigned to her fate than eager to improve her lot. Bobby wished there was more she could do.

'If Dad moves out, that ought to help,' she said. 'I'll speak to Charlie about clearing his equipment out too. Then you can have that room for storage and Dad's old room for a nursery.' Bobby held her sister back to look into her tear-stained face. 'Things will get better, Lil. I promise.'

## Chapter 18

Bobby supposed she ought to feel relieved after her conversation with her sister. It had contained two pieces of good news – that Lilian was no longer taking tonic wine, and that her relations with George Parry were no more than they ought to be. And yet Lil had sounded so unhappy, in her life and in her marriage. Perhaps spending more time with Tony would help, but Bobby sensed the problem went deeper than something that could be fixed by a trip to the pictures.

Preoccupied as she was with her sister's worries, Bobby didn't forget to stop in at the Hart on the way home and purchase a jug of beer for Charlie. There was nothing left now of the BBC's ten shillings. She felt very extravagant at having spent so much in one day, but if it made Charlie smile it would be worth it.

She wondered how he was feeling after his emotional deathbed visit. Bobby was sure he must be craving a pair of warm arms and the soft, soothing murmurs of a wife who loved him. She wished they were together.

Tomorrow was Saturday, her half day. Bobby had an appointment with Dr Minchin in the early afternoon, but that left plenty of time to prepare Charlie's homecoming tea. If he was lucky enough to avoid too many of the delays that were a hallmark of wartime travel, he could be home by early evening.

The last thing Bobby felt like after her sober conversation with Lilian was trying to be funny, but she hadn't forgotten her plan to write a dozen good jokes before she retired. She couldn't afford to waste any free time she was granted before the baby came – a visit to her sister was enough to remind her how precious a mother's leisure hours were.

Like Lilian, Bobby felt it would be an extravagance to light a fire only for herself. Instead, after a frugal supper of bread and dripping, she carried her hot water bottle and the wireless set into the bedroom. There she put on several layers and some gloves, found her notebook and the fountain pen Don had given her when she left the *Courier* and tuned in to the Forces Programme. There was a new episode of *ITMA* on at half past eight. Bobby hoped listening to it would set her creative juices flowing.

'Oh!' she said, quarter of an hour into the broadcast.

It had been so fast she might have missed it. It was during one of Tommy Handley's conversations with another character: Mrs Mopp, the eccentric, gravel-voiced charlady. And it was her joke! Thrown in among the other one-liners had been one of the gags the programme had paid her five shillings for. Even with the BBC letter, Bobby hadn't quite believed her words could be on the air, heard by thousands of listeners.

Even the king would have heard it! Everyone said he never missed an episode of *ITMA*. Had he laughed at her joke? And had Charlie heard it, wherever he was?

Bobby remained in a starstruck daze, still unable to quite believe that her words, her actual words, had been broadcast across the country. But once it sank in, it did more than anything else to bolster her confidence. As soon as the programme was over, she took up her pen and started to write.

–

When Bobby awoke, she was still in her gloves and three warm jumpers, her notepad under her cheek. She had stayed up writing far later than she'd intended, eventually falling asleep with her uncapped pen still in her hand.

Woozily she reached for Charlie, then opened her eyes when she encountered a wet patch.

'Oh hell!'

She jumped out of bed and yanked on the light pull, assuming her hot water bottle must have leaked, but it was her fountain pen that was to blame. There was ink everywhere. When Bobby looked in the mirror, she saw that the impression of a joke was emblazoned like a bad tattoo on her right cheek where she had slept on her notepad.

What had she written anyhow? She snatched up the notepad and skimmed the smudged but thankfully still readable writing.

There were nine jokes there. Perhaps five of them were all right. One was sheer nonsense. Bobby must have scribbled it down when she was all but asleep. The other three needed work, but she might make something of them. She would take the pad to work and type up the good ones. If they still managed to produce a smile after she had slept on them – rather less literally this time – she could send them off by tomorrow's post.

Bobby looked at the bed and grimaced. Ugh, why had she let herself fall asleep holding the pen? God knew how she was going to get that ink out. She'd have to miss her breakfast cup of tea and get the bed stripped down so the mattress could dry off before bedtime.

What time was it anyway? Bobby glanced at the clock and her eyes widened.

Half past eight! She was supposed to unlock the office in fifteen minutes!

The clock couldn't be right. Marmaduke always woke her at half past six, without fail. He was so reliable, she didn't even bother to set the alarm now. The thing must have stopped.

Bobby went to peep behind the blackouts, and blinked at the thin light.

That meant the clock had to be right. Oh Lord, she was going to be so late! She couldn't possibly get to the office in less than three-quarters of an hour, even if she missed breakfast and hid her hair under a scarf. Tony would never let her live it down, after all the times she'd told him off for turning up a few minutes after nine. And there was the bed to strip down, and jokes all over her ruddy face, and no Charlie to help her get everything in order.

'Why did you have to choose today of all days to start sleeping in?' she wailed to Marmaduke.

Bobby was nearly an hour late for work, running all the way. She found the office unlocked, with Tony at his desk looking exceptionally smug.

'How did you get in?' she panted.

'Parry had a spare key. Good thing too or I'd still be outside, freezing my bits off.' He gave her a stern look. 'Well, young lady, what time do you call this?'

Bobby shook her head. 'You've really been looking forward to this, haven't you?'

'What do you think?' he said with a grin. 'So, are you going to confess to Reg or do I need to tell tales?'

'Really? After all the times I've covered for you?'

'Aye, and never let me forget it.' Tony leaned back and lit a cigarette. It was no wonder Lilian struggled on the housekeeping, given the amount he must spend on fags. 'Tell you what, I'll make a bargain with you. I'll say nowt to the old man in exchange for… the next ten tea rounds.'

'I'd rather come clean and make the time up.' Bobby sat down without removing her coat. 'I don't suppose the captain will mind if I stay an extra hour.'

'How come you're late anyway?'

'Oh, Charlie's away visiting an RAF pal in hospital. He usually reminds me to set the alarm before bed,' Bobby said vaguely. 'I dropped off listening to the wireless and overslept.'

'You all right then?' Tony asked, peering at her. 'Thought you might be ill. You don't look too good.'

'Ta very much.'

'Honestly, you're dead pale. Not sickening for summat, are you? Because Lil was counting on you to mind the baby tomorrow night.' He rolled his eyes. 'She's got it into her head for us to go dancing.'

Bobby smiled. 'Has she? Good.'

'Your doing, was it? I'd be happier with the pub, if we must go out.'

'I'm sure you would, but Lil wouldn't.' Bobby met his eyes. 'Just do me a favour and take her out on the town. It's good for you to spend time together away from Annie.' She held up her hand as he opened his mouth. 'Somewhere that isn't the ruddy pub. You spend half the time there chatting to your mates while she sits on her own. If you care about her as much as you say, do something she wants to do for once.'

'Course I care about her. Married her, didn't I?'

'Mmm. You seem to be forgetting that I remember exactly why you married her. It didn't have much to do with romance, I recall.'

'Well, I didn't have to. Plenty of blokes wouldn't have bothered.'

Bobby shook her head. 'Honestly, why do people keep mentioning that like it's some great magnanimous act? Yes, you married her, and so you bloody should have when you were the one—' She took a deep breath. 'Look, never mind. It's in the past. Just take her out and show her you appreciate her once in a while, will you?'

'Aye, all right. I was going to anyhow, so you'd no need to stick your oar in,' Tony said, truculent at being lectured to. 'You going to be able to mind the baby? You look sick as a dog.' He narrowed one eye. 'You weren't out on a spree last night while your other half was away, were you?'

'No I was not. I'm not you. And yes, I can mind the baby.'

'Get the kettle on, then.'

Bobby put a hand to her head. 'In a bit. I'm not getting ill but I do feel dizzy. I suppose it's from running all the way here.'

As the morning wore on, however, Bobby started to worry there was more to the way she was feeling than her rushed start. The feeling of dizziness persisted, and although she'd had no breakfast, she couldn't stomach the thought of drinking tea. There was an unsettled queasiness in her belly that extinguished appetite entirely.

But what worried her most was the lack of movement there. Whenever Tony was engrossed in something, Bobby slipped one hand under her coat so she could run it across her stomach, desperate for some little twitch that would set her mind at rest.

Always Marmaduke woke her, for five weeks now. She had never known him be still for this long. Now she thought about it, she couldn't remember him moving since yesterday morning, when Charlie had rested his head against her stomach and the baby had seemed to still in response. At the time, Bobby had believed he must be comforted by the proximity of his father. But... could there be something wrong?

She found it impossible to focus on her work. The article she was attempting to write swam before her eyes. She was conscious only of her stomach, still and quiet – as if there was no baby growing there at all. Her mind kept returning to one horrible image: Georgia Scott on the night she had been born, lying under a shroud at the foot of her mother's bed.

Bobby's appointment with Dr Minchin wasn't until two, but by eleven she was in such a state that she felt she couldn't stay in the office another moment. She was shaking, unable to type, and it had become a real effort to conceal how she was feeling from Tony. She simply had to see the doctor right away. Oh God, she wished Charlie was here!

What if he came home to discover the baby they had invested so much in, their little miracle of life, was... Bobby swallowed. She couldn't bring herself to think the word.

It couldn't end this way. Not after all Charlie's struggles with impotence, which had made a family seem impossible. Not after his miraculous return from that final op, just one day after his baby had been conceived, so that his very survival felt fated. It felt like everything had been leading up to this, to Marmaduke, the child who was to make their world complete. And now...

If anything had happened to him, would it be her fault? Charlie had warned her again and again about working during her pregnancy, but like a fool Bobby had pushed to remain at *The Tyke*. Not because of the money but because she wanted to be there – had cared more about the work she loved than keeping her baby healthy. If it was her fault, Charlie would never forgive her. She wouldn't deserve to be forgiven.

'Tony, I've got to go,' Bobby said, well aware that her voice, like her hands, was trembling. 'Can you lock up?'

'Go? You've only been here an hour.' Tony peered at her. 'You're white as owt, Bob. You're shaking. What's up, love?'

'I... I feel a bit fluey, that's all. I think I spoke too soon when I said I wasn't coming down with anything. I need to go home and rest.'

Even Tony looked concerned now.

'You'd best not walk home by yourself,' he said. 'I'll come with you.'

'There's no need for you to lose an hour's work. I need fresh air, that's all.' Bobby hurried to the door, hoping he wouldn't press the point. She felt like she might faint, and clung to the doorframe. 'Don't tell our Lil I left early, will you? I don't want her to worry.'

'Sure? You'd better have her or Mary sit with you if you're not feeling right.'

'I told you, I just need rest.'

Bobby hurried out before Tony pressed more questions on her. She had to get to the doctor's surgery in Smeltham, and pray Dr Minchin could fix whatever was wrong.

It was over two miles to the neighbouring village, however, and Bobby felt very dizzy indeed now she was on her feet. She wasn't sure how she was going to make it. There were no buses, and no one with a vehicle she could beg for a lift. But she had to get there.

Bobby was very wobbly as she staggered along the road to Smeltham. Her hands shook as badly as Charlie's. She had barely gone a mile when the sick, dizzy feeling overwhelmed her and she was forced to stop to vomit.

She fell to her knees as she retched, but nothing came up after a day without food: just bitter-tasting bile. When the fit was over she remained kneeling, slicked with sweat and with no energy to move. Her throat felt swollen and sore from tears she was too weary to shed. She just slumped against a tree, overcome by numb despair.

Marmaduke was dead. She knew he was. He was dead, because she hadn't listened to Charlie when he had insisted she stop working. She had as good as murdered him. Her little miracle. Her baby.

Everything was over now. Their beautiful dream had ended. She must have been the biggest fool alive to put her faith in miracles. If there was such a thing, there wouldn't be a war killing young men in droves every single day.

Bobby's body shuddered with grief. She felt as weak as a newborn kitten, with no strength to move from this spot. She would die here, she was sure: at the side of this lonely road, leaning against the bare, skeletal tree that was her only means of support.

There was a rumble in the distance, as of a truck. It would be military, Bobby guessed. Since the abolition of the basic civilian petrol ration, there were few vehicles on the road that didn't belong to the armed forces. She pulled in her knees to allow it to go by.

The vehicle that appeared was indeed military: a Tilly truck with Air Force roundels. Bobby waited for it to go past, but it didn't. Instead it slowed to a stop, and a familiar face appeared out of the window.

'Slacks. Funny place to stop for a picnic.'

It was Ernie King, of course, grinning as ever. His grin faded when he noticed the state of her, however.

'What the devil is wrong?' He jumped out immediately and turned to the driver. 'Give me two minutes, Cloutier.'

Despite her distress, Bobby smiled with relief. The arrival of someone strong, someone she knew cared for her, was very welcome. Ernie was here – solid, frank and reassuring – and she no longer had to deal with this thing alone.

'Sorry,' she whispered as he bent over her, concern written all over his face. 'I was walking to Smeltham and I… had a funny turn. I'll be all right in a minute.'

'The hell you will. You look like death, kid.' He sat down and stretched an arm around her, which she sank into gratefully. 'Tell me what you need.'

'I don't like to hold you up. I suppose there's somewhere your station expects you to be with that Tilly.' She flashed him a weak smile. 'But if you could make a telephone call to Topsy and tell her I'm here, I'd appreciate it. I've got no energy to walk further.'

'I'm hardly going to leave you at the side of the road. Let us give you a ride home. I'll gladly take the rap for it.'

'No.' Bobby forced herself to sit up straighter. 'I can't go home. I have to get to Smeltham.'

'Why Smeltham?'

She flushed. 'Because… because that's where the doctor is.'

Ernie's face was full of worry. 'You're that sick?'

'I… don't know. I hope not, but I have to see him.'

Ernie was silent for a moment.

'About the baby, I guess,' he said.

She met his eyes. 'How did you know there was a baby?'

'I started thinking about it that night you told me you felt sick from my smoke. I noticed you'd abandoned your favourite legwear recently as well. I guess skirts are better when you've got something to hide.' He looked searchingly into her face. 'Is it an emergency?'

'It might be. I haven't felt him – the baby, I mean – move all day.' She closed her eyes. 'I'm so frightened, Ernie,' she said in a whisper. 'You don't know how much this baby meant to Charlie – to us both.'

Ernie stood up and held out his hand. 'Come on.'

With an effort, Bobby got to her feet. She could feel herself swaying, and was grateful when Ernie put a supportive arm around her waist. He seemed to notice the thickness there, and his face filled with tenderness.

'Where are we going?' she asked in a faint voice.

'To the doctor, of course. Don't worry about a thing, kid. I'll get you there.'

He supported her to the truck and helped her in, then turned to the young Canadian warrant officer driving.

'Cloutier, get in the back,' he ordered. 'I'll drive the rest of the way. We've got an unscheduled stop to make.'

'Does the CO know?'

'No. It's on my responsibility.'

The lad looked worried, but since Ernie outranked him, he didn't have any choice except to do as he was told. He got in the back of the truck and Ernie climbed in beside Bobby.

'I'm so sorry about this,' she murmured, slumping against the hard seat. 'I'd hate you to get into bother on my account.'

'Oh, I can cope with a few days of peeling potatoes.' He took his hand from the gearstick to press her arm. 'I hope it isn't bad news.'

'I'm praying it isn't.'

## Chapter 19

Half an hour later, Ernie stopped the Tilly outside the cottage from which Dr Minchin ran his general practice.

'I'll walk you to the door.'

'People are going to gossip fit to burst if they see you escorting me into the doctor's and I announce I'm having a baby right after,' Bobby said, with an attempt at a smile. She pressed a hand to her forehead. 'Still, you better had. I might fall down otherwise.'

Bobby clung to him as he walked her to the cottage. Her knees felt like they'd been replaced with jelly.

'I'd better not come in with you or there really will be talk,' Ernie said. 'We'll wait here to give you a ride home.'

'No, please. You're liable to get into enough trouble thanks to me. I'm sure the doctor will help me get home. He's got a car.'

'Nonsense. The doc's got patients to see to. I'll take you.'

'Please, Ernie,' she said, looking up at him. 'I don't know how I'd explain you driving me home to the neighbours, especially when Charlie's away.'

'Well, if that's the way you want it.' He rapped at the door then bent to kiss her cheek. 'It doesn't seem the right moment to offer congratulations so I'll save them for another time. But it'll all work out, you'll see.'

'You've been a real knight in shining armour today, Ernie. That girl of yours doesn't know how lucky she is.'

'I wouldn't know about that.'

The door opened and the doctor's wife appeared. Mrs Minchin acted as secretary-cum-nurse to her husband during consulting hours.

'Oh,' she said on seeing Bobby. 'Morning, love. We weren't expecting you while two.'

'I know. Is Dr Minchin free now? I have to see him.'

Mrs Minchin took in Bobby's drawn, sickly looks. 'Why, is summat up?'

'I don't know. Perhaps.'

'He's with another patient but I'll send you in right after.' She squinted short-sightedly at Ernie. 'This is your husband?'

'Just a friend,' Ernie said. 'Look after her, won't you, ma'am? Make sure she gets home OK.'

'Um, yes,' the woman said, puzzled at encountering an unexpected accent.

'See you, Slacks. Take care, all right?' Ernie saluted before heading back to his truck.

Without his support, Bobby felt unsteady again. She was glad to follow Mrs Minchin to the waiting area and sink into a seat.

After what seemed like an age, the patient who had been in with the doctor finally left. Dr Minchin put his head round the door to speak with his wife, who was sitting behind a desk filing prescriptions.

'Well, Gertie, who's next?'

'Mrs Atherton had better go in, Dick,' his wife said. 'She's not due while two, but it's an emergency.'

The doctor beckoned to Bobby and she followed him into the surgery.

'Take a seat, Mrs Atherton,' the doctor said, gesturing to a chair, 'and let's hear what's worrying you.'

'It's Marmaduke,' she said at once, then flinched at having used the foolish nickname she and Charlie had given the baby. 'Sorry. I mean the baby.' She gasped back a sob. 'Dr Minchin, I'm so frightened.'

'Now, let's try to stay calm,' Dr Minchin said in his gentle voice. The shrewd, intelligent eyes behind homely round spectacles were instantly reassuring. 'Working yourself up into a state certainly won't do – what did you say his name was, Marmaduke? – any good. What's worrying you?'

'He's stopped moving, I'm sure he has. I don't think he's moved since Charlie left to go to London yesterday morning.'

The doctor frowned. 'As long as that?'

'I don't know. I mean, I'm not sure.' Bobby rubbed her head. 'I wasn't paying attention until this morning. He always moves around half past six.'

'Bladder pressure, I imagine. Not uncommon, although many babies are more active at night.' The doctor noticed her frightened expression and stopped. 'Sorry, I shouldn't interrupt. Go on.'

'Well, this morning I overslept because I was so used to him waking me, and I realised I couldn't remember him moving for ages.' She sobbed again. 'I can't feel him at all, Doctor,' she said in a whisper. 'I've been pressing against my stomach since I woke up and I can't feel a thing. Not a thing. I'm so scared he's... that he's... dead.'

'Let's not jump to conclusions,' the doctor said evenly. 'Take off your coat and lift your blouse, please.'

Bobby did so, exposing her rounded stomach. The doctor rested his hands on it and moved them around, pressing with his fingertips. Then he put on his stethoscope and moved the cold metal against her skin, an inscrutable expression on his face.

'Is it all right, Doctor?' she asked breathlessly. 'Can you hear him?'

Dr Minchin didn't answer. He just went to fetch a tub of Vaseline, rubbed some on her and started again with his stethoscope.

'Everything all right with your health in other respects?' he asked, in a measured tone that gave nothing away.

'I don't know,' she murmured. 'I felt awful today, but before that everything seemed fine. Only a little tiredness, and needing to visit the lavatory more often. I assumed that was normal.'

'You haven't noticed anything when using the lavatory? Any bleeding?'

'No, nothing like that.'

The doctor fell silent again, sliding his stethoscope over the arc of her belly.

'Ah, there we are,' he said after what felt like a year. 'A strong, regular little heartbeat, just as it ought to be. You know, you had me worried for a moment.'

'You mean… he's all right?'

'Keep monitoring his movements over the next twenty-four hours, but yes, he seems to be. And very much still alive – that I can tell you for certain.'

'Oh, thank God. Thank God.' Bobby laughed with relief. 'Oh, I could hug you, Doctor. I'd never have forgiven myself if anything had happened to him.'

He smiled. 'Save the hug for young Charlie, eh? Now, what's all this about not forgiving yourself?'

'I was terrified it was my fault. That I'd made the baby ill because I would insist on working after Charlie begged me to give it up. But we needed the money, and I felt healthy enough so I…' She flushed. 'I just… kept on.'

'I shouldn't think your office job would have done you any harm. Or is there a lot of fieldwork involved?'

'I often have to go out to conduct interviews, take things to the printer and that sort of thing.'

'It's not ideal for you to be on your feet too much but even so, it isn't exactly manual labour. Husbands do tend to worry about these things more than they need to, especially with a first pregnancy. Nevertheless, you ought to think about giving up now you're approaching your final three months, Mrs Atherton. At the very least, you might speak to Reg about allowing you to work from home.'

'Yes. After today's scare, I've learnt my lesson.' Bobby pressed a hand to her stomach. 'Why had he stopped moving, Doctor?'

'Babies can be a law unto themselves in that respect. Sometimes they're restless; other times they want to be still. I suspect that Marmaduke was tired from the exertions of growing a healthy little body and decided he needed a rest.'

'But he's always been such a wriggly baby, especially in the mornings. He's never failed to wake me in five weeks.'

'Every baby has its own cycle, but it won't necessarily remain static throughout the pregnancy. You can trust me, Mrs Atherton, when I tell you that your baby seems absolutely fine. He ought to be about the size of a large baked potato by now.' Dr Minchin applied the stethoscope again and smiled. 'Ah, there we go. A little kick.'

'Was there?' Bobby hadn't felt a thing.

'A gentle one, but yes. He may not be quite as "wriggly" as usual, to borrow your word, and perhaps you have become somewhat desensitised to his movements, but he is still moving around. As I said, though, keep monitoring him. If he's still quiet tomorrow, give me a call.'

'I will.' Bobby paused. 'And… there definitely is only one baby, isn't there? You know twins run in my family. I'd love two healthy babies, but with Charlie not working, I'd be grateful if the Almighty could see His way clear to spacing them out.'

The doctor smiled. 'No, nothing to worry about there. Only one heartbeat, and your stomach is exactly the size I would expect.'

Relief flooded Bobby as the doctor's words sank in. Everything was all right. Marmaduke was fine, and she wouldn't have to break Charlie's heart.

'If there's nothing wrong, why did I feel so badly today?' she asked, buttoning up her blouse.

'In what way did you feel badly?'

'I felt horribly faint and trembly, and then I sort of collapsed by the side of the road.'

The doctor frowned. 'You lost consciousness?'

'No, although I felt like I might. I knelt down to be sick, but I hadn't eaten so nothing came up. Then I just felt too weary to get up again. If it hadn't been for an airman friend giving me a lift, I'd probably be there still.'

'And how do you feel now?'

Bobby paused to take stock of herself. Certainly the sickly feeling had disappeared, and her hands, when she held them up, were no longer shaking so violently. She could feel a headache beginning, but there wasn't the tight sensation that had left her feeling she might lose consciousness.

'I feel… all right,' she said. 'My head's throbbing, but I don't feel faint or sick like before.'

'I thought as much. Anxiety, that's all. In its worst form, it can feel as bad as the flu.'

'Like Charlie,' Bobby murmured.

'Yes. His attacks are not dissimilar to what you experienced today.' The doctor stood up. 'Now go home, have something nutritious to eat and get some rest. No more missing meals, or you and I will be having words. By tomorrow morning, I'm certain both you and Marmaduke will be as right as rain.'

—

Bobby thanked Gertrude Minchin profusely when the doctor's wife dropped her off at Church View. She noticed a few curtains twitching along the row of houses. No doubt the neighbours had recognised the doctor's car and would be whispering about what that Mrs Atherton at Number 4 was doing clambering out of it, but they would know soon enough.

After today, Bobby accepted that she couldn't continue doing her job. Her pregnancy would have to be made public before gossip spread. That ought to answer the question of why the doctor's wife was driving her around. Thank goodness she had dissuaded Ernie from bringing her home though. That could have given rise to some very awkward rumours.

There was a letter for Charlie on the mat, as well as a couple from Bobby's correspondents in the forces: one from Don Sykes, down south with the Pioneer Corps, and another from John Ellis, a Wykeness friend. Nothing from Jake again. Her head throbbing, Bobby threw them on to the coffee table unopened.

Poor Charlie, she thought as she examined her wan face and hollow eyes in the mirror. It had been a long journey for him, and a solemn task he'd had to perform. No doubt he was looking forward to coming home to a neat, jolly wife, not this spectre. There wasn't enough rouge in the world to give her the appearance of health after the day she'd had.

And how she had felt today was how Charlie felt much of the time. Bobby had witnessed several of what the doctor called his anxiety attacks. She had pitied him with her whole heart, but she hadn't fully understood how he must feel. Now she knew. That sensation of losing control, of lifeforce being sapped, of utter helplessness and a fear that could never be quelled – how could he bear it?

Bobby tried to do as Dr Minchin had advised, although it was difficult to force a meal down. The sick feeling had gone, but she was still in a highly nervous state and it had killed her appetite. She was eating for Marmaduke too, though, she reminded herself. He hadn't had any sustenance since her supper of bread and dripping the evening before. The doctor was right: she needed to take better care of them both.

With an effort, Bobby managed a bowl of soup and a slice of bread. Then she went into the bedroom to rest as the doctor had said. The mattress was still covered in ink, but she had no energy to deal with that. She only barely had energy to remove her clothes. Once she was in her nightie, she lay on the stained, sheetless mattress and threw one blue-mottled cover over her.

Still she worried about Marmaduke's lack of movement. The doctor said his heartbeat was strong and healthy, but then why didn't he move? He couldn't be sleeping all the while, surely.

For an hour Bobby lay with her nightdress hitched up and one hand on her belly, alert to any movement, but there was nothing. Eventually, she fell into a restless sleep.

—

Bobby awoke to the sound of the front door being unlocked.

Charlie was home! How long had she slept? She pulled her nightie over her belly.

It was completely dark now. She must have been asleep for hours, although she didn't feel rested. She had so wanted to make herself neat for Charlie, take some of the pallor from her cheeks and prepare his special tea. Now she would have to meet him in her nightdress, looking like the ghost of Old Mother Riley.

'Bob?' she heard him call. He sounded weary, as she would expect. Bobby went out to him.

'In bed already?' he said with a wan smile, sliding his stick into the umbrella stand. 'You might have waited for me.' He frowned when he took in her appearance. 'But something's wrong. What is it, darling?'

Bobby couldn't help herself. She threw herself into his arms and burst into tears.

'Bobby, what is it?' he asked in alarm. 'Is it the baby?'

'No... no,' Bobby gasped through her tears. It felt like the crying fit she'd been holding back had finally broken through the floodgates, and now there was no keeping it in. 'I've just been... so frightened. I'm sorry, Charlie. I didn't mean to scare you.'

'Go and lie down. You look awful. I'll join you in a minute.'

'Yes. All right.'

Bobby did as he said. She felt guilty that the house was so dark and cheerless, but what she mainly felt was relieved, because Charlie was here and nothing bad could happen when Charlie was here. Yet still she couldn't stop crying.

She pulled the covers over her and hugged her knees. Charlie joined her a moment later, now divested of his coat, hat and shoes.

'Now tell me all about it,' he said, gathering her in his arms. He didn't seem to notice all the ink, his attention was so wrapped up in her.

'Charlie, I'm sorry,' she whispered. 'I was going to have everything nice for you. I had a whole plan.' She sniffed. 'There's salmon and… and beer. I ought to have had it ready.'

'Never mind that. It's you I care about, not salmon. Tell me what happened.'

'It's all right. Dr Minchin says it's nothing to worry about. But the baby stopped moving, and I was really scared he might be… you know.'

'Did you see the doctor?'

'Yes, I ran away early from work then had a funny turn on the road. I couldn't move for trembling and retching. If it hadn't been for Ernie King and his Air Force truck, I might be there still.'

'Oh my God!' Charlie held her back, looking frightened. 'Are you going to be all right? What did the doctor say?'

'He said it was an anxiety attack, like the ones you have. I'd got myself worked up into such a state that it affected my nerves. I'm not ill, and Dr Minchin says the baby's fine. A good, strong heartbeat.'

Charlie still looked worried. 'But he's not moved since then?'

'I still can't feel him,' Bobby whispered. 'The doctor said I'd probably become desensitised. He wants me to ring him tomorrow if there's no change though.'

'Let me feel.'

Bobby lowered her knees for Charlie to rest his head on her stomach. Almost as soon as he did, there was a kick strong enough to make her shudder.

'Oh!' Bobby laughed through her tears. 'Oh my goodness! Charlie, did you feel that?'

'I couldn't fail to.' Charlie lifted his head and rubbed his face. 'Socked me right in the jaw. Me and that boy will be having words.'

Bobby once again burst into tears, but these were tears of relief.

'He really is all right,' she whispered. 'Oh, Charlie…'

He shuffled up to kiss her.

'There now,' he said softly, wiping away her tears with his thumb-tip. 'I'm here, and I won't leave you again until Marmaduke's safely with us. I'm so sorry I went away, Bob.'

'You were right to go. But… do you know what I think?'

'What?'

She smiled damply. 'I think Marmaduke was sulking about you being gone. The last time I remember him moving was yesterday morning, when you said goodbye, and then he was still the whole time you were away. He must have been missing his dad.'

'A fine way to show it, I must say,' Charlie said, rubbing his jaw.

'That proves he must be a man in the making, if he's throwing sulks about not getting his way.'

'You've not been well so I'll let that comment pass. But just you wait until it's two boys against one girl around here.'

Bobby held him tight. 'I'm so glad everything's all right. I thought if anything had happened to the baby, it would be my fault for not giving up work like you wanted me to.'

'And now?' Charlie said softly.

She sighed. 'Yes, I have to. Dr Minchin said it wouldn't do me any harm to work from home, but I shouldn't be on my feet too much in my last few months. Besides, it's getting too hard to hide it now. Two people in the last two days have guessed the secret.'

'Which two people?'

'Jolka and Ernie. I'm not sure Mary doesn't suspect too, and there's bound to be talk among the neighbours after they saw

Mrs Minchin bringing me home. I don't want gossip spreading before I've told the family. We'll announce it tomorrow at dinner, shall we?'

Charlie frowned. 'Did you say Ernie King knows?'

'He knows for sure now, but he already suspected.' She smiled tremulously. 'Oh, he was a saint today, Charlie, when he found me in trouble. You must shake his hand and buy him a drink when you see him.'

'I will. It sounds like he did our little family a big favour.' For the first time, Charlie seemed to notice the ink-stained bed. 'Bobby, what on earth has happened to our sheets?'

'Ugh. I fell asleep writing a piece for work and my fountain pen leaked,' Bobby said, pushing her hair away from her overheated face. 'I was going to sort out fresh linen before you got home. And I was going to light the fire and press your suit for the wedding tomorrow and make salmon sandwiches...' She sighed, resting her head on his chest. 'I'm so sorry. I got some treats on points especially to give you a good welcome home, then I had such a day that all I did was sleep.'

'It sounds like you needed it.' He kissed her forehead. 'I'll build the fire and make some food. You stay here. I'm going to make sure you rest and eat properly from now on, if I have to watch you every minute.'

'I'll make the food. Honestly, I'm a lot better now Marmaduke's back to his wriggly self – only a little washed out. If you feel up to building the fire, though, that will help. I got you a jug of beer from the Hart, and a pack of the cigarettes you like.'

He blinked. 'Beer and cigarettes as well as salmon? You're certainly the Lady Bountiful tonight. You shouldn't spend money on luxuries for me when we need to be counting our pennies.'

'Don't worry, I didn't take it out of the weekly budget. My aunt sent me a ten-shilling postal order for my birthday, so it's bonus money.'

Bobby crossed her fingers under the covers, hoping God would forgive the fib. She would tell Charlie everything when the time was right, but that time wasn't now.

'Still, we ought to save as much as we can, even if it's unexpected,' Charlie said.

'I know, but surely a few treats are allowed sometimes. I didn't want you to come home to brown bread and margarine after seeing your friend.' She took in his tired, solemn looks. 'How was he?' she asked softly.

'Let's get our chores done before I tell you about it. I don't want you cold and hungry when you've not been well.'

## Chapter 20

Bobby felt her spirits rise as she laid out the treats she had bought for Charlie on the kitchen table. It looked like the contents of a Red Cross parcel. They would have salmon on toast with fried tomatoes and onions, followed by tinned peaches and custard for a pudding, then a glass of beer each and a cigarette for Charlie. Now her worries about Marmaduke had settled, Bobby's appetite had returned with a vengeance. She felt quite ready to do the little homecoming feast justice.

Once she had prepared the food, she carried it into the parlour on a tray. Charlie was holding a sheet of newspaper against the fireplace as he coaxed the coke in the grate to catch.

'We won't eat at the table,' Bobby said. 'Let's have it picnic-style in front of the fire.'

Charlie smiled. 'That sounds lovely.'

The fire was crackling to life by the time Bobby had arranged a blanket on the floor, lit a candle and poured them each a glass of beer. Marmaduke had woken up properly now, full of energy as he danced inside her. Bobby shivered happily with every movement.

She made a silent vow that after today, she would never again complain about her lot. All her worries about her job, the wistfulness over her aborted WAAF career, paled into insignificance beside the welfare of her little family. As long as Charlie and Marmaduke were healthy and safe, she would remember to be grateful.

'This is a real party tea,' Charlie observed, picking up a finger of salmon on toast. 'It feels like the war's over already.'

'Well, what are you waiting for? Tuck in.'

Bobby was pleased to see that whatever emotions had been wrung from him over the past two days, they hadn't affected Charlie's appetite. He made short work of the salmon, onions and tomatoes, and she only seemed to blink for the peaches and custard to disappear. She, too, was hungry and ate her tea with relish, washed down with refreshing mouthfuls of beer.

'How was it?' she asked Charlie when he had finished.

'I don't think I've eaten so well since I left the Air Force.' He gave her a peach-and-custard-flavoured kiss. 'Thank you. But let's keep treats for very special occasions, shall we? We'll be living off our savings now you're leaving work.'

He spoke gently, but Bobby felt chastened all the same. Perhaps it had been rather rash to spend all of her ten-shilling windfall so quickly.

'I had thought of one way of adding to our savings pot,' she said. 'Your surgery.'

'What about it?'

'I know it'll be a wrench for you, love, but there's no point hanging on to your equipment until it's obsolete, is there? We can always invest in new instruments if you feel up to practising again,' Bobby added hastily, seeing his solemn look. 'We need money, and Lil and Tony are desperate for space. They can barely move for baby things.'

Charlie sighed. 'I suppose you're right.'

'Will it upset you to part with it?'

'It just feels... final, you know? As long as I had my surgery, it felt like my vet days might not be entirely behind me.' He held up his hand and watched it shake. 'But you're right, it isn't very fair on your sister. Bill Lawrence might buy the equipment for the Smeltham practice, or put me in touch with someone who'd be interested. I'll speak to him.'

'Do you want another drink?' Bobby asked, seeing that he'd finished his beer. 'Or a cigarette? I managed to hunt down a packet of Woodbines. I know you prefer them when you can get them.'

'Just now I want my wife.'

Bobby smiled as he wrapped his arms and legs around her from behind, his hands resting on her stomach.

'I wonder what everyone will say when we tell them about the baby tomorrow,' she said, rather dreamily.

'Oh, I know exactly. The girls will squeak and jump up and down, and demand the right to choose the baby's name and clothes. Mary will hug you so tight it'll leave a bruise, and immediately start picking out layette patterns. Your dad will be gruff but secretly thrilled to pieces. And Tony will probably make some off-colour joke about the conception.'

'It's Reg I'm worried about. I hope he's not cross.' Bobby sighed. 'I will miss the magazine. I wish your brother would consider letting me write for *The Tyke* at home. The doctor said it wouldn't be dangerous, but Reg is so stuffy about those things.'

'You might try asking.'

'I might, but I'm not convinced it's going to help.'

'We ought to think about choosing some godparents, oughtn't we?' Charlie said, kissing her neck. 'We haven't had a conversation about it yet. Or about names, for that matter.'

'I feel like I'll know the name when I meet him or her. Like there'll only be one it could be.'

'Perhaps he really will be a Marmaduke.'

'Perhaps,' Bobby said, smiling. 'I'm not sure what a Marmaduke would look like.'

'What about godparents?'

Bobby pondered the matter. 'I'd like to ask Topsy and Teddy, if you approve. Teddy's a Catholic, of course, but I don't think he'll say no.'

Charlie nodded. 'I was going to say the same. Who for the other two? Tony and your sister? I'm not sure how I feel about Tony Scott as the spiritual guardian of my firstborn, but I guess you'll want Lilian.'

'I wasn't going to suggest Lilian. She's already his aunty so I don't think it would offend her if we asked someone else. The same with your brother and Mary.'

'Who then? Jolka and Piotr? Or Don Sykes and his wife, since you're godmother to their little lad?'

'Not for this baby. I think...' Bobby looked over her shoulder at him. 'This might sound strange, but I'd like to ask Ernie King.'

Charlie frowned. 'You want your old flame to be godfather to our child?'

'He's not an old flame — not exactly,' Bobby said, smiling. 'He was so good today when I needed someone, Charlie. It feels like it would draw a line under everything that's happened between us. But if the idea upsets you, we'll ask someone else.'

'If it's Ernie King you want, then Ernie King it is,' Charlie said, stroking her cheek. 'I'll leave you to ask him, shall I?'

'Thank you.' Bobby rewarded him with a kiss.

Charlie seemed to drift into a reverie, his hands absently massaging her stomach. Bobby watched them move, feeling how the baby shifted in response. He did know when Charlie was holding her, she was sure. She wondered how.

'What happened with your friend, love?' she asked softly. 'Did he know you were there?'

'Yes, he was in surprisingly good spirits,' Charlie told her. 'He couldn't talk much but he was still able to rib Willis about the NAAFI girl he's been walking out with, and flirt with his nurses. He always did have an eye for the ladies.'

'Did he look very frightening?'

'The poor lad was wrapped up like a mummy. Every inch of him burnt. I can't imagine the agony.' He shook his head, brow lowering. 'Too many boys are ending their lives that way. It isn't right.'

'He knows, doesn't he? That he's... that he doesn't have long left?'

'He knew.'

Bobby frowned. 'Knew?'

Charlie hid his face on her shoulder. 'We were only just in time,' he whispered. 'We got word the next morning that he'd gone in the night. I hope wherever he is now, it's a better world than this one.'

'Oh, Charlie. I am sorry.'

'I'm not,' he muttered grimly. 'Every minute he stayed alive was pain.'

Bobby shuffled around. 'Let's leave the washing-up and have an early night, shall we? We can take the wireless in and have a cuddle. It's the wedding tomorrow, and I'll be in no mood to celebrate it if I don't get some rest.'

'I'd like that.' He let her go so he could start collecting up the tea things.

'By the way, you'll be pleased to know I wrote to the Air Ministry on the train home,' he said as he did so. 'I popped it in the box in Leeds.'

'Oh.' Bobby had been so preoccupied with other things, she had forgotten about the DFC. 'And... you accepted?'

'Said I would, didn't I? Not that I needed to write – they presume acceptance for things like this. I felt like I wanted to though.'

'I thought seeing your friend might have changed your mind.'

'I have to put my duty as a father and husband first. I do feel guilty, but Hynesy would have understood.'

Bobby remembered the letter that had come for Charlie, which she had thrown on to the coffee table with the rest of the post. She went to retrieve it.

'I forgot that this came for you,' she said, holding it out. 'It's a Skipton postmark. It couldn't be about that job at the bank, could it?'

'If it is, it'll be a rejection.' Charlie put his tray of crockery down to open the letter.

He frowned while he read it, Bobby watching him anxiously.

'Well?' she asked. 'Is it a rejection?'

'It's... no. Well, yes, but...' He sounded bewildered. 'Here, you read it.'

Bobby took it from him.

> Dear Mr Atherton,
>
> I would like to thank you for meeting with me concerning the role of junior clerk at Skipton Penny Bank. Unfortunately, it was felt your war injuries were such that it would not be possible for you to perform this role to the bank's high standard. However, on a personal level, I was impressed by your neat appearance, education and head for figures. I would therefore like to ask you to consider another role.
>
> My secretary, Miss Cummings, will be leaving the company when she marries next month, and I would take it as a favour if you would consider filling the vacancy. The role does not involve significant amounts of time on your feet, nor handling money. You would be responsible for typing, correspondence, office administration, taking dictation and keeping my appointment book. The bank would also invest in shorthand training for you.
>
> The salary may be lower than you are used to but is nevertheless a generous wage for the work: £3 per week, plus an additional £10 per annum marriage allowance. You would also be entitled to an allowance of £10 per annum on the birth of your first child, with smaller allowances for subsequent children.
>
> I would be grateful if you could write with your decision at your earliest convenience.
>
> Yours sincerely,
> Wm. Miller
> Manager, Yorkshire Penny Bank

Bobby stared at the letter for a long time. Charlie had sunk into a chair.

'A secretary,' she said at last.

'Women's work,' Charlie muttered. 'Miller's trying to do me a favour.' He gave a hollow laugh. 'I suppose he feels sorry for me. He knows a hopeless unemployable when he sees one.'

'Three pounds a week,' Bobby said, her eyes still fixed on the letter. 'And an extra four bob a week marriage allowance, with another four when Marmaduke comes. He's right, it is a good wage for the work. The *Courier* only paid me thirty bob as a typist.'

'It's a good wage for a single woman. For a married man, it's insulting.' Charlie rubbed his face. 'Twenty-eight years old and the head of a family, and I'm expected to work for three quid a week.'

Bobby went to sit on the arm of his chair.

'I know it's not ideal, but it's work, isn't it?' she said gently. 'And while it might not be a great wage, it's a quid more a week than I get on the magazine. We can make it stretch.'

'But having to tell people I'm a secretary – a secretary, for God's sake, and working for a woman's wage!' He laughed grimly. 'I imagine Tony would crack a few jokes at my expense.'

'Pay no attention to him. He can hardly mock your wages on what Reg pays him, and I know for a fact he was only on three pounds a week at the *Courier*.'

'But it's still a woman's job. I'll never hear the end of it from the lads round here.'

Bobby put an arm around his shoulders. 'You don't have to take it.'

'Of course I have to bloody take it. What else is there?' He sighed, and gave her arm a squeeze. 'Sorry, I shouldn't swear. It's just hard to feel like the head of the family doing a job like that. And then I'm to be grateful for it, and take it as a favour!'

'It doesn't have to be for long. You can be keeping an eye out for other jobs.'

'What other jobs? It'll be even worse once the war ends and I'm competing with hundreds of demobbed men with two working arms and legs each.'

'I'm sorry, Charlie.' She stroked his hair. 'You're worth so much more.'

Charlie sat silent, his face dark. Gradually his expression started to lift, however, until he looked up with a smile.

'I'm being an ungrateful swine again, aren't I?' he said softly. 'Here's fate, stretching out her hand with the means to provide for my wife and baby, and I'm turning my nose up because it doesn't satisfy my pride.'

'It's understandable, when you've got a brain you're desperate to use. I've felt that way all my life. That the world refuses to let me do what I'm capable of.'

'And I should count myself lucky to be one of the more privileged sex, I know.' He planted a kiss on her lips. 'There. Take that as an apology, and consider me duly reprimanded for my ingratitude. I must admit, it's a relief to know you can leave *The Tyke* without plunging us into destitution. I couldn't bear to have you working after what nearly happened today.'

## Chapter 21

Bobby was careful to set her clock before bed, now Marmaduke had blotted his copybook as an alarm. Tomorrow was the wedding of Gil Capstick and Mabs Jessop, and she would feel dreadful if anything happened to make them late. However, the baby had returned to form now his dad was home, waking her as ever at half past six.

The first thing Bobby did on waking was disable the alarm so Charlie could sleep on, then she went to get ready for the wedding. The hectic nature of yesterday had left no time to prepare. There was Charlie's shirt and suit to iron, and she hadn't had time to adjust her best pale green twinset. After today, when she had come clean to her family, she could stop going to such lengths to hide her blossoming figure, but for the next few hours she needed to keep up the pretence.

Bobby glanced at the letter Charlie had received from the bank as she ironed his suit.

It ought to be a relief to know her husband had a weekly wage packet beckoning. Despite Charlie's hurt pride, it wasn't such a terrible salary. It was more than a private in the army received, at least, and the family allowance was a generous addition. Yet Charlie had sounded so unhappy that it worried Bobby how he would settle to the work.

In the early days of their acquaintance, Bobby had felt she and Charlie were too different to ever be more than friends. As she had come to know him better, she had begun to feel it was in their very differences that they suited. She was too fond of work, he of play, and they exercised a healthy moderating influence on one another. That was before the war had taken them, and made them the people they were now – more solemn and thoughtful, but closer than they had ever been as sweethearts.

But there was one respect in which Bobby and her husband had always been alike, and that was in their craving for stimulating work. This had always been more of a problem for Bobby than Charlie. As a man he'd had a world of employment open to him, whether it was healing animals or flying bombers. No one expected him to give it up to boil napkins and scrub linen. No one pushed him into passive roles that didn't interest him, like typing or filing.

Whereas Bobby had had to fight all her life to do more than the world deemed appropriate to her sex. She well remembered how dull she had found her typing role on the *Courier*, longing to do what the male reporters were doing. She remembered, too, how she had defied her commanding officer when the WAAF had tried to condemn her to shorthand typing for the duration, fighting instead to be trained as a plotter.

And now it was Charlie who was compelled to take a job typing while his eager, active brain went to waste. Bobby supposed it was worse for him in some ways. She was a girl from a working-class family, long taught that she ought to consider herself privileged to be doing clerical work rather than earning her crust in the mills. Charlie, as a boy with a private education, had never been set such limits.

It was this, she imagined, that humiliated him as much as the low wage or the fact he was doing a woman's job. That notion his brain was no longer enough, now the body that went with it was broken. He'd been taught to expect the world, and had seen the opportunities it offered as his by right. Whereas no little girl was taught to see a future beyond her own hearth.

But there wasn't much Bobby could do about that. All she could hope was that the work wouldn't push Charlie into a funk he would find it hard to get out of.

She thought of the medal Charlie had finally, reluctantly, decided to accept. He might write to say he'd changed his mind now, since his ultimate aim had been to secure a job. Still, Bobby harboured a hope that Charlie would make his peace with the DFC somehow. It would be such a proud thing for his family.

But it was in Charlie's hands now. Let him write a refusal if he must. She was done trying to change his mind.

—

Bobby just had time to adjust her best skirt before the ceremony. She felt like she owed it to her good friend Andy Jessop, the bride's late grandfather, to show herself up well.

It wouldn't be long, she supposed, before she would have to abandon her current clothes for maternity items. Bobby had never been a worshipper of fashion the way her twin was, but the idea of those shapeless, sack-like dresses still made her grimace.

Inside the chapel, Charlie joined Gil by the altar to perform his duties as best man. Meanwhile, Bobby slipped into a pew next to her sister.

'Are you all right?' Lilian whispered. 'Tony said you weren't well at work yesterday. Annie and I called on you but there was no answer.'

Bobby shook her head. 'I told Tony not to worry you with it.'

'Well, where were you?'

'At the doctor's,' Bobby said, as quietly as possible. 'But everything's fine. It was a storm in a teacup in the end. Just my silly brain getting worked up over nothing.' Bobby pressed her sister's hand. 'Charlie and I are going to have something to announce at dinner though. Be ready, all right?'

'You're announcing it today?'

'Yes. It's time.'

A hush fell on the congregation as the organ began to play.

Bobby glanced around the Wesleyan chapel. It was significantly smaller than St Peter's, the Anglican church, but quite a crowd had been packed in. The Jessops were a large clan and half the pews were taken up with Andy's children, grandchildren and great-grandchildren. His second wife Ginny was there as well, of course, damp-eyed as she waited for her stepgranddaughter to appear.

Topsy had naturally been invited – she always did receive an invitation to village weddings, as lady of the manor. She was sitting with Jolka and Mrs Hobbes. Teddy, whose wheelchair would struggle to fit into the small space, was at home enjoying a visit from Piotr and young Tommy.

The chapel quickly became so crowded that it was standing room only. Gil was well-liked in Silverdale, his job as postman bringing him a wide circle of friends. The groom was grinning in a dazed manner by the altar, as if he still couldn't believe his luck.

Ernie and Sandy, both fleeting objects of Mabs Jessop's affection, had been invited too. Bobby caught Ernie's eye and smiled. She hoped he would understand what this meant – that all was OK with the baby after all. He smiled back. Bobby vowed to seek him out during the reception, and speak to him about what she and Charlie had discussed.

-

It was a simple wedding, but emotional. The recent death of Andy seemed to hover over the event.

Mabs sounded choked as she said her vows. It was clear she had developed a real love for the man she was marrying. Gil beamed like a man whose horse had come in at a hundred to one, leaving no one in doubt that this was the happiest day of his life.

After the service, everyone proceeded to the church hall by St Peter's for a lunch of ham sandwiches and lemonade. The hall belonged to the Anglicans, but they didn't begrudge a loan to any local Methodists with a wedding, christening or funeral to observe.

'We'd better not stay long,' Mary whispered to Bobby after they'd congratulated the new Mr and Mrs Capstick. 'I've the roast to get on. I did suggest to the childer we might have a light supper, since they'd be filling their tummies with jelly and blancmange this afternoon, but they wouldn't hear of missing Sunday dinner. Honestly, you'd have thought I was suggesting starving them to death.'

'I'm on their side. Best meal of the week,' Bobby said. 'Besides, it's nice to have the family together on Sundays.'

'Aye, there is that.' Mary smiled. 'I remember when family meant only me, Reg and young Charlie, when he deigned to give us his company. Now the kitchen barely holds us all. Everything seemed to change when I talked my Reg into taking on some city lass who turned up sobbing and covered in coal dust one afternoon.'

Bobby smiled too. 'I imagine you're sorry you ever persuaded him.'

'I'd love to tease you, Bobby, but that's a fib too big,' Mary said, giving her a squeeze.

Bobby flinched at the arm around her well-rounded abdomen, but Mary didn't seem to notice anything amiss. Her gaze had drifted to Jess and Florrie, who had skipped the sandwiches and were queuing with hungry expressions for the sweet things.

While Gil and Mabs's wedding feast couldn't compare with the spread when Topsy had married Teddy the year before, they had still done themselves proud. Silverdale folk were always generous when a couple were to be wed. There was even a cake: small but rich-looking, with real sugar icing.

'Where on earth did they get that?' Bobby asked Mary.

'I think it was Topsy's present. As for the sweet things, they'll have come from the two Canadians, I expect. Their rations seem a mite more generous than we civilians get.' Mary shook her head at Jess trying to fit a whole jam tart into her mouth. 'All this and she still wants a dinner. I'd better make sure they don't wolf down their food. Their father's obviously too busy with his lady friend to keep an eye on them.' She bustled off.

There was still that note of disapproval when Mary regarded the captain and Miss Simpson, who was his guest for the reception. Bobby had wondered if her friend might warm to the woman now she had shown herself to be a steady sort, but apparently not.

She was as keen as Mary to make this a short stay. She wouldn't be able to relax until she and Charlie had broken their news to the family. As long as they were all here, there was a risk that someone would let the secret slip. Bobby knew she could trust Jolka and Ernie, but a couple of the gossipy neighbours who had spotted her being driven around in the doctor's car were also here.

There were a few people she wanted to speak to before leaving though. One of them, Ginny Jessop, was standing alone gazing out of the window. Bobby approached her.

'How are you feeling, Mrs Jessop?' she asked gently, resting a hand on the old lady's shoulder.

'Oh. Miss Bancroft.' Ginny pulled her eyes from the window. 'I'm sorry, I must've been away wi' t' fairies.' She shook her head impatiently. 'Miss Bancroft, now what am I on about? It's Mrs Atherton, isn't it? How long is it you'll be married now?'

'Coming up to nine months.'

'As long as that already!' Ginny's gaze drifted to the window again, which looked out on the fells rising up into a steely Dales sky. 'Time does seem to run faster the older you get,' she said dreamily.

'How are you feeling?' Bobby repeated. 'It must be an emotional day for you.'

'It is.' Ginny smiled in Mabs's direction. The young bride was holding her husband's hand and beaming as she received the hearty congratulations of their many friends. 'But a proud one. Andy would be proud enough to burst if he were here. He had a soft spot for that little lass out of all on 'em, wayward as she could be.'

'I'm sure he is here.'

'Aye, happen so.' Ginny laughed, a little brokenly. 'He used to despair of seeing the child settled. Always she'd be running after lads wi' more brass buttons than brains, caring for nowt but a handsome face. It took losing someone she loved to make her understand the value of the heart underneath. He'd be glad o' that, any road. Glad it were him as brought them together.'

'You must miss him a lot.'

'That I do. Don't seem fair we got so little time. Then again, we were lucky to get that much. Andy had a long life, and he fit a whole lot into it.' Her gaze drifted once again to the towering fells, turning in the direction of Newby Top, Andy's old farmhouse. 'He were allus fond of thee,' she said quietly.

'I was fond of him.'

'Forever boasting of knowing thee, he was,' Ginny said with a little smile. 'That clever lass from t' paper, who knew all the words anyone could think of. He'd laugh hissen silly at your bits in our paper when I read them to him. "She'll do great things, our Miss Bancroft, Gin. Just tha watch and see." That were what he said to me near the end. Gave you all the credit for the wooing of me. I think he was as attached to you as one of his own.'

Bobby felt a lump rise, thinking about the friend she had lost.

She hadn't been sad to say goodbye to Andy for his own sake. He had been content, even happy, as the end of his life approached, feeling he had been blessed in both years and loved ones. But for her own sake Bobby had been sad, because even the knowledge that someone you care for has had a long and blessed life doesn't prevent you from missing them when they're gone.

He had been so proud to know her. So sure she would do something of real note one day. Would she? Could she? Was it too late, now she was to be a mother?

'I miss him too,' Bobby said, swallowing a tear. 'I really do.'

Ginny smiled, and turned to give her a hug.

'You know, I reckon you're right,' she whispered as they embraced. 'I reckon in his own way, he is here today.'

—

When Ginny had left her, Bobby went to pluck Charlie's elbow. He was smoking among a gaggle of men from the local farms, friends from veterinary days, and seemed to be enjoying himself. She felt guilty about interrupting, but she didn't want to speak to Ernie without telling Charlie where she was going. If the village gossips spotted her slipping away with Ernie King while her husband was distracted, they'd have a field day.

'What's up, Bob?' he asked. 'Did you want to go home?'

'Soon, but not yet. I wanted to tell you I was going to speak to Ernie about what we discussed, so if you find I've disappeared, I'll be outside with him.'

'All right.' He gave her a kiss. 'When you want to leave, just let me know.'

'I will. You enjoy yourself with your friends.'

She left Charlie to the ribbing of his pals, who seemed to be unleashing a store of wife-related wisecracks. She made a mental note to write a few jokes about husbands for the wireless to get her own back.

Ernie was congratulating the bride and groom. Bobby waited for him to finish before waving to claim his attention.

'Bobby,' he said when he approached. She noted the concern in his tone, as well as the absence of nickname. 'Everything all right, kid?'

'It is, but... can you come outside? I want to talk to you in private.'

He frowned. 'Your other half going to be OK with that? I prefer weddings that don't include a sock in the puss.'

'Charlie's given his blessing for me to sneak off with you, don't worry,' she said with a smile.

Ernie let out the deep laugh that always reminded Bobby of when she had first got to know him, in the winter of 1941 when they had appeared in Topsy's pantomime together. She couldn't remember anything that had brought her as much joy as that little production.

'That's mighty liberal-minded of him,' Ernie said. 'Come on then.'

'Is Barbara not with you?' Bobby asked as they ventured out into a chilly winter afternoon.

Ernie shrugged. 'I could hardly drag the girl here without an invite.'

'The invitations to single folk said they could bring someone, didn't they? I know Captain Parry's did.'

'Can't say I noticed. I'm sure the happy couple will be glad not to have another mouth to feed.' He looked keenly into her eyes. 'I guess from the way you were smirking at me in church that I'm safe to offer those congratulations I was saving?'

'Yes, it was all OK. Just babies being babies, the doctor said, and I'd got into such a panic that I'd made myself ill. Once I could feel the baby moving again, I was soon my old self.'

'In that case, my heartiest congratulations to both of you.' He shook her hand, making her smile.

'We're going to tell the family later today,' she told him. 'Don't give us away, will you?'

'Sure. I know how to keep my mouth shut.'

'Ernie, I wanted to ask you something,' Bobby said. 'I hope you won't think it's strange.'

'What is it?'

'Well, we thought… that is, Charlie and I decided we'd like you to be the baby's godfather. If you wanted to be.'

'Gee,' Ernie said, blinking. 'Godfather? Me?'

'We'd be honoured if you would. We're going to ask Topsy and Teddy to be the others when we've made the news public, but I wanted to ask you first.'

'Why me?'

'Well, you're important to me,' Bobby said, flushing. 'That is to say, I'm fond of you. I don't know what I would've done without you yesterday, honestly. I'd like you to be something to my baby, and him to you.'

Ernie seemed to swell, the chest of his dress uniform expanding with pride.

'I've never been a godfather before,' he said. 'What if I mess it up?'

Bobby smiled. 'You won't. You'll be wonderful.'

'And I guess I'd be Uncle Ernie, would I?'

'If you like.'

'Heh. That sure sounds strange. I'll do my best to live up to it though.'

'So you will?'

'Yeah, if you really want me. It'd be an honour, Slacks.'

Bobby beamed at him. 'Oh, thank you. I am glad. Charlie will be too.'

'What happens now? Do I need to sign anything, or do we just spit in our palms and shake?'

'I think that comes at the christening,' Bobby said with a laugh. 'But I'm willing to risk village gossip and give you a hug. You saved my life yesterday, and I was so shaken that I barely said thank you.'

'I don't think you were quite at death's door, but I'll take a hug if it eases your conscience,' Ernie said, smiling. 'You'd better start it though, then I can claim to be the innocent party if your Mr Atherton files for divorce.'

Bobby wrapped her arms around him. He didn't embrace her in return, but smiled down at her with a protective tenderness.

'You know, Slacks, you're going to make one hell of a mom,' he whispered.

'Thanks, Ernie. I'm glad things worked out for us. I'm glad we both got to be happy.'

He brushed his lips against her cheek. 'All the happiness in the world, kid. You deserve it.'

—

Bobby was anxious to leave after her conversation with Ernie, but Charlie was having such a merry time with the other men that she didn't like to drag him away. It was good for him to socialise. Instead she sought out Topsy, who she hadn't seen since Jolka had passed on the news that Mrs Hobbes would be leaving her.

The blow had softened a little with time, although Topsy still seemed stunned at losing her much-loved nanny. Mrs Hobbes was to leave her at the end of the month, when she had arranged to move into a cottage in the village – by the beck for the benefit of her pet goose Norman and his family, just as Bobby had predicted. Topsy soon began talking animatedly about her and Teddy's plan to adopt a child, however.

'I've written to one of Father's friends on the board of the Waifs and Strays Society for advice,' Topsy said. 'Oh, but it is frustrating having Maimie leave just when I need her. Of course I'll have to give up nursing. Teddy will need me at home, and I'll have the house to keep. I've never tried being a housewife before. Maimie's always been there to divide the chores with.'

Bobby had private suspicions that Maimie Hobbes had taken on more than her fair share of chores at Topsy's cottage. The former nanny did seem to act as unofficial housekeeper there. However, she kept quiet on this point.

'Shan't you miss nursing?' she asked Topsy.

'I'll miss doing my part to help those poor boys, but when I've got my own wounded hero at home, it's hard to feel too guilty.' Topsy popped a shortcrust finger in her mouth, as usual eating like someone with no time to waste. 'I think it will be rather an adventure, don't you? I wish Maimie didn't have to go but I'm looking forward to getting started on motherhood.'

Bobby would never cease to be amazed at the breeziness with which her friend considered such matters. Bobby was perpetually worrying herself into knots about how the changes in her life would affect her, but to Topsy, every change was just the next big adventure. Why couldn't she be that way?

It felt strange, too, how little changed Topsy was. Bobby often felt like a whole other person than that girl who had first come to Silverdale, and Charlie had changed even more. Everyone she knew had changed to some extent, because two years of war did change people. Mary had become more independent, Reg softer, her father happier, Lilian more serious and Tony more responsible. Only Topsy seemed never to alter.

And yet Topsy had altered – a great deal, under the surface. Loving Teddy had taught her softness, and selflessness. Bobby could never have pictured the Topsy Sumner-Walsh she had met on New Year's Eve 1940 as a mother, a nurse or the wife of a disabled man.

Topsy had matured, but she had managed to retain her colour, her buoyancy of spirit and youthfulness of heart – all the things people loved her for. No amount of war and hardship seemed able to rob her of them. Bobby felt sure her friend would have the same happy disposition all her life, and it gladdened her to think of it.

## Chapter 22

'Are you ready?' Charlie murmured later that day, when he and Bobby arrived at Moorside for their family dinner. The time had come, finally, to share their big news.

Bobby didn't know if she was or not. It felt strange that soon, everyone would know about Marmaduke. She was filled with worry about how the family would react when she revealed not only her pregnancy, but the sneaky way in which she had endeavoured to conceal it.

'I suppose so,' she whispered back. 'Let's go in. We're a little late.'

In the kitchen, they found everyone already seated around the table: her father; Lil and Tony, with Annie in her high chair between them; Captain Parry and his daughters; and Reg of course, with Mary at the oven checking on the joint. The sound of merry chatter instantly made Bobby feel better. Everyone seemed in good spirits after today's happy event.

Bobby wondered how they were actually supposed to announce their news. Ought she to bang her fork against her glass, as people did at weddings? She would feel so foolish. Perhaps she should leave it to Charlie.

'Well, you're here at last,' Mary said as they each took a seat. 'In that case, I can start serving up.'

'Just a moment. Before we eat, there's something I'd like to tell you all.'

Bobby glanced at Charlie in surprise. It wasn't him who had spoken. It was Captain Parry, seeming to snatch the words right from their mouths.

Mary frowned. 'Everything all right, George?'

The captain looked rather bashful. 'Um, yes. I only wished all of you to know, before anyone else, that Miss Simpson and I... well, the fact is we're engaged to be married. She did me the honour of agreeing to be my wife this afternoon.'

This was met by a shocked silence. Of course Bobby had known George was considering a proposal, but she hadn't expected it to happen quite so soon. He and Miss Simpson had barely been walking out five weeks. Quick engagements weren't unusual in wartime, but Captain Parry seemed such a sensible, cautious man.

The silence was broken by Lilian.

'Congratulations, George,' she said, smiling warmly. 'She's a wonderful girl. Every happiness to you both.'

This seemed to break through the collective daze, and a moment later Reg and Rob were slapping George on the back while everyone offered their congratulations.

'You ought to have said summat, Ginger,' Reg said. 'I'd have got a bottle in to toast the happy news.'

Florrie, however, was staring at her father in horror.

'You're not really going to marry *her*, are you?' she asked in a disgusted tone.

George rested a hand on her shoulder. 'Now, Florrie, don't be that way. You'll like her ever so much when you know her better.'

The child's lip wobbled.

'I won't let you,' she said. 'I won't, so... there.'

Jess, who looked no happier about the situation, nodded in agreement. 'Nor me either. We'll... we'll run away if you marry her. I bet you'll be sorry then.'

'I'm afraid it isn't up to the two of you who I marry,' their father said sternly. 'We'll talk about it at home.'

'If you loved us then you wouldn't marry no one without asking us,' Florrie said, the tremble in her lip becoming more violent. 'And you wouldn't want to replace our ma with someone like *her*. That's cruel, and it's wrong and... and I'll hate you forever.'

'Florence Parry, I know you don't mean that,' Mary said, frowning. 'You mind how you speak to your father.'

'I do. I mean it more than anything. And I won't let him, I won't!'

Sobbing, Florrie ran from the table. They heard her thundering upstairs a moment later. Jessie looked like she might follow, but a look from Mary kept her in her chair. The younger child had always been more concerned about pleasing the grown-ups than her more wilful sister.

Captain Parry sighed. 'I'll go after her. I am sorry, Mary. I didn't expect her to take on like this.'

'Let me go, George,' Lilian said quietly.

'If you think that's best. She'll be more likely to listen to you or Mary than to me at the moment, I think.'

'She'll be in the attic,' Mary said. 'Would you rather I went, Lilian?'

'I think she might listen to me, if I take the baby to her,' Lilian said. 'You serve up, Mary. I won't be long, I hope.'

She took the smiling Annie from her high chair and disappeared.

By the time Mary had served them all, Lilian had reappeared with Annie against her hip and Florrie beside her. The little girl looked pale, but she was no longer crying.

'Florrie has something she would like to say,' Lil told them.

Florrie sniffed. 'Sorry if I ruined dinner, Mary. And Dad, I'm sorry I said I'd hate you forever. I won't really.'

The captain couldn't help smiling. 'Well that's certainly a relief.'

'But I wish you didn't want to get married though.'

He drew her to him and planted a kiss on her curls. 'We'll talk about it at home, all right, sweetheart? Let's have no more tears now, when Mary has been kind enough to cook dinner especially because you asked her to.'

'All right.'

Lilian passed the girl a handkerchief before sitting down, and Florrie blew her nose.

'Well!' Mary said cheerily, in an attempt to shift the lingering awkwardness. 'Another wedding on the horizon, and only just back from one. I'll barely have time to press Reg's suit.'

Bobby gave Charlie a significant look. He nodded, and opened his mouth to speak. But before he could do so, Rob cleared his throat.

'Happen you'll need to press it sooner than you think, Mary,' he said, turning red. 'I, um… I've a little summat to tell all of ye as well.'

Bobby blinked at him. She had forgotten her father had said he'd let everyone know about his plan to move out of the cow house today. But what did he mean about suits?

'What is it, Rob?' Mary asked.

'Well, the fact of it is, I'll be flitting next month. Not far, like. We've taken a little place on the beck. But anyhow, we'd like all of you to be there, although it won't be much. At our age, we thought summat quiet would be best.'

'Dad, what are you talking about?' Lilian asked.

Rob rubbed his neck. 'When I told you and your sister I'd a mate from t' pub I was aiming to set up home with… that's true enough, but I didn't quite tell you all of it. Anyhow, now she's given me a yes I can come clean.'

Lilian frowned. 'She?'

'Oh my goodness!' Bobby said, the penny dropping. 'Dad, you're not saying… not Mrs Hobbes?'

'Aye, well, she's a fine old girl, and we rub along well together. I hope you'd never think I was trying to replace your mam, but at my time o' life… I'd like to spend what's left of it wi' someone I can look after, and someone as can look after me.' His neck was starting to look rather sore under constant rubbing. 'So, um, I asked and she said yes. That's about all there is to it. The wedding's booked at the registry in Skipton for three weeks' time.'

'Three weeks!'

Bobby didn't know whether to be pleased or to run sobbing from the room as Florrie had done. She was so surprised, she didn't know what to feel.

It was Charlie who recovered first, breaking the second stunned silence of the afternoon. He leaned across the table to shake his father-in-law's hand.

'Every happiness, Rob,' he said. 'I won't think of it as losing a father-in-law so much as gaining a goose.'

Rob smiled. 'Aye, it'll be an experience sharing a home wi' that pet of hers. Still, she's worth it for all her funny ways.'

Tony looked rather thrilled, which Bobby assumed had more to do with no longer having to share a home with his father-in-law than her dad's news. He shook Rob's hand heartily.

'We'll miss you, old man,' he said.

Rob laughed. 'Like heck you will.' He glanced from Bobby to Lil. 'And what do you pair have to say about it?'

'Well, I mean... congratulations,' Lil said, planting a bewildered kiss on his cheek. 'Every happiness and all that. But I wish you'd told us sooner, Dad. Three weeks isn't long to plan a wedding.'

'Oh, it's plenty for a couple of old fogies like us. We've been talking about setting up home for months, but Maim wouldn't commit till she'd squared it with Her Ladyship. I told her I'd be ready with the licence as soon as she gave me the nod.'

Bobby finally recovered enough to smile at him. 'You sly thing. So that's what's had you in a good mood the last few months, is it? I wondered what could be putting the grin on your face.'

'You approve then?'

'You could knock me down with a feather but yes, I've always liked Maimie Hobbes. Does Topsy know?'

'Not yet. Maim's breaking the news now.'

The rest of the family chimed in with congratulations, and Rob was beaming by the time they settled down to eat. Bobby was so knocked for six that she was halfway through her meal before she remembered that she, too, had some news to break at what was turning into a highly eventful family dinner. The thought seemed to occur to Charlie at the same time.

'When?' he murmured.

'Wait till everyone's eaten,' she whispered back.

Bobby hoped that by the time everyone had finished their puddings, they would have recovered enough from the previous bombshells to be ready for one more.

'Well, shall we gents go into the parlour for a smoke and leave the girls to have a gossip?' Reg asked when everyone had cleared their plates. 'I feel like we've all been too much surprised to chip in with the required amount of back-slapping and hand-shaking, but there's plenty of time to set that right. It's only a shame we've got no cigars.'

'Happy to donate a few fags from my supply,' Tony said.

Mary shook her head. 'Oh no you don't, Tony Scott. I've just got that ceiling clean. If you boys want to smoke those smelly Egyptian things, you can do it outside.'

Bobby nudged Charlie before the family began to disperse.

'Yes. Right.' He cleared his throat. 'Um, Bobby and I are expecting a baby.'

She shook her head at him. 'You couldn't have built up to it a bit more?'

'I thought there'd been enough suspense for one afternoon.'

'Fair enough.'

This announcement didn't seem to produce quite the shockwaves the previous two had. Lilian had been expecting it, of course, and Mary didn't seem excessively surprised. The men looked a little dazed, perhaps. The girls, as Charlie had predicted, squealed with delight.

'Is it a boy or a girl?' Florrie demanded to know.

Bobby laughed. 'Yes.'

'I hope it's a boy.'

'I hope it's a girl,' Jessie said. 'If it is, will she be called after me?'

'No, she should be called after me,' Florrie said. 'I'm oldest.'

'I'm committing to nothing until he or she arrives,' Bobby said with a smile.

'When will it be born?'

'It ought to be mid-May.'

Mary frowned. 'You must be five months gone already then.'

'Six months come Valentine's Day.' Bobby shot her an apologetic grimace. 'I'm sorry, Mary. I ought to have told you all sooner.' She glanced at Reg. 'I hope you're not angry.'

Reg remained silent, however.

'It's wonderful news,' Lil said, beaming. 'Isn't it, Tony?'

'Oh, aye,' Tony said. 'You're leaving the mag then, are you, Bob?'

Lilian glared at him. 'Really, that's the first thing you think of to say?'

He shrugged. 'Got to be a conversation about it, hasn't there?'

George Parry shook Charlie's hand, then pressed Bobby's shoulder. 'Heartiest congratulations to you both. I'm sure we can't wait to welcome him or her.'

Mary gave Charlie a hug, then Bobby. 'Aye, congratulations, you two. Although rightly I ought not to speak to either of you. You've left me barely any time to get some knitting done.'

'Congratulations to you, Nana,' Bobby whispered as Mary embraced her. 'Please don't be cross. I so wanted to tell you, but...'

'I know.' Mary brushed a tear from her cheek. 'Don't worry about Reg. I'll talk him round.'

'You guessed, didn't you?'

'Let's say I had my suspicions.' She held her back. 'Now be sure you leave everything unlocked if you have the babby at home, back and front door and any other lock in the house. It'll ease the birth. You must turn over your mirrors as well.'

Bobby smiled, accustomed to Mary's store of old superstitions, and promised it would be attended to.

'Bobby, will the baby like stories?' Florrie demanded. Her eyes were glittering, already thinking about how many new tales she could add to her book before the baby's arrival.

'I'm certain of it,' Bobby said.

'Tha reminds me of another little lass, Florrie,' Rob told her, getting up. 'Always wi' her it were stories, stories, stories.'

'Who is she, Mr Bancroft?' Florrie asked.

He smiled at Bobby. 'Well, happen she's a mite bigger now. You remember, Bob? They were always about little girls with brown hair and twin sisters and their heads full of books, cracking spy rings and whatnot.'

'I remember,' Bobby said softly.

She had been worried that her dad, too, might be resentful she hadn't shared her news sooner, but since he had been nursing a secret of his own for months, he had less cause to take the moral high ground than Reg and Mary. Anyhow, he didn't look angry. He was smiling as he pressed her shoulder, although there was a sad, tender expression in his eyes.

Bobby waited for his congratulations, but he didn't offer any.

'Come over to t' cow house when you've done here, lass,' he said. 'Summat to give thee.'

'All right.'

After shaking hands with Charlie, Rob disappeared.

Bobby turned to Reg, who had remained silent in his chair while the rest of the family fussed about. 'Um, can I talk to you in the parlour?'

'Aye.' Reg blinked a few times, then reached for his stick. 'Aye, let's get it over with.'

He followed her to the parlour, which felt oddly bare without their desks. Reg's wolfhound Barney, who had been banished here with his sister while the family ate, sidled up to Bobby's legs and she tickled him absently between the ears.

'Reg, I'm so sorry I didn't tell you,' she said. 'I felt terrible about it, but...'

'But you wanted to keep working.' He shook his head, scowling. 'Bloody stupid of you, five month in.'

'You're angry,' she murmured. 'But what could I do, Reg? I knew you'd never keep me on if you knew. Charlie was out of work, and we needed the money.'

'I'd have given you the damn money, lass. You think I'd leave my own brother scrambling for pennies with a bairn on the way?'

'I didn't want you to give it to us. I wanted to earn it.'

'Striding over the fells in that condition,' Reg muttered. 'Suppose you'd lost the babby, eh? How d'you think I'd feel, knowing it was me who sent you out there?'

'Honestly, you men act like we're as fragile as eggshell once we're expecting,' Bobby said, her patience fraying. 'Dr Minchin told me it wasn't dangerous to keep working, as long as I didn't over-exert myself.'

'Aye, well, it's not only that.' Reg pushed his fingers into his thinning hair. 'I never should've taken you on again when you came back from war. You were supposed to be at home, looking after our Charlie. That's why they let you out, isn't it?'

'Well, yes. But the best way for me to look after him while he was out of work was by earning money. Charlie would hate being forced to take charity from you and Mary.'

'That's summat, I suppose,' Reg said, in a less harsh voice. 'I remember when the boy wasn't too proud to beg a loan so he could waste it on girls and horses. Good to know he's finally grown up.'

'He's a different man these days,' Bobby said quietly.

Reg sighed. 'I knew it was only a matter of time, but Lord knows how I'll manage without you. Not that I'd ever admit it to the missus, but I was starting to enjoy retirement. I'll have to step back in now. Scott does all right but I wouldn't trust him in an editor role.'

Bobby felt a sadness at this. She would miss being the deputy editor, plotting out each issue. She felt bad for Tony too, who would be counting on a promotion.

'Will you take on a junior reporter?' she asked.

'Huh. Where from? I had trouble enough getting you pair, with war taking all the lads. Now it's even come for the lasses, if I was minded to try that again after the trouble it caused last time.'

Bobby flashed him a smile. 'Come on, Reg. I wasn't so bad in the end, was I?'

He smiled back, unable to keep up his bad temper. 'You've certainly been good for our Charlie. Can't say I regret the way you turned things upside down around here, all told.'

'You're not so cross with me that you'll go on grandad strike then?'

'Grandad.' He rubbed his cheek thoughtfully. 'Aye, suppose I am in a way.'

'That's what Charlie and I were hoping you'd be. Like I told Mary, you two would always be Nana and Grandad to any children of ours.'

This seemed to shift the last of Reg's grump. He looked pleased, and a little touched.

'Well, look after yourself then,' he said to Bobby, covering for his emotion with gruffness. 'No more of this nonsense about working. Charlie told me he'd got that clerk's position. No cause for you to be anywhere other than at home now he's earning.'

'He told you that?'

'Aye. Shame he can't get more with his fancy education, but better than sitting on his ar— on his backside at home.'

So Charlie had told Reg he was to be a clerk. Well, a clerk wasn't a million miles from a secretary, Bobby supposed. If it helped the boy's pride then she guessed it didn't matter what he called himself.

'And what about the magazine?' she asked. 'How will you manage?'

Reg shrugged. 'Make up the difference with freelance pieces, same as before. Not the cheapest way of doing things but it'll have to do till the war's over.'

Bobby put a hand on his arm. 'You won't consider...'

'What?'

'You won't consider keeping me on? Not as deputy editor but just part-time, working from home. If you only paid me a third of my salary, I know I could produce twice as much quality copy as any freelance.'

Reg snorted. 'Don't talk daft. I need someone who can go out and get me stories.'

'Tony can write those pieces, but there's plenty I could do. Half of what goes in the mag is from desk research alone. Charlie can fetch me books from the library when I get too big to go. It would help supplement his wage, and I'd love to stay involved.'

'You think like that now, when you've not got a bairn demanding your constant attention. I'm sorry, Bobby, but you won't be able to have everything. That's just the way things are.'

'I don't want everything. I just want...' She sighed. 'I just want a bit of what you have – what men have. Something to do with my brain between changing the baby and cooking the dinner. The ability to earn by doing what I'm good at. Is that really too much to expect?'

'Should've thought about what you had the right to expect before you were expecting,' Reg told her shortly. 'You really think that when you've been up five or six times in the night, cooking and cleaning all day on a few hours' sleep, you'll want to sit down and write me a piece on drystone walling?'

'You might at least try me. If I produce shoddy work, I promise there'll be no hard feelings about terminating the arrangement. But I'm sure I could find a way to make it work – I'm sure of it, Reg.' She met his eyes. 'Just think about it.'

He shook his head. 'No, Bobby. You can work next week to get everything finished off, then that's an end on it.'

'Why not, though? You used to think a woman couldn't make it as a reporter out here, until I proved you wrong. You said yourself it had forced you to change your ideas. Why can't you change your ideas about this? I just want to do something that matters with my life, the same as you did when you started the mag.'

Reg lifted an eyebrow. 'Raising the next generation don't matter?'

'I mean something that matters to me, as a person in my own right.' Bobby pressed a hand to her forehead. 'I'm sorry. I don't mean to sound impatient. It's just frustrating that something has to be done a particular way solely because that's how it always has been done.'

'Oh, shoo, dog,' Reg said, rebuffing Winnie as she attempted to snuffle in his pockets. 'What worries me isn't doing things the way they've always been done. What worries me, lass, is you.'

Bobby blinked. 'Me?'

'Aye. So eager to be always working, working, working. You'll never be a mam first and foremost while your mind's half on your job. A wife and mother has her own work to do and it's not writing ruddy articles.'

'Yes, but—'

He patted her arm. 'Look, I'm not saying I aren't sorry to lose you. You're a damn good writer. Happen in fifteen year or so, when your bairns can fend for themselves, you might put your hand to summat. But I'm sorry: it's time now to think of your family.'

## Chapter 23

Bobby felt solemn after her conversation with Reg. She had known what answer he would give, but still she had harboured a hope she might change his mind. Now she had to accept that her association with the magazine she loved was really, finally coming to an end.

There was a loud hum of chatter from the kitchen when she and Reg emerged into the hall. It sounded as though the Parry-Scott-Atherton clan had at last absorbed the happy news that their ranks were about to swell by two brides and a baby. Bobby could make out the excited voices of Jess and Florrie, subjecting Charlie to a barrage of questions.

'And will the baby like drawings?' Florrie was asking.

'I should think so,' Charlie answered.

'And hens?' Jess demanded.

'Tell you what, Jess. Make me a list and I'll wire the stork asking him to make sure we get one that meets all your requirements, all right?' Charlie said with a laugh. Bobby smiled.

Reg pressed her arm kindly. 'Try not to take it too hard, lass. You've got better things in your life now than my daft old magazine. Come and celebrate with your family. I'll send Scott to the pub for a jug or two of summat for us.'

'Yes.' Bobby roused herself. 'In a moment. I told my dad I'd meet him over the way.'

'Don't be long, eh? And bring Rob back with you. Hard to celebrate when we're missing a groom.'

In the cow house, Bobby found her father sitting by the unlit fire with a duster, polishing something. He slipped it into his pocket when she came in and looked up to smile at her.

'Pull up a chair, if you can battle your way through t' babby's bits,' he said. 'Don't suppose your sister will miss me once she's got an extra room to dry her washing in.'

Bobby moved one of the clothes horses aside and sat on the settee by him.

'It'll certainly be a big change.' She paused. 'I suppose... you have talked to Mrs Hobbes?'

'Better get used to calling her summat else. She'll be Mrs Bancroft in three week.'

Bobby blinked. The new name sounded strange.

'So she will,' she said. 'I suppose I ought to call her Maimie, as Topsy does. That's going to take time to adjust to.'

'What is it you want me to talk to her about, then?'

Bobby hesitated. Her dad's struggle with shell-shock wasn't an easy subject to broach.

She thought of the years she and Lilian had been responsible for him, after their mam had become ill. At only fourteen they had been forced to step into their mother's shoes, caring not only for their two younger brothers but their father, whose mind had never recovered from the horrific things he had seen in the trenches. Bobby remembered all the times they had soothed him after a nightmare with soft words and strong drink. And she remembered that dreadful day two years ago, when, reeling from the loss of his job, her dad had attempted to take his own life. He was a lot better now, but still, Bobby would want his new wife to be aware of everything she needed to be aware of if she was to share a home with Robert Bancroft.

'I only wondered if she knew that you... slept badly at times,' Bobby said, trying to phrase her worries in the way he would find least humiliating.

'Does the poor mare know what she's let herssen in for, you mean?' her dad said, with a small smile. 'Aye, Maim knows. She had a husband in the last lot. Knows how us old soldiers can be.'

This was about as frank as Bobby had ever heard her father when it came to an acknowledgement of his mental state. She wondered if it was Mrs Hobbes – or Maimie, as she ought to get used to calling her – who had encouraged him to open up.

'I'm glad of that,' she said, pressing his hand. 'Have to make sure you'll be looked after, don't I?'

'Me and Maim understand one another. Just a pair o' lonely old folk with bairns grown, who've found we'd rather have each other's company as not. We're not sentimental, but I think we'll make each other happy.'

'I'm pleased for you, Dad,' Bobby said softly. 'Mam would be as well. She wouldn't want you to be alone.'

'Aye.' Her dad turned away as he struggled with emotion. 'She were always big-hearted, were my Nell.'

'What was it you wanted to give me? There's a bit of a party at the house. Tony's going out to fetch something to drink. I was told by Reg to make sure I returned with one bridegroom ready to have his health thoroughly toasted.'

'Two things actually.' Her dad took a fat envelope from his pocket. 'First is this. There's one for each of the four of ye, but I'll keep Jake's while he's settled. He'll only waste it on that bike of his if I give it him now. Happen those of you with families have got more important things to do wi' it.'

Bobby peeped into the envelope and stared at the contents.

It was filled with money. Five-pound notes, a whole stack of them! Even one would have been unimagined riches.

'Bloody hell, Dad!'

'All right, young lady, language.'

'Sorry. But where on earth did you get this?' She frowned. 'You haven't been messing about with Pete Dixon again, have you?'

'Nay, nowt like that. Sold our house, di'n't I?'

'Gosh.' Bobby peeped again into the envelope. 'How much is here?'

'Little over thirty-five quid each. I got four hundred for the place. After paying my share for our cottage and putting a little into the pot me and Maim are saving for old age, there were a hundred and fifty left to share among you bairns.'

'Dad, that's... I don't know what to say.' Bobby gave him a hug. 'You've got no idea how much this is going to help. Charlie and I have barely got ten pounds left in our savings.'

'Aye, it's come at a good time.' He fixed her with an earnest look. 'And now I'm going to tell thee same as I told thy sister, and it's no reflection on young Charlie so don't take it that way. I've always liked the lad. But if you'll take my advice, you'll keep a tenner to buy stuff for t' babby and squirrel the other twenty-five away for a rainy day.'

She blinked. 'You mean, not tell Charlie about it?'

'Up to you but I'd think on if I were you. Women don't have the temptations us lads do when it comes to unspent money. In fact, I'll tell thee a story, our Bobby.'

'A story?'

'Aye, of me and your mam. When we'd been married nobbut a year, Nell told me she'd been left summat in an old aunt's will. Ten pound, she told me. Well, that were a heck of a lot in them days. It came in right handy – especially when Nell's doctor told us we'd be getting two babbies for the price of one. When you and Lil were about two year old and your mam getting ready to have our Ray, I got laid off. I thought it'd be the end o' t' world when that happened. The ten pound were long gone by then, o' course. We'd barely a few bob in savings, and I had no idea how I was going to support three little 'uns till I was back in work. That was when Nell – God bless her, just days from giving birth – pulled up the mattress and presented me with an old tea tin, tied wi' string.'

'What was in it?'

'I'll tell thee. A little under forty pound. That were a small fortune to a working man in the twenties – nigh on five months' wages. Turned out, the ten quid were just a little bit of what your mam had been left. She'd put the rest aside in case the family ever fell on hard times.'

'Blimey! Weren't you angry she hadn't told you?'

'Happen I were grieved at first, but I soon saw sense. She'd kept it safe for nigh on three year. If I'd known about it, can't say as I wouldn't have ended up dipping in for one thing or another until there were nowt left when we needed it. Women are better at saving, I reckon. They've got that instinct, feathering nests.' He patted her hand. 'Like I said, up to you, but your Charlie will be happy enough if it gets him out of a spot.'

'I suppose so,' Bobby said vaguely, thinking of her plan to keep a little pot of earnings from her writing work. Perhaps that was what had been in her mind: holding back a few feathers in case her little nest were ever to need them. 'Shall we go and join the celebrations?'

'Got summat else for thee first. Had to hunt around a bit for it, mind.'

From his pocket, Rob took the thing he'd been polishing. Bobby had thought it was a coin, but now he put it in her hands, she could see it was a silver medal on a faded red, white and blue ribbon. It bore the image of the old king, George V, and when she turned it over, she found the king's crest above the words *For bravery in the field*.

'Dad, this isn't...'

'Aye,' he said, blushing deeply. 'Long time since I last looked at that old thing. Thought it'd be half rust, but it's polished up all right.'

'Your Military Medal,' Bobby said wonderingly. 'Mam told me you'd been awarded one. I'd started to think she must've dreamt it. Why did you never show us before?'

'I wasn't ready,' her dad said simply. 'Wasn't ready to think about what I got it for.' He shuddered. 'Hellish time that were: the Somme. Like world's end or worse. I've not had it out in nigh on quarter of a century. But now... I think I'm ready to make my peace with it.'

'Why are you giving it to me?' Bobby said, rubbing her thumb over the laurel wreath on the back.

'I aren't; I'm giving it into your care. It's as much your brothers' and sister's as yours, but happen it might bring thee luck with a babby on t' way.' He smiled. 'Besides, I don't trust Tony not to pawn the thing if I leave it with our Lil.'

'I'll take care of it, I promise.' She looked up at him. 'Mam told me what you did. Those men whose lives you saved. That was incredibly brave of you, Dad.'

'Brave.' He cast a blank look at the medal. 'Aye, folk use words like that. Don't feel much like that when you're in t' thick of it though.'

'How does it feel?'

'Like… nowt, really. There's no time to think, about being brave or owt else. You just… do what you have to. You do what's in front of you. Don't see it makes me better nor worse than any other lad they didn't bother to pin one o' them things on. Half on 'em never come home to get it pinned on.'

'Charlie's said something very similar.'

'Aye, he knows it as well as I do.' Her dad nodded to the medal. 'Be sure to show it to t' bairns when they're big enough, won't you?'

'I'll be proud to. What started you thinking about it?'

'Reckon it were what you said, about having my picture taken in uniform for the young 'uns.' He rubbed his neck, as he always did when he felt bashful. 'I never cared much about the thing for my own sake, but after I'm gone it won't matter what I felt, will it? But it'll matter to the next generation that they had a grandad they can feel proud of. Happen they'll treasure it for the sake of that old grandad who loved them, and pass it to their own bairns in their turn.' His brow lowered. 'And I hope none on 'em, Annie's generation or the ones to follow, are called on to fight another war like the two I've been cursed to see. This time, let's hope it's truly an end.'

'I've never heard you talk this way before,' Bobby said.

'What way's that?'

'As if you're... more at peace with yourself. More understanding of the things that happened to you. Is that Maimie Hobbes's doing?'

He smiled. 'Suppose it is. She's a good woman under that mad feathered hat. Knows how to get the best out of me, same as your mam.'

'Oh Lord, the hat,' Bobby said, laughing. 'Will she wear it to the wedding?'

'I told her it's all off if she doesn't,' he said with a grin.

Bobby's gaze drifted back to the medal.

'Thanks, Dad,' she said softly. 'I promise I'll look after it for you – for all of us. I know your grandchildren will be just as proud of you as your children are.' She gave him another hug. 'I hope you and Mrs Ho— Maimie will be very happy together.'

–

'Well that was quite a day,' Charlie said as he and Bobby walked home, Bobby's arm through his and her blackout torch in her other hand. 'You might have to help me to bed. I'm feeling a little... merry.'

'I can tell,' Bobby said, laughing as she stopped him meandering into a ditch.

Their evening at the farmhouse had turned into quite a party. After the men had finished the beer Tony had brought from the Hart, the captain had remembered a bottle of port he'd been given when he left his regiment and gone to fetch it. The girls had been allowed to stay up late, and everyone present had toasted to happiness, marriage and new additions. Bobby hadn't got too 'merry', as Charlie put it, but she had enjoyed seeing her husband being sociable with the other men: cracking jokes, sharing smokes, slapping backs. Tonight, he had seemed like the old Charlie – the carefree lad he had been before he had gone to war.

'We had a little windfall today,' Charlie told her. 'Reggie gave me five pounds to buy things for the baby. That ought to be a big help, don't you think? I can order us a cot tomorrow.'

'That makes two windfalls then,' Bobby said. 'My dad gave us ten pounds as well. He's rather flush after selling our old house in Bradford.'

Bobby had reflected on what her dad had said about the thirty-five pounds, and come to the conclusion it was good advice. She didn't relish keeping secrets from her husband, but a little money Charlie didn't know about could be a big help if an emergency befell them.

'That was what your dad wanted to talk to you about?' Charlie asked.

Bobby thought about the Military Medal, wrapped in newspaper in her handbag. She wanted to think over what her dad had said about his decoration before she talked it over with Charlie.

'Mostly that, yes,' she said.

'Well, then we're quite rich, aren't we, Mrs Atherton?' Charlie said, leaning a little unsteadily to plant a kiss on her cheek. 'Tell you what, why don't we treat ourselves to a night out next week? I'll take you dancing, and when we're tired of that we can go to the pictures. I'll even buy us fish and chips, just like when we were courting.'

'I'd like that,' Bobby said with a smile. 'We ought to be careful with any extra money, though, Charlie. It'll soon go once we start buying everything the baby's going to need. Don't forget the dressing-down you gave me for the sheer extravagance of spending a few bob on tinned peaches and beer for you.'

'Ahhhh, but that was when I was an impoverished jobless waif,' Charlie said with a sweeping gesture, filled with gregariousness and beer. 'I ought to be allowed to take my wife out and enjoy her once in a while. It won't be so easy once the baby comes.'

'True.' Still, Bobby was glad to think of the twenty-five pounds she had hidden away. The fact that Charlie didn't know about it would be an inducement to frugality.

'I suppose you were talking about the magazine when you dragged Reggie off,' Charlie said. 'What did he say?'

She sighed. 'Exactly what I expected. He's determined that if I so much as lift a pen once I've got a baby, Marmaduke will be poking his eye out with scissors or setting fire to his cot. I did think your brother might be willing to at least send a bit of freelance work my way. He says to ask him again when I'm eighty-five and all our great-grandchildren are grown up.'

Charlie slipped his arm around her waist.

'You could bamboozle him,' he said. 'Become Ronald Cosmopolis: freelance writer, gentleman adventurer and all-round man of mystery. I can mail Reggie your articles from Skipton so he won't suspect.'

'Ronald Cosmopolis?' Bobby said, laughing. 'What kind of pseudonym is that?'

'A darn good one. I wish I could be called Ronald Cosmopolis.'

Bobby smiled.

'What are you smirking at, young lady?' Charlie asked, grinning affectionately at her.

'You remind me of someone I used to know, that's all.'

'Old boyfriend?'

'That's right.'

'What was he like?'

'Oh, trouble in trousers. Not bad-looking, I suppose, but far too fond of a pretty girl. Still, he could always make me laugh.'

'Miss him?'

'Sometimes. But I prefer the man I ended up with.' She stood on tiptoes to plant a kiss on the white scar across his cheek. 'Still, it's nice to have the Charlie Atherton I first fell for pay a visit from time to time.'

Charlie smiled. 'Well, what do you think? Is Ronald Cosmopolis going to be making his debut on the pages of *The Tyke* in the near future?'

She sighed. 'It's tempting, but no, I couldn't lie to Reg. I'm just going to have to find something else to do to stop me going mad.'

## Chapter 24

Bobby had worried the time might drag when she was at home all day with nothing to do but scrub and think too much, but the weeks that followed seemed to pass rather quickly. Charlie began his new routine, travelling daily to the bank in Skipton, and things settled into a fresh pattern at Number 4 Church View.

Before Bobby knew it, it was early March – just eleven weeks before they expected to welcome the baby. The days had grown longer and daffodils nodded by the side of the road. It was strange to think that when the trees were once again clothed for summer, she would be a mother.

Bobby got up when Charlie did at 6:30 a.m. – Marmaduke kept up his habit of early rising. She began by making his breakfast, then there was the house to air, grate to sweep, ornaments to polish, lav to scrub, clothes to wash and darn and iron, meals to prepare, and a dozen other jobs that wreaked havoc on her aching back and swollen ankles. In the evenings, her needles clicked away making things for the baby.

Monday was washing day, which left little time for anything else, and Friday was the day Bobby went shopping in Settle. Yet in spite of the many jobs that had to be done, she found she still had a few hours each day to herself. The doctor had urged her to prioritise rest now she was well into the final stage of her pregnancy, but Bobby didn't feel guilty about using the time to write. It wasn't strenuous, and it kept her mind off worry about the birth.

The fact she was still managing to write only made Bobby more irritated when she read *The Tyke* and noted the decline in quality. Tony's work was... well, fine. He wasn't a bad journalist when he committed to doing some work. But he had never really understood what the little magazine was all about, and besides that he was no Dalesman, either by birth or adoption. Circumstances may have dropped him in Silverdale, but Tony Scott was a townie through and through. His articles lacked heart, Bobby felt. The freelance reporters produced good work, but as Bobby knew from her stint as deputy editor, that came at a higher price than using staff writers.

She could do so much better! Reg might at least have considered keeping her on at home until the birth, while there was no baby to care for. What could have been the harm in that?

Bobby had seen a little success in her new endeavour of writing for the wireless, but not enough to compensate for the loss of her work on the magazine. Whenever she had a spare hour, she set herself the same goal: a dozen jokes, which she would aim to sell to one of the radio comics. She didn't confine herself to *ITMA*, but sent material for the attention of all the great and the good – even Arthur Askey, the BBC's golden goose. Sometimes Bobby's letters fell on stony ground, but other times she received a response – occasionally accompanied by a very welcome postal order.

Her success rate, Bobby supposed, was about twenty per cent. If she wrote a dozen gags, perhaps two or three would be considered good enough. Not all the comics paid five bob either. If her work was rejected by Askey or Handley then Bobby might try her luck with one of the up-and-coming names, but from them she would be lucky to get half a crown.

Still, while the money didn't flow in as fast as Bobby might have hoped, it gave her a buzz to hear her work broadcast. The fact it was a secret only added zest. And she was increasing the twenty-five pounds her dad had advised her to put away, little by little. By the time she had passed the seven-month point in her pregnancy, Bobby had earned an additional three pounds for her rainy-day pot. She might have hoped for more, but it wasn't bad for a few hours' work every week.

It also performed a valuable function in occupying her mind. As the date she was due to give birth drew nearer, Bobby was becoming increasingly anxious – almost to the exclusion of everything else. She couldn't help being haunted by that night Lilian had given birth. Lil had nearly lost her life that night, and then there was what had happened to poor Georgia. Writing had become a lifeline to Bobby at a time when her worrisome brain badly needed something to dwell on other than the potential for catastrophe.

Her writing sessions did carry a feeling of guilt, however, that she could derive so much pleasure from them. It made her think of Reg's words the day she had begged him to keep her on: that she'd never fully commit to motherhood while she had half her mind on her job.

It had started Bobby thinking: would she be a good mother? It wasn't something she had questioned before. She had cared for her brothers when they were young, she often minded Annie, and she loved helping Jess and Florrie with their problems. It was the Parrys' presence in her life that had made her realise how much she wanted a child. But her thoughts had always been about herself: how much she wanted to be a mother. She hadn't considered it from the child's point of view. Would it be bad for Marmaduke to have a mother who wanted to do more in her life than care for him? Would he feel neglected, and resent her for it?

And yet Bobby knew she did need more than motherhood. It was frustrating to have the pleasure of creativity swamped by feelings of guilt. She wished she could be like Jolka, who stood defiant as she claimed her right to be more than simply a woman and a mother. Bobby couldn't detach herself from the weight of society's expectations the way her bluestocking friend seemed able to do.

She worried about Charlie too. He had been working at the bank for over a month, but although he rarely complained, Bobby could sense he wasn't entirely happy there.

He seemed to have made his peace with his role, although he would still describe himself as a clerk when asked. He was grateful to be earning a wage, even if the salary wasn't what he had been used to. He admired his boss, Mr Miller.

The big problem, Bobby could tell – and she could tell because she had been in that position herself – was that Charlie was bored. There was little to challenge him in typing and filing. She knew he missed his veterinary work, and would give anything to be able to practise again. Bobby wished there was some miraculous cure for the tremor in his hands, but there wasn't.

The only part of Charlie's new job that produced a spark of interest was learning Pitman's shorthand. Forming the symbols was easier for him than writing longhand, and like Bobby when she had first studied it, he enjoyed feeling he was learning a sort of secret code. One of Bobby's favourite parts of the day was when Charlie asked her to help him in his learning. He would attempt to write her love notes in those strange-looking symbols. Bobby laughed as she corrected them, rewarding him with a kiss for every word he got right.

Today was Friday, Bobby's shopping day. The post hadn't arrived when she left to get the bus into Settle, but there were two letters on the mat when she returned.

One was for Charlie and one for her, both with typewritten addresses, which usually heralded something official. Charlie's letter bore those always significant initials: OHMS.

Could it be about his DFC? He hadn't confided whether he had written again to the Air Ministry now he had a job, turning down the decoration. To be honest, Bobby had forgotten all about it in the flurry of things that had happened recently: leaving her job; her father's wedding to Mrs Hobbes, a low-key affair that had taken place the previous month; helping

Captain Parry with the arrangements for his own wedding in late May. Bobby wondered if Charlie had forgotten too. She put the envelope on top of his newspaper for him.

The name 'Bancroft' caught her eye on the other envelope. That meant it must be from the BBC.

She tore it open, hopeful it might contain another welcome postal order, but there was only a letter.

> *Dear Miss Bancroft,*
> *I have been asked to thank you for sending your work to Mr Jenkins. However, I'm afraid he feels it would not be suitable…*

Bobby didn't bother reading on. It was a standard rejection: she'd had too many like it not to recognise the format. She sighed and stuffed the thing into the pocket of her voluminous maternity housecoat.

It was a shame, though. Bobby had been proud of her last lot of jokes, persuaded they were some of the best she had written. There had been twenty in total, and all of sufficient quality for broadcast, she had felt. Yet not a single joke had met with approval.

Bobby frowned as something in what she had read registered. She pulled the crumpled letter out and looked again at the first line.

> *Dear Miss Bancroft…*

Miss! Why would they address her as Miss? She always sent her work in under a male name.

She took out the envelope. That, too, was addressed to Miss Roberta Bancroft.

Oh Lord. Had she inadvertently signed her real name? Pregnancy did seem to be making her absent-minded.

Well, that accounted for the rejection then. What an idiot! Why hadn't she checked her letter over before sending it off? She could slap herself.

Bobby's irritation with herself quickly shifted to anger with the comic who'd rejected her work, however.

Twenty good jokes, rejected for the utterly ridiculous reason that the brain that had come up with them was lodged inside a woman's head rather than a man's! It was absurd to think someone would rather throw away good work than admit a woman had written it for him. What a world this was.

She couldn't even enjoy a cathartic rant about it to Charlie, since she had kept her joke-writing so deadly secret. She would have to pour out her rage in a letter to Scarlet, and wait until her friend could reply for the soothing, sympathetic words she needed.

She shoved the crumpled letter in the salvage bin rather violently, pushing it under some old newspapers so Charlie wouldn't spot it, then went to lie down. Her back was very sore after a morning of shopping.

Bobby felt tears start to rise at the unfairness of it all. That outlet would be closed to her henceforth, she supposed, now those in charge knew the secret of her sex. No amount of signing herself 'Robert Bancroft' could undo that slip of the pen. She would never sell another joke again.

It wasn't right. Her brain was the same one it had been when they had believed her a man, and her work had been deemed good enough then. Why should this change anything? Men were so proud of being the more logical sex, yet there was no logic to this at all.

She had needed this, damn it! She had lost her job at *The Tyke*, and now it felt like the one thing that had been keeping her going in lieu was being taken away from her.

Bobby had been planning to write that very afternoon. There would have been enough time before she needed to cook the tea to pen a good nine or ten jokes.

But there was no point now. Her gaze landed on her notebook lying on the bedside table, and she swallowed a sob.

Some words of Jolka's came back to her as she lay staring at it.

*You can write for other publications as well as you can write for* The Tyke, *I suppose...*

Which was all very well, but which ones? There wasn't much she knew about apart from life in the Dales, and no magazine other than *The Tyke* would be interested in that. Perhaps she could write about other things — she had briefly been a newspaper reporter, after all — but it was difficult to chase down stories when she was the size of a house.

Bobby's attention was drawn to a periodical under her notebook: not one for adults but a story magazine for children, *The Girl's Own Paper*. Charlie had brought it from Skipton as a present for Florrie, and Bobby had put it by the bed to remind her to give it to Lilian when she saw her.

She slid it out and flicked through.

The stories were just what Bobby had loved when she had been Florrie's age — the sort she had striven to emulate in all her early jottings. Bobby, too, had been an avid reader of *The Girl's Own* when she had been in pinafores and long socks.

Her interest in journalism had been sparked by a piece in that publication, now she came to think of it: an account of the exploits of the woman reporter who had become Bobby's idol, Dorothy Lawrence. But it was fiction stories that had been her first love, and made her dream of a writing career.

The tales in *The Girl's Own* were filled with action, usually featuring a plucky heroine uncovering a mystery, winning a hockey match for her school, taking first place at a gymkhana or — in these days of war — bringing down Nazis. Tales with titles like 'Susan of St Agatha's', 'The Cravensdale Mystery' and 'Jane Does the Job'. Bobby spent an informative hour reading the magazine from cover to cover.

*People before things*, Reg had always told her — that was what made for a compelling magazine article. Bobby was sure it applied as much to fiction as non-fiction. That was why there was so often a Jane or a Susan in the titles of these tales — because it told readers that here they would find a friend, someone they could aspire to emulate. More importantly, it told them that here was someone *just like them*. If you could craft a heroine readers could root for, she would carry the story on her back.

Bobby put the magazine aside and reached for her pen.

## Chapter 25

By the time she needed to start cooking tea, Bobby had covered several pages of her notebook.

What she had produced was a more mature version of the stories she'd written in childhood. It drew heavily on her experience in the Women's Auxiliary Air Force. Bobby was a little worried it might be too similar to a story *The Girl's Own* had already serialised, 'Worrals of the WAAF', but since she had little other experience to draw upon as the basis of a thrilling adventure story, she had decided to stick with what she knew.

Besides, her WAAF heroine – Lindy Langstaff, Bobby had named her – wasn't much like well-to-do Worrals. She was from a more humble background for a start, which Bobby hoped would make her relatable to girls from lower-class families. She well remembered how she had longed to read about girls like herself as a child, rather than the plummy heroines she seemed to encounter in every tale. She had also drawn on her experience in The Flying Aces concert party and given Lindy theatrical aspirations.

The story dealt with Lindy using her experience as a ventriloquist to outwit a Nazi paratrooper, throwing her voice in order to lure him to her commanding officer. Of course, the CO then rewarded the plucky teenage airwoman with instant promotion. Bobby smiled as she thought how her ventriloquist friend Ellis would appreciate that. She had tried to infuse her story with humour too, which she modestly felt she wrote well.

Bobby had no idea if the story was any good, but writing it had significantly improved her spirits. For so long, writing had been something she had done as part of her job, always striving to earn the approval of those above her – whether that meant Reg Atherton, Don Sykes or the nobs at the BBC. This was the first time in ages that Bobby had written something solely to please herself.

It had been enormously satisfying to lose herself in the world she had created. Stuck in the house as she had been since passing the six-month point in her pregnancy, sighing as she watched the fells putting on their spring garb through the window, it had been liberating to join Lindy for her adventures. Even if, when she read it back, Bobby felt the story wasn't something *The Girl's Own* could be interested in, she felt she was now in a state of mind to bite her thumb at the BBC brass with aplomb.

Her sex wouldn't count against her with the *Girl's Own* editress. There were a few male authors who contributed, but the majority of its stories were written by women. She could abandon subterfuge, submit material under her own name and experience the pleasure of seeing that name printed under the story's title – if, of course, the story was deemed good enough. Many writers for the periodical were professional authors, like Captain W. E. Johns, the creator of Biggles, who wrote the Worrals stories. That was some stiff competition. But the magazine did have a wide pool of contributors, not all of whom were famous names, and after all, she was a professional writer. Bobby decided that she would read her story back with fresh eyes after a few days, and if she felt it had a future, she would take a chance and send it in.

By the time Charlie arrived home, Bobby was in the kitchen, humming merrily as she stirred a pan of stew.

'You sound happy,' Charlie said when he came in, wrapping his arms around her sizeable belly and kissing her neck.

'I am,' Bobby said, rather surprised to find this was true. Whether her story was accepted for publication or not, writing it had done wonders for her spirits. Not to mention that her brain had been kept too busy to let her worry about the imminent delivery of her baby once.

Of course this immediately brought on the familiar feeling of guilt about the pleasure she had got from writing, losing herself in it to the exclusion of thoughts of her child.

'Really, you're not worrying about anything today?' Charlie said. 'Are you sure you're my wife?'

'Well, I never said I wasn't worrying about anything.'

'Go on, what is it this time?'

Bobby turned to face him. 'Charlie, do you think I'll be a good mam?'

'If I didn't, I'd hardly allow you to carry my baby. I don't think you've ever thanked me for that, by the way.'

She smiled. 'You're all heart. I mean it though. Do you think I will?'

'Don't be daft. You'll be the best mam there is. Why, do you think you might have suppressed Fagin tendencies and set Marmaduke to work stealing hankies as soon as he can walk?'

'It's something your brother said to me, I suppose. About how I could never be a good mother while I had my mind on work.'

Charlie frowned. 'Reggie didn't say that, did he?'

'Not exactly, but that's what my brain filed away. I worry that because I do want to do things other than be a mother, it means I won't be able to do it well.' She looked up at him. 'But I do need more, Charlie, the same way you do. That isn't wrong, is it?'

'Of course it isn't. Reggie's talking out of his hat. Didn't you tell me your mam worked in the mills nearly all your childhood?'

'That's right, and took in washing when she wasn't able to. A lot of mothers down our way worked after having families. They had to.'

'So she must've been a bad mother then.'

'She was not,' Bobby said, glaring at him. 'I'd never have been the person I am without my mam to tell me I could make something of myself. She was an incredible woman. The best mother there was.'

'And so is her daughter an incredible woman who'll be the best mother there is. I don't know why you listen to Reggie's Victorian nonsense when you've got your own mother to inspire you.'

Bobby smiled. 'All right, clever clogs. That was a devious way to make a point, getting me all cross.'

'But it worked, and now you're smiling again.'

She gave him a kiss and turned to stir her stew.

'What's brought on the good mood then?' Charlie asked, resting his chin on her shoulder.

Bobby wished she could confide in him about the story she had written. She would love to have him read it, but she was still determined to keep her writing endeavours secret until the time felt right. She wanted to see if she would have any success submitting to *The Girl's Own* before she said anything.

'Going out shopping, I suppose,' she said, grimacing slightly at the fib. 'Not that there's much fun in queuing forever and eternally, but I do get sick of being in the house.'

'You should ask Mary or your sister to pick up our rations now you're seven months gone. The doctor says you oughtn't to be on your feet too much. And suppose Marmaduke decides to arrive early and you give birth in the middle of the grocer's?'

'Please, Charlie, don't take this away from me. It's the only freedom I still have. I swear I'm about to start talking to the faces in the wallpaper, stuck indoors constantly.'

'What faces in the wallpaper?'

'Exactly.' Bobby sighed. 'It was lovely seeing all the spring flowers starting to appear. I wish I could get out more to enjoy them.'

'I wonder when we can go up into the fells again,' Charlie said dreamily. 'Every time I see Dick Minchin, I ask if he thinks my leg's recovered enough to do a little modest hiking. I hardly need to use my stick any more. But it's always "Soon, Charlie, soon."'

'I doubt I'm going to be able to make it to the peak of Great Bowside for a while yet,' Bobby said, putting her hands over his on her stomach. 'I'm surprised you can still wrap your arms around me.'

He turned her around to kiss her. 'You're beautiful.'

'I'm huge.'

'Well, yes, but I like that in a wife. Makes me feel I'm getting my money's worth.'

Bobby smiled. 'Tea's nearly ready. How was work, love?'

He sighed. 'Humiliating.'

'Why, what happened?'

'Ugh. Bill Lawrence came in for an appointment with Miller. He wants to arrange a mortgage so he can move his practice to bigger premises.'

'Why should that be humiliating?'

'It's humiliating when I've told everyone I'm a clerk and Bill finds me taking dictation. He just had this expression on his face, you know? Like "how the mighty have fallen".' Charlie rested his forehead against hers. 'We always had a healthy rivalry when we were running neighbouring veterinary practices, and now I have to see that look of pity where there used to be respect.'

'I'm sure there wasn't anything of that nature. Bill knows why you had to stop practising. That alone merits his respect.'

'Perhaps it was my imagination, but I couldn't help feeling that way.' He closed his eyes. 'And then there was Phil Reynolds.'

'Who?'

'A farmer from Skipton way I know a little. He came into the bank today too. He didn't know I'd left the Air Force. Of course, the first thing he wanted to know after we'd exchanged "good mornings" was why.'

'What did you tell him?'

'That they'd invalided me out. Phil took one look at me trembling and drew his own conclusions.' Charlie laughed bleakly. 'Didn't even shake my hand. No doubt it's all over Skipton by now that the RAF kicked me out as an LMF case.'

Bobby felt her protective hackles rise. She scowled at the unknown Farmer Reynolds.

What right did this man have to judge Charlie when he knew nothing of his injuries? When he had no idea of the horrors her husband had seen, or the friends he'd lost? And that went for Bill Lawrence too, if he'd really dared to show Charlie pity. It was easy for men in reserved occupations to stand in judgement, when they got to remain safe at home.

It made her wish Charlie would accept the DFC, and wear it with pride. Then men like Phil Reynolds would be forced to acknowledge him a hero. She knew it was no good saying this to him, though. He would rather accept Reynolds' sneers than exploit his decoration to score points.

'I know I ought to be grateful to have a job,' Charlie said. 'And I am, Bob, honestly. The work's not exactly enthralling but it's comfortable. But when someone turns up from my old world, it does bring it home that this is a long way from what I wanted to be doing with my life.'

'Oh Charlie, I'm sorry.'

'Well, one good thing came of it. After Bill had seen Miller, he stopped to pass the time of day and I asked if he'd have any interest in those instruments. I've been trying to get hold of him for ages.'

'And he did?'

'No, but he told me there's a friend of his son's from veterinary college who's opening a new practice ten miles away – Roger Turner. He's starting from scratch so he'll need a full set of everything. Bill thinks he'll take the lot.'

'That's good news. When will you see him?'

'Bill gave me his number and I rang him from the box outside the bank. I'm meeting him in the Hart Tuesday week,' Charlie told her. 'Do you think your sister would mind me taking him round? I doubt he'll agree a price without seeing the condition.'

'I'm sure she won't, if it means there's the chance of an extra room,' Bobby said with a smile. 'Annie's finally got her nursery now my dad's moved out, but I know Lil's dying for somewhere to hide the clothes horses. I'll ask for you.' She kissed his nose. 'Now sit down and rest your leg. I'll serve up in ten minutes.'

'All right.'

'Oh,' Bobby said as he turned to leave. 'There's a letter on the coffee table. OHMS.'

Charlie frowned. 'OHMS?'

'I'm afraid so. Could it be about the DFC?'

He sighed. 'I should open it and find out, I suppose. I thought once I left the RAF, I'd never have to see that miserable set of letters ever again. Some hope.'

Bobby found Charlie looking rather grim when she entered the parlour to let him know his stew was ready. The letter lay open on the table.

'Well, what is it?' she asked.

'You're right, it is about that ruddy gong. They want me to be invested at Buckingham Palace in seven weeks' time.'

Bobby perched on the arm of his chair. 'Will you go?'

'I don't know, Bob. Honestly, I'd forgotten I ever said I'd take it.'

'You could change your mind. Now you're in work, you don't need it to impress employers with. Although it might help if you decided to look for something else.'

'Hmm. I'd rather stay where I am than brag about my feats of so-called heroism to get me into something better.' Charlie eyed the letter listlessly. 'But I suppose it's too late now to turn it down. I'll write and say I can't attend the investiture though. They can post it to me if they must, then I can stick it in a drawer and forget all about it.'

Bobby stretched an arm around his shoulders. 'Are you sure you don't want to go, love? It's the sort of opportunity that comes along once in a lifetime. Having your photograph taken with the king and everything. The village would be so proud, and your family and the girls. Wouldn't you like that?'

Charlie scowled. 'What do you think?'

'No, I suppose not,' Bobby said with a sigh.

'I'd feel like the biggest fraud alive, standing there with the king like a genuine hero. No, Bobby. I couldn't.'

Bobby thought about what her dad had said, the day he'd given her his Military Medal. How he had felt similar about his own prestigious decoration, but that in the end it hadn't been about him. It had been about his legacy to his grandchildren.

'It would be an incredible thing to show Marmaduke when he's old enough,' Bobby said. 'For me too. I'd be as proud as anything.' She looked at his grim expression. 'But it's up to you, Charlie.'

'I couldn't go even if I was minded to.'

'Surely Mr Miller would grant you a holiday for something so important.'

'Not because of Miller, because of you,' Charlie said with a small smile. 'I promised I wouldn't leave you until after the birth and I meant it, Bob. If the king's so desperate to meet me, he's welcome to hop in his golden coach and come up to Silverdale. I'll even stand him a pint at the pub.'

'But you wouldn't be leaving me, would you? I'd be coming too.'

'What?'

'You think I'd stay at home while you were being decorated by the king? I'm not going to miss that, even if I do have to look like a sack of flour for it.'

'Don't be daft. You couldn't travel to London that close to the birth. What if the baby comes in the middle of the ceremony? Are you planning to ask the queen to midwife for you?'

Bobby smiled. 'I won't be that close to the birth. If it's in seven weeks, that means there'll be a whole month until Marmaduke's due to put in an appearance. I'll check it's all right with Dr Minchin, but I'm sure it wouldn't be dangerous.'

'I'm serious. What if you went into labour early?'

'There's a slim chance, I suppose, but I guess they have maternity hospitals in London too. I'll keep my legs crossed for the investiture.'

'All right, and what if there's an air raid?'

'There hasn't been a proper blitz for ages, just nuisance raids. I'm willing to take a risk.'

Their conversation was interrupted by a knock at the door.

Charlie frowned. 'You're not expecting anyone, are you?'

'It'll be one of the family, I suppose. I'll get it.'

Bobby eased herself to her feet and went to answer it.

'Heyup, Bob,' the young man on the doorstep said.

Bobby stared at her youngest brother, who was in his battle-dress uniform with a bag over one shoulder. 'Jake! What on earth are you doing here?'

'Got some leave, didn't I?' He blinked at her well-rounded belly. 'Flaming Nora, you're huge.'

'But what're you... when did you... oh goodness. Why don't you write and say you're coming, you ass?'

He shrugged. 'Thought I'd surprise you. Aren't you pleased to see me?'

'Where are you staying?' Bobby asked, ignoring this question for the moment.

'Well, here.'

She blinked. 'Here?'

'That's all right, isn't it?'

'There isn't much room, Jake. You'd be better off with Lil, or Dad.'

'Lil's got the baby, and I don't want to bother Dad and his new missus. Don't worry, I can bed down in the living room.'

Bobby tried to gather her wits after her brother's unexpected appearance.

'You'd better come in,' she said. 'We were just going to eat. Lucky I cooked enough for two days.'

'Hang on. Brought someone to meet you.'

Jake beckoned to someone standing out of sight. A young woman appeared at his side, smiling shyly.

'Um, how do you do?' she said to Bobby, in a lilting Irish accent.

Jake put a proud arm around her. 'This is Kathleen, my girl. Kath, this is my big sister Bobby – my very big sister at the moment. That ought to give the two of you summat to talk about, any road.'

But Bobby was too flabbergasted to say hello. All she could do was stare at the girl's round belly, almost as big as her own.

## Chapter 26

'Oh my word!' Bobby stared at the girl's stomach.

'Aye, all right, you can give me a sermon later,' Jake said. 'Can we come in or what, Bob? Cold out here.'

'Um, yes,' Bobby said. 'Yes, come in, both of you.'

She ushered them into the parlour. Charlie looked up from his newspaper.

'Hullo, Jake. Didn't expect to see you today.'

'All right?' Jake went to shake Charlie's hand before guiding Kathleen to the fire.

Charlie didn't seem nearly as dazed at the unexpected appearance of his brother-in-law as Bobby, although his eyes, too, flickered to Kathleen's stomach.

'This your young lady?' he said.

'Aye.' Jake regarded Kathleen proudly. 'Soon to be my missus. Kathleen Brady.'

Charlie stood up to present the girl with his hand, and she shook it shyly.

'You're very welcome, Miss Brady. And congratulations.' He glanced at her stomach. 'Double congratulations, it seems. Can I get you both a cup of something?'

'Thank you,' Kathleen said in her soft voice. 'I'd love a cup of tea, if it wouldn't be too much trouble.'

'I'll make it. Charlie, go and have your stew in the kitchen.' Bobby, who had recovered her equilibrium finally, shook her brother's fiancée's hand as Charlie disappeared to have his tea. 'I'm sorry, you must think I'm frightfully rude. It was only the surprise of seeing my no-good baby brother. Welcome to our home, Kathleen.'

'It's a lovely place you have,' the girl said politely.

'Thank you. Now I wonder if you wouldn't mind covering your ears?'

Kathleen blinked. 'Covering my ears?'

'Yes. I need to say a few words to our Jake that I'm afraid are going to turn the air rather blue.' Bobby spun to face Jake, who was scuffing his feet as he awaited the earful he knew was coming his way. 'What the hell do you think you're playing at? I've barely had a line from you for months, then you turn up with a fiancée you haven't told us about and a baby on the way? Dad's going to play pop.'

'Why do you think I came to your place?' Jake said, with an attempt at a grin. 'Look, can you save it, Bob? I'm knackered. You can tell me off when I've had some sleep.'

He did look tired, and haggard too. It had been some time since Bobby had seen her youngest sibling. Now she examined him properly, the change in his appearance was rather shocking. He had lost weight, she was sure. Although his face was still boyish, his eyes seemed to carry more than their twenty-one years.

It reminded her that the war on the home front could do as much damage to a man as the battlefields of Europe and Africa. Months of defusing bombs had clearly taken their toll on her little brother.

'Come and sit down,' she said in a softer voice. 'How long are you both here for?'

'Three days.'

'As long as that?' Bobby rubbed her head. 'Lord knows where I'm going to put you, but we'll make it work somehow. I'll have to go into town again tomorrow and see what food I can get. You'd better give me your ration card.'

Jake grimaced as he sat down. 'Forgot it. Sorry.'

'Oh, you are hopeless. I thought they gave you one with your leave pass.'

'They did, but I left it somewhere. It don't matter, I don't eat much these days.'

'Well you ought to. You're as skinny as a rake. I'll have to see about fattening you up before I send you back.'

'I've got my book,' Kathleen said. She took it from her handbag and handed it to Bobby. 'Sorry to be so much trouble to you, Miss. Jake said it would be all right if we stayed here.'

Bobby smiled as she put the ration book away. 'It's Bobby, not Miss. Don't worry, love, no one's blaming you.' She sat down by Jake and ruffled his hair. 'I'm blaming this one. Still, it's good to see you, Jake, even if you are a… but I won't go into that. You know what you are.'

'We can stay then?' he asked.

'I'm not going to throw you out into the street, am I?' She glanced at Kathleen. 'I'll have to think about sleeping arrangements though. What possessed you to just turn up?'

'We needed your help.' Jake beamed at his fiancée. 'We've come to get married. I thought you and Lil could help us sort it out.'

Bobby pressed her forehead. 'You're wanting to arrange a wedding on this leave? In three days? Oh my word.'

'Well, we need to do it fast, don't we?'

Bobby glanced at Kathleen's swollen stomach. 'So I see.'

'Look, we meant to do it properly. Have the wedding first and that. But the army wouldn't let me out for it, so… things ended up sort of the wrong way round.'

Jake looked so genuinely puzzled as to how this could have happened that Bobby couldn't help a smile.

'I'll make your tea,' she said, heading to the kitchen.

Charlie was seated at the table, finishing a bowl of stew.

'Well this is a turn-up,' he said quietly.

'You're telling me,' Bobby muttered back. 'Honestly, I don't know whether to hug the lad or strangle him.'

'He looks like he needs the hug more. Poor kid.'

'I know, he looks dreadful. I suppose you heard all that about the wedding, did you?'

'I did. Why would he come to you?'

'Me and Lil did our share of raising him,' Bobby said, rubbing her forehead. 'He was a bairn when our mam got ill. I suppose it's natural he'd look to us when he needed help.'

'Not to your dad?'

'Their relationship's always been a bit strained. Jake found it hard to understand why Dad was… the way he was. Struggled to respect him.' She shook her head. 'Honestly, could he not send a ruddy telegram to say he was coming? Where on earth are they going to sleep?'

'They'll have to bed down in the parlour.'

'They can't share, can they? They're not married yet.'

Charlie laughed. 'She must be six months pregnant, Bobby.'

'I suppose so,' Bobby conceded. 'Still, I'd like to do things properly until after the wedding. She ought not to sleep on the floor in her condition anyway. She'll have to share with me and you can sleep in the parlour with Jake.' She pressed her aching temples. 'I can't imagine how I'm to feed them. Typical of the boy to forget his ration card. And how can we arrange a wedding at this short notice?'

'Registrars are used to last-minute arrangements these days. We'll take them into Skipton tomorrow. I'll go to the registry and organise it while you hunt down provisions.'

Bobby glanced through the door at her brother, who was sitting with Kathleen on his lap. 'I'd be minded to give him a serious ticking-off about getting that poor girl into trouble if he didn't look so awful. But he's trying to do the right thing.'

'You can tell he thinks the world of her.' Charlie got up and gave her a kiss. 'And since I feel much the same about my own wife, I'm going to insist she eats her stew while I brew the tea.'

'Yes, I ought to eat.' Bobby rubbed her eyes. 'I dread to think what our Lil's going to make of all this.'

Bobby slept badly that night. She found it hard to relax, sleeping beside a stranger.

Kathleen was a quiet sleeper, but this only made things worse. Bobby had grown used to Charlie's restlessness. The lack of movement felt eerie, now. She listened carefully for any sound from the parlour to indicate her husband was having an unsettled night, but she couldn't hear anything. Charlie's nightmares were different from her father's: more a quiet whimpering than outright screams.

Oh God, her father. He would have to be told about this. Rob's relationship with Jake had always been difficult, but Bobby would like Kathleen to be welcomed into the family properly. There was also the thirty-five pounds her dad had put aside for his youngest child. The lad had more important things to spend it on now than his Triumph motorcycle. She made a mental note to send a message to Lilian tomorrow, and enlist her help.

—

By 9 a.m., Bobby, Charlie and the prospective newlyweds were in Skipton. Bobby hadn't neglected to send a note to Lil via Gil Capstick, explaining that Jake had turned up for some leave and to call round later.

'You three had better get to the registry and find out what you need to do,' Bobby said. 'Don't wait for me after, just get the bus back. I'll head home once I've scoured the shops for supplies.'

'Don't you need witnesses though?' Jake said. 'You'd better come with us, Bob, in case you have to sign owt.'

Bobby was surprised her eternally clueless little brother was even this well-informed about weddings.

'I doubt they'll be able to do it today, Jake,' she said. 'You have to get a licence first. Once you've got that, you can arrange the ceremony when you're next able to get leave.'

He shook his head. 'We want it done right away. Don't we, Kath?'

The girl nodded. 'I don't want my baby born without a father. My family wouldn't ever speak to me again. They're strict Catholics.'

'They don't know you're engaged?' Bobby asked.

'No. I came over here to go into service, but I lost my job last month.'

'The toffs she worked for gave Kath her ticket when they noticed… well, you know,' Jake said, looking rather guilty. 'I've been supporting her on my pay, but a guinea a week don't go far. I'll get more once we're married.'

'And if I have the baby here then, um…' Kathleen flushed. 'Well, there'd be no need for my mam and da to know we didn't do things proper. I'm of age.'

'We'll do everything we can,' Charlie said. 'Let's start with buying the licence. You'll need the special one for servicemen if you want a wedding this weekend.'

'Buying?' Jake cast a worried look at his bride. 'Here, does it cost money to get married? I spent all I had getting us here.'

'Never mind the money. You can owe it us.' Bobby gave him a kiss, and one for Kathleen. 'Once you're safely married, we can spend your next leave celebrating. But for now, just try and get yourselves wed, all right?'

Bobby left them to walk to the register office while she went to scour the shops. It had been slim pickings in Settle yesterday. She was hoping there might be a wider selection in the bigger town.

As it happened, she did rather well. The greengrocer had not only carrots and potatoes but that rare thing, an onion. Bobby hadn't used up any cheese yet and she had Kathleen's book to get another portion, which ought to make a decent supper of Welsh rarebit with fried onion.

But her real lucky find was in the butcher's. Bobby and Charlie were registered at the butcher's in Settle for their rations, but she'd entered with the forlorn hope the Skipton butcher might have an off-the-ration oxtail to sell her. It was the butcher's wife who had been behind the counter, however, and she had taken pity on the heavily pregnant woman struggling around town with her shopping. With a wink she had produced two sausages from under the counter, and sold them for thruppence each. Half a sausage with their rarebits would be a treat indeed.

Bobby felt weary after making her purchases, and her ankles had swollen painfully. She was hobbling in the direction of a bench when a Canadian voice hailed her. She turned to see Ernie King, jogging to catch her up.

'Oh. Hello, Ernie.' Bobby felt suddenly very conscious of her bloated figure, her ugly swollen ankles and the unbecoming maternity dress she was wearing. She hadn't seen her friend since she had been forced to abandon her pre-pregnancy wardrobe. No doubt she looked a fright, especially compared to the Dorothy Lamour lookalike Ernie was engaged to. He beamed at her like old times, however.

'Here, give me that,' he said, taking the basket. 'A man can't let the mother of his godchild lug heavy baskets around.'

'It isn't that heavy.'

'Baloney. Now, take my arm. Where are you headed?'

'I was going to find a bench. I'm rather tired.'

'I don't wonder,' he said, glancing at her stomach. 'You're huge, Slacks.'

'I wish people would stop telling me that,' Bobby said impatiently. 'I know I'm huge. I've never felt huger in my life. Everywhere I turn, there's some man waiting to tell me what a great ugly lump I am.' She rubbed her head. 'Ugh, sorry. I had a bad night's sleep.'

'You're right, it wasn't very chivalrous. You look great, kid.' Since Bobby had ignored the instruction to take his arm, Ernie did it for her, tucking it through his. 'What's been keeping you awake? Has my godchild been kicking you?'

It made Bobby smile to hear his repeated use of 'godchild'. He swelled every time he said it.

'No, unexpected visitors,' she told him. 'My brother turned up to pay his wedding visit.'

Bobby chose not to mention that the wedding was yet to come rather than in the past, in case Jake and Kathleen should be spotted in the village.

'In that case, congratulations to your brother.' Ernie guided her to a bench opposite the Plaza cinema. 'Here, rest up a minute.'

She flashed him a weary smile. 'Thanks. When is your wedding to be? I'm still waiting to meet this girl of yours.'

He shrugged. 'Everything in its season, as the Good Book has it. Seems hard to ask a girl to tie herself to me when I never know if I'll be coming back. If I get through this tour, perhaps.'

Bobby examined his face. Ernie looked wistful behind the broad grin, and there were heavy bags under his eyes. In fact he looked more exhausted than she did.

'You've been working too hard, Ernie,' she said gently. 'What is it they've got you on? The Ruhr?'

'Not sure I'm allowed to tell but yeah, I've been flying a lot. Nearly every night.'

'You must be wiped out.'

His gaze was blank as he stared ahead. 'You know, Slacks, I do a roll call in my head when I'm in bed. The name of every guy I've met since we started this thing who's gone – I memorised them all, so they weren't forgotten. The list's so long now that I'm always asleep before I get to the end. It's as good as counting sheep.'

The mingled expression of grief, defiance and exhaustion was too familiar. Bobby had seen it on Charlie's face, and on dozens of airmen who had been in the privileged yet often deadly position of being selected as aircrew.

'And Chip last of all,' she said softly.

He gave a bleak laugh. 'You'd think, but no. We're dying like swatted flies up there. Two more pals gone since Chip's Lanky came down.'

'Poor Ernie,' Bobby said with a sigh. 'Poor all of you. I wish there was something I could do.'

He summoned a smile. 'Sorry, kid, didn't mean to go all morbid on you. Can't help feeling like there's been some terrible mistake is all, that I'm still around when so many are gone. Especially these days, when it seems to be op after op. Butcher Harris isn't letting up at the moment.'

'You must have a guardian angel.'

'Then that means someone must be remembering me in her prayers,' he said, squeezing her shoulder. 'Where do you need to be now, Bobby? I don't like to leave you here.'

'If you don't mind walking me to the bus stop, I'd be glad of your company and basket-carrying services.'

Ernie helped her to her feet and hooked her arm through his. They were about to set off when Bobby's attention was caught by someone emerging from the cinema. She instantly recognised the clipped moustache, pipe and flaming red hair as belonging to George Parry. His hair alone made him a hard man to miss.

Bobby was surprised to see him in town, and by himself. She had seen the Parry girls a few days ago, and had understood their father had a date arranged with Miss Simpson after today's shift at the department store. This information had been accompanied with the customary grimaces and eye-rolls from Florrie and Jess, who were still struggling to warm to their father's fiancée.

A moment later, however, a woman emerged to join him.

So he was on a date after all. Bobby wondered why the captain would bring his young lady out to Skipton when there were many more cinemas in Bradford.

'Who is it, Slacks?' Ernie asked, squinting to see what she was looking at. The sun was in their eyes, and Bobby, too, had to squint to see properly.

'George Parry and his fiancée,' she told him. 'I suppose I ought to go and say—'

But Bobby stopped short as the sun disappeared behind a cloud, and she was able to get a better look at the woman with Captain Parry.

Because of course, the woman who had accompanied the captain to the cinema wasn't Miss Simpson. It was Lilian.

## Chapter 27

Bobby quickly dragged Ernie away, hoping he wouldn't notice anything amiss. She managed to make polite conversation until her bus arrived, but her brain was awash with concern for her sister.

Lil had been adamant that there was nothing untoward in her relationship with the captain. Despite Bobby's qualms, no one else in the family seemed to think there was anything improper about it. Even Tony, a jealous husband if ever there was one, didn't suspect anything.

Why? Bobby knew it wasn't really about Lilian. It was because the captain – officer, war hero, fond father, model of an old-fashioned English gentleman – seemed in every way above reproach. Even after seeing what she had seen with her own eyes, Bobby could hardly believe that George Parry would pursue a married woman.

It had worried her enough when she had spotted the two of them in Settle, talking so earnestly, but Lilian had sounded genuine when she had told Bobby she'd been advising the captain on engagement rings. But the pictures – that was different, wasn't it? Bobby would need to be delusional in the extreme to persuade herself that Lil and George must have run into each other there coincidentally. True, they hadn't looked exactly cosy, but they had without a doubt been at the place together. What else was she supposed to think, except… but even now, Bobby wasn't ready to give a name to what she thought.

Oh, she could curse her family today! It felt like every time something went right with them – Charlie's new job, Marmaduke, her father's marriage to Mrs Hobbes – something else went wrong to balance it out. The doctor had said she must try to avoid shocks at this stage in her pregnancy, and here was her little brother turning up out of the blue with a pregnant Irish Catholic girl while her twin sister was sneaking around with another man behind her husband's back.

'Take care of yourself, Slacks,' Ernie said as he handed Bobby on to the bus. 'Keep me in your prayers.'

'Hmm?' Bobby roused herself. 'Oh. Yes. I will, Ernie.'

'See you soon, OK? Look after that godkid of mine.'

Bobby managed a smile, although she was a million miles away.

When Ernie had gone, she paid her fare and went to sit at the back. She had no energy for small talk if a neighbour were to get on. At the back, she could slump down in her seat and hopefully stay unnoticed until it was time to get off.

She almost slid right off her seat, however, when her sister and Captain Parry got on at the very next stop. They didn't notice Bobby, hiding at the back. She watched to see how the pair would behave together.

They weren't touching – in fact almost suspiciously so. Any man who possessed a degree of chivalry would hand a woman to her seat on an unsteady bus, even if she were a stranger. The captain didn't. He seemed to be consciously maintaining a degree of distance from his companion.

'I had a wonderful time,' he said in a low voice.

Lilian smiled, but she didn't speak.

'Lilian, I wish it didn't have to be this way.'

'So do I, George,' she said quietly. 'But it does. Give Veronica my regards, won't you?'

'I'll be sure to do so. Thank you again for your company.'

And that was it. The captain left Lil and went to sit at the front. The two didn't so much as look at one another for the rest of the trip. George got off at the stop before the one closest to Silverdale, as if anxious they shouldn't be seen walking into the village together. Lilian, Bobby assumed, would get off at the Bull.

She didn't know what to make of it. If it was an affair, it seemed a rather odd one. It reminded her of that Fred Astaire song, 'A Fine Romance'. Like the couple in the song, Lil and George had hardly seemed overcome by passion. Nor were mistresses known for sending good wishes to their lovers' wives on parting.

When their stop approached, Bobby let Lilian stand up first before following with her shopping basket. She tapped her sister on the shoulder.

'Oh!' Lilian patted her heart. 'Bobby. You gave me the fright of my life.'

'Mmm, I bet.'

'Where did you spring from? Were you hiding under the seats?'

'I was at the back.' Bobby glanced at the driver as they slowed to a stop. 'We'll talk when we get off.'

They alighted and the bus drove away.

'We can hitch a ride with Bert in the coal wagon,' Lilian said, a rather forced brightness in her tone. 'You ought not to walk. It isn't good for you in your condition.'

'Do you know what's not good for me in my condition?' Bobby said. 'Sudden shocks and surprises.'

'Yes, I got your note about Jake turning up. You ought to have sent him to us. He can sleep in the nursery if we bring Annie's cot into our room. Do you want me to take him tonight?'

Bobby glared at her. 'You can jolly well stop trying to change the subject, Lilian Scott. That wasn't the shock I was referring to and you know it.'

Lilian sighed. 'You saw then.'

'I did, and it's no use trying to tell me to mind my own business.' She folded her arms. 'What's going on, Lil? You swore to me there was nothing between you two.'

'There isn't. I mean... look, it isn't what you think.' Lilian glanced round at the sound of the coalman's horse and cart trundling towards them. 'We'll get a lift to your cottage, then I swear I'll tell you everything. But don't be all cross and Bobby about it, will you?'

'I'm making no promises until I know what there is to be cross and Bobby about.' She lowered her voice as Lil flagged down the cart. 'I only hope you know what you're getting yourself into, that's all.'

—

As soon as the cottage door had closed behind them, Bobby turned to her sister.

'Well?' she demanded.

'Can't I at least put the kettle on?'

'There isn't time. Charlie might be back any minute with Jake and Kathleen, the girl he brought. I want to hear all about it while we're able to talk freely.'

Lilian frowned. 'Our Jake brought a girl?'

'Never mind Jake. You're not going to distract me, Lil. Tell me about you and George Parry.'

Lilian sighed. 'Sit down first. You must want to get the weight off your feet.'

'Well, all right,' Bobby said grudgingly. 'But no making a bolt for it. If I have to lock you in to get the story out of you, I will.'

Bobby sat on the settee and Lilian, smiling, sat beside her.

'I pity poor Marmaduke, being born to such a terrifying specimen of a mother. I dread to think how you'll be when the poor boy starts taking out girls.'

Bobby opened her mouth, but Lil raised a hand.

'All right, I'm telling you,' she said. 'It really isn't as bad as it looks.'

'I saw you coming out of the cinema, Lil. How can that possibly not be as bad as it looks?'

Lilian frowned. 'Have you been following us?'

'No. I was shopping.'

'Friday's your shopping day.'

'That was before our Jake turned up without his ration card and his ribs showing,' Bobby said. 'I popped in to see what extras I could pick up, then I bumped into Ernie King and he insisted I have a sit-down opposite the cinema.'

Lilian examined her with concern. 'You do look tired. Are you getting enough rest?'

Bobby glared at her. 'That's neither here nor there. What had you been doing at the pictures?'

'Watching Gary Cooper in *Pride of the Yankees*.'

'All right, and what else?'

'That's it.' Lilian shuffled to look into her eyes. 'That really is it, Bobby. I know what it must look like, but I swear that man has never so much as held my hand. We're friends, that's all. Just… good friends.'

Bobby shook her head. 'Friends don't go to the cinema. Lovers go to the cinema.'

'Don't be daft. Friends go to the cinema all the time.'

'Not when one's a man and the other's a woman. Especially not an engaged man and a married woman.'

Lilian turned away, scowling. 'Honestly, I can't believe you sometimes. Who did you say you were with when you saw us?'

'Ernie King.'

'Arm in arm, I suppose?'

'Only because I was weak,' Bobby said, flushing. 'That's what any gentleman would do.'

'But he's not your husband, is he? It wasn't so long ago he wanted to marry you.'

Bobby laughed. 'He's unlikely to swing me on to a stallion and ride off into the sunset with me now, is he? He'd damage his back.'

'If people saw you arm in arm, there'd be talk.'

'I'm seven months pregnant, Lil.'

'Which is exactly what there'd be talk about. Why am I always getting the lectures while you act like you're the respectable one? You're not Mam.'

'You know it isn't the same. There wasn't anything secretive in my meeting Ernie. He just happened to be there.'

'Isn't it the same?' Lilian demanded. 'How many times have you been to the pub with one of your men friends, just the two of you? Even married men, like Don Sykes?' She was glowering now. 'And am I to be denied the one thing that truly makes me happy? The one thing that makes it worthwhile getting out of bed each morning? Why must it be one rule for me and another for you?'

'You can't compare this to my relationship with Don. He's never behaved in any way that wasn't brotherly. He doesn't give me fur coats and knicker elastic for presents either.'

'He gave you a fountain pen.'

'That was a leaving gift. He was my boss, Lil. We never went for a drink without the blessing of his wife. I'm godmother to their child.' Bobby raised an eyebrow. 'I take it Tony doesn't know about your cinema dates with the captain?'

'Well, and what if he doesn't? He expresses precious little interest in anything else I tell him about my day.'

'Look, I don't want to have a row over it,' Bobby said soothingly, putting one hand over her sister's. 'I'm sorry if I sounded like I was accusing you. It's because I'm worried for you, Lil.'

Lilian's black expression lifted slightly. 'All right.'

'How long has it been going on?'

'Since not long after that day I told you about, when he found me drunk and was so kind. It was an accident really. We bumped into each other while he was in town hunting for a gift for Veronica's birthday.' She smiled fondly. 'Poor man, he looked so thoroughly bewildered that I couldn't help taking pity on him. I said I'd be happy to help pick something out, and we chose a gift for her together.'

'How does that end up at the pictures?'

'George was so grateful, he asked what he could do to pay me back – what my favourite little treat was. I tried to brush it off, but then he remembered I'd told him how much I used to adore the movies. When I said Annie was with you for the afternoon, he insisted on paying us both in to see a new Humphrey Bogart. He said a break from my routine was exactly what I needed, and… well, I felt it was what I needed too.'

'So you went?'

'I didn't think it was wrong. He wanted to repay a favour, and I couldn't resist an afternoon away from my life.'

'Did he try anything?'

'He never touched me.' Lilian flushed. 'After that… it just sort of turned into a regular thing. It became the bright spot in my week.'

'He's really never kissed you or… you know, anything?'

'I told you, we've never even held hands. We just meet at the cinema, watch the film and catch the bus home.' She smiled sadly. 'Perhaps I was wrong in agreeing to go again after that first time. But physically there'd been nothing between us, and I knew there never would be as long as George remained the man he is. Even if I said it was what I wanted, he wouldn't. It was within the letter if not the spirit of my marriage vows, so… I just allowed it to keep on happening.'

'I heard him say he wished things could be different,' Bobby said softly. 'He'd have wanted to be with you, under other circumstances?'

'Oh, what does it matter what he wants?' Lilian pressed her temples. 'Tony's my husband, and soon George will be married to Veronica and that'll be an end of it all.' She whispered a sigh. 'But I wish things could be different too. I'm sorry, Bobby, but

I can't help it. When I spend time with Annie and the girls and then take them home to their father, I just think… we could have been such a perfect little family.'

'Oh, Lil.' Bobby absorbed her sister into an embrace.

'I've let you down, haven't I? I ought to have told you, but I knew you'd force me to face up to the fact it was wrong.'

'You haven't let me down.' Bobby held her sister back. 'You know it has to stop, though, don't you?'

'I know.' Lilian took out her handkerchief to blow her nose. 'I don't know how I'll explain to George. He can be rather naive. It's not like either of us has been unfaithful.'

'Maybe not in the physical sense, but in spirit. You promised your heart to your husband as well as your body.'

'I think Tony knows deep down that he's never really had my heart,' Lilian whispered. 'When I look at the difference between him and George… I can't love a man I don't respect, and Tony's such a hard man to respect sometimes. Every time he does something to make me admire him, he undoes it the next minute through some bit of petulance or folly. I dread feeling that one day, I might end up actively despising him.'

Bobby was silent. On this point it was hard to speak up in Tony's defence.

'I know it's strange, but the cinema trips with George have made being married to Tony easier to bear,' Lilian said. 'I was content to make his meals and wash his clothes, even to tolerate sharing his bed, as long as I had those to look forward to. It made me less irritable, so he was happier for me being happier.'

'I doubt he'd see it that way.'

Lilian sighed. 'No.'

'Do you love him?' Bobby asked quietly. 'The captain?'

'I… honestly, I don't know. I don't know if I love him as a man or more the idea of him. He's just so admirable and kind and…'

'…and not like Tony,' Bobby finished for her.

'But he does make me happy,' Lil said with a small smile. 'I enjoy his conversation. He makes me laugh. I'm going to miss him terribly.'

'You're going to end it then?'

'I have to, don't I? Otherwise I really am going to fall for him, and that's going to break nobody's heart but my own.'

Bobby squeezed her hand. 'You do right, Lil. I know it's not easy, but you could make a world of trouble for yourself if you keep seeing him. If you're lonely, I'll be your steady date for the cinema.'

Lilian gave a damp laugh, wiping her eyes. 'I doubt you could fit into the seats.'

'Don't you start.'

They were interrupted by a loud knock.

'Charlie must have forgotten his key,' Bobby said. 'Lil, you'd better fix your face before our Jake sees you crying. I haven't had time to fill you in on his affairs, but you might be in for a shock.'

Lil had gone to the window to twitch aside the net curtains. Her eyes widened.

'You're telling me,' she said. 'Bobby, there's a gang of Redcaps outside.'

## Chapter 28

'Redcaps!' Bobby hurried to the window as fast as her large frame and sore ankles would allow her.

Lilian was right. There were four military policemen on the doorstep, all wearing grim, set expressions. The sergeant at the front gave another urgent rap.

'What do we do?' Lilian whispered.

'We have to open up, don't we?' Bobby whispered back. 'Otherwise they might break the door down or something.'

'What can they want with you and Charlie?'

'I have a hunch,' Bobby muttered darkly. 'Just follow my lead, all right?'

Hastily she chucked Jake's bedding roll and kitbag into the bedroom, then went to answer the door.

Bobby tried to make sure she looked good and pregnant before opening up. The fact there were only two women here, one of them in the most vulnerable of conditions, meant the men would be less likely to force entry.

'About time,' the sergeant at the door said gruffly. But his scowl lifted when he saw who had opened it. 'Oh. Sorry, Miss.' He whipped off his cap.

'It's Mrs, as I thought would have been obvious,' Bobby said coldly, one hand on her stomach.

'Yes, well, you never know these days. No offence meant, Miss— er, madam.'

'It's Mrs Atherton. This is my sister, Mrs Scott.'

'May I speak with the man of the house?'

'He isn't at home,' Lilian said. 'Can we help you, Sergeant?'

The sergeant looked irritated that he would have to deal with a woman, as if he thought he might have to speak extra slowly. If Bobby hadn't been so keen to get rid of him, she would have made him repeat himself a few times just to teach him a lesson.

'Either of you ladies know a Private Jake Bancroft of the Royal Engineers?' he asked. 'We were told he had family at this address.'

'He's our brother.' Bobby tried to adopt a surprised expression. 'Oh goodness, he isn't in any trouble, is he?'

'I'm afraid to say he is. Can we come in and look round?'

'I'd rather you didn't, if you don't mind. Our husbands are away from home, as I said. There's only me and my sister in the house.'

'Not that we're suggesting anything improper, Sergeant,' Lilian said, with the arch smile that had always won her admirers in her spinster days. 'It's only that my husband can be rather jealous. I wouldn't want it to get back to him that I'd been seen entertaining four handsome soldiers the minute he left me alone.'

The flirting seemed to pacify the sergeant a little. His mouth almost moved, although it would be a stretch of the imagination to call it a smile.

'Well, I wouldn't want to upset a lady as is expecting,' he said, with a glance at Bobby's stomach. 'Can you tell me when you last saw your brother?'

'Not since last summer,' Lilian said, exuding guilelessness. Bobby was glad Lil was here. Her twin was much better at this sort of thing.

'Any letters giving his current whereabouts?'

'We haven't had a letter in weeks,' Bobby said, glad that this question, at least, she could answer truthfully. 'Why, what is it he's done, Sergeant?'

'I don't suppose you girls know what being absent without leave means, do you?'

Bobby tried not to let her annoyance show. Aside from the fact she had been in the WAAF for six months and Lilian had spent nearly a year in the Wrens, who nowadays didn't know what 'absent without leave' meant? This was someone who patronised women simply because he could.

'We're familiar with the term, yes,' she said coolly.

'All right, then I can tell you that your brother had a late leave pass Thursday night after the expiration of which he failed to return to barracks. That makes him officially AWL as of 2 a.m. Friday morning.'

Bobby and Lilian both tried to look shocked.

'Our Jake wouldn't do that,' Lilian said. 'He's always been a good lad.'

'Well, he did,' the sergeant told her shortly. He narrowed one eye. 'You're certain he hasn't been here?'

'Absolutely positive,' Lilian said, with so much conviction that even Bobby half believed her.

'Hmm. Any other family in the neighbourhood?'

'There's only our father, but he and Jake are estranged so there's no chance he'd go there,' Bobby said, significantly overstating the difficulties in her father and Jake's relationship. 'He might go to our sister-in-law in Bradford – that's our other brother Raymond's wife. He's fighting in North Africa.'

She was hoping this might get rid of them. If Jake were to turn up while the men were here they would haul him away, still unmarried, and probably lock him up for a few months as punishment. There would be no guarantee he'd make it out in time to legitimise his baby. The sergeant was still eyeing them narrowly, however.

'All right,' he said at last. 'We'll be going now. But I ought to tell you, madam, that if your brother hasn't returned to his barracks within seven days of going AWL, it's likely steps will be taken to have him classified a deserter. That'll mean a court martial and up to two years in the nick. You might pass that on, if he does turn up.'

'I will. Thank you.'

'What happens if he does return within seven days?' Lilian asked.

'Loss of privileges and maybe a spell in the glasshouse, but nothing more serious.' The sergeant fixed her with a knowing look. 'Best thing you can do is persuade him to get back as soon as he can and hope his CO deals lightly with him for a first offence. That's if you hear from him, of course.'

'Of course,' Lilian said sweetly. 'But I doubt we will. Goodbye, Sergeant.'

The policemen departed, and Bobby leaned against the door.

'I think he knew we were hiding something,' Lilian said.

'I'm sure he did, but he seemed to be telling us he was leaving it in our hands. Is he still out there?'

Lilian went to the window and flicked aside the curtain.

'No, they're walking up the road,' she told Bobby. 'There's an army Tilly parked at the top. It looks like they're really going.'

'We'd better hope they don't run into Jake on the way.' Bobby shook her head. 'Honestly, wait till he gets back. I'll bloody kill him!'

'What could he have been thinking?'

'I suppose he was hoping to get the wedding over with and back to his camp before they classed him as a deserter.'

'Wedding? What wedding?'

Bobby sighed. 'You'd better sit down. There's been… a development.'

—

'Oh, the poor lad,' Lilian said feelingly when Bobby had filled her in. 'I suppose the army wouldn't give him leave so he took matters into his own hands. His CO's bound to be lenient when he knows the circumstances.'

'Let's hope so, but we need to get him married and back there first,' Bobby said. 'I hope Charlie was able to arrange it. I really don't think Jake will go back to his barracks until he's married. He and Kathleen are worried to death the baby's going to be born illegitimate.'

'No wonder you look tired,' Lilian said, with a concerned look. 'Tell you what, let me take Kathleen tonight, then you and Charlie can have your bed. We've got a spare room, and I'd like to get to know her. I know how scary it is to find yourself in that position.'

'She might appreciate that. She seems an isolated little soul, with her family all back in Ireland.'

'How old is she?'

'Twenty-one, I think, same as Jake. She's ever so sweet.'

'Tony's going out to some Home Guard thing so it'll be just me, her and Annie. And if our Jake kips on your settee, that keeps things respectable until they're married, doesn't it?'

'If you really wouldn't mind,' Bobby said. The idea of having no one in her bed tonight but Charlie was very appealing.

'Of course not. Let me pick Annie up from Mary and get the nursery room ready, then you can send her over. I've not got much food in though.'

'I'll feed her. I was able to buy enough to make a good tea. Then I can ask Charlie to walk her round to yours.'

Lilian grimaced. 'One of us needs to tell Dad about this.'

'Yes,' Bobby said, sighing. 'I wonder how he'll take it. I remember what a row we had when I told him you were expecting Tony's baby.'

'That was as much about Tony as the baby though.'

'True. He ought to warm to Kathleen. She's a gentle little thing.'

'Fathers are never as protective over sons' virtues as daughters',' Lil observed. 'Besides, Dad's mellowed since he took up with the new Mrs Bancroft.'

'Things have always been awkward between him and Jake though.'

'I'll break it to him gently. I can walk over with Annie in a bit. If he takes it well, Maimie might invite the pair of them to dinner tomorrow.'

Now that the combined ranks of the Atherton-Scott-Parry clan had grown beyond what could be accommodated by Mary's kitchen, Sunday dinner worked on a rota, with Bobby and Charlie alternating between their respective families. Tomorrow they were to join Rob and his new wife, along with Lilian, Annie and Tony.

'Thanks, Lil. I don't know what I'd do without you.' Bobby gave her sister a hug. 'And I'm sorry for telling you off before. I was worried, that's all.'

'You were right. I ought to have known better,' Lilian said with a sigh. 'I can try to justify it to myself this way and that way, but I know Tony would never see it like that. I just… couldn't help it.'

'I'd hate to see you hurt,' Bobby said softly. 'If I sounded stern, that's the reason. There's no happy way it could end for you, Lil.'

'I know. I was foolish to give in to it.'

They were interrupted by the arrival of Charlie and the young couple.

'Well?' Bobby demanded, getting to her feet with difficulty. 'Are they married?'

'No,' Charlie said. 'But they will be soon. I sorted out the special licence and the registrar has got an opening first thing in the morning. He took one look at Kathleen and took pity on them.'

'Oh, thank goodness.'

Jake threw himself down on the settee next to Lilian. 'Heyup, Lil. What're you doing here?'

Lil turned to glare at him. 'Don't give me "Heyup, Lil", you little sod. Give me a hug, then after that I've a good mind to box your ears, big lad though you are.'

'That's if I don't box them first.' Bobby turned to Charlie. 'We saw off four Redcaps not less than an hour ago.'

Charlie blinked. 'What, here?'

'Redcaps?' Kathleen said, looking worried. 'You mean, policemen?'

'That's right,' Bobby told her. 'Your young man there is absent without leave. And if he doesn't get back to his barracks by Thursday, he could be looking at two years inside for desertion.'

'Two years?' Kathleen turned to glare at Jake. 'You told me you had four days' leave!'

'I did it for you, Kath,' Jake said, looking at her with pleading in his eyes. 'I won't have my baby being born without a dad. I mean I am his dad, but I want it to be legal and everything.'

'A dad's no good to our baby in jail, Jake. You ought to have told me. I'd never have let you break the law.'

'I know you wouldn't,' he said with a weak smile. 'Why d'you think I didn't tell you?'

Kathleen continued to glare. Jake looked like a cornered rabbit as he faced stern looks from two sisters and one fiancée. He turned to Charlie, who unlike the women only looked rather bewildered.

'It weren't my fault,' Jake said. 'The buggers wouldn't let me have the leave. I had to do summat, didn't I? What if the baby came before they let me out long enough to get married?'

'OK, let's all calm down,' Charlie said, taking control of the situation. 'It's not ideal, admittedly, but it isn't the end of the world. I'm with Jake. This is for the best.'

Bobby shook her head. 'You're not taking his side? He could get into serious trouble for this, Charlie. So could Lil and I, since we lied ourselves blue for him to those Redcaps.'

'I'm sure the army won't punish him too harshly once they know why he did it,' Charlie said. 'A few weeks confined to barracks, perhaps, as long as he goes straight back after.'

'You are going straight back, aren't you?' Lilian demanded of Jake.

'Said I was, didn't I?' he said. 'We'll go soon as we've got the certificate.'

## Chapter 29

Bobby couldn't leave her brother in the doghouse for long. He looked so dejected and tired, she didn't have the heart to stay angry. It stirred everything that was motherly in her to see the lad in distress. There was still so much in him of the little boy he'd been when, as girls of fourteen, Bobby and Lilian had found themselves responsible for his care. She ruffled his hair when she served him his rarebit supper, to let him know he was forgiven.

Kathleen, too, seemed to have forgiven him – at least, so Bobby assumed when she noticed the young lovers holding hands under the kitchen table. They were a sweet pair. Bobby felt sure her dad would like this new addition to the family, even if he didn't approve of the way she had been brought into the Bancroft fold.

After they had eaten, Bobby commissioned Charlie to escort Kathleen to Lilian's. She gave him whispered instructions to find out if Lil had seen their dad, and what his reaction had been to the news.

–

'Well, what did she say?' Bobby demanded when Charlie arrived home. He had sought her out in the kitchen, where she was elbow-deep in the washing-up. Jake had gone to buy a packet of smokes from the Hart, so they could talk freely.

'She couldn't say much in front of Kathleen but it sounds all right,' Charlie told her. 'At any rate, the kids are invited to dinner tomorrow.'

'Jake said they were going back as soon as the ceremony was over.'

'He can stay for dinner, surely, and introduce Kathleen to your dad. The army won't declare him a deserter for the sake of a few hours.'

'I suppose not.' Bobby wiped her hands on her pinny and turned to him. 'I hope he'll agree to come. He hasn't met Maimie yet.'

'Why wouldn't he agree?'

'It's like I said – he and our dad have had a difficult relationship ever since Jake got to an age where he could understand why Dad was the way he was.'

Charlie put his arms around her waist.

'Meaning the way your dad used to drink, I suppose,' he said quietly.

'His drinking, the screaming nightmares, the way he shakes...' Bobby sighed. 'A hundred times I've tried to make Jake see that Dad can't help being that way, but it was no good talking to him about combat fatigue or shell-shock or any of those terms. Jake was growing into a young man and all he understood was that his dad, who ought to be someone to admire, was screaming in the night because of things that happened to him twenty years before. In the eyes of a boy who got his ideas about what made a man from thriller comics, his dad was a coward. It hurt me to see him so ashamed, for both their sakes.'

'I hadn't realised it was as serious as that,' Charlie said, frowning.

Bobby ran a hand over her forehead, beaded with sweat from the steaming washing-up water. 'They're not estranged, exactly. Our Jake loves his dad in his own way; I'm sure he does. But he can't admire him, and I wish there was some way to fix that.'

'Does he know what your dad went through?'

'He knows Dad was in the trenches but that doesn't mean he understands. He never saw Dad's nightmares first hand as Lil and I did, or heard him raving about the horrors he'd seen. He was the baby, so we did everything we could to shield him from it. I wonder sometimes if that only made things worse.'

Charlie looked rather thoughtful. He seemed about to say more, but Jake arrived back with his cigarettes and the conversation came to an end.

—

Bobby was hoping Marmaduke would settle that night and let her have some uninterrupted rest. With Charlie back at her side, there was no reason for the baby to make a fuss about the absence of his father.

Unfortunately Marmaduke, while quiet enough, seemed to have decided to make a mattress of Bobby's bladder. It must have been around midnight when she admitted defeat and slid noiselessly from under the covers to use the privy. Charlie was sleeping soundly for once, and she didn't want to risk waking him by making use of the jerry under the bed.

In the parlour, the embers of the fire were still in the grate, lending the room a mellow illumination. Bobby believed her brother to be asleep on the settee when she tiptoed to the kitchen so she could let herself out of the back door, but once she had visited the outhouse and crept back in, she realised this wasn't the case. The red glow of his cigarette rather gave him away as awake.

'Hiya, Bob,' he said in a toneless voice. 'Want to sit down? I wouldn't mind some company.'

She put a finger to her lips.

'Don't wake Charlie,' she whispered. 'It isn't often he gets a proper night's rest. Here, shift your bottom.'

Jake sat up and Bobby took a seat beside him.

'You ought to be asleep,' she said sternly. 'Big day for you tomorrow.'

'Aye, I guess. Why doesn't Charlie get a proper night's rest? He doesn't work nights, does he?'

'No. No, he...' Bobby looked at her brother in the dim fire glow, taking in his haggard appearance. 'He sometimes struggles to sleep, that's all.'

'Why?'

'He just does.'

Jake was silent, staring into the fire as he smoked.

'Do you want me to make you some warm milk?' Bobby asked gently.

Jake smiled. 'You going to sing me a lullaby as well?'

'If you like.'

'I'm not eight any more, Bob.'

'You know that to me and Lil, you'll always be the baby no matter how big you get. To Dad too.'

'Huh.'

'You are staying to dinner before you go, aren't you? Dad ought to meet Kathleen, and we can introduce you to Maimie.'

'Who's Maimie?'

'Dad's new wife.'

'Oh. Right.' His gaze was still fixed on the fire. 'I forgot. What's she like then?'

'Not much like Mam,' Bobby said with a smile. 'But she's good for Dad. She's a brisk, sensible, kindly sort, in spite of some odd ways. You'll like her.'

Jake rubbed his hair, no more long and slicked as it had been in civilian life but trimmed to the harsh army-regulation short back and sides.

'I can hardly remember Mam now,' he said. 'I can't remember her reading to me or owt. Can barely remember how she looked when she was well, except from photos. I just remember her being in bed all the time, dying, and you and Lil looking after me. That's bad, isn't it?'

'It isn't bad,' Bobby said softly. 'You were a little boy.'

'I keep thinking, will he remember me if I don't make it? The baby, I mean. Kath'd find herself another feller, I suppose.

I hope she would, and not stay on her own. But then the baby probably wouldn't ever think about the dad he'd had before.'

'We wouldn't let him forget. We'd still be his family.'

Jake swallowed a sob. 'I've seen some stuff, Bob.'

Bobby put an arm round his broad shoulders. 'I know, love.'

'I had this mate. Terry. We were working on this UXB in Tottenham Court Road: a five-hundred-pounder from a tip and run the night before. Chatting about football and joking about each other's girls, sharing fags and that. Weren't supposed to be a high-risk job but summat must've gone wrong because… well, he sent me to fetch a couple of teas from the WVS wagon round the corner.' Jake closed his eyes. 'There were a bang, and… when I went back he was in bits, Bob. Actual bits, lying all round. Hands and feet and… and guts. That used to be Terry, and he was my mate. He didn't deserve that, did he?'

'No, sweetheart. No one deserves that.'

'I always swore I'd never be like Dad when I grew up. But when I thought about Terry, and imagined the bits of him might've been bits of me…' He turned wide, damp eyes on her. 'I really thought about not going back,' he whispered. 'Just taking Kath and running and running, hoping the war wouldn't catch up with me. Bet you're ashamed of me now, are you?'

'Come here.' Bobby gave him a hug. 'Stop talking daft. I'm proud of you and I always will be.'

He gave in to sobs as he hid his face on her shoulder.

'Suppose I'm more like Dad than I realised,' he muttered. 'Cowardice must run in the family.'

'You mustn't say that. You're not a coward, and neither is Dad.'

Jake continued as if he hadn't heard her.

'If it hadn't been for the baby, I honestly might have deserted,' he murmured. 'Only I couldn't stand thinking that then he'd grow up knowing his dad was a coward, the way I had to. I wanted him to have a father he could respect, even if it meant lying the rest of my life about how frightened I was every time they sent us out to another damn bomb.'

Bobby let him go. 'Do you really think that being afraid and being a coward are the same thing?'

'Well, what's the difference?'

'The difference is... I honestly don't know, because I'm not sure I really believe in cowards. That is to say, I've met a lot of men since this war started – and women too – who have done things the world would call brave, but I've never met one who hasn't been afraid.' She shook her head. 'It's my fault for reading you all those Bulldog Drummond stories when you were little. They've given you the idea that heroes are men who don't know the meaning of fear, when in real life there's no such thing. If there are men who feel no fear, they're probably in the funny farm where they belong.'

'What are you on about, funny farm?'

'Everyone feels fear in the face of death, Jake. Everyone. It doesn't mean there's something wrong with you. If you didn't feel fear when you were defusing a bomb, *then* there'd be something wrong with you. Anyone who says they're not afraid in that situation is either lying or touched in the head.'

'Running away makes you a coward though, doesn't it?'

'Perhaps, in some circumstances. But you didn't run away.' Bobby dipped her head to catch his gaze. 'You didn't, did you? You are going back?'

'Only because I have to. Because I don't want my kid to find out his dad was a deserter. Don't see how that that makes me less of a coward.' He put his neglected cigarette out in the ashtray before it burned his fingers. 'I'll probably wind up like Dad, screaming like a bairn and shaking all the time.'

'You think Dad's the only man from the last war who ended up that way? The only man from this war?' Bobby demanded. 'That's what happens to someone when they've been dragged to hell and back, Jake. Any good, modern doctor will tell you it's the sign of being pushed to the limit of what the human mind can stand, not cowardice.' Bobby paused, wondering whether she ought to talk about this without her husband's permission, then decided Jake's need was greater. She knew her brother admired Charlie, and it might help the boy to understand. 'You've noticed Charlie's hand shaking when he smokes, I suppose.'

'That's because his arm was burnt when his plane caught fire.' He frowned. 'It is, isn't it?'

'Not only that,' Bobby said quietly. 'He has... the doctor calls them attacks. Nervous attacks, like Dad has after a bad dream.'

Jake stared at her. 'But Charlie climbed out of his plane to put the fire out and saved those other men. That's what you told me.'

'He did, and the fact he was afraid doesn't make him any less of a hero for it. If anything, it makes him more of one.' Bobby rested a hand on her belly. 'I hope our baby will always understand how brave his father was, no matter how Charlie might shake or cry in his sleep.' Something occurred to her. 'Hang on. There's something I want to show you.'

She tiptoed to the bedroom, where Charlie still slept soundly. Quietly she took her dad's Military Medal from a drawer, then carried it back to Jake in the parlour.

'Here,' she said when she was again sitting by him, opening the newspaper the medal was folded in. 'Look at this.'

'What is it?'

'Take it to the fire and see.'

Jake did so, blinking at it in the red glow.

'It's a medal,' he said. 'Is it Charlie's?'

'No, it isn't Charlie's. And it's not just any medal, it's the Military Medal. They were awarded in the last war to soldiers who'd carried out acts of gallantry under fire. A very great honour, and one of the rarest decorations there were.'

'Well, whose is it then?'

'It's Dad's. He was awarded it for saving the lives of three men at the Somme, even though he was bleeding heavily from a shoulder wound that could have killed him. I'd never have known about it if Mam hadn't told me on her deathbed – at least, not until he gave it me a few weeks ago.'

Jake stared at the medal with something like reverence. 'This is really Dad's?'

'It is. Turn it around and see what it says.'

Jake did so. 'For bravery in the field,' he murmured, reading the inscription.

'That's right. He's a hero, Jake.' Bobby stood up to put a hand on his shoulder. 'And so are you,' she said quietly.

'How come he never told us he'd got a medal?'

'He lost a lot of friends in that battle, in quite horrible ways – the way you lost your friend Terry, but many times over. All his medal does is remind him of living through hell, and the men he knew who never came home. It's hardly surprising he didn't want to think about it.'

'But he gave it you, didn't he?'

'To look after on behalf of us all, yes. I think his new wife might have helped him make his peace with it, but the main reason was for the sake of his grandchildren. So that when he's gone, they'll have this to show them their grandad was a brave man.'

'And he kept it secret all this time,' Jake said wonderingly. 'Why'd he take it if he didn't want it? I guess he had a choice.'

'I'm not sure he understood himself until recently. He came to the conclusion that it was never for his own sake, because how he felt wouldn't matter once he was gone. It was for the sake of those who came after.' She smiled. 'That includes your baby too. And I'm sure he'll be just as proud of his dad as he is of his grandad.'

'Wish I'd seen this before,' Jake murmured. 'Wish I'd seen it when I was a kid.'

'I wish you had too. But Dad was always a brave man, Jake. It doesn't need a decoration to make that true.' She pressed his shoulder. 'It just needs us to understand that there's a difference between fear and cowardice. Even the bravest man's nerves will break after he's been through horrors. That's not weak or womanish or shameful. It's natural, and it's more common than you know.'

Jake summoned a shaky smile. 'Reckon I ought to know that, after the stuff I've seen.'

'You'll stay for dinner, won't you? Take Kathleen to meet Dad?'

'All right.' He gave the medal a last lingering glance before handing it back to her. 'I guess Kath'd like that. And... I'd like to see Dad.'

'Good lad,' Bobby said with a smile. 'Now go back to sleep. You're getting married tomorrow.'

## Chapter 30

Jake and Kathleen's wedding was a quiet affair: just the bride and groom, with Bobby and Charlie as witnesses. The groom was in the same crumpled battledress he had been wearing since he arrived, and Kathleen wore a loaned twinset and skirt: the outfit Bobby had adjusted for Mabs Jessop's wedding when she had been at a similar point in her pregnancy. Celebrations could follow another time, when it would feel more appropriate.

And yet, rushed though the whole thing was, it was as moving a wedding as Bobby had ever been to. She didn't often cry at weddings but she cried at this one, even though the ceremony barely lasted ten minutes. The young couple's eyes were so filled with love as they said their vows that she couldn't help letting slip a tear.

Charlie smiled at her as they waited for Jake and Kathleen to sign the register.

'They grow up so fast, eh?' he whispered.

'I'm just glad it's done with,' Bobby whispered back. 'Nothing says true love like a race against the clock to legitimise your baby.'

'Don't pretend to be cynical. I saw you having a little weep.'

'You looked rather damp around the eyes yourself, come to that,' Bobby said with a smile.

'Well. They're sweet, aren't they?' Charlie's gaze drifted to the young couple. 'They ought to be happy together.'

'Yes, it's worked out as well as it could given the circumstances.' Bobby glanced at him. 'Thanks, Charlie.'

'For what?'

'For being so helpful with my family crisis, getting the wedding arranged. You've been a real pillar of strength.'

'Well, your family's my family. I'm sure you'd have done the same for my brother if he'd turned up with a pregnant girlfriend and the Redcaps on his tail.'

She laughed. 'What, Reg?'

'All right, if I had another brother.'

Bobby looked up into his face. 'Are you OK, love? You were a little quiet on the bus.'

'I'm OK. Just in a thoughtful sort of mood.'

'What are you thinking about?'

The newlyweds had done their bit now, and the registrar was beckoning Bobby and Charlie over.

'We'll talk about it later,' Charlie said, taking her arm. 'Let's get your brother on a train first, then I can have you to myself again.'

—

Bobby felt nervous as the four of them made their way to her dad's cottage afterwards.

She couldn't help thinking about the awful row she'd had with her father the day she'd broken the news that Lilian was not only married to Tony Scott but also several months pregnant with his baby. Yes, Lilian was a girl and her father naturally more protective. Yes, Tony had seemed a poor choice for a son-in-law at the time. But weighed against that was Rob's affection for Lilian, which Bobby had been confident would ultimately overcome his disappointment. He had never been as close to Jake, for exactly the reasons she and her brother had discussed last night.

Her dad was there to greet them when they knocked on the door of the cottage by the beck that was his new home. Maimie was beside him with Norman in her arms, and Lilian, who had gone over earlier to smooth the way, was next to her: cradling Annie in much the same way as her stepmother was cradling her pet goose. If Bobby hadn't been so anxious, she wouldn't have been able to avoid laughing at the scene. But her anxiety was alleviated when her dad stepped forward and shook Jake vigorously by the hand.

'Good to see you, son,' he said in his heartiest voice. 'Why don't you write, eh? But never mind that now. Your sister tells me congratulations are in order.'

Jake looked dazed by his father's enthusiastic greeting. 'Um, well, I got married this morning.' Kathleen was gripping his hand, and he gave her a little nudge. 'This is Kathleen Brady, my— no, that's not right, is it? Kathleen Bancroft, now. My, um, my wife.'

'Welcome to the family, love.' Rob pressed her hand warmly.

'It's very nice to meet you,' Kathleen said. 'Jake told me he had a lovely family. I thought he must be exaggerating, but he wasn't a bit.'

'Here, come and meet another Mrs Bancroft. That's my missus.' Rob guided Kathleen proudly to Mrs-Hobbes-as-was, who smiled and nodded with utmost affability. Marriage seemed to agree with her almost as well as it did with her new husband.

'Is that the Sunday dinner?' Jake asked, nodding to Norman in her arms.

'Nay, young man, that's your new stepbrother,' Maimie told him. 'Say hello, Norman.'

Norman honked in disgust, making Bobby laugh. He was the only resident of Silverdale who never changed. Jake laughed too, and consented to be brought forward by his father for an introduction to his stepmother. Bobby exchanged a smile with Lilian as she followed the others into the house.

'Well, lad, I think we've time for a smoke before we eat,' Rob said to Jake, putting an arm around his son's shoulders. 'We'll leave young Charlie to squire the women while me and thee have a little talk, father to son.'

'I'd like that. Ta, Dad.' Jake smiled gratefully at him. 'I mean, really, thanks for everything.'

Lilian nudged her sister as they watched the two men disappear into their dad's study.

—

'Straight to bed, I think,' Charlie said when he and Bobby arrived home. 'I don't care if it's barely five o'clock. I've never felt more in need of an early night.'

They had seen Jake and his new wife safely on board the bus into Skipton after dinner, the envelope containing Jake's share of the money from the house sale now stashed in Kathleen's purse. The girl couldn't have looked happier if she'd married into the royal family, with this unexpected windfall, the warm welcome she had received from the Bancroft clan and of course her long-desired new surname.

'All right but don't get any ideas,' Bobby warned her husband. 'I'm so exhausted I think my knees have stopped working.'

'What I had in mind wouldn't have involved your knees.'

She smiled. 'I can manage a cuddle. That's all I'm good for today, I'm afraid.'

Charlie massaged his forehead. 'I think it might be all I'm good for as well, sadly.'

'I ought to make tea first,' Bobby murmured. She felt like she barely had energy to open her lips after all the drama of the last few days.

'Why, are you hungry?'

'Not really. I ate plenty at dinner.'

'Then rest first. I can make sandwiches later for a supper.'

Bobby glanced around the parlour. It felt strangely bare, now Jake had gone. As dramatic as it had been, she had rather relished having a little brother who needed her help. She had always thrived in a crisis, and it had given her something to focus on other than worry about having the baby.

'It feels quiet without the children, doesn't it?' she said dreamily.

Charlie smiled. 'I'm not sure how your brother and his wife would feel about being called "the children" at twenty-one.'

'I can't help it. Jake feels like such a boy still. I suppose mothers always do feel that way, even after their children are grown up.'

'Go and lie down, darling. You look dead on your feet. I'll bring you a cup of tea.'

'Yes. Thank you.' She could feel her eyes trying to close.

Bobby was asleep almost as soon as her head touched the pillow. She didn't know how long she slept, but it was dark when she awoke. Charlie lay beside her, leaning on his elbow as he watched her sleep.

'Oh Lord.' She rubbed her eyes. 'How long was I off for?'

'Well your tea's gone cold. Do you want another cup?'

'Mmm. In a minute.' She rolled on to her side. 'I'd prefer a cuddle first.'

'A request I'm always happy to grant.' He wrapped her in his arms, or as best he could around her big belly.

'It went well today, didn't it?' Bobby mumbled, fighting off the lingering stupor of sleep. 'My dad and Jake, I mean. Jake and I had a heart-to-heart last night that I think did some good.'

'I know,' Charlie said quietly.

Bobby frowned. 'What?'

'Sorry, Bob. I couldn't help overhearing. I woke up when I heard you talking.'

Bobby thought back to her conversation and grimaced.

'I'm so sorry, Charlie,' she said. 'I know I shouldn't have talked about your problems without discussing it with you. It's just, Jake admires you. He knows what you did on that last op. I thought it might help him make his peace with everything if he knew our dad's problems weren't unique.'

'I don't mind. It just made me think, that's all.'

He drifted into a reverie, rolling on to his back to stare at the ceiling. After a while, Bobby tried to reclaim his attention.

'What did it make you think about, love?' she asked.

'About what you said to Jake. About your dad's medal.' He turned over again to look into her face. 'And it made me realise… you were right, darling. I ought to go to the palace. Have my picture taken for the papers and everything you wanted. Because it is complicated – heroism and cowardice and all those daft notions that are more storytelling than reality. And because it isn't really about me, is it? It's about Marmaduke.'

'It took overhearing my conversation with Jake to make you realise that?' Bobby said, shaking her head. 'I've been telling you all that for ages.'

'I know. Honestly, I thought you were just trying to make me feel better about myself.'

'I did want you to feel better about yourself, but I still meant every word.'

'It wasn't only that, though.' He ran a hand over the swell of Bobby's stomach. 'It was what your brother said. How he'd struggled to understand the way your dad was when he was a kid, and the difference it obviously made when you showed him that medal.'

'Go on.'

'When you're a child, everything's black and white, isn't it? There are heroes and cowards, goodies and baddies, and you play with toy soldiers and dream of the battlefield as if it isn't something monstrous. It made me think… I do want our child to admire me. I've never believed I was a hero over and above any other man. In the thick of things, it felt like I was operating on my instincts rather than any conscious idea of bravery.' He met her gaze earnestly. 'But I always tried to do what was right, Bobby. I fought hard when I was in the RAF to make sure this damn war didn't brutalise me the way I've seen it do to others. And if that makes me weak or womanly, I'd rather be that kind of weak than the sort of brave that means not having compassion – even if that compassion extends to the enemy as well.'

Bobby smiled. 'Which is exactly why I love you.'

'I hope, one day when Marmaduke's a man – or a woman, if that's the way it turns out – that he or she might be able to understand all this,' Charlie went on. 'But he won't be able to understand it when he's a kid. He'll just want to know what Daddy did to help beat the bad guys. That stuff matters, when you've got a head full of stories and a child's understanding of the world. I couldn't bear for him to see me shaking and have that come between us like it did for your dad and Jake. I couldn't bear for him not to have a proud story about his old man to tell his grandchildren after I'm gone.' His face took on a determined expression. 'So I'm going to take that gong, and I'm going to have my photograph taken with the king, and one day I'm going to show it to my son. I'm going to tell him I got it for saving lives, because that's a damn sight more heroic than taking them. Because it won't matter if I felt like a hero sixty years from now when my kid's an old man, but it'll matter that I always tried to do what was right. If he remembers me for anything, I want him to remember me for that.'

'Oh Charlie, I am glad.' Bobby gave him a kiss. 'I know it isn't straightforward, when you've lost so many friends, but I do think it's the right thing to do. And I'll be bursting with pride on behalf of both Marmaduke and myself when I see you invested.'

'I'm really not sure you should come, Bobby,' Charlie said, running tender fingers over her stomach. 'It's a long way to London.'

'I'll check with the doctor first. Would that satisfy you?'

'I suppose so, if Dick Minchin says it's all right,' Charlie said, although still a little doubtfully.

She nestled into his arms. 'I'm glad you were able to make your peace with the DFC, but words matter too, Charlie. Help Marmaduke to understand when he's old enough, won't you? I want him to grow up to be exactly the sort of compassionate, sensitive man his father is.'

Charlie smiled. 'You didn't always describe me in such glowing terms. "Irresponsible" is a word I remember you using. "Flirt" is another.'

'If he grows up to be a flirt then I suppose that's only to be expected,' Bobby said, smiling too. 'But as long as he's a good man, I can cope with him having an eye for a pretty girl.'

'Or her having an eye for a handsome lad.'

She laughed. 'If she does, she didn't get it from her mother.'

'I take great offence at that,' Charlie said, flicking her ear. 'I think there's another Marmaduke-related worry you can put to bed now as well, after what I heard last night.'

'What?'

Charlie brushed her hair back from her face. 'Whether you'll be a good mother,' he said softly.

'How do you mean?'

'I heard how you were with your brother, Bob. That mix of tenderness and no-nonsense that was just what he needed. You reminded me of Mary.'

'That might be the nicest thing you've ever said to me.'

'I mean it. He needed guidance and you said just what you ought to say to make sure he got it. You were perfect.' He kissed her. 'You've already had plenty of practice in the maternal arts, I can see that. And I can tell that no amount of other things in your life would stop you putting your child first. So no more worrying about it, all right?'

Bobby smiled. 'Thanks, Charlie. You know, that was exactly what I needed to hear.'

## Chapter 31

Bobby received a telegram from Jake the next morning, letting her know he had arrived at his barracks safely. She also received a rather longer letter from Kathleen a few days later, thanking her for her kindness and letting her know that Jake had been confined to barracks for a month as punishment for going AWL. This was lenient, considering. Bobby guessed the CO had been sympathetic when he heard the story of the two young lovers and imposed the minimum punishment. She was thankful Jake's confinement would be over by the time his baby was born.

One Tuesday over a week later, Bobby woke rather late. Now she was drawing closer to the birth, Marmaduke seemed to have decided he might as well enjoy sleeping in. She was going to have to stop relying on him and start setting the alarm, or she'd never manage to get everything done. It would be a mere two months now until the baby arrived, and only a month until Charlie would be travelling to London to receive his DFC.

Bobby had seen Dr Minchin, and while he had reminded her there was no guarantee Marmaduke wouldn't decide to arrive ahead of time, he had said there was no significant danger in making the journey. That was good enough for Bobby, who informed Charlie she would be coming with him whether he liked it or not. Major blitzes were rare these days, with only the occasional 'tip and run' raid, so she wasn't worried on that score either.

She hoped Marmaduke's new-found tardiness didn't imply any unwillingness to come out. She was heartily sick of being big and sore and having ankles the size of oranges. As afraid as

Bobby was of giving birth, she was beginning to feel the day couldn't come soon enough.

Charlie's side of the bed was empty, but Bobby could hear him bustling about so she knew he hadn't gone to work. She pushed her feet into her slippers before seeking him out in the parlour. He was bent over the coffee table, writing.

'Morning,' she said, yawning. 'Sorry I overslept. Have you had breakfast?'

'Yes, I made myself some toast.'

'What are you writing?'

'A note for you. You might as well read it now you're here.' He handed it to her.

> *Don't forget I'm seeing Roger Turner in the Hart after work so will be later than usual.*

This was followed by some Pitman's shorthand. Charlie's skills hadn't progressed enough yet for him to write the whole note that way.

'What's this supposed to say?' Bobby asked him.

'"I love you". Doesn't it?'

'Not quite. You've got some of your strokes the wrong way round. What you're actually telling me is that you vole me.'

'Oh. Well, that's close enough.' He came to take her in his arms. 'I'd better go for my bus.'

'Good luck with Roger. I hope he buys the instruments.'

'So do I. I'll give him my finest spiv patter, quite worthy of a Peter Dixon.'

'Good idea, and pay for his beer as well.' Bobby gave him a squeeze. 'Have a good day, darling. You do really, truly vole me, don't you?'

'You and only you, Mrs Atherton.'

He pressed a kiss to her hair before grabbing his hat and hurrying out.

Bobby was sitting down to a breakfast of boiled egg, toast and orange juice when the post arrived.

Along with extra eggs and milk, orange juice was one of the few perks of her pregnancy, since what supplies there were of the precious vitamin-filled liquid were available only to expectant mothers and young children. You couldn't always get it even with one of the special green ration books, but Bobby had been lucky enough to find some put aside for her under the grocer's counter on her last shopping day. She tried to savour it, knowing her days of enjoying this particular treat were numbered.

The soft 'flump' of the post suggested a well-stuffed envelope was among the letters. Bobby abandoned her breakfast and went to the front door to see what it might be.

She hadn't neglected her writing ambitions in the wake of her brother's tempestuous visit. The very day after he and Kathleen had departed, she had read her WAAF story over and found that not only did she think it well worth sending in to *The Girl's Own*, but also that it might be the best thing she had ever written. She had longed to show it to Charlie, but had forced herself to hold on to her excitement until she had an answer from the magazine.

Their submission guidelines had been on the back page, although there had been nothing about fees. Bobby would have liked to know how they compared to the five shillings per joke she had received from the BBC. She was instructed to send her story and a covering letter to the editress, along with a stamped, self-addressed envelope.

Bobby's heart sank as she bent her poor sore knees to pick up the single envelope.

The address wasn't typed, as she would have expected from a professional publication. It was handwritten, and in a hand she knew well. Her own.

That could only mean a no. The self-addressed envelope she had sent had been for the return of her story if it was deemed unsuitable. Bobby took the letter back to the parlour and stuffed it under Charlie's paper, unable to bring herself to open the thing and read those depressing words of rejection.

She tried to curtail her feeling of disappointment as she nibbled her toast, but honestly, she felt like crying. When she had approached the BBC she hadn't allowed herself to get her hopes up, hardly daring to believe that her words could be good enough for that illustrious institution. And yet they had been – some of them, anyhow. Perhaps that had made her over-confident, but Bobby hadn't been able to help letting her imagination run away with the notion of her story being printed in *The Girl's Own*. This time it would have carried her byline, unlike the anonymity of the gags she had sold to the BBC. This time she could tell her friends and family, and bask in the knowledge she wasn't just a published writer but a published author. Perhaps Florrie and Jess would read her story, and boast to their schoolmates of her. Perhaps it would lead to more and better things, until she really was managing to bring in a decent income from her pen alone.

But the daydreams had been for nothing. The magazine didn't want her work. There was no anti-woman prejudice at play – not at *The Girl's Own*, for goodness' sake, with a woman editor and mostly female contributors. No, her story must have been rejected for the standard of writing alone. And if even this, which Bobby had been so convinced was the best thing she had written, wasn't good enough, there was precious little point in her striving to do more.

A gloom settled on her as she began her chores – those she could still do, at least. Now she was the size she was, she and Charlie had been forced to invest some of their weekly budget in engaging a home help for a few hours a week. Bobby had been considering speaking to Charlie about making the arrangement permanent, and perhaps confiding in him about her little pot of money – the twenty-eight pounds she had hidden in her biscuit tin under the bed. It would have freed up some of her time to write so she could bring in badly needed cash.

But there was no point now. If she wrote, it would be solely for her own amusement. They couldn't justify paying a home help so Bobby could dabble in her hobbies.

By the end of the day, however, Bobby's depression of spirits had turned into annoyance.

She was sure that had been a good story. She was sure of it! What possible reason could the editress have for turning it down? Was it because Bobby was an unknown where so many contributors were established authors? Or was her WAAF heroine too similar in nature to Captain Johns' Worrals? She had to know. If it was the latter, and not to do with the standard of her writing, she might at least be encouraged to try her luck with a different periodical.

Putting down her duster, Bobby waddled to the coffee table – at least, her walk felt like a waddle these days, as if the baby had caused her to become half duck – and took the envelope from under Charlie's paper.

She slid out the contents. Yes, there was her story, returned as she had thought. Only now it was covered in notes in blue pencil. It looked like one of her pieces for *The Tyke* after Reg had subbed it.

Bobby looked at one of the margin notes.

> *Love Lindy's pluck here, but what is she feeling? More interiority please.*

What did it mean?

Under her story were three other things. One was a letter from the editor. One was a legal document of some kind. And the other... Bobby almost dropped it when she saw what it was, and the amount written on it. It was a cheque, not a postal order, made out to Mrs Roberta Atherton. And the amount on it was four pounds.

Bobby slumped on to the settee.

Four pounds! It had taken her months to earn anywhere close to that writing jokes. Four pounds was two weeks' salary on *The Tyke*.

When she had recovered, Bobby took up the letter.

> *Dear Mrs Atherton,*
> *I would like to express my sincere gratitude to you for sharing Lindy's story with me. I don't believe I've smiled so much while reading a submission in a long time, or been quite so on the edge of my seat waiting to see what would happen. As you can imagine, many of the submissions we receive these days feature a heroine who is either a WAAF, a Wren or an At – more than I could ever cram into my pages even if the standard were sufficiently high. But Lindy is something special. Pending some minor revisions, I would very much like to include her story in a future number of* The Girl's Own Paper.

Bobby stared at the words. Truth be told, it hadn't occurred to her that the periodical might be swamped with military stories among which hers could be lost, yet they had loved it in spite of so much competition. She had never had such fulsome praise from the BBC: only a yes or a no. None of her editors – neither Clarky, Don nor Reg – had been prone to excessive praise. She swelled under this vote of appreciation from the editress of such a prestigious and long-established publication.

She read on.

> *I see from your letter that your writing background is primarily in newspapers and non-fiction periodicals, which does rather come across in your work. The prose is spare, clean and readable, and you write emotion well*

*where it is included, but I did feel that I would like to venture more into Lindy's head at times. I have taken the liberty of noting these on your manuscript. I would be grateful if you could return the revised draft along with the enclosed contract under our standard terms, which commissions another five stories in the Lindy series. Should these prove popular with readers, as I do not doubt they will, I would be very keen to discuss the possibility of a serial. Do let me know when you and your agent (if you have one) would be free to visit my offices in London.*

*Once I have received your revised manuscript, I will arrange for the other half of your payment to be sent to you.*

*Sincerely,*
*Phyllis Flagg (Mrs)*
*Editress,* The Girl's Own Paper

Bobby almost swooned for the second time that afternoon when she read 'the other half of your payment'. She snatched up the contract that had been enclosed with her manuscript.

Yes, it was true. The fee was to be *eight pounds* per story for first publication rights, whatever that meant – eight pounds each! And they wanted another five stories, and a Lindy serial to follow perhaps. That meant nearly fifty pounds for the stories in total, and who knew how much for the serial? Bobby could hardly imagine such riches.

She didn't know what to do. Her heart was jumping about like a mad thing. She started pacing the room.

She needed to lie down. No, no she didn't. She needed to get an agent. The letter said she ought to have one. Where did one find agents? Was there some equivalent of a marriage bureau for writers where they paired you with one? What to do, what to do! Should she walk to the Bull, where they had a telephone, and ring up Charlie at work? Oh Lord, she was all of a flutter! It was like a dream, but it was real. It was real, and it was happening to her, now. Marmaduke was squirming inside her, as if he, too, was fidgeting with excitement.

A glance at her watch showed her she couldn't telephone Charlie, as he'd be on the bus back from Skipton. Still, she had to tell *someone* – right away, this instant. She might burst if she didn't.

Not even bothering to change out of her pinny and headscarf, Bobby threw on her overcoat and hurried to her sister's.

## Chapter 32

It took Bobby rather longer these days to walk the half-mile to Cow House Cottage. She hadn't realised how much she relied on Charlie's arm for support until she reached the packhorse bridge and had to stop to catch her breath.

She felt like she weighed a million tons. If she had been thinking clearly, it might have occurred to her to commission one of the boys playing football near her cottage to take a note over for a sixpence fee, and get Lilian to come to her. But she had been too impatient to wait.

She knew her sister would be in. It was Tuesday, the night of Tony's Home Guard parade. Lilian always made sure she was at home to prepare his sandwiches and Thermos.

Bobby frowned as she descended the track to the cow house, however. Even at the top, she could tell that there was an almighty racket coming from the place. The door stood open, and sounds drifted out to her – raised voices, the baby screaming. The voices belonged to Tony and Lil. And there was something on the ground outside – some sort of animal, it looked like, although it wasn't moving. What on earth could be going on?

Bobby sped up, at least as much as she was able to. She wondered Reg and Mary hadn't come out to investigate. The row must be audible from Moorside. She wouldn't be surprised if it could be heard even as far as the Parrys' house.

No sooner had she thought of the Parrys than a pale, frightened face belonging to Jess peeped round the cow house door. When she caught sight of Bobby, she came running up the track and flung herself into her arms.

'Jess, sweetheart, what on earth is going on?' Bobby asked, hugging her tightly.

'It's Mr Scott,' Jess whispered. 'He's gone mad, Bobby. He keeps shouting and shouting. I ain't never heard him shout before. Aunty Lil told me and Florrie to take Annie over to Mary, only Mary ain't in, nor Reg. And Dad's gone out in town with that Miss Simpson so he ain't in either. He was supposed to come for us soon. I was looking to see if he was coming and I saw you.'

'Where's Florrie?'

'She's watching Annie. Aunty Lil told her to. But Annie won't stop crying and Mr Scott won't stop shouting and me and Florrie don't know what to do.'

All thoughts of the exciting news that had filled her brain moments ago had been forgotten now. Bobby took the child's hand and hurried with her to the cow house. As she drew closer, she saw that what she had taken to be a sleeping dog was in fact Lilian's fur coat.

'Oh God, no,' she muttered.

She could hear what Tony and her sister were saying now.

'Just tell me how long it's been going on,' Tony was demanding.

'Tony, please, not in front of the children. Calm down and we'll discuss it sensibly.'

Tony gave a hollow laugh. 'Sensibly! Bit late for being sensible, don't you think?'

Bobby hurried in with Jess. Florrie was there, white and frightened, with the screaming Annie in her arms. Tony was standing over Lilian in his Home Guard battledress, white with rage and hurt.

'What on earth is going on?' Bobby demanded. 'I could hear you yelling halfway over the bridge, Tony.'

Tony spun on her, and she winced at the look on his face. Bobby had only seen him look so utterly overcome with emotion one other time – the night Lil had been in labour, and they had so nearly lost her. She still remembered Tony, almost brutish in his grief, muttering angry prayers demanding God take his worthless life instead of his wife's.

'Ask your sister,' he growled.

Lil flushed. 'He found my coat. The one Geor— that Captain Parry gave to me.'

'So you knew too, did you?' Tony said to Bobby, in the same voice of strangled rage. 'Well, of course you did. Thick as thieves, you two, aren't you? You've been covering for them, I suppose. Pete told me what he'd seen. The two of them coming out of some teashop in Skipton.'

Bobby turned to her sister. 'What?'

'I met George there to break it off, like I told you I was going to,' Lil said in a low voice. 'That's all.'

'Break it off?' Tony turned to face her again. 'So there was something. How long has it been going on?'

'It hasn't. I swear to you, Tony, that man has never so much as touched me.'

Tony gave a grim laugh. 'Right. He dresses you up in fur coats as a token of appreciation for making such a good cup of tea, I suppose.'

'He gave me the coat because I was pregnant and miserable and he thought it might make me smile. It was damaged stock from his shop.'

'And you accepted it. You, a married woman. A *fur coat*, Lil! You know what people would think if they knew, right?'

Lil flushed. 'I know, it was wrong. It was so long since I'd had anything really nice to wear that I couldn't help it.'

'The clothes I slave away earning money for you to buy aren't good enough, are they?'

'I never said that.'

'And what did he want in return for this fur coat, as if I couldn't guess?'

'He never asked me for a thing, Tony,' Lil said quietly. 'I'll swear to that on my daughter's life. He's never asked me to go to bed with him. He's never tried to kiss me. He's never even held my hand. He was just kind to me when I needed kindness, and...' Her blush deepened. '...and occasionally we'd go to the cinema. That's all there was to it.'

'To the cinema?' Tony shook his head darkly. 'I don't bloody well believe this.' Something seemed to dawn on him. 'That's who you named her for, isn't it? The other baby.'

'Georgia,' Lilian whispered. 'Yes. He was there that night my labour started. He brought help – saved my life.'

It was this, even more than the fur coat and cinema trips, that seemed to knock Tony reeling. He stared at his wife with a look of impotent horror that was as piteous as it was frightening. Bobby almost thought for a moment he might strike Lilian, he looked so wild.

'You'd even take her from me,' he whispered. 'Even her, Lil.'

All the while, Annie had been crying at the top of her lungs. Florrie jiggled the little thing helplessly, white and scared, while Jessie lurked by the door as if preparing to flee.

'Tony, can you please stop?' Bobby begged him. 'You're upsetting the children.'

'Nobody asked your opinion,' he snapped. 'Go home, can you, Bob? This doesn't concern you.'

Bobby approached Florrie and held out her arms.

'Here, my love, give me the baby,' she said gently. 'I think you girls ought to wait outside for your father. You shouldn't be listening to this. Florrie, take care of your little sister please, and don't wander off.'

Florrie nodded soberly and took Jessie's hand to lead her outside.

Tony showed no sign of calming down. He was pacing in long strides from one end of the room to the other, hands over his ears, as if to shut out the sound of his thoughts.

'My mam told me you were no good,' he was saying. 'And me, I told her to shut her mouth. Took your part while all the time you were...' He turned to face Bobby. 'You're no better either.' He sneered. 'My friend, eh? And all the time your sister's running around like a tart while you lie through your teeth to me.'

Bobby didn't answer. She couldn't trust herself to say anything that wouldn't make matters worse.

She supposed she shouldn't be here during this intensely private confrontation, except that there was no chance she was going to leave her sister alone with Tony in this mood. So she just shushed the poor baby, whose cries had settled to a dull whimper, pressing Annie's soft cheek against her own.

'Bobby hasn't lied to you,' Lilian said quietly. 'She didn't know a thing about it until a few weeks ago when she saw us in Skipton, and she took your part right away, Tony. That's why I ended things – not that there were things to end, really. You're right, it was wrong of me to hide things from you. But in spite of how it must look, George and I were never more than good friends.'

Tony snorted. 'A friend who takes you out to the pictures and gives you fur coats. Men who give gifts like that always expect to get paid, Lil – that's if he hasn't been paid already.'

'You don't believe me?'

'Any reason I should, after all the other lies?'

Lilian sighed, looking suddenly weary. 'No, I suppose not. But it's true, all the same.'

Tony stood there, looking at her with a helpless expression. Then he burst into tears. Bobby and Lilian stared at him, neither knowing what they ought to do.

'Why though?' Tony asked after a moment, when he had got his outburst under control. 'I've been good to you, haven't I? I don't get roaring drunk or beat you or run around with women. I work hard to get you and the baby what you need. I never complained when you insisted on having your dad live here with us. Never questioned it when you told me Annie was mine, though I knew you'd had plenty of other boyfriends.' Tony's voice broke. 'I've done everything for you,

Lil. Everything. I've loved you more than I thought I could love someone. And you pay me back with this.'

'I know,' Lil murmured. 'And for what it's worth, I'm sorry, Tony. The last thing I wanted was for you to get hurt.'

'Aye, but you didn't go out of your way to prevent it, did you? Why did you do it? Can you just tell me that?'

'I told you, I didn't *do* anything. There was no affair. Just… companionship. Conversation.'

'Why with him? Why not with me? I'm your husband.'

'Because… because…'

'…because you don't love me,' he finished for her. 'Do you?'

Lilian bowed her head. 'I'm sorry. I tried, really I did, but…' She trailed off in a sigh.

'Do you love him?'

'I… I honestly don't know. I admire him a lot. I respect him.'

'You respect him but you don't respect me.'

'I didn't say that.' She met his eyes. 'You're my husband, Tony. I accept that. I won't be so foolish again, I promise.'

He snorted. 'You *accept* it?'

'What more do you want me to say?'

'I want you to say you're happy about it. That I'm the one you'd choose.'

'I can't. I'm sorry. I wish I could, but I just… can't.'

'Why not?' he demanded in a choked voice.

'I want to love you, Tony. I even try to. I suppose I just can't forget how things began for us. The way you exploited the information you had on my dad to get to me.' She turned away sadly. 'I know there's a good man in you somewhere. I know you love me and I know you adore the baby. But… I'm sorry, but I can't quite manage to forgive you for the way we ended up here.'

There was the sound of manly footsteps striding down the track, and two squeals of 'Dad!' from the Parry sisters outside.

'Right,' Tony muttered to himself. 'Right.' He turned and strode out of the door.

Bobby frowned at Lilian. 'Where's he going?'

'I can guess. Put Annie in her pram and come on.'

Lilian ran out after her husband. Bobby put the whimpering baby down and followed.

George Parry was hurrying down the track to his daughters, but Tony sprinted up to him and blocked his way.

Lilian came jogging up the track behind him, Bobby behind her with the two girls gripping a hand each.

'You,' Tony muttered to the other man.

The captain examined him coldly. 'Can I help you?'

'You can. You can keep your damn hands off my wife, for a start.'

The captain stared at him. He looked unsure how to respond while Tony squared up to him.

'I've never touched your wife, Scott,' he said at last. 'I respect her far too much.'

'Tony, please, leave the man alone,' Lilian said, putting a hand on her husband's shoulder. 'It's true, I swear it. He never touched me. Come back to the house and let's discuss things calmly.'

Tony ignored her, pushing the hand on his shoulder roughly away.

'You wanted to, though, didn't you, Parry?' he demanded with a sneer. 'Who the hell gives a fur coat to a woman and doesn't expect to get into her knickers? Bringing your kids over to play happy families every day. Is she your wife? Is she?'

'My wife is dead,' George said stiffly.

'So you thought you'd fill her place with mine, did you?'

'Daddy, I'm scared,' Jess whispered. 'Can we go home please?'

The captain took his house key from his pocket and handed it to Florrie. 'Here. Take your sister home. I'll be there soon, when I've finished my discussion with Mr Scott.'

'We don't want to leave you,' Florrie said.

'This gentleman and I need to have some grown-up talk. I won't be long, sweetheart.' He looked at Tony. 'I suppose it's all right with you if my daughters leave before we continue this… conversation?'

'Aye, get them out of the way. Some things it's best bairns don't see.'

'All right, girls, go on.'

Florrie hesitated before taking the key from her father. She took her sister's hand and they ran off towards their cottage.

'And now I suppose you're going to demand satisfaction,' the captain said calmly to Tony. 'Would you prefer pistols or swords?'

'What I'd prefer is to plant my fist in your smug face, you bastard. You've been watching my wife ever since we came here. I've seen you. Maybe summat happened between you and maybe it didn't, but I know well enough what was in your mind.'

'You never could understand what a treasure you had in Lilian.' The captain paused. 'But for what it's worth… I apologise. I did wrong in seeking out your wife's company behind your back. I knew it was wrong, and unbecoming of a gentleman, yet selfishly I pursued it because… well, because her company was pleasant to me. You have every right to be aggrieved, but I can assure you Lilian has behaved impeccably. If it wasn't that she had so few pleasures and holidays, I'm sure she would have told me to go to the devil long before now.'

Tony gave a hollow laugh. 'But that's no good, is it, mate? Because now she loves you. How can she not, with you standing there talking all posh with your pipe and your moustache and your sodding war wound, when it's me she's got to come home to? I mean, I'm no war hero, am I? I've never had a bullet put in my shoulder by a Luftwaffe pilot on the beaches of Dunkirk. I'm just Tony bloody Scott, that's who I am. Anybody back where I used to live can tell you who I am.' He swallowed a sob. 'Couldn't it have been anyone else, Parry?' he asked in a whisper. 'I've had one damn thing to love in my entire waste of a life, and you… you had to take her away from me.'

The captain flashed Lilian a helpless look. 'I really am so sorry.'

Tony laughed. He turned away, as if he was going back to the house, but Bobby knew better. She had seen the clenched fist. A split second later he had swung, his knuckles catching the unprepared captain full in the face. There was a cracking sound and George fell backwards with a sharp groan, clutching his stricken nose. Blood streamed from his nostrils.

'I had to do that,' Tony said in a strangely detached tone as he stood over his bleeding rival. 'Wouldn't be a man if I didn't.'

'Tony, for God's sake, stop this!' Lilian ran forward to wrap her arms around her husband's back, trying to wrestle him away. George was staggering to his feet now, and Tony's fist was still white-knuckled at his side.

'Lil, get off me,' he said, pushing against her with his shoulders. 'Take Bobby and go back to the baby. This is between me and him.'

'He's bleeding, Tony! I swear you must've broken his nose. Just get the hell away from him.'

'It's men's business. It doesn't concern you.'

Still she held on to him. 'I won't leave you here to beat him to a bloody pulp. Come home, can you?'

'Lil, I said get off!' Tony gave her a rough shove, using all his strength to free himself. Lilian lost her grip and fell to the ground, hitting her head against a rock on the gravel track.

'Oh my God!' Bobby dropped to her haunches. 'Lil, sweetheart, are you all right?'

'I'm… fine.' Lil put her hand to the back of her head, then stared woozily at her red fingers. 'Oh. I'm bleeding.'

Bobby shook her head darkly at Tony. 'What the hell did you do?'

Tony was staring at his injured wife, a horrified look on his face.

'It was an accident,' he said helplessly, to no one in particular. He looked from Lilian lying on the ground to Captain Parry holding the bridge of his gushing nose. 'It was an accident.'

He bent down to try and help his wife, but Bobby pushed him away.

'You've done quite enough. Get away from her.' She turned back to Lilian. 'Can you walk, love? Are you dizzy at all?'

'It could be a concussion,' the captain muttered nasally. 'Scott, if you want to help then go for the doctor.'

'It was an accident,' Tony repeated again.

'Leave, Tony, can you?' Bobby said. 'Walk to the Bull and ring for Dr Minchin. And don't even think about coming back until you've remembered how to behave like a civilised human being rather than whatever that caveman nonsense was.'

'I never meant... never would've... Lil, I am so, so sorry.'

'Please,' Lilian whispered. 'Just go, Tony. I can't be near you at the moment.'

Looking utterly defeated, Tony turned to head up the track.

'Can you both walk?' Bobby asked the two casualties. 'We ought to get back to the cow house. There'll be bandages and things in Charlie's cupboards. I think I still remember how to apply a nasal splint. Thank God for the WAAF.'

'I can walk,' Lilian said, wincing as she pushed herself into a sitting position. 'I need to get back to my baby.' She looked at the captain. 'George, are you all right?'

'Don't worry about me,' he said, sounding as if he had a heavy cold. 'A bloody nose is no more than I deserve for my part in this. Still, he's certainly broken it. I don't want the girls to see me gushing blood if I can help it, so anything you have in the way of bandages would be appreciated.'

Lilian shook her head, then grimaced from the pain of moving it. 'I'm so sorry. You left them in my care and now they've been exposed to all this. How will we ever explain it to them?'

'I'm the one who ought to say sorry. I've caused a lot of trouble for you, one way or another. I don't know how you can bear to look at me, Lilian.'

'Never mind all that,' Bobby said firmly. 'The more immediate concern is the fact you're both bleeding all over the place. Let's get inside.'

## Chapter 33

At the cow house, Bobby pillaged some bandages from Charlie's surgery, as well as cotton wool and a bottle of antiseptic. She was able to fashion a nasal splint for the captain from a couple of matchsticks.

She was relieved to find that Lilian's head didn't look too bad: just a small cut at the back, and the beginning of a rather fine lump. Still, Bobby hoped Dr Minchin would be able to come. She remembered from her first aid training that concussion could be a difficult thing to diagnose, and was dangerous if left untreated. There were various ways to test for it, asking about spots behind the eyes and so forth, but Bobby couldn't remember what they were.

An hour later, however, the doctor still hadn't arrived. There was no sign of Tony either, although Bobby had hardly expected him to come home after what had happened. She imagined he had either gone to his Home Guard parade or – and this seemed more likely – he was drinking away his woes in a pub somewhere. Wherever he was, she hoped he was having a long, hard think about what he'd done.

She might have understood him thumping Captain Parry, given the provocation. She had even felt rather sorry for him when he had looked so very broken at the thought George might have secured Lilian's love when he had been striving for it all this time. But what he had done to his wife was harder to forgive.

Lilian had finally managed to soothe the baby, who was sleeping quietly. Lil's head was bandaged from eyebrows to crown – the cut was small, but Bobby had been liberal in her use of Charlie's dressings nonetheless. Meanwhile, the captain had two matchsticks either side of his nose secured by a strip of plaster, with cotton wool in both nostrils. The bleeding finally seemed to be slowing.

'Look at the pair of us,' Lilian said when she had put down the baby. 'We look like we've escaped the pyramids, George.'

The captain smiled. 'Yes, we are rather Tutankhamun-like. How does your poor old head feel, darling?' He winced. 'I'm sorry. Lilian. I hadn't meant to call you that.'

'It aches, but it should be all right by tomorrow,' Lilian said. 'It'll only be a little tender for a while, I think.'

'I ought to get back to the girls. They must have been frightened before, and I owe them an explanation. If I stay any longer, they'll wonder what's become of me.'

'You ought to see the doctor first,' Bobby said. 'I don't know if I've dressed your nose right at all, George. I can go to the girls and tell them not to worry about you.'

'No,' the captain said, a little more sharply than he was accustomed to speak. 'Sorry, but I wouldn't want Scott to hear I'd been alone here with his wife. Besides, you've done enough rushing about today for someone in your condition. You can send the doctor to me when he's treated your sister.'

'Why did you come over?' Lilian asked, turning to Bobby. 'I forgot to ask in all the drama.'

Bobby thought of the news she had been so excited to share. What had seemed like the beginning of a whole new life hardly seemed to matter, now. She had no idea what the future would hold for her sister and Tony, after this.

'Just for a chat,' she said vaguely. 'It wasn't important.'

'I'll leave you to wait for the doctor,' the captain said, getting to his feet. 'Lilian, I'm so sorry again for all the trouble I've caused you. I've been a very selfish man, I see that now. I don't know what made me act so rashly.'

'Why did you?' Bobby asked. She was tired and annoyed after the scene earlier, and in no mood to mind her own business.

And while Tony was currently top of her grudge list after the way he had hurt Lilian, the captain certainly wasn't in her good books either.

The captain sighed. 'I suppose I thought I could have my cake and eat it too, to coin a hackneyed phrase. I admired your sister, and I felt that if we remained strictly and carefully platonic in our relations then I could enjoy her company without violating the sanctity of marriage.'

'It didn't occur to you that feelings were involved as well as marriage vows?' Bobby demanded. 'That it was always going to be more complicated than that?'

Lilian shot her sister a look, but Bobby ignored it.

'I don't suppose it did,' the captain said, his eyes fixed on Lilian. 'Or at least, I didn't allow myself to think about it.' He approached Lil to take her hands. 'I'd like to say I had enough decency in my soul to regret it. But when I think of the time we spent together, Lilian, I honestly can't. It was precious, every moment. I thank you for it.'

'You sound like you're saying goodbye,' Lilian said quietly.

'Yes. I'll make other arrangements for the girls after school. I suppose you and I must be merely nodding acquaintances henceforth. Neighbours and no more.'

'You're right. It's the only way.' Lilian summoned a watery smile. 'But I want you to know, George... I don't regret it either. Those memories are precious, as you say, and I'll be living on them the rest of my life.'

'And I pray with all my heart that it will be a long and happy life, filled with love. I've never met anyone who more deserved it.' The captain hesitated, then planted a soft kiss on her cheek. 'Take care of yourself, my dear.'

'I know Veronica will make you happy. I'll never forget you. Tell the girls I love them, and...' Lilian bit her lip. 'Goodbye, George.'

'Goodbye, Lilian.'

The captain gave her a last lingering glance before he left. Lilian watched him go, staring at the door for some time after it had closed.

'So it was love after all,' Bobby said quietly.

Lilian started. 'Bobby. I'd half forgotten you were here.'

'I'm so sorry, sweetheart. What happens now?'

Lilian sat down beside her. 'I suppose... I put it behind me. Keep it my special, secret little memory, like a lovely dream I once had, and try to muddle along with Tony. Try to love him if I can.'

'Do you think you ever could?'

'I don't know.' Lilian touched one hand to the back of her bandaged head. 'I don't know.'

—

A little while later there was a knock at the door. Bobby expected to see the doctor when she answered it, but instead it was Charlie, accompanied by a young man she didn't recognise.

'Bobby,' he said with surprise. 'You're here.'

'I am. And so are you.' She cast a puzzled look at the stranger. 'And, um, so are you. Well, come in.'

'Is everything all right?' Charlie asked, looking anxious as he followed her inside. 'There's a fur coat on the ground out there and I was sure I saw blood on the track.' He clocked Lilian's bandaged head and stared. 'Hellfire! What have you girls been doing?'

'Never mind that. You're needed,' Bobby said. 'In the absence of a doctor, a vet will have to do. Do you know much about concussion?'

'I know how to check for it. Why, has Lil got a concussion?' He looked at Lil. 'Have you got a concussion?'

'I don't think so, but I'm no expert,' she said.

'Right. Well, let's take a look.' He came forward and started unravelling her bandages.

Bobby looked at the other man, who was taking in this scene of chaos with a bewildered look on his face. 'Who's this, Charlie?'

'Roger,' Charlie said absently. 'Your sister told me I could bring him to the surgery. Remember?'

'Oh.' Bobby rubbed her head. 'Yes. Sorry, I'd forgotten.'

'Is anyone going to tell me what's going on?'

'I'll tell you all about it once you've checked our Lil over.' Bobby summoned a smile for Roger. 'I'm so sorry about this, Mr Turner. Let me show you into the surgery. Charlie can join us when he's done with his patient.'

'She makes me sound like a poorly spaniel,' Lil muttered while Charlie pressed his fingers against her lump.

'Right,' said the dazed-looking Roger. He followed Bobby to the surgery.

'Um, so these are the instruments,' she said when they were inside, gesturing vaguely. 'All in excellent condition, as you can see. A real bargain at… whatever Charlie said he was willing to sell them for. This one's a bull emasculator and the rest are for, er… sheep. Sheep things.'

Roger smiled. 'I take it you didn't meet him working as a veterinary nurse?'

'Well observed,' Bobby said, smiling too. 'I'm sure he'll be here in a moment to tell you what everything is. My sister had an accident earlier and my first aid skills are rather rusty, I'm ashamed to say.'

'Not at all,' the man said politely. 'Your bandaging looked first rate.'

He seemed young to be starting his own practice, Bobby thought. Roger Turner couldn't be more than twenty-two.

'I know, barely out of the cradle and already opening a surgery of my own,' Roger said with a laugh, as if reading her thoughts. 'My old man died recently and left me some money, so I thought why should I be slogging my backside off for any other sod, pardon my French? The problem is finding someone to come in with me. I could use an old hand at my side who'd be able to weigh in with knowledge and advice, but practically everyone not in a practice of their own seems to have gone off to the veterinary corps.'

'Oh,' Bobby said, disappointed. 'So there's a chance you won't need to buy Charlie's instruments after all, then.'

'Well, I haven't quite given up hope of finding a partner.' He looked at her keenly. 'I was hoping your husband might be interested, but he tells me he doesn't practise any more. Any idea why?'

Bobby flushed. 'Well, um, he was injured in the RAF. I shouldn't say too much when it's his business, but the injury makes it difficult to do work that requires a steady hand. That's why he's selling his instruments.'

'That's just it. He wouldn't need to be involved much on the practical side. I'm after more of a silent partner, if that's the right term — someone with the experience I lack who'll take an advisory role, and help train up an apprentice when we're in a position to take one on. But he turned me down flat when I suggested it.'

'Really?'

'Perhaps you could talk to him? The offer's still open if you think he might change his mind.'

'Why did he turn you down?'

'I couldn't say.'

They were interrupted by Charlie.

'It's all right,' he said to Bobby. 'No concussion, just a nasty bump. How did she get it anyhow?'

'She had a fall. I'll tell you how it happened later.'

Bobby cast another puzzled look in Roger Turner's direction. Why on earth would Charlie turn down a role that sounded so eminently suitable for him, when she knew he longed to return to veterinary work? A partnership where his role was advisory rather than practical sounded ideal — more than ideal. It could have been made for him. Bobby couldn't understand why he wouldn't bite this new friend's hand off.

'So, did you show Roger everything?' Charlie asked her.

'I showed him the bull emasculator.'

Charlie shook his head. 'It really worries me that that's the only one you ever remember. Come on, Roger, let me talk you through it all.'

—

Dr Minchin eventually turned up and was able to confirm that Lilian wasn't suffering from a concussion. After he had been over to the Parrys' to see to the captain's nose, he had kindly offered to drive Bobby and Charlie home in his car.

Bobby hadn't liked to leave her sister alone, and had been making plans to stay at the cow house overnight. Tony had arrived home, however, chastened and surprisingly still sober, which had changed matters.

'You'd better go, Bob,' Lilian had said quietly. 'He and I ought to talk.'

So Bobby had left with Charlie and the doctor, but not without a glare that told Tony exactly what she currently thought of him.

'Well that was quite a day,' she said to Charlie when they were home.

'I can see that,' Charlie said, glancing at her dirty, bloodied pinny. 'Sit down, Bob. I don't know what happened today but I'm sure it can't have done you any good.'

'I'm jolly glad I was there, though.' She sighed. 'What a mess it all is.'

Charlie guided her to the settee. 'What on earth went on earlier? I saw that look you gave Tony. He didn't do that to your sister, did he?'

'He did.'

Charlie shook his head darkly. 'That bastard. I wish I'd been there. I might have thought Tony Scott was a lot of things, but I never had him down as a wife-beater.'

'It was a little more complicated than that. Hold me, can you?'

Charlie sat down beside her and guided her into his arms.

'Well, what happened?' he asked.

After Bobby had filled him in, Charlie looked rather stunned.

'Gosh,' he said at last.

'I know.'

'Your sister and Captain Parry! I'd have thought he'd be too stuffy for anything as exciting as an affair.'

'It wasn't an affair. Not exactly.' Bobby sighed. 'I felt so sorry for them when they said goodbye. I think they've fallen quite deeply in love. And now they can never see each other again, except to nod to in the village. Lil's had so much bad luck, it doesn't seem fair that there won't be any happy ending for her.'

'She ought to leave him. Tony,' Charlie said grimly. 'I've got no time for men who hit women. I heard you tell your brother you weren't sure you believed in cowards, but I do. Men who prey on the weak. Men who beat women. They make me sick.'

'I don't believe Tony's a bully by nature. He looked horrified when he realised what he'd done.'

'Good. He should do.'

'What do you think will happen to them? Could they ever be happy?'

'I don't know, Bob. It draws a line, something like what happened tonight. The fact Tony hurt you sister, I mean. Everything afterwards will be coloured by it, even if it never happens again.'

'You might be right,' Bobby said with a sigh. 'I wish there was something I could do.'

'You can't fix everything, darling. It's between Lil and Tony now.'

'I know.' She stroked his hair. 'Why don't you rest your head in my lap? Marmaduke always sleeps when he feels you there.'

'All right, but not for too long. You need to eat, Bob.'

He lay down, and Bobby let out a deep sigh. She could feel the tension of earlier dissipating with Charlie's head in her lap and the baby settling in response. Once again, she wondered how Marmaduke always seemed to know when his dad was near.

She felt rather sleepy herself. Her eyes started to flicker, but Bobby forced herself to remain awake. There was something she wanted to ask Charlie before she let herself relax.

'Did Roger say anything about that equipment?' she asked.

'He seemed impressed by the bull emasculator. I think you rather oversold it.'

Bobby smiled. 'Don't joke. Do you think he'll take it?'

'He was definitely interested, but he had some things to arrange first. He's going to let me know when he's made a decision.'

Bobby hesitated, wondering how to proceed.

'It must be galling for you,' she said. 'Seeing him making plans to open his own practice. I know how much you miss veterinary work.'

'I do,' he said with a sigh. 'Still, if he takes everything, that's ten pounds. We'll be quite rich, won't we?'

'Yes,' Bobby agreed, thinking guiltily of her biscuit tin containing nearly three times that. 'That's if he takes it though. He told me he was having trouble finding a partner, with so many vets gone to war. If he can't find someone then it could be all off, he said.'

'He told you that?'

'He did.' Bobby paused. 'And he told me… he told me he'd offered it to you. Is that true?'

'Yes, it's true. What of it?'

'I just can't understand why you'd turn it down, darling. Roger said it was more an advisory role than a practical one, suitable for someone with a lot of experience. I can't think of anything more perfect. I know you're unhappy at the bank, and how much you miss your old work. And to be a partner in your own practice too.'

Charlie gave a bleak laugh. 'He didn't tell you about the money then.'

'What money?'

'The investment money to get the thing started. It's a hundred pounds, Bobby. Roger's putting in fifty and he's looking for a partner to put in another fifty. Where am I supposed to get money like that?'

Bobby almost laughed. 'That's what's stopping you?'

'You say it like it's nothing. Even if Roger took my instruments in part payment, where would I get the other forty quid? Reggie doesn't have that kind of money to lend, and there's no one else I'd ask. Even if the bank would consider giving me a loan, it's a big risk. I'd be giving up a guaranteed salary of three pounds four a week – three pounds eight when the baby comes – in the hope this new practice will be successful.'

'Do you think it will?'

'I think it's got a good chance,' Charlie told her. 'There's no practice within ten miles of where Roger will be setting up, which works in his favour.'

'So if you had the forty quid, and you weren't worried about bringing in a regular wage to support your family while you grew the business, would you do it?'

He laughed. 'You mean if I was a completely different Charlie, with no family and wads of ill-gotten cash under the mattress? Yes, Bobby, then I'd do it. Unfortunately I'm this Charlie, which rather puts the kibosh on the whole idea.'

All Bobby's excitement about the news she had to share, forgotten during the scene between Lilian and Tony, had returned stronger than ever. Because now that news could really make a difference.

'All right, sit up and brace yourself,' she told Charlie. 'I've got a surprise for you.'

'If it's a secret fortune of forty pounds, you and I are going to have words, Mrs Atherton. The scandal of where your sister got that fur coat would pale by comparison.'

'You'll see,' Bobby said, with a grin she couldn't manage to suppress.

She went to the bedroom and retrieved the biscuit tin under the bed. When she had taken it back to Charlie, she removed the lid and tipped it out on the coffee table. Bank notes and postal orders, bound together with elastic bands, tumbled out. Charlie stared at them.

'Well?' Bobby said after a moment's silence.

'Pardon my language, but bloody hell!' Charlie said. 'What... where... I mean, how much?'

'Twenty-five pounds in cash and three pounds in postal orders.'

'But where on earth did you get it? I hope you haven't been selling your favours to Ernie King.'

'They'd never fetch so much,' Bobby said with a smile. She picked up the bundle of banknotes. 'This is from my dad. I'm sorry, Charlie, but I wasn't completely honest about my share of the money from the sale of the house. It was thirty-five pounds, not ten. My dad told me this story about him and my mam that made me think... well, I wanted to put it aside as rainy day money, just in case. I knew it would be too tempting to spend it otherwise. And it worked, you see? Because now we need it, there it is.'

Charlie stared dazedly at the money before picking up the stack of postal orders. 'What about these?'

'There's a story attached to each one.' Bobby drew out one of the five-shilling postal orders. 'This one, for example. Do you remember last month when we were listening to *ITMA* – how you laughed at that joke of Funf's about careless talk?'

'Vaguely,' Charlie said, blinking. 'What does that have to do with anything?'

Bobby beamed. 'Now guess who wrote it.'

He stared at her. 'No!'

'Honestly. I must have sold over a dozen jokes to radio comics since Christmas. You don't know how hard it was not to tell you.'

'But why didn't you tell me?'

Bobby sat down by him.

'I'm sorry, darling,' she said softly. 'I was desperate to have some writing to do when I left work, and I did hope I could bring in money by it while you were unemployed. But I knew it got you down, the way you weren't able to support your family. Then when you got your job at the bank, and felt so humiliated doing a woman's job... I was worried it might upset you.'

'Upset me?' Charlie looked again at their riches, and started to laugh. 'You daft apeth. I'm as proud as anything.'

Bobby kissed his cheek. 'I hoped you would be.'

Charlie became sober. 'This doesn't really change things though, Bob. I mean it does, in a lot of ways. We won't need to worry about buying things for the baby, and any extra you can earn at home will help. But this is still some way short of what I'd need to go into business with Roger. Even if it was enough, the postal orders you've been getting would be a pretty unpredictable source of income if I couldn't bring in a regular wage. You don't have any sort of contract with these radio comics, I suppose.'

Bobby grinned at him. 'No. Not with them. The money in the tin is actually only half my news. The other half came this morning, and I've been bursting to share it with someone all day.'

'What is it?'

Bobby went to fetch the envelope she had received from the *Girl's Own* editress. She extracted her story and handed it to Charlie.

'Here,' she said. 'Read this first. Ignore the bits in blue for now.'

Bewildered, Charlie took it from her and read it through. Bobby watched him keenly, alert for every change in his expression.

'Well?' she demanded when he was done. 'What do you think?'

'It's very good,' he said. 'The sort of thing Florrie likes. Funny too. Is it yours?'

'It is. It came in the post today with those editorial notes, and a letter and contract. Not to mention a cheque for four pounds – half of what I'll be paid for it in total.'

Charlie blinked. 'Four pounds? You earnt four pounds for this? That's more than I make in a week.'

'It'll be eight pounds when they send the other half. Plus they've sent a contract for five more stories, and the editress says she'd be interested in a serial if the readers like them.' She sat by him, smiling. 'That ought to get you enough for your practice, don't you think? And with a contract in place, it makes for a more secure income than selling gags. We can afford to keep Jenny on as home help, so I can make a little time for writing each day. I hope it might turn into something I can make a proper career out of – something that won't interfere with my duties at home.'

Charlie was silent for a long time, his head in his hands. He was staring at her contract as if he couldn't believe his eyes. Bobby had started to worry he was upset, until eventually the dazed look faded and he started to laugh.

'Oh my God,' he said. 'I'll tell you what, it's a wonderful thing to have a clever wife. I'll be recommending it to all the young bachelors.'

'You'll do it, then? You'll telephone Roger and tell him you want to take the partnership? If we cash the cheque and postal orders and add the six pounds left in the baby pot, that's thirty-eight pounds. If Roger's willing to take your instruments in lieu of another ten, I'm sure Reg would loan us two to make it up. I can pay him back when I get the four pounds I'm owed.'

'I think...' Charlie stared at the contract. 'I think... yes. If you honestly don't mind funding me, darling, then I'd really like to do it. I know it's a risk, but I've always been a vet first and foremost. I don't think I can be happy doing anything other than tending beasts, the same way you need your writing.'

'I know.' Bobby gave him a hug. 'I'm so pleased, Charlie. I've hated to see you unhappy in your work. I just know you'll make a success of it. You can make a success of anything you turn your hand to.'

Charlie smiled. 'Says Agatha Christie over here.' He kissed her. 'Thank you,' he said softly. 'I'll do everything I can to make sure you never regret it.'

## Chapter 34

It was five days later when Bobby looked out of her window to see Florence Parry moving furtively around the graveyard opposite.

Charlie was out, meeting with Roger Turner to discuss the arrangements for their new practice, and Bobby had pulled her chair to the window while she worked on the second Lindy story. She was hoping to find inspiration among the crocuses and primroses in the churchyard. If she couldn't get out to enjoy the springtime, she could at least make sure Section Officer Langstaff was able to do so.

It was Sunday, but there were to be no family dinners that day. Word had quickly spread of the row that had taken place between Lilian, Tony and the captain. The news that George Parry had had his nose broken by the jealous husband of 'that Mrs Scott' was being spoken of in whispers all over Silverdale, much to Bobby's chagrin. She hated to think of her sister being the subject of gossip, especially when the connection with the captain had been – from a physical point of view, at least – entirely innocent.

Of course Reg and Mary knew what had occurred, and it was unavoidable that Bobby's dad would get to hear of it. Neither he nor anyone else knew about Lil's head injury, however, which Bobby was grateful for. She felt sure there'd be another broken nose in the family if her dad got wind of it, and this time it would belong to Tony Scott.

The whole family – Scotts, Parrys, Bancrofts and Athertons – were in a state of collective shock about the business. No one seemed to know how they ought to behave: whether they ought to still be on speaking terms with either Tony or the captain, how to keep George's daughters within the fold now he and the Scotts were estranged, or who was ultimately to blame for what had happened. No one even knew what had happened, exactly. Only that Tony had suspected his wife and the captain, and had broken the man's nose in a fit of jealousy. On top of that had come news of the breaking of George Parry's engagement to Veronica Simpson. No one knew why, but gossip said it had been he who ended it.

Bobby, fingers itching as ever to fix things, was at a loss as to how they could move forward. Lilian and George had said their goodbyes, and yes, their relations would have to be different from now on, but where did that leave the children? It would be impossible to sever relations with George without losing Florrie and Jess, and no one could bear the thought of that. Mary was in some distress about it all. But how could things be managed, after what had happened? A sort of numb inertia seemed to have descended on the family, with no obvious next step.

Bobby watched as Florrie scuttled around the graveyard. What could the child be up to? After a moment, she put down her notepad and heaved herself to her feet to find out.

'Florrie!' she called on entering the graveyard, waving to the girl.

'Hullo, Bobby.' Florrie came running over to hug her around her huge belly.

Bobby smiled and bent to kiss her hair. 'It's nice to see you, sweetheart. But what on earth are you doing in the churchyard?'

'I was looking for Georgia. I can't remember which one's her grave.'

'Well, let me help you.' Bobby guided her to the right plot. 'Here she is, look. Why did you want to see her?'

'To talk,' Florrie said quietly. 'Aunty Lil told me she always talks to Georgia when she's sad and it makes her feel better.'

'Are you sad, my love?'

Florrie nodded, brushing a tear away. 'I thought I'd be happier than anything if Dad only said he wouldn't marry that Miss Simpson, but I wish he would marry her if it meant... if it meant...' She broke off to swallow a sob, and Bobby pulled her into a hug.

'If it meant what, sweetheart?'

'If it meant we could stay,' Florrie whispered.

Bobby frowned. 'Stay? Where are you going?'

'Dad says we're to go back to London. He says he's caused trouble here and now we have to go.'

Bobby held her back. 'Your father's planning to move you back to London?'

Florrie nodded miserably. 'Because of what happened with Mr Scott, when he hurt Dad's nose.' Her face took on an expression of defiance. 'But I won't go, Bobby. I'll... I'll hide and not go. I want to stay here, with Mary and you and Aunty Lil. I don't see why me and Jess should have to go away just because Dad did something wrong.'

'No,' Bobby said absently, her thoughts on this new development.

It had never occurred to her the captain might take his children away as a result of what had happened, but of course it was logical. She knew he blamed himself for the trouble Lilian had found herself in. But to take the girls away from their new family, where they were so loved... that was far worse than his ill-judged liaison with her sister. Mary would be devastated if the girls were taken away. Everyone would be in a state of grief.

'Bobby?' Florrie murmured, her eyes fixed on the gravestone.

'Yes, my love?'

'What did Dad do to make Mr Scott want to hit him? I know it's about Aunty Lil, and Georgia as well because she was named after him. And I know that, um, there's something where ladies who are married aren't allowed to have man friends who are sort of like their husbands, and kiss them and things. Like our

Aunt Sadie used to have, where she had boyfriends and Uncle Jack never knew about it. But Dad says he didn't do any of that with Aunty Lil. They just went to the pictures sometimes.'

Bobby wondered how she could explain. Florrie was growing into a young woman, but she wasn't one yet and her view of the world was still very much that of a child. It would be hard to make her see how Lilian's friendship with her father was different to Florrie's innocent friendship with Louis Butcher, her favourite playmate from school.

'It's a little complicated,' Bobby said. 'Sometimes it's about more than kisses.'

'Like the thing people do to make babies. I know all about that,' Florrie told her, sounding rather proud of the knowledge. 'Aunty Lil told me about it.' She pulled a face. 'It sounds horrid.'

Bobby smiled. 'No, I don't mean that. I'm talking about feelings. Sometimes when men and women are friends, even without kisses and… and the thing they do to make babies, they have feelings which make them different to ordinary friends.'

'You mean like love?' Florrie said, with another disgusted grimace.

'Yes, I suppose I do.'

'Dad doesn't love Aunty Lil like that, does he?'

'I don't know, sweetheart. It's hard to know what other people feel unless they tell you. But I suppose Mr Scott thought he might do, and that's what made him angry.'

'So if Dad tells him he doesn't love her, then that'll be all right, won't it?' The girl looked at her hopefully. 'Then we could stay.'

'I'm not sure it's as simple as that. But I hope your father changes his mind, all the same.' She glanced at Florrie. 'Does he know you're here?'

'No, I sneaked out. I was going to run and see Mary, but Dad says I'm not allowed to go to Moorside. Then I remembered what Aunty Lil said about Georgia. I'd rather talk to you about it though, Bobby.'

'We ought to get you home, before your dad worries. I hope you won't get into trouble.'

'Don't care if I do anyhow,' Florrie muttered darkly. 'Are you coming too?'

'Let me lock up the cottage, then yes. I'd like a word with your father.'

After Bobby had locked up, she walked – or rather, waddled – with Florrie to the cottage by the bridge. From a little distance, she could see the shepherd's hut behind it where she and Tony had worked. She breathed a sigh.

Tony was to be pitied in this too. What was tragic about it was that no one was entirely to blame. Lilian and George couldn't help their feelings any more than Tony could help his. It was all such an awful muddle that there didn't seem any happy way out of it.

When they reached the cottage, Bobby knocked on the door. The captain opened up a moment later. He still wore a dressing on his nose, which looked very bruised.

'I have something that belongs to you, I think,' Bobby said, nodding to Florrie.

The captain shook his head. 'Florence Parry. Now where have you been running off to this time? You know I expressly forbade you to go bothering those poor people, and that includes Bobby too.'

'Don't care,' Florrie said, looking belligerent. 'Didn't go to Bobby's house anyhow.'

'That's true,' Bobby said. 'I found her wandering in the graveyard.'

'Well you can come inside this minute, young lady, and help Mrs Wilcox prepare the dinner,' the captain told Florrie sternly. 'And no more running off.'

'Fine.'

'Say goodbye to Bobby.'

Florrie turned wide eyes on her. 'You'll tell him, won't you, Bobby? That he's not to be allowed to take us?'

Bobby smiled sadly. 'I'm afraid I don't have that right, my love.' She gave the girl a kiss. 'Go on inside as your father says. I'm sure I'll see you soon.'

Florrie went inside, her eyes filled with angry tears.

'I'm so sorry you've been troubled,' the captain said. 'I can't think what possessed her to go to the churchyard.'

'She said she was visiting Georgia.'

'Was she?' He paused. 'And, um... your sister is well, I hope?'

'She's been better. Could I come in a moment?'

The captain looked hesitant.

'It won't take long.' Bobby rested a hand on her stomach. 'There's no scandal in you and me being seen alone together, I suppose.'

'No. I'm sorry, I was being thoughtless. Do please come inside and rest awhile.'

Bobby followed him into the house, where he showed her into the parlour.

'Would you like a drink of tea, or some water?' he asked when she was sitting down.

'No, thank you. I just wanted to ask about... well, Florrie said you were thinking of moving back down south. That can't be true, can it?'

The captain sighed as he took a seat opposite her. 'I'm afraid it is.'

Bobby shook her head. 'But you can't! I mean, I'm sorry, of course you can do whatever you like. But I really wish you wouldn't.'

'You heard about my engagement being broken off, I suppose?'

'Yes. I was sorry to hear it.'

George looked past her out of the window, as if half his thoughts were somewhere else. 'It seemed only fair. I couldn't tie a young girl like that to me knowing my heart was somewhere else. Besides, she never had been able to win the admiration of the children. It was them I was thinking of more than myself when I formed the connection – their need for a mother.'

'When you say your heart was somewhere else…'

'I doubt I need to explain it to you, do I?'

'No,' Bobby said quietly.

'I was naive,' he said with a sigh. 'The intention was innocent, in the beginning. Your sister reminded me of my Rose, and how I'd longed to pamper her after Jess was born. When I saw something I knew Lilian would like – the coat – I thought, well, where is the harm? She made me smile, in a way I hadn't smiled in so long. Then before I knew it, I… felt for her in a way I wasn't able to change.' He met her eyes. 'It wasn't planned, Bobby. None of this was planned. It just seemed to happen.'

'I am sorry. You acted unwisely, as did my sister, but neither of you can help your feelings being what they are.'

'If I could, I'd change them in an instant.'

Bobby leaned forward. 'But do please reconsider moving back to London. This business has brought you pain, I know, but it will bring so much more to so many people if you take the girls away. They belong here.'

'What else can I do? I know it must be as hard for Lilian to see me as it is for me to see her, and while I'll always believe Tony Scott to be a boor entirely unworthy of her, he is nevertheless her husband. It complicates things for me to be here, and it gives rise to gossip that affects your sister's standing in this community. I won't be responsible for bringing her further unhappiness.'

'It isn't only about you and Lil though. Do you have family in London?'

'None of any significance, now,' he told her. 'There was only my brother Jack, who as you know was killed in the war. His widow has a new husband, and no interest in her former family.'

'And yet here you've found a large family. Mary Atherton loves those girls like a mother. We all love them, and we've grown fond of you as well, George. It will break the children's hearts and ours if you take them away.' Bobby looked earnestly into the solemn, honest green eyes above his broken nose. 'Please, please do stay. You've got a good job, and people who care about you. If you and Tony can make it up, perhaps we can move beyond this.'

'It wouldn't change the way I feel about his wife,' the captain said quietly. 'Nor the way I believe she feels about me. As long as I'm here, it must cause problems between Mr and Mrs Scott. I acted very wrongly in my dealings with them. It's right that I remove myself from their lives so they can be happy with one another.'

'But what of your children? What of their happiness?'

'Young people are generally resilient. The girls may be sad for a time, but no doubt they will find happiness in their new life after a period of adjustment. So, I suppose, will everyone here.' He closed his eyes. 'Still, I will miss this place. We could have been content here, if I had only been stronger. What a damn fool I was to give in to it!'

'Please, George, I wish you'd reconsider. For the children's sake.'

'I'm sorry, Bobby. I made a poor choice in allowing myself to grow close to a married woman. Now it's time to choose what's right.'

## Chapter 35

Bobby knew it was no use remonstrating further. The captain had made up his mind, and she had no idea what she could say to alter that.

She almost walked into Tony going over the bridge – or more accurately, he almost walked into her. In fact he almost knocked her over. Her brother-in-law looked a million miles away, his brow furrowed in thought.

'Oh.' He stopped short before he careered into her. 'Sorry, Bob. Didn't see you.'

He looked tired, but not sad particularly. Perhaps wistful.

Bobby knew from Lilian that the two were no longer sharing a bed. Tony himself had been the one to move his things into the nursery, while Annie went to share with her mother. Lil had confided to Bobby that she was unable to see Tony's absence from her at night as anything other than a blessing.

'Are you all right?' Bobby asked him.

'Hmm?' Tony's attention seemed to have wandered as he gazed out over the beck. 'Pretty here this time of year, isn't it?'

'Um, yes. Are you all right?' she asked again. 'You look... strange.'

'Fine. Fine.'

'Have you been somewhere?'

'Bradford. Man I needed to see there about summat. Been to see your sister, have you?'

'No, I was taking Florrie home. I found her wandering in the graveyard, all upset.'

'What's she upset about?'

Bobby sighed. 'The captain's moving them back to London. You know, because of... well, you know. I tried talking to him, but I couldn't get him to reconsider.'

'Taking them to London?' Tony said, frowning.

'Yes. It'll break Mary's heart if they go.'

'Lil's too, I reckon. She loves them kids nearly as much as she loves her own.'

'We'd all miss them. They're part of the family.' Bobby looked at him. 'I don't suppose you'd consider talking to George and trying to smooth things over, would you?'

'Huh. I'd make it worse. He don't think much of me.'

'You could try.'

'Aye, I could.' Tony fell silent for a moment. 'Parry was never the cause of the thing, I know that now. He was only ever a symptom. Mind, I'm not going to apologise about his nose. He deserved it.'

'That's what he says too. But you might be able to find some way to move on from this, for the family's sake.'

Tony went to the edge of the bridge and leaned on it as he looked out over the beck. It was chattering merrily after a heavy fall of spring rain, and there was a fresh, mossy smell in the air.

'Sorry I shouted at you that night, Bob,' he said. 'You know I've always thought you were all right. I'm even fond of you, in a way.'

'Never mind about me. I'm not important.'

'Funny you still talking to me,' he murmured without looking at her. 'Never thought you'd look at me again after what happened.'

'I wasn't sure I would either.' Bobby went to stand by him, inhaling the scents of early spring.

'It really was an accident.'

'It was an accident that didn't need to happen.' She shook her head. 'I never thought you could've been so rough with someone you claim to love. I could have forgiven the rest of it, but that...'

'I was always disgusted at the sort of man who could hit a woman,' he said quietly. 'Lil don't look at me the same now. Happen I don't deserve her to.' His face took on a determined expression. 'But I'll be a better man from now on, I swear it.'

'I've heard that before, Tony.'

'I know, and I tried. I did try, Bob, after I found out about the baby. If I'd only been able to make Lil love me, maybe I could've stuck it.'

'What made you fall in love with her? I've always wondered.'

He shrugged. 'Well, there was a baby coming, wasn't there?'

'I didn't ask what made you marry her. I asked what made you fall for her. You two are so different.'

Tony watched the beck in thoughtful silence.

'I never amounted to much, did I?' he said quietly. 'I do know that. Honestly, Bob, I couldn't believe my luck the day your sister told me she was expecting and needed me to step up for her. That made me... made me someone, you know?'

'So you loved her because she needed you?'

'Not only that. My mam and dad made a rough job of bringing up me and my brother. Never cared much about us, I reckon, and they hated each other. I thought that Lil and the baby were my chance to do better.' He paused. 'I loved her because I wanted someone to love, and she was mine.'

Bobby sighed. 'I'm sorry, Tony.'

'I was wasting my time though, wasn't I? She'd never have been able to forget how it all started. And now this has happened...' He closed his eyes. 'Well, it is what it is. But for my daughter's sake, I want to do better. I will do better.'

Bobby put a hand on his arm. 'If you mean it, you might start by having a man-to-man talk with the captain. With your voice this time, not your fists. You're the only one who can make him change his mind.'

'Aye, I will. No point both of us buggering off.'

Bobby frowned. 'What do you mean, both of you?'

He finally turned to face her, his eyes filled with weary resignation. 'I'm off, Bob. That's what I was in Bradford for today. In two weeks, I'll be leaving here. I don't suppose Reg will cry too much at losing me from the mag.'

'I don't understand. You're not leaving Lil?'

'I think we both know Lil left me a long time ago, if I ever had her,' he said with a sad smile. 'No point kidding myself about it till we're two old people sharing a house and hating each other, like my parents. Some things you can't move on from, Bobby. For her sake and mine, I have to let her go.'

'But they're your family, Tony!' Bobby stared at him in disbelief. 'I can't believe you'd abandon Lil and the baby, after everything the three of you have been through.'

'I'm not abandoning them. I'll send money to support them – a fair bit more than she gets in housekeeping now, once I start work. Pay's not much but it's better than here.'

'You've got another job?'

'Aye. Pioneer Corps.'

'You're joining the army? I thought you couldn't serve because of your asthma.'

He snorted. 'Told you that, didn't I? Told you a lot of things – you and others. No wonder your sister can't respect me.'

'I don't understand, Tony.'

'The night our Annie was born, I told you I'd done things I was ashamed of. I thought God must be punishing me by taking Lil. Remember?'

'I remember.'

'Well, this was the worst. The quack who did my medical said I wouldn't be A1 because of my asthma but he could certify me fit for home front duties with the Pioneers. I'd just got my job at the *Courier*.' Tony was quiet for a long time, watching the beck. 'Told the doc I'd rather stay as I was. Hinted I'd make it worth his while. Risky but I'd heard he might be bent. Well, so he was.'

'You bribed an army doctor to get out of serving?' Bobby stared at him. 'My God, Tony.'

'Aye, now you're disgusted. Don't wonder, after your Charlie nearly died for this thing.'

'So you told them what you did? That means prison, surely.'

'No, I just asked for another medical. They'll review exemption cases if you ask, now they're desperate for men.' He swallowed. 'Late to start doing the right thing, I guess. I don't suppose she'll ever respect me – Lil. I know now she'll never love me. But that little baby loves me. When I see her smiling at me, her eyes full of trust… I want Annie to respect me, Bob. I want her growing up proud to carry my name. That's why I'm going. Not for Lil. For her.'

His face was working with emotion. Bobby put a hand on his arm.

'I think… that's the right thing to do,' she said gently.

'I know it is.' Tony roused himself. 'I'll talk to Parry. Happen he'll reconsider when he knows I'm going. And after a bit, if Lil wants to make a change, she can cite desertion or adultery or whatever she wants. Put it all on me, I don't care. I guess I deserve it, after the way I pressed her into marriage. Bound to be gossip but she'll get along all right if folk think I'm the one to blame. Divorce don't bring the shame it did ten year ago.'

'I'm so sorry it had to end this way.'

'So am I. I did hope she might learn to love me. It took this business with Parry to make me realise she never would.' He turned to look at her. 'But I'm not sorry. We did it for Annie. If it ends in divorce, my daughter can still hold her head up. That's all I wanted.'

Bobby summoned a smile. 'I'll miss you, Tony. It won't be the same here without you to beat at darts.'

'Will you write to me? Tell me how Annie's getting on? I won't half miss her. I don't suppose Lil'll want any more contact with me than necessary once I'm off.'

'I'm sure she'll always want you involved with your daughter, whatever else might happen.'

'Still, I'd rather hear from you,' Tony said. 'It'll hurt Lil to write, and it'll hurt me to hear from her. Tell me all about my little girl, all right? Don't let her forget me. I trust you, Bob.

You've always tried to do what's right, which is more than I ever did.'

'I won't ever let her forget she's got a dad who loves her.' Bobby squeezed his arm. 'Goodbye, Tony Scott. And good luck.'

—

There was a formal goodbye two weeks later, as Tony prepared to leave for basic training. The family lined up outside the cow house: Bobby, Charlie, Rob, Reg and Mary. Out of respect for the Scotts, Captain Parry had decided it was best if he and his daughters stayed away.

The situation with the Parrys had been resolved, although no one was sure what had been said – not even Lilian. All anyone knew was that Tony had called on his erstwhile love rival, and after he emerged, all plans involving relocation to London had been scrapped.

The official story was that Tony had secured a place in the Pioneers after demanding a further medical to see if there had been any improvement in his chest. No one except Bobby knew how he had dodged his duty years ago, and she had no intention of sharing it with anyone. Tony was doing the right thing now. There was no cause to bring shame on either him or, by association, his wife and child.

No one had been told that Tony's departure also signified the end of his marriage. That would come later, when claims could be made of desertion or infidelity to smooth the way for a divorce. But it seemed to be tacitly understood by the people present today that this was what was happening.

Tony emerged from the cow house, suitcase in hand, looking bashful in his new uniform. Lilian followed with the baby. She looked as though she had been crying. So did Tony.

'Now, Tony, have you got your tea and sandwiches?' Lilian asked, fussing round him as she brushed imaginary specks from his uniform.

Rob laughed. 'He's not off to a Home Guard parade this time, our Lil.' He came forward to shake his son-in-law's hand. 'Good luck, lad. About time you joined the ranks of the proper soldiers. You'll miss your stripe, though, eh?'

Tony summoned a smile. 'I'll soon get another one.'

'See you do. And now I've to find another mug to help me get my traps up, I suppose. You'll be missed, son.'

'Aye,' Reg said, coming forward to take his turn at shaking hands. 'I've only got half a ruddy magazine for next month, for a start. Going to cost me a fortune in freelance fees. Still, I reckon you'll make a better soldier than a writer.'

Tony laughed. 'Doesn't sound like much of a compliment, Reg.'

'Depends what sort of a soldier you make, don't it?'

After everyone had wished Tony luck, Lilian handed the baby to Bobby so she could embrace her husband.

'Goodbye, Lil,' Bobby heard Tony whisper. 'I'm sorry for everything. I hope… well, I hope you'll be happy.'

'I'm sorry too.' She held him back to look into his face. 'Do you have to go? We could try again.'

'Would there be any point?'

She sighed. 'No. I don't suppose there would.'

Tony rubbed his eye rather gruffly. 'Look after my daughter, all right?'

'I will. Come home when you're on leave. She'll…' Lil swallowed. '…she'll want to see you.'

'We'll see. I'll write when I get there.'

And that was that. Ten minutes later, Tony Scott was gone and out of their lives, almost as if he'd never been a part of the world of Silverdale at all.

## Chapter 36

After Tony's departure, things settled back into a happier routine in Silverdale, although there was a certain wistfulness in the air. It didn't exactly feel like something was missing – Tony had always felt rather wedged into their lives here, as if he didn't quite belong. It was more a sort of regret at the way things had turned out, even though everyone accepted it had been the best of all possible outcomes. It meant the Parrys could stay without the captain feeling he was rubbing salt in the wound of the husband he'd wronged, and although he and Lilian cautiously limited the time they spent in each other's company, it nevertheless freed her from the unhappiness of her marriage. Still, she was quiet and thoughtful after the departure of her husband.

Apart from Lil, the wistfulness in the air affected Bobby most. She was the one who had been closest to Tony, other than his wife: his friend and colleague of several years. He hadn't always been an easy man to like, but she had felt she understood him. She was fond of him in her way, just as he was of her. She was glad he had gone – glad he had decided to do the right thing and answer the call of duty, and glad he had set Lilian free. But she missed him all the same.

It was now 20th April, just four weeks before Marmaduke was due, and Bobby had never felt more uncomfortable in her life. Despite Dr Minchin's assurances that she wasn't expecting twins, she still worried about it. If it wasn't twins, then why was she so darned big? There must be room for a football team's worth of babies in her belly. If it was only one, he must be the size of a small elephant.

And she was due to travel to London in two days' time. Bobby was still determined to see Charlie awarded his DFC but she was dreading the journey, and for one simple reason: what if the train didn't have a lav? If it didn't then she had no idea what on earth she was going to do when she needed to use the privy, as she now seemed to do several times an hour. Should she pack the jerry from under the bed, and ask Charlie to hold up one of her enormous maternity dresses as a screen whenever she felt yet another call of nature? Suppose she needed to go in the middle of the investiture? Ought she to put up her hand and ask the king if she might be excused?

'Well? Did you do it?' she demanded of Charlie as soon as he came home from work. The fact he was beaming from ear to ear seemed to suggest he did, but she wanted to hear it from him.

'I did.' Bobby was washing up, and Charlie spun her around to wrap her arms around his neck, suds and all. 'My notice has been given at the bank and I am officially a vet once more. Well, I suppose it won't really be official until we cut the ribbon on the new practice, but I'm counting it from today all the same.'

'Wonderful.' Bobby gave him a big kiss. 'I've got good news as well. My third Lindy story was accepted, and with no edits this time. I must be getting better. So, that's another eight pounds for the pot.'

'That's my clever, hard-working wife.' He kissed her again. 'Hey, what do you think to investing in a second-hand gramophone and a few records? We can spare ten pounds, can't we?'

'We still have to be careful, Charlie. We don't know how long it will take for the practice to start paying out, and we need to keep as much as we can aside for the baby.'

'It's the baby I was thinking of. Since I won't be able to take his mother dancing for a while, I thought it would be a good idea to rectify the deficiency at home. I'm sure Marmaduke wouldn't want the family scandalised by a divorce.'

Bobby grimaced. 'Oh Lord, please don't joke about that. Not after everything that happened with Lil and Tony.'

'Sorry,' he said in a softer voice. 'That was tasteless. I wasn't thinking.'

Bobby sighed. 'I mean, I do think it's right, them separating. I'd rather they got a divorce and we had to deal with wagging tongues than that Lil stayed with him to be unhappy. Still, the marriage deserves a certain mourning period, such as it was.'

'You're right. Tony leaving was the best outcome, but that doesn't exactly make it a happy one.'

There was the sound of a vehicle pulling up outside. That in itself was unusual enough for them to frown at each other. A moment later, there was an urgent knock at the door.

'I know that knock,' Bobby said ominously. 'That's the knock of someone with a crisis they want one of us to solve for them. I've heard it too many times recently. I was really hoping we could be free of drama until after the baby was born.'

'If that's your other brother with a pregnant fiancée and the Redcaps on his tail, I'm putting him straight on a train back to wherever he came from,' Charlie announced.

'I don't think the trains run as far as North Africa,' Bobby said with a smile. 'His wife might be rather put out as well. We'll both go, shall we?'

She wiped her hands on her apron and went to answer the door, Charlie following. They found neither Redcaps nor AWL brothers on the doorstep, however, but Topsy Nowak, looking incredibly pale.

'Birdy, darling, you have to come at once,' she said breathlessly. 'I borrowed a car from the hospital to fetch you.' She glanced at her friend's stomach. 'Oh. But you're huge.'

It had been a month since they had last seen one another, when Topsy had called round with the exciting news that she and Teddy had been approved to adopt a baby. And while Bobby did feel as if she'd doubled in size since then, she didn't see why everyone had to be constantly pointing it out to her. She did own a mirror.

'I know I am,' she said. 'Is something wrong, Topsy? Teddy's all right, isn't he?'

'Teddy's fine. He's at the hospital with Maimie, waiting to go in. But it's you he's been asking for, Birdy. Can you come? He won't linger long, the doctor says.'

Bobby cast an alarmed glance at Charlie.

'Who won't?' Charlie asked. 'You aren't making sense, Tops.'

Topsy ran a hand over her head. 'I'm sorry. I've been so terribly out of sorts, I… it's all come out in the wrong order.'

Bobby grabbed her by the shoulders. 'Who, Topsy? Just tell me, who is it that's at the hospital?'

'It's Ernie,' Topsy said in a whisper. 'Ernie King.'

—

Bobby swayed when Topsy delivered the news. It was only Charlie's arm around her that stopped her from keeling over.

'For God's sake, Topsy,' Charlie snapped. 'Don't you know she shouldn't be given sudden shocks? Here, Bob, come and sit down.'

'Oh, I am sorry,' Topsy said, following them inside. 'I… didn't think. It's all been so horrid, my brain's everywhere. Birdy, can I get you some water? That was very stupid of me.'

'No. No, I don't want water.' Bobby looked at Topsy, who was swimming before her eyes. 'Tell me what happened.'

'Don't, Tops,' Charlie warned. 'She shouldn't be upset.'

'I have to know everything, now,' Bobby murmured. 'It'll be worse not to know. Please, Charlie.'

Charlie hesitated, then nodded to Topsy to go on.

'They brought him in this morning,' Topsy said. 'I wouldn't have known anything about it now I'm not nursing, but as luck would have it I'd gone over to talk to the matron about repairs to the house and I heard them say his name.' She fixed her helpless eyes on Bobby's. 'They've brought him there to die, Birdy. He told them he wanted to die at Sumner House. There's only just time to say goodbye.'

Charlie knelt down in front of his wife. 'Are you all right, Bob?' he asked gently. 'What do you need?'

Bobby felt like the room was spinning. Ernie King! Of everyone she had prayed to come through this war, other than Charlie and her brothers, she had said the most prayers for him.

He couldn't die, could he? Not Ernie. He was so strong and young and… and alive. He was going to be married when he finished his tour, and take his beautiful bride to Canada to run the family farm. Bobby had only seen him a few days ago in the village, teasing her and swelling with pride as he talked about being godfather to the baby. It wasn't fair. It wasn't fair…

'Is he really dying?' she asked Topsy in a whisper.

'I'm so sorry,' Topsy said. 'His plane caught fire on impact and he was trapped inside. They don't think he'll live two days, if that.'

'And he asked for me?'

'That's what the doctor says.'

'Then take me to him.'

Charlie seized her hands. 'No, Bobby. I won't let you go. You aren't well.'

'I am well. It was a shock, that's all. I want to say goodbye to my friend.'

'It's dangerous, darling. You're eight months pregnant. Be sensible.'

'Please, Charlie.' She squeezed his hands. 'You know how much it meant to you to say goodbye to Hynes. You called it a privilege. If I don't do the same for Ernie when he's asked for me, it'll haunt me until my dying day.'

Charlie hesitated.

'All right, then I'm coming with you,' he said finally.

'You don't need to. Topsy will look after me.'

'Rubbish. I'm going with you and that's all there is to it.'

—

The matron was silent and solemn as she showed the three of them to the hall outside Ernie's private room. Bobby found herself wondering vaguely what the room had been before, when this had been Topsy's house. A study? A closet? The closets of Sumner House were probably larger than her bedroom.

She felt like she needed to cry, but she couldn't. Her reflection in the glass of the portraits that lined the walls made her look like the ghost that haunted this old place, with her pale face and huge grey maternity dress. She certainly felt like a ghost.

Teddy was already waiting, with Maimie Bancroft, formerly Hobbes, in charge of his wheelchair. They both summoned weak smiles.

'Well, here's my stepdaughter,' Maimie said softly. 'I'm sorry we had to meet like this, Bobby. You had better take a seat.'

'We are to wait until called,' Teddy told them. 'Ernie is sleeping now, his doctor says. You ought to go in first, Bobby. It is you Ernie particularly wished to see.'

Teddy looked sober, yet not exactly sad: only resigned. It was different for him, Bobby supposed, just as it was different for Charlie. They had been airmen. They had lost friend after friend in this war. Teddy had witnessed the deaths of almost his entire crew the night he had lost the use of his legs. Grief was different, when you were one of the men who had flown.

Bobby sank into a seat. She felt like she didn't want to be here. She felt like she would rather die than have to see that handsome, strong young man who had once loved her in pain, with his life draining away. But he had asked for her, and if he wanted her here when he was dying then she would never dream of letting him down.

'It seems a strange place to offer congratulations, but I think I ought to,' Charlie said to Teddy and Topsy, in a muted tone appropriate to their setting. 'You're to have a new baby soon, my wife tells me.'

Bobby was grateful to him for taking up the conversation. She felt some talk was preferable to silence, but she had no energy to make it herself.

'This is right,' Teddy said, with a proud smile for Topsy. 'Those in authority have decided we will make suitable parents in spite of all this.' He gestured to his paralysed legs. 'Now we wait only for them to decide which baby they feel will suit us most.'

'We told them we don't mind what it is,' Topsy said. 'If it needs two loving parents, nothing else is important.'

'Is that the way it works?' Charlie asked. 'I wondered if they didn't have you pick one out for yourself.'

Teddy smiled. 'But this would be no good, because my wife would come home with a whole orphanage's worth. I know she could never choose one from among them all, and our little cottage would have babies spilling out of every nook and cranny.'

Topsy smiled too. 'You know me too well, husband of mine. Just you wait until I get this big old house back. Then you'll see how many babies I can squeeze in.'

They were recalled to their sober purpose by an RAF doctor emerging from Ernie's room.

'He's awake for the moment,' he said in a solemn voice. 'If you want to say your goodbyes, I would advise you to do so quickly. Who will go in first? No more than two at a time.'

'I will,' Bobby whispered. 'I'm told he asked for me.'

The doctor glanced at her stomach. 'Are you sure? He's heavily bandaged, and on a lot of morphine. You may find his appearance upsetting.'

'I won't go without seeing him. I was in the WAAF; I'm sure it isn't worse than anything I've seen before. Please, Doctor.'

'I'll be going in with her,' Charlie said. 'I'm her husband.'

The doctor gave a slight nod and beckoned them in.

Bobby wasn't sure what to expect. She assumed Ernie could talk a little, if he had asked for her. But would he know her?

The light was low in the room. There was a bed and a window and little else. The window was open, letting in a blossom-scented April breeze. Bobby knew the windows at Sumner House were usually kept shut, to maintain a sterile environment. She imagined that didn't matter for Ernie.

He was on the bed. She supposed it was him. All she could see were bandages in the rough shape of a man.

'Can he hear us?' she asked the doctor in a whisper.

Ernie answered this before the doctor was able to. There was a low rumble from the bandages, then a hoarse, harsh growl.

'Hey.' There was a deep, pained intake of breath, a long pause, then, 'Slacks.'

'Ernie! Oh my God!'

Bobby rushed over to take his hand. It was covered in bandages, like the rest of him, but his fingertips were exposed. They were red and tender, more like tissue than flesh. Bobby tried not to touch them in case she hurt him, but she gave a gentle pressure on the thickly bandaged hand.

'Bobby?' the harsh whisper came again. It didn't sound much like Ernie's voice, except in the tone. Bobby felt she would know him however parched and burnt his throat was, if he sounded that way.

'Don't try to talk, darling,' she whispered, sinking into the chair by his bed. 'I'm here. Charlie's here too.'

'All right, King?' Charlie said in a jovial voice. 'Anything to get out of buying me that pint, eh? Thought I'd better come along and make sure you didn't try to steal my girl again.'

There was a deep rumble from the bandages that sounded like a laugh.

'Lucky,' came the harsh growl.

'I know I am,' Charlie said softly, looking at Bobby. 'Save us a seat on the other side, OK, old man? Sorry you didn't make it.'

Ernie inclined his head in what Bobby guessed was a nod of acknowledgement. She felt that something was happening now that she wasn't a part of. A bond that came not from friendship but comradeship. Ernie needed Charlie to be here just as much as he needed her.

'Kid,' was the next mumbled word, and Bobby knew what that meant.

'Of course,' she whispered, pressing his hand. 'We'll save your place at the christening. They'll still be your godchild. We know you'll be watching over them.'

'You had better say your goodbyes,' the doctor said in a low voice. 'He can't stay awake for long, I'm afraid.'

'Wait,' Ernie rasped. 'Slacks.'

'I'm here, Ernie,' Bobby said. 'What is it?'

'Barbara.'

'Barbara – your fiancée? Oh yes, of course. I'll write to her and tell her… tell her everything. What's her last name?'

'No… Barbara.'

Bobby frowned, and looked at Charlie. 'What can he mean?'

'I think I know,' Charlie said quietly. 'There is no Barbara, is there, King? There never was.'

A slight shake of the head.

'Bobby,' he whispered. 'Always.'

She didn't understand for a moment. Then she met Charlie's eyes, and she did.

'Oh, Ernie,' she whispered. 'I'm sorry. I'm so sorry.'

'Be… happy,' he rasped. 'Live. For me.'

'I'll miss you.' Bobby let out a weak laugh. 'Every time I put on a pair of trousers, I'll think of you. Every time I hear "The Lambeth Walk". Every time I look at the baby.'

'See you… later.'

'Yes. Later.' She held his hand to her cheek, feeling those oddly inhuman fingertips against her skin. 'Goodbye, Ernie. Goodbye.'

## Chapter 37

'Are you sure you're all right to come with me?' Charlie asked for the hundredth time as he and Bobby stood on a platform at Skipton railway station two days later. Reg and Mary had come to see them off, and were watching them proudly. In fact, Reg had been so proud when his brother had told him he was to be awarded no less a gong than the DFC that Bobby had thought he might pop every button on his waistcoat.

She shook her head impatiently. 'I told you I was. I don't want to miss this, Charlie.'

'Bob, you look all in. It isn't too late for us to go home with Reggie and Mary. I'd rather keep you healthy than meet any number of kings.'

'I'm only tired, that's all. After losing Ernie and... and everything.'

Topsy had sent a note the day after Bobby had said her final farewell to the other man who loved her, letting her know that Ernie hadn't survived the night. Bobby had been glad, for her friend's sake, that he hadn't lingered on in pain. Yes, she had been glad. And then she had cried and cried until she thought she might burst.

She couldn't stop thinking about him. Ernie King, strong and brave and kind and alive, so, so alive, dying in a bed far from home with the whisper of a Dales springtime on his poor burnt fingertips. Ernie King, who had never again got to see the country he loved and the family he'd left behind. Just one more life extinguished by a war that had killed so many, but a life Bobby had prayed for every night.

Perhaps it was an indulgence, when so many had died, to grieve so deeply for one person. But grieve she must, all the same. She could have been Ernie's wife, under other circumstances. If he hadn't stepped aside for Charlie with that nobility and selflessness typical of the man, she might even now be wearing his ring.

And he had loved her, all this time. Had never stopped loving her. Yet it had only been on his deathbed that Bobby had realised how deep and unchanging his feelings had been. She wished she had known, before. She wished there was time for one final conversation.

But... *see you later*. Ernie's last words came back to her as she blinked on a tear. Yes, she would see him later. One day, hopefully a long time in the future, she would see him again. And then... yes, then there would be time for conversation.

She hadn't forgotten his other words either. *Live for me*. Ernie had lost his life, but she had hers. Currently she was the custodian of two lives: her own and the one growing inside her. The baby would be Ernie's godchild, even if that relationship had never had the chance to be solemnised. That was why she was determined to go with Charlie to London, and make sure neither of them missed an opportunity that came along once in a lifetime.

Their train was due in five minutes. Mary stepped forward to say goodbye, giving Charlie a hug first.

'Now be sure your uniform's brushed before you go to the palace,' she warned him. 'I'll not have it said any boy of mine was looking shabby for the king. And take a clean handkerchief, and don't forget to stand up straight when they take your photograph. Oh, and the girls told me to remind you that you promised them some of the spice they like back from London.'

Charlie smiled. 'All right, Mam, I won't forget.'

'And this is for you, Bobby,' Mary said, handing her a box tied with string. 'I made it special out of a bit of material I had off one of the WVS girls.'

'What is it?' Bobby asked.

Mary smiled. 'Open it and see.'

Bobby did so, and blinked at what was inside. It was a dress – a dress for someone just her current size. But it wasn't one of the ugly, shapeless maternity dresses that were all the shops felt women in the later stages of pregnancy ought to shroud themselves in. This was silk – parachute silk, she supposed – dyed royal blue and trimmed with ribbon. It was huge, and it was fit for a ballroom.

'Mary, it's beautiful,' she breathed.

'Well, you want to look nice for the palace, don't you? A girl likes to look her best no matter what size she is. Now, now, don't make a fuss,' Mary said with a smile as Bobby fell on her neck. 'Just be sure to bring me and Reg a healthy grandchild next month. Then I'll call myself repaid in full.'

Reg stepped forward to shake his brother's hand.

'I'm right proud of you, lad. Right proud of you,' he said, with no sign of wanting to give over his firm pumping of Charlie's hand. 'So would our old man be.'

'Thanks, Reggie. That means a lot.'

'Now then. Before you go to this fancy do at the palace I'd better give you the benefit of my years as a newspaperman, writing about the nobs and their swank,' Reg told him with authority. 'You don't want them laughing in their toff sleeves when you start quaffing from the finger bowl like some country oik.'

Charlie smiled. 'Go on.'

'If you meet an archbishop, it's "Your Grace". If you meet a prince or princess, it's "Your Highness". If you meet a king or queen – and I'm pretty sure you will – it's "Your Majesty". And if you meet the Duke of Devonshire, tell him he still owes me that five bob.'

'I think I can remember that,' Charlie said, laughing. 'Anything else?'

'Aye. If there's food, you start from the outside and work your way in with the cutlery. And if it's real silver, stick it in your sock right quick before the butler gets his greasy kid gloves on it.'

'It pays to be related to socialites, doesn't it?' Bobby said with a smile.

Reg approached her now to say goodbye. 'Look after yourself, lass. Take good care of that baby while you're down south. They're proper heathens down there, tha knows.'

'I will. Thanks, Reg.'

He looked a bit awkward. 'You know, young Florrie showed me your bit in her comic. Good, that was.'

'You mean "Lindy Gulls the Hun"?'

'Aye. Nice little tale for the bairns. Florrie was about bursting showing it off to all her pals.' He paused. 'Good fee, I suppose?'

'Um, yes,' Bobby said. '*Girl's Own* pay eight pounds a story. They've given me a contract for five, and I hope more to follow.'

'A lot more than I could ever afford to pay. Shame, that.'

Bobby frowned. 'Reg, are you saying... do you mean you'd have liked me to write for *The Tyke* again?'

'Aye, well, maybe I were a bit hasty,' Reg said, blushing fit for anything. 'I mean, you're a canny lass, head screwed on and that. You've dealt with a lot this past few month, and you in the family way an' all. I reckon it's not for an old dinosaur like me to say what you can do and what you can't. I reckon you know well enough for yoursen.'

'So you're saying... what are you saying?'

'It's left me in the lurch, young Scott going for a soldier like that. Costing me a fortune in freelance writers to keep the mag running. So if you wanted to do a bit of writing, four or five articles a number at ten bob a week, just when you can fit it in around the babby...' He rubbed his neck. 'I know it's not much, now you're getting big cheques from the real papers. But we do miss you at *The Tyke*, and if nothing I can say is going to stop you writing, well, I'd rather you were doing a bit of that writing for me.'

'Reg, really?'

'Aye, keep it in the family, like. I mean, it'll go to you and Charlie one day, the mag. Happen it'll even make you money, when this ruddy war's over. Best to keep your hand in, if you'll be in the editor's chair one of these days.'

Bobby beamed at him. 'Reg, I'd love to. I'd really love to.'

—

To Bobby's enormous relief, the train that took them from Leeds to London was a corridor train with a lavatory at the end of each carriage. She made sure to claim a seat near it, so she would be able to make a dash there if there was an urgent call of nature.

Marmaduke was incredibly wriggly at the moment. Bobby supposed he was reacting to her excitement about the trip to the capital. It was rather uncomfortable, though, like the cramps she used to get with her monthlies. She hoped he would settle in time for the ceremony tomorrow morning.

'May I see the invitation again?' she asked Charlie, who was reading a book beside her.

'If you like.' He fished it from one of his pockets.

The letterhead stated that it had come from the Central Chancery of the Order of Knighthood at St James's Palace, and it was marked confidential. Bobby experienced a thrill of pleasure as she read it.

> *Sir,*
>
> *The King will hold an investiture in the ballroom of Buckingham Palace on Friday 23rd April 1943 at which your presence is requested. It is requested that you be at the palace no later than 9:30 a.m. Please attend in either service dress, morning dress, civil defence uniform or dark lounge suit, as appropriate.*
>
> *I am desired to inform you that you may be accompanied by up to two relatives or friends to witness the*

*investiture from the spectators' area. Please retain this letter as your card of admission.*
*Your obedient servant,*
*Flying Officer P. Fredericks, DFC, RAF*

It truly felt real when she read the invitation in all its formal language. They were really going to the palace, where Charlie would be decorated by the king. Her Charlie! No wonder Marmaduke was dancing a jig, when he had such a father to be proud of.

—

It was Bobby's first visit to London. She wasn't able to see much of it when they arrived that evening, deep in the blackout. She peered curiously from the window of the cab as it took them to the palace next morning, however, looking for all those famous buildings she had seen so many times in photographs: the Palace of Westminster, Nelson's Column, the dome of St Paul's.

'Oh my word,' she murmured as the car sped through the streets.

She had never seen a city on such a scale. It felt a hundred times bigger than Bradford or Leeds. Some buildings here stood nine or ten storeys high. There were vehicles everywhere: cabs, buses, trams, all rushing workers to their destinations.

And so many people! City men in suits and bowler hats, hurrying to the office. Market traders and white-coated shopkeepers. Housewives pushing prams. Lads in their shirtsleeves lounging on street corners, smoking and whistling at the girls.

Yet this vibrant place was so scarred by rubble and ruins. Skeletons of what had been buildings lined the streets. It looked like Westgate in Bradford the night after the city's one and only blitz, back in the summer of 1940, except here the destruction went on for streets and streets.

The people walked through the wreckage as if it was the most normal thing in the world. Bobby had seen bomb damage in newsreels, but it wasn't until she had witnessed it with her own eyes that she had really understood what it must be like to live in London in wartime. The people here had experienced a very different war to the one taking place in sleepy Silverdale. It made Bobby think of Jake, and the important, dangerous work her brother did here in the capital.

Charlie sat quietly at her side, arrayed in RAF service uniform for what would almost certainly be the last time. Demobilised men were encouraged to wear uniform for the presentation of military honours. He had turned rather pale – from nerves about the investiture, Bobby supposed. She held his hand tightly.

'First visit to the smoke, is it, missus?' the jovial cabby asked her.

Bobby smiled. 'Is it obvious?'

'Not for me to say. What do you think, then?'

Bobby shook her head wonderingly as she watched the crowds of people going about their business. 'It's so… big. And there's so much rubble everywhere. Yet people hardly seem to notice the damage at all.'

'We ought to be used to it by now,' the cabby said cheerily. 'Got to keep buggering on, as they say, pardon my language. Now then, duckie, palace, was it?' He winked. 'Having tea with the queen, eh?'

'Not far off.' Bobby puffed herself up. 'My husband is to be awarded the DFC.'

–

At the palace, Charlie was led away by a man in RAF uniform to be given instruction on protocol. Meanwhile, Bobby was shown into the spectators' seating area in the ballroom by one of the palace ushers.

There had been a crowd of sightseers at the gates when the two of them had shown their invitation to the sentry. Bobby was glad she had on the silk dress Mary had made for her and her mother's pearls, as well as a fur stole that Topsy had loaned for the occasion. Now she could really feel like a lady. Perhaps the folk at the gates thought she was some visiting dignitary or titled person. They would never guess that here was someone from a Bradford mill family.

Bobby looked around her with wonder as she was shown to her seat. She had never been in such an opulent room before. So much gilt and crystal and velvet! Even the chair she was instructed to sit on was probably worth more than her house.

Charlie stood nervously a little distance away. He was with four other men awaiting investiture, all in RAF service dress. There were seven spectators including Bobby, seated in one long row. Various other people were present: several in RAF uniforms, an official palace photographer – press photographs would follow outside after the ceremony, they had been told – and others who Bobby assumed worked in the royal household. There was no sign of the king, however.

The palace ushers were very stiff and proper, but one of them approached Bobby's seat and bent to speak to her, dropping his formal manners.

'No need for you to stand when they play the anthem, darling,' he whispered in her ear. 'His Royal Majesty will understand. He's got two of his own, after all.'

Bobby gave the man a grateful smile. 'Thank you.'

A moment later, 'God Save the King' began to play, and then... there he was. The king, George the Sixth, dignified and statesmanlike in his RAF uniform.

Bobby was glad the usher had said she might remain seated. She felt sure she would faint if she tried to stand, just through sheer disbelief that she – humble, insignificant Bobby Bancroft from Bradford – could actually be here: sitting in this opulent room inside a royal palace, clothed in silk and furs, waiting to see her husband decorated by a king.

Two other men were invested first, and then it was Charlie's turn. Bobby held her breath as she watched him approach the illustrious personage who was to present him with his medal.

Charlie stepped forward and saluted. He looked so very smart and handsome that Bobby could have burst for pride. Marmaduke seemed to agree, bouncing up and down inside her. The king spoke a few words to Charlie that Bobby couldn't hear, then pinned the medal above his left breast pocket. Charlie saluted again, and returned to his place.

It had taken only minutes, yet it was something Bobby would remember all her life. Her Charlie and the king. For all his doubts about accepting the decoration after he had lost so many friends, Bobby couldn't help feeling when the king pinned on the medal that it wasn't only for Charlie. It was for all of them: every man who had died in this war to keep the world free for her baby to grow up in. It was for Teddy's crew. It was for Bram. It was for Chip. It was for Hynes. It was for Ernie King. Every one was a hero, and in seeing her husband decorated, Bobby felt that each lost man was being recognised for his sacrifice. When she swelled with pride, it wasn't only for Charlie. It was for all of them.

## Chapter 38

'I can't help feeling that every day I don't meet a monarch after this is going to be a disappointment,' Charlie said when they were on the train home, in his civilian clothes once more. There weren't many fellow travellers, and they had managed to get a compartment to themselves.

Bobby laughed. 'Yes, you looked to be bosom pals. Will you invite him for Christmas dinner?'

'If he brings his own sprouts.'

'What was it he said to you?' she asked curiously.

'Just congratulations, and...' Charlie flushed. 'And that he knew what I'd done and he thought I was a brave man.'

'Quite right too.'

'By the way, you're definitely letting me get that gramophone after the daft sum you spent ordering pictures from the photographer.'

Bobby smiled. 'Can I help being proud of my brave, handsome husband? I want one for everyone in the family and some for the local newspapers. Come next month, there won't be a person in Yorkshire who doesn't know the name Charles Atherton, DFC.'

'Well, I think you can say "I told you so" now,' Charlie said, lounging back against the antimacassar. 'In spite of my catastrophic predictions of air raids and you giving birth during the ceremony, we seem to have survived our trip to the capital relatively unscathed.'

'Don't tempt fate. We're not at home yet.' Bobby grimaced, and pressed a hand to her stomach. 'Ugh.'

'What's up? Do you need the lav again? You might as well just lock yourself in for the whole journey.'

'Very funny.' She rubbed her belly, trying to soothe her restless baby. 'It's Marmaduke. He won't keep still today. It's giving me terrible cramps.'

'Perhaps he's homesick,' Charlie suggested. 'We're coming through Peterborough now. If we're lucky and there aren't too many delays, we ought to be in Skipton for the last bus.'

They weren't to be lucky, however. It must have been some way past Sheffield, deep in the blackout, that the train stopped. An hour later, they were still there. Bobby's cramps were showing no sign of letting up, and Marmaduke felt low in her belly, pressing against her bladder. She had needed to visit the privy four times in the hour they'd been stuck here. There had been blood on her underwear the last time, which worried her, but she hadn't said anything to Charlie.

'We're going to have to find a room for the night in Leeds at this rate,' Charlie muttered. He opened the door of their compartment and called to the conductor outside. 'Excuse me. Do you know what the delay is?'

'Now, sir, you know I can't tell you that,' the man said indulgently. 'Careless talk, et cetera et cetera.'

'Are you at least able to tell us how long it's going to be until we start moving? My wife is expecting and she's very uncomfortable.'

'I couldn't say, I'm afraid, sir. As soon as we know more, I'll be sure to inform you. In the meantime, your wife should feel free to lie down and rest.'

Charlie closed the door. 'He says you can lie down.'

'Very kind of him,' Bobby muttered. 'Charlie, I... I don't feel well.'

He frowned. 'What's the matter, darling?'

Bobby shuddered as another cramp ripped through her. These were so much worse than anything she'd experienced with her monthlies, although those could be bad enough to put her in bed. Her stomach felt hard and tight whenever another one came.

Her eyes widened as she felt a sudden dampness between her legs. Dr Minchin had told her what that meant.

'Charlie,' she whispered. 'I think… I think he's coming. The baby.'

Charlie stared at her. 'What?'

'I just felt my waters breaking. He's coming, Charlie.'

'But… he can't be. He isn't due for a month.'

'Well perhaps if you try explaining that to him, he might change his mind,' Bobby snapped, pain making her irritable.

'Right.' Charlie stared at her. 'Oh God. Right. Um… OK, stay calm. I'm a vet, I know about births.'

'I'm not a bloody calving heifer, Charlie.'

'All right, you should, um, lie down. Take off your underclothes and lie on the floor.'

'Would it help you if I was on all fours?' she asked dryly.

'There's no need to pick on me about it. It isn't my fault.'

'Of course it's your fault. It's your damn baby.' Bobby took the hand he held out and let him help her lie on the floor.

'I'll speak to the guard,' Charlie said. 'There must be a way to get you to a hospital. You stay here and… breathe deeply or something.'

'What if he's born while you're gone?'

'He won't be born just like that. Labour takes hours. Days, sometimes.'

Bobby stared at him. 'Days? Did you say days?'

'It probably won't be that long. Stay calm, all right? I've delivered hundreds of babies.'

'They weren't babies, Charlie, they were lambs. Get me a doctor, now. A proper, human doctor.'

'I'll do what I can.'

Charlie disappeared to speak to the conductor. Bobby wriggled out of her stockings, girdle and knickers, trying to slow her panting breaths. Another cramp-like sensation tore through her and she cried out.

Her husband reappeared shortly after.

'He's going to arrange for a message to be sent to the next signal box.' Charlie took her hand, and she gripped his fingers tightly. 'Just hold on, Bob. It'll be all right.'

Bobby cried out again as her stomach jolted, feeling like it was tearing her in two. Her brain was screaming. She could feel the baby right against the wall of her womb, she was sure. He felt so heavy, and his movement through her body entirely outside her control. Charlie said labour ought to last hours, but it felt like the baby might arrive at any minute. She hoped he would, and end this blinding animal agony that was like nothing she'd ever experienced.

The conductor arrived soon after. Bobby could barely focus, but she could make out the blur of a railway uniform.

'Oh my word,' the man said when he saw her lying there, pain-wracked and slicked with sweat. He pulled himself together. 'Um, a message has been sent to the next signal box to have a car waiting at the station, sir. It will mean an unscheduled stop.'

'I don't care what it means,' Charlie snapped. 'I just want to get her to a doctor. Why can't the car come here? Or let me out and I'll flag someone down.'

'We're in the middle of nowhere – in the midst of the Peaks. There's nothing out there but hills and sheep.'

'Then get this bloody train moving, can you? That's your job, isn't it?'

'We'll be moving again as soon as we can,' the man said stiffly. 'I'm afraid there has been significant bomb damage to the line.'

Bobby screamed. The pain no longer felt like cramps. Now it felt like being torn apart, limb by limb, organ by organ.

'I won't make it,' she gasped. 'He's coming, Charlie. I think he's coming now.'

'Is there a doctor on this train?' Charlie demanded of the conductor.

'I'll make enquiries.'

'Make them fast.'

The man disappeared, and Charlie knelt by Bobby to take her hand.

'It hurts,' she whispered. 'Oh God, it hurts.'

'I know, love,' he said soothingly, stroking her hot forehead. 'I'm here. It's all right.'

'You won't leave me, will you?'

'They'd have to drag me away.'

The conductor came back ten minutes later, escorting a no-nonsense young woman in a VAD uniform. She carried a medical bag over her arm.

'This young lady has midwifery experience,' he told Charlie. 'I'll leave her to… yes. If you need anything, Miss Hunter, just call.'

The man fled, as if desperate to get away before a baby popped out. Bobby didn't blame him.

'Deborah Hunter,' the nurse said by way of an introduction.

'Charlie Atherton,' Charlie said. 'This is my wife, Bobby.'

The nurse nodded. 'You may leave now, Mr Atherton. I can take things from here.'

'I'm not leaving.'

Bobby let out a cry.

'You ought to,' Deborah said. 'From the state of your wife, I'd say the baby might be here any minute. You'd rather not see that, I suppose.'

'I'm a vet; I'm sure I've seen worse. And I'm not going to leave my wife while she's in pain.'

'Please,' Bobby gasped. 'Please, Nurse. I want him to stay.'

Deborah shrugged. 'I can't make him leave, I suppose. Just try not to get in the way, Mr Atherton. Now then, Mrs Atherton, when did your pains begin?'

'I started noticing cramps yesterday morning. They… they weren't too bad then.'

'It sounds as though you may have been in labour for some time without realising it. How far apart are the pains?'

Bobby cried out again as the sensation of being torn apart shot through her.

'I think... every five minutes or so,' she panted.

'Then we must be close.'

'He's a month early, Nurse,' Charlie said. 'Is that bad? It must mean there's something wrong, does it?'

'Not necessarily. He may be rather small on arrival, that's all.' Deborah looked up at Charlie. 'If you really want to make yourself useful in the birthing room, call the guard and tell him I need hot water, soap and any clean towels he can find. Quickly.'

Charlie nodded and went to do as he was asked.

Time seemed to blur for Bobby after that. She might have been in labour for hours, or it might only have been minutes. She had a sensation of Charlie holding her hand, squeezing tightly on his fingers with each fresh burst of pain, and a woman's voice telling her to push.

She had almost forgotten she was giving birth. There was only the pain she was trapped in, and a feeling it was going to last forever. Her body was being split into two pieces and she'd never be able to put it back together again. She felt delirious with agony.

And then, just as she was about to give up and wish herself dead rather than another minute of this, it was over. The pain subsided, and her body, weak and sore as it was, was under her control again. She could hear Charlie laughing softly, the whisper of scissors, the gentle coo of the nurse, then a wail as from a good, healthy pair of little lungs.

'My baby,' Bobby gasped. 'Is he...'

The nurse put a towel-wrapped form into her arms. 'He's a fine, strong baby boy. But you seemed to know that already.'

The baby's cries ceased the moment Bobby held him. She stared with wonder at the tiny red face blinking at her with deep black eyes.

'It's a boy.' She laughed, looking at Charlie kneeling by her side. 'Charlie, it's a boy.'

'It is. The most beautiful little boy there ever was.' He kissed her soaked forehead softly. 'You were wonderful, darling.'

'I'll leave you alone for a moment,' Deborah said, getting to her feet. 'I need to speak a few words to the conductor about cleaning up in here.'

Charlie got up to pump her hand. 'I don't know how I can ever thank you enough, Nurse.'

Deborah smiled. 'Well, I'm still not convinced husbands in delivery rooms are a good idea, but I'd say you have the makings of a fine midwife, Mr Atherton. Congratulations to you both.'

When the nurse had gone, Charlie knelt again by Bobby and the baby.

'I thought he was bound to be a girl,' Bobby whispered. 'We nearly always have girls in my family.'

Charlie ran a tender finger over his new son's tiny nose. 'I've never seen anything more beautiful in my life, except perhaps his mother. I'll tell you what, you can keep your kings. Nothing will ever compare to meeting this little man.'

'He's perfect. Absolutely perfect.'

'I have to say, though, darling, he doesn't look much like a Marmaduke.'

'I know what he looks like,' Bobby said softly.

'I can guess what you're going to say. Ernest, after his godfather.'

'If you approve.'

'Yes, it suits him.' Charlie smiled as the baby gripped his finger. 'He looks a serious little soul. What about a middle name?'

'I'd like to name him after your brother, if it's all right with you.'

Charlie laughed. 'I'd be perfectly happy with that if my brother wasn't called Reginald.'

'Well, does he have a middle name?'

'David, after our grandfather. I could live with David.'

'Ernest David Atherton.' Bobby spoke the name slowly, trying out the sound. 'Yes, I like that.' She smiled at the wrinkled, beautiful, miraculous, gummy little face that belonged to her and to Charlie. 'Welcome to the world, Ernie Atherton.'

## *Epilogue*

### *8th May 1945, VE Day*

'A little higher,' Bobby said to Topsy as her friend stood on a ladder, attaching Union Flag bunting to the balcony in the ballroom at Sumner House.

'I'm sure you time your babies on purpose to get out of the difficult jobs, Birdy,' Topsy called down.

Bobby smiled and rested a hand on her lightly pregnant stomach. 'If you'd been there during my last baby's dramatic arrival, you'd know what a jolly difficult job this is.'

'There.' Topsy climbed down to examine her handiwork. 'A little lopsided but I think we've made the place suitably festive.'

'It is perfect,' said Teddy, who was supervising proceedings from his wheelchair. 'We will celebrate the end of that terrible war in fine style, as it is right we should.'

Topsy took his hand, and a look of quiet understanding passed between them. Bobby had noticed many such looks since the news had reached them that all of Teddy's Polish family had been murdered in one of Hitler's horrific extermination camps. In tenderly supporting her husband through his grief and even more through raising their child, Topsy seemed to have become softer and more thoughtful than she had been before.

Lilian came in, hand in hand with Annie, who beamed on everyone present with all the sunshine in her little soul.

Lil stopped to speak to Florrie and Jess, who were making paper chains on the carpet. Ernie sat between them, patting out a drumbeat on his round two-year-old belly. His awed admirer

– Topsy and Teddy's little girl, Abigail – watched in wonder at the cleverness of his music-making.

'I don't want to get you too excited, but I've just seen a trifle the size of Blackpool Tower being prepared in the kitchen,' Lilian told her stepdaughters, the two Parry girls. 'It's so high that I could barely see Maimie behind it.'

'Is there cream in it?' Florrie asked.

'And jelly?' Jess chimed in.

'There's real whipped cream, an absolute mountain of it, and custard made with real eggs, and so much jelly you'll have tummy ache for a year just from looking at it. It's a proper trifle, with silver balls on top and everything, just like I remember from before the war.'

'Gosh!'

'And cakes too. Proper cakes, with egg and sugar and icing.' Lilian lowered her voice. 'I'll see if I can pinch one to take one home with us. We can serve it to Dad as a lovely surprise with his evening pipe, can't we?'

'I want to give Dad the cake,' Jess said at once.

Florrie, who at fourteen was indifferent to privileges like serving her father cake when she had hairstyles and film stars to think of, only shrugged.

Lilian left Annie with the other children and went to join Bobby, Topsy and Teddy. Bobby nodded at her son, patting his little bare belly to impress his friends. Annie seemed just as amazed as Abigail at this incredible skill.

'Look at him there, flirting,' Bobby said. 'I ought to have known he'd take after his father.'

'Let's hope the next one's a girl, then she can take after you,' Lilian said with a smile.

'What time is Tony coming?'

'He's travelling up from his barracks on the midday train. It was good of George to offer to forgo the party. We're very civilised, but it still feels awkward to have my former husband and my current one mingling in company.'

Topsy smiled at her little blue-eyed daughter, who was trying to eat a paper chain link. Florrie spotted this in time, however, and quickly took it from her.

'It'll be lovely to see this place filled with children,' she said dreamily. 'We ought to have quite a collection to do justice to Maimie's tea. Jolka and Piotr are bringing Tommy and Maria, and your brother and his wife will be here with their little one, Birdy, and there'll be Mabs and Gil's boy Andrew, plus I don't know how many from the village.'

'Aren't you worried about your beautiful home being destroyed when they start romping?' Lilian asked. 'I must say, I thought it was very brave of you to offer to host the party when you have so many precious things.'

'Or very foolish,' Bobby said with a laugh.

'Oh, no, not a bit,' Topsy said. 'It's felt as quiet as anything since the RAF went away. After years in a cottage, I can't even describe how big Sumner House feels to me now.' She smiled, and took Teddy's hand. 'But we're going to do something about that, aren't we, darling?'

'What do you mean?' Bobby asked.

'I told you that all Teddy and I wanted was to fill this place with children. Well, so we will. I've decided to turn it into a home for war orphans. It's foolish for just we three to be rattling around here when I could be doing some good with it. I'm meeting with the trustees of a children's charity next week to plan it all out.'

'Oh, I think that's a lovely idea.' Bobby gave her friend a hug. 'This would be a wonderful place for children to grow up. If I can do anything to help, let me know.'

'I'm sure there'll be lots our celebrated author can help with,' Topsy said with a smile. 'I'm engaging you to cut the ribbon when we open the place, for one thing.'

Bobby laughed. 'I'm not sure my name's going to be much of a draw, but I'd be happy to.'

'Come on, darling,' Topsy said to her husband. 'There's still bunting to put up in the library. You had better make sure you're there to catch me if I fall off my ladder.'

'Your wish is my command, as always,' Teddy said, kissing her hand. Topsy took charge of his wheelchair and they left Bobby with her sister.

'Where could Dad and Charlie have got to?' Bobby asked. 'They were supposed to be helping put up the decorations, but they went out an hour ago on some secret mission and I haven't seen them since.'

Lilian smiled. 'Ah yes, the secret mission. You'll see.'

'What are you up to?' Bobby asked, narrowing one eye.

'Like I said. You'll see.'

Charlie and Rob turned up twenty minutes later, along with Mary and Reg. All four were grinning in a way that made Bobby highly suspicious. Charlie was hugging a large cardboard box.

'Why are you all smiling like that?' Bobby asked. 'And what's in there?'

'Come and see.' Charlie put the box down.

Too curious not to comply, Bobby went to open the box. She drew out a hardback book with a colourful cover: one of several. The title was *Lindy Langstaff, Pride of the WAAF*, and the name underneath it was Roberta Atherton.

'My author copies,' she whispered. 'Where did you get these? The publisher told me it would be at least a fortnight until they reached me.'

'Pete Dixon were making a trip down to London yesterday for some shady business or other,' her dad told her. 'Slipped him a quid to pick these up and bring 'em back for you. We thought you'd get a thrill from having them today.'

Florrie came over to see what was going on, Ernie holding her hand and tripping over his feet in his hurry to reach his mother.

'What is it, Bobby?' Florrie asked.

'It's my story,' Bobby said, showing her the book. 'The serial I wrote for *The Girl's Own*. A publisher contacted my agent and told him they wanted to make it into a book.'

Florrie stared at it. 'Gosh. You wrote a whole book?'

'I did.' Bobby took a copy from the box and handed it to Florrie. 'Here, this one's for you. You know, it was really you who gave me the idea.'

'Was it?'

'That's right. Seeing the wonderful stories you wrote for Annie made me remember how much I'd loved writing them myself when I was your age. That was when I came up with Lindy.'

'Gosh,' Florrie said again. 'Will you sign it for me, Bobby? Then everyone at school will have to believe me when I tell them I know you.'

Bobby swelled. She had never been asked to sign her work before. Signing her own book, with her name right on the cover, would make her really feel like an author.

'If you like,' she said. 'I'll come over to you when I've hunted down a pen.'

'I hope I get my name on a book one day.'

Bobby smiled. 'Keep writing as well as you do and I'm sure you will.'

Ernie was fussing to be picked up, turning red in the face as he stood on tiptoes and stretched up to his mother. Bobby lifted him into her arms.

'Look, Ernie,' she said, showing him the book she was holding. 'Your mam wrote a book. What do you think to that, darling?'

'Trifle,' Ernie said in a matter-of-fact tone.

He had clearly picked up the word from the conversation earlier, and although Bobby was sure he had never seen a trifle in his life, the reaction of the Parry girls had obviously conveyed the idea that it was something to be desired.

'That's rather rude,' Bobby told him. 'It certainly wasn't a trifle. Actually it was quite difficult, with your lordship demanding all my attention.'

Charlie laughed. 'Sorry, Bob. When you're two, pudding is always going to come higher on the list of priorities than books even if your mam did write them. But I'm proud of you.'

'We all are,' Mary said. 'Well done, Bobby.'

Her dad nodded. 'Hear hear.'

'Bobby, give Charlie the baby,' Reg said. 'I want a word.'

Bobby passed Ernie to his father. 'Here. Try not to let him catch sight of any trifle before the tea, though, Charlie. I wouldn't put it past him to scoff the whole thing by himself, even if it is as big as Blackpool Tower.'

'All right, my lad, come with me,' Charlie said. 'At your age, it's high time you learnt the proper way to make a paper aeroplane.'

'What is it, Reg?' Bobby asked when they were alone.

He rubbed his neck. 'Well, happen this won't mean much to you now you've got your books and that. But with the war over and the paper ration hopefully on its way out, this could be a new era for our little mag. I've got a list of potential subscribers a mile long, just waiting till I could get the paper to print enough magazines for them.'

'I know, you could make it a good little business once they lift the restrictions.'

'Nay, not me. I'm getting to be an old man now, lass. And I must confess, while I wouldn't mind contributing the odd bit now and then, I'd rather be up a hill looking for wood warblers or laiking with my grandson than subbing copy.'

'You're not selling the business?' Bobby asked, frowning.

'Not selling it. Giving it. That's if you want it, like.'

Bobby blinked. 'You want to *give* me *The Tyke*?'

'Aye, if you'll have it. Happen you'll turn me down, now you've other interests that pay better. Not sure what I'd do with it then. Can't really stomach the thought of some bowler-hatted type who don't know what it's all about taking it over. Anyhow, if you want it, it's yours.'

Bobby laughed. 'Reg... do you mean it?'

'Course.' He frowned. 'Not saying you'll take it, are you?'

'Of course I'll take it. I love that magazine – I always have. And it won't stop me writing my stories, now I can afford care for Ernie.' She beamed at the prospect. 'I won't let you down, Reg. I know I can really make it something.' Bobby rather shocked her brother-in-law by throwing herself at him for a hug.

'Aye, well, no need to be soft about it,' Reg muttered, patting her awkwardly on the back. 'Congratulations, Bobby. You've always been a good lass.'

He wandered back to Mary, leaving Bobby to think over what he had said.

Her own magazine! She could hardly believe it. And she was an author too, a real one. An actual book had her actual name on the actual cover. Bobby still held one gripped in her hand. She felt like she needed to be touching it, just to believe it was real.

She looked around the ballroom, festooned with bunting as her loved ones prepared to mark the end of a war that had raged for more than five years. A gramophone was playing music suitable to the occasion – 'There'll Always Be an England', 'The White Cliffs of Dover' and other patriotic yet jolly tunes. Finally, a war that had felt like it might go on forever had ended. Fascism had been defeated in Europe, and all over the continent, people who had lived under the yoke of the Nazis were being liberated once more.

Everything Bobby had ever wanted seemed to be represented by what was in the room. She had her books, she had her magazine, and best of all, she had her family. The war was over and the children who were to celebrate here today would grow up in a world at peace.

Bobby looked at Charlie, sitting with Ernie on his lap as he showed the little boy the proper way to fold a paper aeroplane. Smiling, she went to join them.

## *A letter from Betty*

Hello, and thank you for choosing to read *Brighter Skies in the Dales*. Sadly, this is the last book in the series of six following Bobby's experiences during the Second World War, and it's been a real wrench to say goodbye to characters I've grown to care so much about over the past few years.

In this story, Bobby and her husband Charlie return to domestic life after doing their wartime duty with the RAF, but this doesn't mean their experiences of war are behind them. Like so many of those who served, Charlie has been left scarred both mentally and physically by what happened to him as a bomber pilot, and he struggles to find his place in the civilian world again. Bobby, meantime, tries to juggle emotionally supporting her husband with her first pregnancy, her ambition as a writer and a number of crises in her wider family. Bobby and Charlie's war may be over, but its legacy remains for them to deal with side by side.

It's been difficult writing this while knowing it would be the last book following Bobby and her circle, who feel almost like family after four years telling their stories. However, I hope readers will also fall in love with a new set of characters in the stories I am going on to write – more of which very soon!

I'd absolutely love to hear your thoughts on this book in a review. These are invaluable not only for letting authors know how their story affected you, but also for helping other readers to choose their next read and discover new writers. Just a few words can make a big difference.

If you would like to find out more about me and my books you can do so via my website or social media pages:

Facebook: /BettyFirthAuthor
Instagram and Threads: @BettyFirthAuthor
BlueSky: @maryjaynebaker.bsky.social
Web: www.bettyfirthauthor.co.uk

Please do stay tuned for announcements about further books by Betty Firth. Thank you again for choosing *Brighter Skies in the Dales*.

Best wishes,
Betty

## *Acknowledgements*

As always, I'd like to thank my talented and hard-working editor at Hera, Keshini Naidoo, as well as my agent, Louise Buckley at Hannah Sheppard Literary Agency, and the rest of the team at Hera and Canelo for all the work they have put in on this book. Special thanks go to my clever author friend Kirsty Bunting for her research help with one aspect of the plot!